The old lady sniffed or as near as elegance allow. 'Poor family background, I believe, and that is so important. One has to think of the children of the marriage and how they would turn out.'

'Which brings us to Beth.'

'I had hoped we had finally got rid of that girl.'

'Beth does a very good job for me, Mother. In fact I would go as far as say I would be lost without her. We have come to depend on her. Caroline feels that she cannot leave Beth out of the guest list.

'No, don't say what you were going to: Beth is a working girl and no longer a threat to Caroline. To be honest I feel very offended that you should think so little of your grand-daughter's charms that you would consider Beth a threat.'

'I do consider it. I always have. You, my dear, are blinded by love of your daughter and her resemblance to Margaret. I am not, I see what is there. Caroline is pretty, Beth is beautiful. Take it from me that there will be no invitation going to Beth Brown and you can leave Caroline to me . . .'

Beth

Nora Kay

CORONET BOOKS
Hodder and Stoughton

First published in Great Britain in 1995
by Hodder and Stoughton
A division of Hodder Headline PLC
First published in paperback in 1996
by Hodder and Stoughton
A Coronet Paperback

10 9 8 7 6 5 4

British Library Cataloguing in Publication Data

Kay, Nora
Beth
I. Title
813.54 [F]

ISBN 0 340 76593 3

Typeset by
Letterpart Limited, Reigate, Surrey
Printed and bound in Great Britain by
Mackays of Chatham plc, Chatham, Kent

Hodder and Stoughton
A division of Hodder Headline PLC
338 Euston Road
London NW1 3BH

For Bill and Raymond and my brother Syd

Chapter One

The last of the children to come out of Sandyneuk Primary School were two small girls. One of them pointed to a woman standing alone and well apart from the young mothers gossiping at the school gate.

'Is that lady your mummy?'

'Yes,' Beth answered shortly, and her small mouth buttoned. Mary Watson had no need to ask, she knew it was her mother.

'My mummy thinks she's your gran and not your mummy.'

'Well, she isn't, she's my mummy,' Beth said indignantly.

'She looks old, that's why. She looks like my gran only she doesn't because my gran looks nicer.' Having said her say the child skipped ahead and out of the gate.

Beth watched her go, wanting to put out her tongue, but afraid to in case her mummy saw her and Beth knew she'd be very cross. Her mummy did look old, that was the worst of it, but Mary Watson didn't have to go and say so. Crossing to where her mother stood Beth wished with all her heart that she had a mummy who was young and wore pretty clothes.

Harriet Brown smiled to her daughter, then frowned.

'Must you always be last, Beth?' She wore a drab brown coat on this bright, breezy April day, with a cloche hat of the same colour.

'I couldn't help it, my shoe lace came undone and I had to stop and tie it.'

'At your age you should be able to tie them so that they don't come undone.' They moved off together, the tall, thin woman and the child. For all her drab clothes Harriet Brown was a good-looking woman with a smooth, oval face and a nice figure. The child with her long, skinny legs would likely be tall, too. Beth resembled her mother in all but her hair which was dark like her father's. Harriet's was light brown with traces of grey.

Beth was deep in thought. Should she or should she not tell her mother? She decided she should.

'Mummy, do you know what Mary Watson said?'

'That's just silly, Beth, how could I possibly know since you haven't told me.'

With the tip of a pink tongue Beth moistened her lips and said the words into herself first. It was important to get them right. 'She said that – her mummy – said that my mummy – looked like a grandma.'

Beth watched the angry colour flood her mother's face. 'That was an extremely rude thing to say.'

'Are you very old, mummy?' Beth persisted.

'No, I am not very old, I am not old at all, just older than – than—'

'The other mothers,' Beth added helpfully.

'Yes.'

'Is daddy very old?' Beth thought about her daddy and decided he must be a hundred.

'No, he is not. We are what you could call older parents, dear. Do you understand now?' But of course the child didn't, it was obvious she didn't, her little face was puckered in concentration.

'No, I don't, mummy, I don't really understand why you had to wait until you were old to have me borned.'

Harriet had to smile. The child could be quite amusing, some of the things she came away with.

'I wasn't old,' she said sharply, 'just old to be having a first baby.'

'You're hurting my hand,' Beth complained, 'you're holding it too tight.'

'Sorry, I didn't mean to,' Harriet said letting the small hand go free, 'but do keep up.'

Beth was almost running. 'You don't need to meet me from school. I can come home all by myself.'

'If I were to allow you to do that, would you promise to come straight home and not have me worried?'

'Yes, mummy, I promise.'

'Very well, Beth, starting Monday I won't come to meet you.' Harriet smiled to herself as she said it. She had been thinking about allowing the child to find her own way home but she was pleased that Beth had suggested it herself. Though it wasn't far from number three Sycamore Lane to the school, the double journey and the waiting about dug into her day. Then there was the embarrassment of being so much older than the other mothers and feeling their eyes on her.

As for six-year-old Beth, she was just hugely delighted with her victory. No one would call her a baby now or worse, say that her mummy looked like a grandma. They wouldn't if they didn't see her.

Running ahead, Beth went round to the back door of the neat little cottage that was home to George, Harriet and Beth Brown. The front door, with its shining brass door knob and letterbox, was seldom used. Only the occasional visitor or the minister, who visited his flock twice a year (more often if they were ill), came in that way. All the houses in the lane were similar but the garden at number three was the best kept.

The garden was Harriet's hobby and she spent as much time as possible in it. To the front of the house there was a small patch of grass kept short, and in spring and summer the borders were a blaze of colour. Just now the long trumpeted golden daffodils were at their best with the tulips alongside just beginning to show their pinks and reds. The ground to the back was long and narrow and on a slight slope and much of it was given over to the growing of vegetables. In one corner there was a chicken coop, and eggs surplus to their requirements were sold.

'Keep your coat on, dear, we'll take a walk to Inverbrae with the eggs.'

'It's too hot, I don't need my coat,' Beth complained.

'Yes, you do, that wind has a real chill in it and I don't want you getting a cold.'

Beth sighed. She knew better than to argue and stood with her coat on watching her mother pick up the box from the pantry shelf with each egg carefully wrapped in newspaper. Then they set off along the lane and up the steep hill to Inverbrae House.

Sandyneuk was a seaside village on the east coast of Scotland and a pleasant place to live. In the summer months day-trippers flocked to the beach laden with baskets of food, thermos flasks of tea, extra cardigans in case the weather got chilly, buckets and spades and all the other paraphernalia so necessary for a family day out. The more affluent holiday-makers rented a house for one or two weeks and did for themselves. At the end of the season, when the visitors had gone, there was a curious silence which took a little time to get used to. Most of the villagers, though not the shopkeepers, were glad to have Sandyneuk to themselves.

Harriet and George were among those who appreciated

the quietness. They were a placid couple, always ready to give a helping hand but who generally kept themselves to themselves.

George earned his living as a clerk with a local building firm. He was very efficient at his job but his heart wasn't in it. He longed for a different life, a worthwhile life spent doing missionary work in Africa, India or wherever the Lord had need of his services. As a lay preacher, George felt himself well qualified and it was at a Prayer Meeting that he had met the woman who was to become his wife. Discovering that they both had an interest in missionary work drew them together. Love didn't enter into it and neither Harriet nor George looked for more than liking and respect. Marriage, however, was desirable. A couple, legally tied, could do so much more and accommodation was less of a problem for a couple than two single people.

Harriet was thirty-eight and George five years older when they married. A year later they were making arrangements to go to Africa when Harriet discovered she was pregnant. It was difficult to know which of them was the more appalled. Nearing forty, Harriet had been so sure that motherhood was no longer a threat, but it had happened. She couldn't go but she insisted that George should go without her. George was torn between his desire to go and his duty to his wife. Harriet did have a sister who might be called on to help, though they weren't particularly close. In the event it was the doctor who made the decision for them. His patient, he said bluntly, was not having a trouble-free pregnancy and there was her age, old to be having a first baby. At a time like this a husband should put his wife first. His own opinion, not voiced, was that visiting heathen countries was a waste of money and that there were plenty of folk in this country in need of spiritual help.

'Mummy, do you think we might see the little girl today?'

'No, Beth, I think that highly improbable. The child won't be allowed to wander about in the servants' quarters, nor the kitchen.'

'Is that because she is better than us?'

'She and her family have advantages that we don't have but if you listened properly in church you would know that in the sight of our Lord we are all His children, we are all equal.'

'Then why does she have a big house and we have a little one?'

Harriet sighed. She shouldn't complain, asking questions was a sign of intelligence, but it was very wearing when the questions went on and on.

'Her family is one where wealth and property are handed down to the next generation.'

'Why doesn't she go to my school?'

'I expect the daughter of the house will have a governess.'

'What's that?'

'Someone who teaches,' Harriet said wearily. Her arms were beginning to ache, not so much from the weight of the eggs, but from the careful way in which they had to be carried.

There was silence while Beth thought this over. 'You mean, mummy, that she has a teacher all to herself?'

'Yes, that is it exactly.'

'Will she be cleverer than me?'

'Not necessarily,' Harriet smiled, 'you have a good teacher.'

The answer pleased Beth, she'd got a star for spelling and all her sums right but she was keeping it a secret until daddy came home. She wanted to tell them together.

They were almost there. Beth wondered what it would be like to live in a big house with servants to do everything. The thought of a little girl like herself living at Inverbrae House fascinated Beth and she longed to see her.

Chapter Two

Set on a rise and sheltered by mature trees, Inverbrae
House was surrounded by acres and acres of land, much of
it rented out. When it was built it was considered a
monument to wealth, though there was nothing vulgar or
showy about it. Rather it had a classic simplicity that was
pleasing to the eye and the ivy, twisted round the pillars at
the entrance, gave it a welcoming look.

The wrought-iron gates were just ahead of them and a
wide, tree-lined driveway led up to the imposing stone
frontage. As always Beth took a long look at all this
grandeur before turning left to walk along a gravel path
that led to the rear of the house. After passing a number
of outbuildings and the stables, they reached the servants'
quarters. The lesser orders had tiny rooms at the top of
the house with windows little bigger than portholes. Each
room was furnished with a cheap wooden wardrobe with a
drawer at the bottom. There was a narrow bed beneath
the fall down roof and many a young maid forgetting the
danger and rising quickly, was reminded of it by a painful
crack on the head.

As befitted their positions, the housekeeper, Mrs
Murdoch and Mrs Noble, the cook, were provided with a
comfortably furnished bed-sitting room. The placing of
Miss Mathewson, the governess, was more difficult since
she was neither family nor servant, but at Inverbrae

House they had solved the problem by giving her a room on the same floor as the nursery. Nanny Rintoul had a room next to her charge.

The outer door was open and Harriet pushed Beth ahead of her. 'On you go, dear, and knock.'

Beth did as she was told and rapped her knuckle on the door as hard as she could.

'Come in,' a voice called.

'Go on, Beth, open it.'

Beth turned the knob and pushed and a wonderful, mouthwatering smell of baking wafted out.

'Thought it might be you, Mrs Brown. Yes, that's right, just put them there on the table. I keep yours for the breakfasts and Cunningham's do fine enough for the baking.' She was a dumpling of a woman with reddish fair hair cut short and her round face was usually smiling. A huge white apron tied at the back with strings enveloped her ample frame.

Harriet had little social chat but it went unnoticed since Mrs Noble had plenty to say. Some would call the cook a gossip and perhaps they were right, but she was never deliberately hurtful.

'I was going to wait until tomorrow to bring them.'

'Glad you didn't, I'm down to my last dozen.' Clouds of white flour rose as she pounded and kneaded the dough and Beth watched in fascination. The punishment went on until Mrs Noble declared it was ready then, picking up a cloth, she opened the oven door and shot the tray in. 'Now I can relax for a wee while and enjoy a cuppie. You'll join me, Mrs Brown?'

'That's very kind of you,' Harriet smiled as she sat down. The cup of tea would be very welcome.

'Undo your coat, it gets that hot in here.'

Beth stood as her mother loosened her coat. Her eyes

10

were on the biscuits cooling on the tray.

'That you just come from school, Beth?'

'Yes.'

Waddling to the pantry she returned with a jug of milk and, after removing the cloth weighted with beads, filled a cup.

'There you are, lass, drink that and help yourself to a biscuit. No, make that two, you're a growing girl.'

Beth had one biscuit in her hand and the other was hovering as she stole a glance at her mother. Harriet gave a slight shake of the head.

'One is quite enough, Mrs Noble.'

'Away with you.' Picking one up she put it in Beth's hand. 'Drink your milk and eat your biscuits outside if that is where you'd rather be.'

Beth smiled and nodded. She liked Mrs Noble and not just because she got something to eat from her, but because she knew that listening to grownup talk wasn't any fun for little girls.

'My, that's a warm winter coat you're wearing,' Mrs Noble said looking at Beth's navy nap coat, 'you must be sweating in that?'

Beth nodded again. Nodding was rude, she knew that, but if she said anything she would have to swallow the piece of biscuit and she would lose all the lovely taste.

'There's a chill air outside,' Harriet said but half-heartedly.

'Bairns don't feel the cold the way we do and I see she has a warm jumper on.' With what could have been a wink she helped Beth off with her coat and opened the door for her.

Once outside Beth began walking without paying any attention to where she was going. Her first biscuit had slipped over too quickly and she was determined to make the other one last as long as possible.

Coming to the high hedge surprised her, she didn't remember coming this way before but she wasn't lost. She could quite easily find her way back to the kitchen. What, she wondered, was on the other side of the hedge? A break in it couldn't be ignored and allowed her to peer through. As she did voices drifted across. Beth kept as quiet as a mouse, she didn't want anyone to know she was there. Moving nearer to get a better view, she was thrilled to see what to her looked like a very big doll's house. The windows of it had pretty flowered curtains, the chairs were cushioned and she could see right in to where a little girl was sitting at the table and chewing the end of a pencil. Beth nearly giggled out loud. She did that and got into trouble.

This, then, must be the little rich girl, the girl she longed to meet, and the woman bending over the table as though explaining something would be the governess. Beth could hardly contain her excitement.

'It's too difficult, Mattie.'

'Of course it isn't, Miss Caroline, you are just not paying attention.'

Fancy being called Miss Caroline! Beth began putting 'Miss' before her own name but it didn't sound nearly as nice as Miss Caroline. She tried it with her real name and decided that Miss Elizabeth sounded even better than Miss Caroline.

'I'm tired, I've been paying attention for ages and ages and when I'm tired I don't have to do lessons. Daddy said so, so there!'

'That was when you were unwell, Miss Caroline, but you are very much better now.' The woman paused then added, 'And what would your grandmother have to say if

12

I were to tell her that you are falling behind with your schoolwork?'

The mention of her grandmother had the desired effect as the governess knew it would.

'You don't have to tell her, Mattie, and truly, truly I'll work very hard tomorrow. No, I won't, tomorrow is Saturday, but Monday, I'll work very hard on Monday.'

'Is that a promise you mean to keep?'

'Yes, honestly it is, and now will you please go away and let me sit here by myself for a little while?'

'Very well,' came in a resigned tone, 'I'll take these things to the schoolroom and come back for you.'

'You don't need to.'

'Nevertheless I intend to. I'll give you ten to fifteen minutes, no more, and keep that rug over your legs.'

Beth watched a pair of thick legs in lisle stockings and brown flat-heeled shoes walk away. She was about to walk away too in case her mother was looking for her, but she was stopped in her tracks.

'I know you are there, I saw you moving so you might as well come out.'

Beth was in two minds. She knew it would be safer to run away but curiosity nagged at her and won. Parting the foliage she stepped out and her eyes widened at what she saw. She was in another world where the explosion of space was overwhelming. Vast areas of grass like green velvet spread out before her and dotted all around were carefully tended flower beds. Further away heads bobbed as the gardeners heaped the cuttings into the barrows to wheel away for compost.

The six-year-olds looked at each other, the one so dark with blue black hair, dark eyes and cheeks that were a healthy pink. The other had pale yellow hair, pale blue eyes and pale skin. The yellow ringlets swung as she spoke.

'What were you doing hiding?' she demanded.

Beth didn't have an answer.

'Cat got your tongue?' It was what her grandmother said to her when she didn't have an answer.

The expression was new to Beth and she thought it funny. How could a cat get hold of her tongue, and anyway she couldn't see one. 'I'm waiting for my mummy.'

'Where is she?'

Beth pointed vaguely. 'With Mrs Noble.'

'Our cook, oh, she'll be ages then,' she said matter-of-factly. 'Grownups do a lot of talking.'

'If that lady finds me here, will she be angry?'

'I expect so but it doesn't matter. Mattie's just my governess,' she said dismissively.

'Mattie's a funny name.'

'That's not her real name, silly, I just call her that.'

'What is her name?'

'Miss Mathewson. What is yours?'

'Beth.'

'Beth what?'

'Beth Brown, but my real name is Elizabeth.'

'Mine is Caroline Parker-Munro.'

'That's a long name.'

'You would have to call me Miss Caroline.'

'Why?'

'Because you would, that's why.'

'Then you have to call me Miss Elizabeth, that's only fair,' Beth said with a toss of her head.

'Is it? Oh, well, you can call me Caroline when nobody is about and I'll call you Beth.'

'Why have you got a blanket over your legs?'

'It's not a blanket, it's a rug and the doctor said I have to keep warm. I'm not very strong, you see.'

14

'You're lucky,' Beth said enviously, 'having a little house to play in.'

'It's a summer house. Mattie doesn't like being outside, she'd stay in the schoolroom for ever, but when the weather is good I make her come out.'

'My mummy says it isn't good to get all your own way.'

'I don't have a mummy, she went to heaven when I was born.'

Beth thought that was dreadful, not to have a mummy. 'Who looks after you?'

'Well, daddy does of course, then there's my nanny, she was daddy's nanny when he was a little boy.'

'She must be very old,' said Beth who was greatly taken up with age.

'I expect so.'

'My mummy and daddy are old.'

'Nanny must be a hundred.'

'My daddy's more than that, he's a hundred and something.' A movement caught her eye. 'She's coming, your governess,' Beth said, alarm in her voice, 'and my mummy will be cross if she's waiting for me.'

'You'll come back? Please say you will?' There was a pleading note in the voice.

'I'll try.'

'Try very hard.'

Beth nodded, then ran back through the hedge and didn't stop running until she was in sight of the kitchen. At that moment the door opened with Harriet saying her goodbyes. She was carrying Beth's coat and the empty egg box.

'There you are, Beth, slip on your coat quickly or daddy will be home and no meal ready for him.'

George Brown was a mild-mannered man who looked his

age. He was of medium build with the beginning of a paunch and had a pleasant face, though it was marred by worry lines. Most of his worries were matters over which he had no control. Disasters that made newspaper headlines gave George sleepless nights. Other people would shake their head and be suitably shocked, but not unduly concerned since it wasn't happening on their doorstep.

When her father joined Beth at the table he had changed out of his dark blue business suit into clerical grey which was more suitable for his duties as a lay preacher.

'Did you work hard at school today, Beth?' he asked as he always did.

'Yes, daddy.'

Harriet was flushed with hurrying. 'Sorry, dear, I spent rather too long at Inverbrae,' she said as she came out of the tiny scullery that was off the kitchen.

'That's all right,' he smiled, 'I'm not in a desperate hurry.'

She served her husband his helping of meat, home-grown vegetables and fluffy boiled potatoes, then went back for her own and Beth's. Harriet didn't eat a lot and her portion was small. Beth, who disliked meat, but had to eat it – how often had she heard about those poor starving people who would be glad of it and how often had she longed to say it, but didn't dare, that they were welcome to hers – had hers cut up small.

Swallowing the meat first was what she liked to do, then she could enjoy forking down the potatoes into the rich brown gravy. But not yet – not a knife or fork could be lifted until the grace was said. Following her mother's example Beth bowed her head, shut her eyes tight, and wished her daddy would say the words a bit quicker.

'Amen.' It came at last and she could open her eyes.

Talking at the table wasn't forbidden but it wasn't encouraged either. Eating was a serious business. One piece of meat on Beth's plate had a horrible bit of fat hanging on to it. She tried to get it off with her knife but it stubbornly refused to move and the thought of it going down her throat right into her stomach made her feel sick.

Harriet had been watching the performance and tut-tutted. 'For goodness sake, child, it won't poison you,' she said as she forked it off Beth's plate and on to her own.

Beth gave a satisfied smile, ate the rest of her meal and decided now was a good time to tell them.

'Mummy, daddy, I got a star for spelling and all my sums right *and* we got our places changed, *and* I'm top of the class,' she said triumphantly.

'Well done, Beth, you're a clever girl,' her father said, his fork arrested half way to his mouth.

'Yes, well done, dear,' her mother added.

'Keep it up, lass, stick into your lessons, there's nothing to beat a good education.' He nodded several times as if to emphasise the point.

Harriet agreed wholeheartedly with her husband. If any good came out of that dreadful war, it was the difference it had made to women. They were just beginning to enjoy a freedom never experienced before. The war years had seen women doing men's work, like driving trucks, working on munitions, and they had shown themselves to be every bit as capable as men. Now there was a marked reluctance to return to the drudgery and boredom of housework and men returning from the war in 1918 were shocked, angered and bewildered to face wives no longer willing to go back to what had been, for them, the bad old days.

Young girls like Beth were the most likely to benefit. No longer would the choice of job be limited to a factory, going into service, or standing behind a counter. The dull jobs would still require to be filled but the less intelligent or those lacking in ambition would be available to do them. The brighter girls would be demanding the right to be as well educated as their brothers.

Before her marriage, Harriet had worked long hours in a draper's shop for a pittance and like everyone else had just accepted her lot, although in her case she had much to be grateful for. She had her Prayer Meetings where she could have intelligent discussions with like-minded people.

It was half past eight and Beth's bedtime. She'd had her glass of milk and taken as long over it as she could, then said her goodnights. The room that was her bedroom was small with the walls painted cream and pretty pink and white curtains at the window. Her narrow bed had brass knobs and beside the bed was a small table with a weak leg. A bookcase had been fashioned out of a wooden box and there was a rag rug to protect small feet from the cold linoleum.

Her mother came up to hear her say her prayers, then Beth climbed into bed. She wished now that she had told her mother straight away about Caroline at the Big House, and she couldn't remember why she hadn't. She would have to now, she couldn't go to sleep without telling her.

Harriet was busy folding up Beth's clothes and putting them on the chair. The school clothes went in the wardrobe since tomorrow was Saturday, and the soiled blouse she took with her for the wash. Beth was sitting up.

'Mummy?'

'Yes, dear?'

'I've got something to tell you.'

'Hurry, then, I have a pile of ironing to do.'

'I saw the little girl and she spoke to me.'

'Who spoke to you?'

'Mummy, I've just told you,' Beth said impatiently. Why was it that grownups didn't have to pay attention and children had to? 'The little girl from the Big House.'

She had her mother's attention now. 'Where was this?'

'You know that place where the high hedge is?'

'Yes, I do know and you've been warned not to stray over that way,' Harriet said severely.

'I didn't know I was walking that way, I just came to it, mummy, and I found a hole in the hedge that I can squeeze into.'

'Why would you want to do that?' The eyebrows shot up.

''Cos I heard someone and I just wanted to peep through.' She paused and her eyes widened. 'And that was when I saw the little girl.'

'And obviously she saw you. Really, Beth, that was too bad of you.'

'I wasn't hiding and I wouldn't have spoken to her only she spoke to me first.'

'Wondering what you were doing there, no doubt?'

Beth ignored that. How did her mummy know, anyway? 'It was nice and warm and do you know this, the girl had a blanket over her legs only she said it wasn't a blanket, that it was a rug and it was because she had been ill. That's funny isn't it, mummy, calling it a rug when rugs go on the floor?'

Harriet didn't trouble to answer. 'If I had been looking for you I would have been frantic wondering where you'd got to.'

'I didn't stay long and I told her you were with Mrs

Noble and she said she was their cook and you would likely be there for ages.'

Harriet's lips twitched.

'And I ran all the way back,' Beth said as if that made everything all right.

'Very well, we'll say no more about it.'

Beth was on the verge of tears. 'She's called Caroline and I like her and she likes me and she made me promise to come back and I said I would try and she said I had to try very hard – and – and – and—' The eyes brightened and the tears overflowed. 'Why can't I play with her? I haven't got anyone to play with.'

Harriet handed her own handkerchief to Beth. 'Wipe your eyes. I didn't expect a big girl like you to act like a baby.'

Beth used the handkerchief. 'I'm not a baby,' she sniffed.

Harriet did feel some guilt. Only a very few of the school children lived up their way and no one in Beth's class. Some lived in the centre of the village beside the Main Street, but most were in the fishermen's cottages clustered down beside the harbour. Harriet knew she wouldn't have a moment's peace if she allowed Beth to play there. It was much too dangerous.

'When you are a little older you can play with your school friends.'

'I'd rather play with Caroline.'

Harriet sighed. 'Although I have nothing against you playing with the girl, I doubt if she would be allowed to play with you.'

'Why not?' The tears had gone and there was outrage in her voice.

'You would not be considered suitable.'

'I would so, but she can't ask her mummy because she

20

hasn't got one. Did you know that, mummy?'

'Yes, Beth, I knew that.' She well remembered the village's grief when the young woman had died in child-birth.

'Next time you go with eggs, it'll be Friday, won't it?'

'More than likely.'

'I can just go and see if she's there, can't I?' she pleaded. 'Please, mummy, and you did say promises had to be kept.'

'Very well, but you are not to be forward or make a nuisance of yourself.'

Beth didn't know what forward meant but the important thing was that she hadn't been forbidden to go.

'No, mummy.'

'Get to sleep now, goodnight, dear.'

'Goodnight, mummy.'

The door closed quietly. Beth never got a goodnight kiss or cuddle. Harriet wasn't the demonstrative type and George was of the same mould. A pat on the head and a smile was all their child could expect.

George Brown took all of his duties seriously and that included making time for his small daughter. Saturday afternoons were devoted to this, when, if the weather was favourable, they would go for a walk. If it wasn't Beth would have to listen to Bible stories. Sometimes she got quite interested and listened eagerly but she much pre-ferred going for walks.

Today it was bright and breezy with a blue sky and no sign of rain clouds. Beth was ready with her coat buttoned and waiting for her daddy to take his off the coatstand.

'Think I'll need it?'

'Your coat? Yes, it's quite chilly out and it'll be worse where you are going.'

'How do you know where we are going, mummy?'

'Isn't it always the harbour?'

'Nearly always.'

'The fresh air would do you good, Harriet.'

'That may well be but I have too much to do and with you both out of the way I'll get on all the quicker.'

George smiled. 'In that case we'll get on our way. Come along, Beth.'

Beth liked it best when it was just daddy. He didn't walk fast the way mummy did and he always answered her questions without sighing. Hand-in-hand they walked down the lane, then down the steep brae to the fishermen's cottages and then along by the harbour wall. There they could hear the screeching of gulls and see the small boats bobbing about the harbour. Far into the distance could be seen the outline of a steamer.

'Breathe in deeply, Beth, let your lungs fill with the fresh sea air, nothing like it to get rid of germs and keep healthy.'

Beth took a deep breath, she loved the smell of the sea and wished that their house was down at the harbour instead of up the hill. They walked on and along the coast road and Beth studied the white house. It fascinated her the way it jutted out and she was filled with a fear that one day it would topple into the sea and disappear.

'How can you be so sure it won't, daddy? What if there was a big wind and it blew the house into the sea?'

This time she heard him sigh the way mummy did.

'Beth, we've been through all this before. The house is perfectly safe and even a gale force wind won't unsettle it. You only think it is in danger because of the angle and the way you are looking at it. Tell you what, one Sunday the three of us will take a walk up to the white house and you will see for yourself that it is nowhere near the cliff edge and absolutely safe.'

'Would you like to live in it, daddy?'

'I would indeed, the house has a superb outlook but we cannot afford to live there.'

'Is it very big?'

'Compared to ours, yes it is, but it wouldn't be considered a large house, just a good family size.'

'When I'm big I'll buy it for you and mummy.'

He smiled down at her. 'And where would you get all that money?'

Her blue eyes looked at him gravely. 'You said I was clever and if I'm clever I'll make a lot of money, won't I?'

'It doesn't always work out that way and remember this, Beth, because it is very important. Money is not, it is not important, we need just enough to cover our basic needs,' he said firmly.

Beth didn't say but she knew he was wrong. Everything in the shops cost money and if you didn't have any then you couldn't buy things.

'Daddy,' she said coming to a stop, 'this is far enough. I want to go back.'

'We could go back home by the top road instead of retracing our steps.'

She looked stubborn. 'No, daddy, the harbour, please.'

'All right, you win this time,' he said, turning round to face the other way.

Back by the harbour wall Beth tugged at his sleeve. 'Daddy, someone is painting, I want to see what he is doing. Please, daddy.'

'He may not object but don't go too near.'

The artist looked up as they approached. He was a tall, gangling youth and he didn't seem to mind at all. Beth went over to the easel to have a good look and turned away disappointed.

'You haven't done hardly nothing,' Beth said accusingly and heard them both laugh.

'Beth, will you never learn to think before you speak. What you should have said is, you've hardly done anything.'

'I finished one earlier on if you would like to see it,' he said eagerly, and before they could answer he had gone to get it.

'That's the harbour,' Beth said excitedly.

'It's very good,' her father said quietly.

'Thank you.'

George pondered. He would like to buy it for Beth but he couldn't afford very much. Still, unless he was very much mistaken the artist was desperate for a sale but trying not to show it.

'Daddy, I like it.'

'How much would you want for it?'

'You are interested?'

'If I can afford it.'

'Make me an offer.'

George did and felt ashamed to be offering so little.

'It's yours.'

'Are you sure you want to let it go for that?' George hated to think he was cheating anyone.

'Absolutely sure.'

'You haven't signed it.'

'Neither I have. I'll do it now.' His hand was shaking as he scrawled his signature.

'Daddy, is it for me?'

'Yes, we'll hang it in your bedroom.'

Beth was flushed with excitement. 'Let me carry it.' Then she looked at the tall youth and remembered her manners. 'Thank you very much. Are you going to paint another one the same?'

'No, no two paintings are ever exactly alike.'

'This one will be best?'

He smiled and Beth thought he had a very nice smile. 'Special anyway,' he said.

'Good luck,' her father said, moving away.

'I have a feeling you have brought me that,' the youth said quietly as he picked up his brush.

Chapter Three

Colonel Nigel Parker-Munro was a tall, handsome man in his late thirties who worried about his delicate small daughter and tried, whenever possible, to spend an hour or so with her each day. Well-meaning friends, his elderly mother among them, hinted that, after six years, it was time he took another wife. For Caroline's sake perhaps he should, he told himself, a girl needed a mother, but he hadn't met anyone with whom he wanted to share his life. Margaret had been very special and losing her in childbirth had been a tragedy that had embittered him for a long time. Some worried that he would blame the baby and have little time or love for her, but they were quite wrong. He saw their child as a living part of Margaret and each day Caroline seemed to grow more like her mother.

Before going down for dinner, Nigel gave a light knock on the nursery door and went in. A small figure usually hurtled herself at him and he would swing her in the air until she was screaming with delight, but not tonight. He glanced questioningly at his old nanny. Miss Rintoul got up stiffly to leave father and daughter together, then caught his eye and shook her head. He knew that look, it said it all, Miss Caroline was being difficult and a good talking to was what she needed. He sighed and forced himself to face the truth. Nanny Rintoul had seemed old when he was a little boy but he remembered, too, that strict though she had been, she could be fun, too. Now she was old and done and sometime soon he would have to make some provision for her and engage someone else. Poor Caroline was surrounded by old people.

'What's the matter, poppet, doesn't daddy get a smile?'

'I haven't got any smiles, I'm too unhappy and it's all grandmama's fault and nanny's, and Mattie's most of all because she told tales.'

'Dear me, I'd better hear about this,' her father said, adopting a serious air. Sitting down in the chair that Nanny Rintoul had vacated he gestured for Caroline to come over. With a whimper she got up on his knee and put her arms round his neck.

'I love you the best in the whole world.'

'Cuddle in then and tell me what is troubling you.'

'I've got a new friend, she's nice and Mattie asked grandmama and I'm not being allowed to play with her.'

'Who is this new friend of yours?'

'Her name is Beth, daddy, she's six same as me, and her mummy brings eggs for Mrs Noble.'

'How did you two meet?'

Caroline giggled. 'She was hiding, she said she wasn't but she was and when Mattie went away I made her come out.'

'That was naughty, making her do something she didn't want to do.'

'I didn't make her, she wanted to.'

Nigel tried to hide his amusement. 'So you two did manage to meet again?'

She nodded vigorously. 'Her mummy said she could play with me but she wasn't to be a – a—' Her brow puckered.

'A nuisance?' Nigel raised an eyebrow.

28

'Yes,' said a delighted Caroline, 'that's what she said, a nuisance.'

For himself Nigel didn't mind who Caroline played with just as long as she was happy, but his mother, Nanny and even Mattie were of the old school. Shades of Upstairs, Downstairs and, in their eyes, this child was plainly Downstairs.

'I'm lonely, daddy, I don't have anyone to play with.'

'That just isn't true, Caroline, your cousins come over and the Watson children.'

She looked scornful. 'They are all older and bigger than me and they are rough. Nanny Rintoul said so, too.'

She had a point, no denying that, and he just wished that she were strong enough to join in a rough and tumble but doubted if that day would ever come.

'Please, daddy, let me play with Beth.'

'Darling, the little girl will go to school and she'll have lots of her own friends.'

'No, she hasn't. She goes to school but her friends all live far away and she hasn't got anybody.' She paused and looked at him with all the wisdom of her six years. 'Everybody has to do what you say.'

'Can't say I've noticed,' he said drily.

'They have to, daddy.'

'No promises but I'll see what I can do.' He glanced at the time. 'If I'm to read you a story we'd better get started.'

'I don't want a story. I want you to tell me what it was like when you were a little boy and you were naughty and climbed up a tree and Nanny Rintoul couldn't find you anywhere.'

'Mother, I honestly don't see any harm in it.'

'No, perhaps you don't, Nigel, and more's the pity.'

'Things have changed,' he said gently, 'the great divisions are no longer there.'

'The war was responsible for that, it was an unsettling time, but the old values will come back, just you wait and see. No, Nigel, it isn't snobbishness, that was what you were about to say, it is a case of knowing one's place. Whatever is said to the contrary, there will always be the gentry and there will always be the servant class. Master and servant, how else could it be?'

Nigel looked at his mother with affection and exasperation. She would never change and perhaps he didn't want her to. She was a proud, imposing woman who held herself very straight and was a firm believer that posture was important to well-being. No member of the family was allowed to slouch in her presence. No member of the family would dare.

'You could be right.'

She smiled and as she did the harshness in her face softened. Nigel was her first born and held a special place in her heart. Her second son had died in infancy and James, three years younger than Nigel, had caused a lot of heartbreak to his parents. He had been the rebel, and even as a schoolboy had just escaped expulsion for some of his pranks that had got out of hand. Many of his misdemeanours would have been overlooked had it not been for his ability to charm others astray.

James had neither the wish nor the brains to follow Nigel to university and his father decided for him that the army would be the making of him. Unfortunately, James had other ideas, he wanted to see a bit of the world but not as a soldier. In the first year of his absence postcards arrived from various places in Europe informing them that he was fine and taking whatever job came his way. Then, quite suddenly, the postcards stopped and they had no means of getting the information to him that his father had died of a heart attack.

Nigel got up and kissed his mother. 'Rest assured, mother, I'll see this friend of Caroline's and satisfy myself that she isn't going to lead your grand-daughter astray.'

Wearing an ancient Harris tweed jacket with leather patches on the elbows and trousers that had long since lost their crease, Colonel Nigel Parker-Munro strode across the lawn and over to the two small figures. It was a Saturday morning and the May sunshine had a lot of warmth in it. Beth and Caroline were sprawled out on the grass and re-arranging the furniture in the doll's house. Both wore summer dresses, white ankle socks and sandals. Beth's dress was pale blue cotton with pink dots and had a white Peter Pan collar. Caroline's dress was pink with sprigs of blue flowers and the cotton of her dress had a lovely sheen to it. Unlike Beth she wore a white cardigan over it to protect her fair skin and give her the extra warmth she always required.

'Silly you, that table goes in the dining-room, not the drawing-room.'

Beth removed it. 'We haven't got a drawing-room.'

'Where do you entertain your guests?'

'We don't hardly have any.' Beth paused. 'We've got a living-room, though.'

Caroline had ceased to listen. 'Look! It's my daddy,' she said excitedly and, dropping the furniture at her feet, ran to meet him.

Beth watched the tall man swing Caroline up high then kiss her cheek before lowering her to the ground. She wished that he would do the same to her, her own daddy never did.

Taking her daddy's hand Caroline dragged him over. 'Daddy, I want you to meet my new friend. She's called Beth.'

Beth had got to her feet and was looking at him shyly. He wouldn't send her away, she was sure of that, because Caroline had said he didn't mind them playing together, it was just her grandmama who objected.

'Hello, Beth, I've heard so much about you from Caroline that I came especially to make your acquaintance.'

'Did you?' she said, then blushed, not at all sure what was expected of her.

'I did indeed.' It was Nigel's turn to search for something to say. 'Spring-cleaning the doll's house are you?'

'Of course not, daddy, the servants do that,' his daughter said scornfully. 'I've been showing Beth where the furniture goes. She isn't very good at it.'

Beth wasn't standing for that. She did so know what went in each room. 'The only one I didn't know was that silly drawing-room.'

'It's not silly,' Caroline said and turned to her daddy. 'Beth doesn't know about a drawing-room because her mummy and daddy don't have one.'

'We've got a living-room,' Beth said defensively.

'Same thing, different name,' Nigel said soothingly though he wanted to laugh. His daughter looked outraged and Beth's mouth was set in a stubborn line. This child, he thought, was going to be good for his daughter, she wouldn't give in to her the way others did, including himself. Because she was delicate they all spoiled her dreadfully, even his own mother who had been so strict with her own.

What an enchanting child had been his first thought on seeing Beth. With those huge, expressive, dark eyes and those incredibly long lashes she was going to grow up to be a real beauty. Beside her dark-eyed friend his pretty little daughter was just a pale shadow. Later he was to learn that Caroline was the older by a month but Beth was taller with her long, thin legs giving her a coltish look.

Lowering himself to the grass, Nigel sat down beside them and began to select pieces of the tiny, exquisitely made furniture, but his clumsy attempts to put them in place had both girls laughing delightedly as they insisted on showing him how it should be done. Perhaps that was when he became Beth's hero. She thought him the most perfect daddy in the whole world. It wasn't that she didn't love her own daddy, she truly did, but he never played with her. Of course, she told herself that it wasn't his fault, he couldn't help being a hundred and something, and Caroline's daddy was young.

Nigel got to his feet and dusted the grass off himself. 'Much as I would like to spend more time with you both duty calls and I have work to do.'

That surprised Beth, she didn't think rich gentlemen worked, only men like her daddy who needed the money. Her Mother had warned her not to be forward and she thought she knew what that meant now. She'd asked and been told that being forward was being cheeky. But asking questions wasn't cheeky and daddy had told her before that asking questions was the only way to learn.

'Do you do real work, Colonel Parker-Munro?' She was glad she had managed to get his name right. Her mummy called it a right mouthful.

'Real work, Beth? Yes, I think you could call it that,' he smiled.

'My daddy does very important work, he looks after the estate. I know that because grandmama told me.' She looked meaningfully at Beth as she said it.

'My daddy has two jobs,' Beth added her bit and it was

true, she didn't have to make it up. 'He's a clerk in an office doing lots of sums and he's a preacher – a lay preacher,' she corrected herself, 'and if I hadn't been borned my mummy and daddy would have been missionaries.'

That was quite a speech for a six-year-old, Nigel thought to himself. A very interesting child, this Beth Brown. Given Beth's background or rather her religious background, his Mother could hardly object, he thought as he prepared to go. Religion didn't play a big part in his own life but his family had always given generously to the church and he'd followed the tradition.

Before he left, Caroline threw herself at him and as he hugged her he caught a wistful expression on Beth's face.

Chapter Four

Beth had been going to Inverbrae House for close on two years. On Mondays and Wednesdays she went straight from school for an hour, and most Saturday mornings were spent there. On good days she walked the three quarters of a mile – there and back – but in rain or darkness a car was provided. Word very quickly spread round the village that Beth Brown was going regularly to Inverbrae House to play with the colonel's daughter. It caused much shaking of heads and not a little jealousy. No good came out of mixing the classes it was agreed, and this would only result in the lass getting ideas above herself.

Having no dealings with the village women, Harriet was unaware of the talk and the undercurrents of resentment, but even had she known it wouldn't have troubled her. She knew that Beth was safe at Inverbrae House and she didn't have the worry of her playing down at the harbour. Mrs Noble, the cook at Inverbrae House, would no doubt have had something to say but the two no longer met. One of the maids collected the eggs.

Beth loved the walk to the Big House. She liked to play make believe and imagine herself the daughter of Colonel Parker-Munro, and with her head held high she would go through the gates and up to the House. Once there a maid would come to escort her along the hallway and then left to a stairway that led to the nursery, now used as a

play-room. There she would usually find Caroline and
Nanny Rintoul and on the occasions when Caroline was
still with her governess, Nanny Rintoul would greet Beth
with a smile and tell her to occupy herself until Miss
Caroline was free.

It hadn't always been like that. The first few weeks had
been a difficult time for everyone but, of course, the
colonel's orders had to be obeyed. Eventually the staff
began to see that life with Beth there was easier than life
without Beth. There were fewer tantrums, Caroline was
more biddable and even her health seemed much
improved.

Disapproval still came from one quarter. Caroline's
grandmother strongly objected to this totally unsuitable
friendship but there was nothing she could do about it
apart from ignoring the girl.

A heavy mist was coming off the sea, shrouding the
buildings and making the October day more like bleak
November. The car came to a halt outside 3 Sycamore
Lane and the young man came round to hold the door
open for his young passenger. Beth was glad that it was
Tommy who brought her home and not the real chauffeur
because he made her feel shy and awkward. Tommy was
fun. He was employed as the head gardener's assistant but
acted as a chauffeur when required. Beth knew all about
him, he had a special young lady he was walking out with
and he was going to marry her one day when he had saved
up a lot of money. And after that he was going to save up
more money and buy a car and charge people for taking
them where they wanted to go.

'Thank you, Tommy,' Beth said politely.

'My pleasure, nothing I like better than having a bonny
wee lass sitting beside me,' he grinned, showing even

white teeth in a face brown from being so much out of doors.

Beth laughed delightedly at the compliment then left him to run round to the back door.

'I'm home, mummy,' she called unnecessarily as she shut the back door and went through the kitchen and into the living-room. 'Daddy, you shouldn't be home yet,' she said showing surprise at seeing him seated at the fireside.

'Took myself off early,' he smiled.

'No, Beth, you do not leave your coat on the chair, you hang it up in the lobby.'

'I was going to later.'

'Do it now. It must be wet.'

'No, it isn't, it can't be because Tommy brought me home.'

'Even a few moments out in this weather would have made it damp.'

'Do as you're told,' her father said irritably, 'hang it up then come and sit down, we have something to tell you.'

Beth picked up the coat and went out, wondering what the something was. When she returned she noticed that her mother had seated herself opposite her husband with her hands clasped in her lap. Her father looked ill-at-ease as he knocked his pipe against the side of the grate.

'George?'

'No, you do it, you'll make a better job of explaining.'

'Explaining what?'

'I'm about to tell you.' Harriet cleared her throat and suddenly Beth was afraid of what she was about to hear. 'We, that is daddy and I, have been asked by the church authorities to go out to Bengal to work there,' she said slowly and clearly.

'Where is Bengal?' Beth asked in a small voice.

'I thought you would have known that. It is in India and

we shall be going as missionaries, spreading the Word of God,' her mother said, quite unable to keep the awe and excitement out of her voice.

'Will there be a school for me?'

'No, Beth, you won't be coming with us.'

'Why not?' she demanded, her voice rising as she became more frightened.

'The life out there is totally unsuitable for children. We shall be in the back of beyond, going from village to village and living in very primitive conditions. No, Beth,' she said, putting up her hand as Beth made to interrupt, 'it is completely out of the question and there is your education to be considered.'

Beth's eyes were round as she stared at her mother, unable to make sense out of what was being said. 'What about me? What is going to happen to me?'

'Your Aunt Anne and Uncle Fred have agreed to look after you. The likelihood is that we'll be home for a short spell after two or three years.'

'Two or three years?' Beth couldn't believe what she was hearing.

'Yes, we'll just have to wait and see what happens then.'

Beth's face showed her horror. Her aunt and uncle and their sons, Adam and Luke, lived in the Lochee district of Dundee. Her cousins were much older than Beth, Adam had started work in the shipyard and Luke hoped to be taken on in eighteen months. She barely knew them for they disappeared with their friends on the rare occasions when Beth and her parents visited Dundee and they didn't accompany their mother and father on the return visit to Sandyneuk. Beth wasn't too concerned about her cousins or her Uncle Fred. Uncle Fred was quite kindly but didn't have much to say for himself. She remembered her daddy saying that it was Anne who wore the trousers and she couldn't understand what he meant. She couldn't imagine her prim, thin-lipped aunt in trousers. Furthermore, she didn't like her aunt and she had the sneaking feeling that the dislike was mutual.

'I am not going to live with Aunt Anne, I don't like her and she doesn't like me, I know she doesn't.' She was pale with shock and fright.

'That is nonsense,' her mother said sharply.

'No, it isn't, and daddy doesn't like her either and that's why he never wants to go to Dundee. And – and – and,' she sobbed, 'I'm not going to live with her and if you try and make me I'll run away.' One look at her father's face told her that she had gone too far. He'd half risen from his chair.

'You will do as you are told, my girl,' he said sternly. 'In this life we all have to make sacrifices. Your mother and I are giving up a comfortable home to work in very difficult conditions.'

'And doing it gladly,' his wife murmured.

'You want to go,' Beth said through noisy tears, 'you've always wanted to go. It isn't a sacri– a sacrifice when you want to do something. It's just horrid for me and you don't care, you don't care what happens to me.' She didn't have a handkerchief, searched her pockets for one to blow her nose, and silently took the one her mother held out.

Her father was pointing to the door. 'Go to your bedroom this minute and don't return until you are ready to apologise for that disgraceful conduct.' After she'd gone, George had the grace to feel ashamed. The child had spoken the truth. They were about to fulfil their own hopes and dreams and the one to suffer was Beth. It was going to be hard on her.

Beth flung herself out of the door, banging it behind her

and in her bedroom gave vent to her rage and frustration by lying on the bed and thumping the pillow. She wasn't ever going to come out of her bedroom. She would die rather than apologise and her parents were hateful. Forty-five minutes later her stomach was rumbling with hunger and with a murmured apology, she sat down to the meal that had been kept hot for her.

'I knew it wasn't going to be easy,' Harriet said to George later in the evening when they were alone, 'but she is being more difficult than I expected.'

'Pity there wasn't someone else we could leave her with.'

'Well, there isn't and I can trust Anne to look after her properly.' Harriet sounded annoyed, which she was.

'I could go alone, Harriet, in fact it might be better with all the unrest there is just now. It could be dangerous.'

'All the more reason for me going. I'm very aware of the dangers, George, and I intend to be at your side.'

George nodded. Harriet was determined and there was nothing more to be said.

'Don't worry so much about her, Beth will get over the shock. She is a sensible child and she'll make the best of it once she realises that there is no alternative.'

They retired to bed to spend a sleepless night.

Next door their eight-year-old daughter was tossing and turning before sleep claimed her and her dreams were of a figure chasing after her and wearing a witch's hat on her head. When hands caught at her, the face under the hat was her Aunt Anne's.

In the morning Beth looked round her bedroom with a vague sense of terror but the sun glinting through the curtains dispelled some of her fears. In that time between sleeping and waking the dream had faded but she was remembering something else. Her parents were going to India in six weeks and they were leaving her behind with Aunt Anne.

It was a silent and unhappy Beth who got through the schoolday and set off for Inverbrae House. Not today did she imagine herself Beth Parker-Munro, she was plain Beth Brown about to leave Sandyneuk to live in Dundee. In six weeks time she wouldn't be coming to Inverbrae House to play with Caroline, maybe she would never see Caroline or the Big House again. A sob escaped her and she swallowed to hold back the rest. She didn't want to cry any more.

When she entered the playroom, Caroline was on her stomach with a colouring book and crayons. She knew it was Beth but she finished filling in the petals of a daffodil with bright yellow before looking up. The greeting died on Nanny Rintoul's lips and her voice held concern.

'Beth, is something the matter, dear?'

The sympathetic voice was Beth's undoing and her eyes filled. Suddenly she was in Nanny Rintoul's arms being comforted, and with her face pressed to the soft bosom. Sobbing with gasps like retches she blurted it all out.

Nanny Rintoul didn't catch everything but she got the main facts.

'Your parents are going to Bengal?'

'Yes.'

'But you're not going?' Caroline said as she came to stand beside them.

'No.'

'That's all right then, you wouldn't want to go to that horrible place anyhow.' Caroline had no idea where Bengal was but she wasn't going to admit to it.

'It isn't all right, Caroline,' Beth said raising her head

and looking a bit self-conscious, 'I'm being made to go and live with my Aunt Anne and Uncle Fred in Dundee and I'll have to go to a new school and I won't ever see you again,' she ended tragically.

'You can't do that! What about me?'

'Miss Caroline, you have nothing to do with it, dear, if Beth's parents wish her to live with her relatives in Dundee—'

'I'll tell my daddy,' Caroline interrupted rudely, 'he'll think of something and Beth,' her eyes gleamed, 'I've just thought of something clever, you can come here and I'll hide you.'

'How do you think you are going to manage that, young lady?'

'I don't know, Nanny, but there's lots of rooms and you wouldn't tell, would you?'

Colonel Parker-Munro was dismayed at the news but like Nanny Rintoul felt it was none of his business. They would all, with the exception of his mother, miss Beth, but life would go on. That, however, was where he was wrong. His daughter had inherited some of his stubbornness, a little of her dead mother's persuasiveness, and her own brand of behaviour to get her own way.

'Daddy, you must do something, Beth doesn't want to go to Dundee and her aunt is a cruel witch.'

'Now, now, Caroline, that is quite enough!'

She burst into tears, sobbed uncontrollably and had everyone in a state when the sobbing turned to hysterics and the doctor was sent for.

He was annoyed at being called away in the middle of dinner, but hid his displeasure. He couldn't afford to offend the Parker-Munros.

'What caused this?' he demanded. 'The child has been so much better lately.'

'Her friend's parents are going to India and leaving their child in Dundee,' Nigel said worriedly. 'As a matter of fact Beth is in a state herself, she doesn't want to go.'

'Ah, the Browns. Going out as missionaries, I believe. I did hear something of the sort.' He paused. 'I'll leave something to calm her but it's only temporary and she is going to continue to be upset until she gets over losing her friend. In the meantime her health is going to suffer.'

Chapter Five

Harriet tapped the letter which had arrived with the morning post.

'It's from Anne, she wants us over on Saturday.'

'Count me out, Harriet, I've too much to do,' George said looking up briefly from reading his own mail.

'No, George, you can't get out of it. She particularly asks that the three of us come and I think it is the least we can do,' his wife said reproachfully.

'Perhaps you're right, what time does she want us?' he said resignedly.

'We're invited for high tea so if we get there late afternoon, we'll have time for a talk before the meal.'

Beth knew that it would be about her but she said nothing, just studiously avoided looking at her mother.

Squally showers in the early part of Saturday meant the wearing of raincoats and Harriet carrying an umbrella to keep her good hat dry. She couldn't go emptyhanded and the previous day had busied herself baking a two-pound sultana cake which, with an unusual touch of humour, George declared had risen to the occasion.

It was now carefully wrapped in greaseproof paper and inside a shopping bag. George had on his best blue suit and carried his raincoat. Harriet wore her Sunday charcoal grey costume under her beige raincoat and Beth had on her navy school trench coat over her dress.

Beth's parents had little in the way of small talk and it was usually Beth who kept up a running commentary when they were on a journey. But not today and it was a silent trio who waited for the bus to Dundee and then a further wait for a tram to take them from the city centre out to Lochee.

After leaving the tram it was a short walk to the home of the Farquharsons at number six Walton Street, a street of tenement dwellings of the better class since they had a bathroom.

'Here we are,' Harriet said with forced cheerfulness as they turned into the close. The close and stairs had been painted a bottle green with a thin yellow line to break the monotony. Harriet went ahead and when it came to the curve she kept to the broader side of the stone stairs. She stopped at a door on the second floor, or two stairs up as Aunt Anne would have it. There she waited until the other two had arrived before knocking.

In a few moments quick footsteps were heard, then the door opened.

'Not too early, are we?' Harriet smiled. It wasn't like her sister to come to the door with an apron on over her dress.

'No, of course you're not,' she said untying her apron. 'Just putting the final touches to the table and I knew it was you, heard the clatter on the stairs. Come in.' They followed her – George closed the door – along a narrow lobby to the front room where a fire burned.

Uncle Fred got to his feet. 'Hello, there, nice to see you all again, it's been a long while.'

'You're looking well, Fred,' Harriet smiled.

'Can't complain. The rain kept off for you, did it?'

'Yes, we were lucky.'

'In that case I won't need to hang up your coats, they

46

can go on the bed,' Anne said as she collected the garments over her arm.

'Sit yourself down, Harriet, over here beside the fire. My Beth, but you're getting to be a big bonny lass. In a year or two, George, she'll be having the lads after her.'

'And me after them,' George laughed, 'seems to me that they are courting these days as soon as they finish school.'

'You're not so daft, are you?' Fred turned to Beth.

'No, Uncle Fred.' Beth sat next to her mother. She had on a pale green dress with tiny brass buttons down each side to the waist. It had been let down twice and no amount of pressing with a damp cloth had taken out the marks.

'And this is you for pastures new, George?'

'That's right, Fred, a big change for us all.'

'It's that all right and I don't envy you. Not that I wouldn't mind a change of scenery but that kind of life isn't for me.'

'I should think not,' his wife agreed and with a sound that could have been a sniff as she brought a straight-backed chair forward for herself, 'but some folk just have itchy feet I'm thinking.'

Beth laughed, she couldn't help it, it was seeing the expression on her father's face, one of tolerant amusement with just a trace of anger.

'Neither of us has itchy feet, Anne, we are going on God's work.'

'If that is the way you like to put it. To me it's just an excuse to see a bit of the world.'

There was an uncomfortable silence eventually broken by Fred.

'I know better than to offer you a refreshment, George, but Anne, lass, how about making a pot of tea, it's a long

47

while yet until we get something to eat.'

Anne got up. 'I'll put the kettle on.'

Harriet got up, too. 'Let me help with the cups and oh, that parcel I put down is a sultana cake I made.'

'Thanks, but you didn't need to. I did a baking myself.'

'I'm sure you did,' Harriet said gently, 'but none of it will go to waste with two big strapping lads—'

They were through in the kitchen by now.

'Like filling a bottomless pit, heaven alone knows where they put it all. Away and get the cake then and I'll put it in the tin.'

Harriet went to collect it from the half moon table in the lobby then left Anne to unwrap it. The look of surprise as she did was unflattering, but even Harriet had to admit that she seldom produced anything so professional looking. The cake was perfectly browned and the fruit well distributed.

'Good for you, Harriet, it might have taken a prize at one of your village fêtes.'

'Never do have a success when it really matters,' Harriet laughed as she took cups and saucers from the press. 'How are the lads?'

'Fine. Adam's got himself a lass.'

'Not serious, though?'

'Better not be, as I told him it'll be a long while before he's able to support a wife.'

'And Luke?'

'A worry, that one, clever like your Beth, but can't get himself away from school quickly enough. I'm tired telling him that paying attention to his lessons will get him a better job.'

'He'll maybe change and you've done your best.'

'I have that. Playing truant, too, would you believe? I was up at the school about that, but enough about Luke.

When I was there I mentioned that my niece would be coming to live with me and transferring from Sandyneuk Primary.'

'Any problems?' Harriet asked anxiously.

'None.' She filled the teapot. 'You take that tray with the cups and I'll follow. A few fairy cakes is all I'm putting out, I don't want to put them off their meal.'

A stool, a wooden one that Fred had made, was put beside Beth to hold her cup in case she spilled. The others got theirs in their hand. Harriet and Anne had long since mastered the art of holding cup and saucer in one hand and eating a cake with the other. Their spouses hadn't and looked for a suitable resting place for their cups. Fred chose the mantelpiece and George put his on the floor beside his feet.

'Got your sailing date?' Fred asked as he waited for the sugar bowl to reach him.

'Yes, Fred, everything is arranged as far as possible and we've managed to get a chest to take our belongings.'

'Will it take the lot?'

'No, Anne, we'll have a case as well but that will go with us.'

'What about your house?'

'A bit of luck there, Fred,' George said as he swallowed the last of the fairy cake, 'the landlord belongs to our church and he is to let the house furnished until such time as we know our future plans.'

'Hope it's someone who will look after your things.'

'We'll just have to take that chance. It would cost us a lot to store the stuff.'

'Anything you want, Anne, you must just take,' Harriet said.

'There's a bed that will do the bairn but I've no spare wardrobe for her clothes.'

'We'll get that over with bedding and various other things.'

Beth was looking from one to the other, taking it all in.

'You haven't much to say for yourself, Beth,' her aunt said sharply, 'I've no time for sullen bairns.'

'Beth's just a bit bewildered.'

Beth bit her lip. She'd finished her tea and cake and was sitting hunched up, looking every bit as miserable as she felt. She had to get out of the room and she was going to make the excuse that she wanted the bathroom, though she did not. She looked hard at her mother who thought she knew the signs and indicated by the faintest of nods that it would be in order to excuse herself.

'Excuse me,' Beth mumbled as she got to her feet and was careful not to come against the stool and send the cup and saucer flying. It wasn't very steady.

Once she was safely in the smallest room of the house with the door locked, she looked about her. Of course she had been in it before, but she was looking at it with different eyes. The bathroom was smaller, though not much, than the one at home and the white bath was the same with its clawed feet. The walls were cream painted and a shelf held Uncle Fred's shaving things. How much water would she be allowed? How far up the bath would it come and how often would she be allowed to have a bath? At home it was Tuesday nights and Friday nights and the rest of the time she had, what her mother called, a good wash.

Then she thought about her cousins, those big boys she barely knew and wondered what it would be like living with them. Mummy didn't allow her to lock the bathroom door when she was having a bath in case she fell getting in the high bath or lost her balance getting out – as if she would. One thing she was absolutely sure about was that

the door would be locked when she was having a bath in
Aunt Anne's house. She wasn't going to let anyone see
her without clothes.

How long had she been? She flushed the toilet then
wished she hadn't. All of a sudden she wanted to go and
she knew it would take ages for the cistern to fill up again.
She knew about these things, her daddy had told her.

'Poor bairn, it's no wonder she's quiet,' Uncle Fred
was saying once Beth had left the room. 'What an
upheaval for her.' He puffed at his pipe, then took it out
of his mouth and jabbed it at them. 'While you're busy
preparing yourselves to go and do your Good Works, I
wonder if you've given much thought to how that lass
feels about it?'

George looked distinctly uncomfortable. He was changing his mind about Fred. The man was far from being
hen-pecked. Probably he just thought it was easier to go
along with his wife than face up to the tirades, unless it
was something he felt keenly about.

Harriet was slightly flushed but she spoke in her usual
calm way.

'You are being rather unfair, Fred. I can assure you that
Beth's welfare has been uppermost in our minds and it is
only because we know she is to be well taken care of that
we can leave with an easy mind.'

'Oh, she'll be that, I promise you,' Anne said and like
the other two was surprised at the outspokenness of her
usually easy going husband. 'I'll see that she doesn't get
up to any mischief. In fact it'll be real fine having someone
to help with the housework.'

'Have a heart, Anne,' Harriet laughed, 'remember
she's only eight.' But for the first time she was feeling
uneasy.

'Going on nine.' Her small eyes darted to Harriet.

'Don't tell me you still do everything for her?'

'Well, yes, I suppose I do.'

'More fool you. My laddies have their tasks to do. Well, not Adam now that he's working, but Luke has to do his before he leaves for school. High time you had that lass doing something, but don't you worry, I'll take her in hand. I'll see she gets a proper training, I'll take a leaf out of mother's book.'

Being the elder daughter with an ailing widowed mother, or one who pretended poor health, the bulk of the housework had fallen to Harriet when she was about Beth's age. Remembering her own lost childhood and the resentment that had built up in her, she had determined that her daughter's life would be different.

'Anne, I have no objections to her helping a little but I don't want Beth neglecting her homework. And I certainly don't want her over-burdened with household tasks. To my mind mother made little effort to do much herself and was far too hard on us. Perhaps not so hard on you since you were the younger.'

'Did us no harm.'

'I don't agree.'

'The trouble with you, Harriet, is that you never liked housework, to you it was drudgery. Believe me the day will come when Beth will thank me.'

They broke off when Beth came in quietly and took her same seat.

No one could have faulted the meal or the way it was set in the large kitchen which was also the family's living-room. Over the white starched tablecloth was a lace-trimmed teacloth embroidered in a lazy-daisy stitch and the best china was set out.

Fred had been well warned by his wife about grace

being said but she gave him a look in case he had forgotten.

'You'll say grace, George,' Anne said from her place at the top of the table.

Before bowing her head and closing her eyes, Beth caught the tiniest flicker of an eye that could have been a wink from Uncle Fred.

Beth enjoyed the home-made meat roll, it was tasty with no bits of fat to put her off. When asked she took another slice and more potatoes. Once the meat plates had been removed the teacups were filled and passed down the table. Beth's eyes were on the three-tiered cakestand. On it were scones, some plain, some with currants, fruit loaf, gingerbread, a cut-up jam sponge and plain Abernethy biscuits.

George wiped his mouth with the linen napkin then sat back.

'That was a lovely meal, Anne, I thoroughly enjoyed it.'

Anne's putty-coloured skin reddened at the compliment. She didn't understand her brother-in-law, never had, but he was always polite and well mannered. Her own men folk ate heartily but without comment. A clean plate, she supposed, was a compliment of sorts.

'It was lovely, Anne, and you went to a lot of trouble,' Harriet added.

'What about you, Beth, did you enjoy your Aunt Anne's cooking?'

'Yes, thank you, it was very nice,' Beth said politely. She wished that she'd managed to get her thank you in before her aunt asked, particularly when she noticed the slight fleeting frown on her mother's face. But it wasn't her fault, she wasn't allowed to interrupt, and she couldn't get a word in anyway.

★　★　★

It was time to go, the coats had been carried through.

'We'll see you at Sandyneuk, there are things we need to discuss.'

Anne nodded. 'I'll let you know which day.' She knew it would be about money for Beth's keep and her clothes. She could say that in their favour, neither of them was mean with money, and spent as little as possible on themselves. Anne felt sure that the authorities would make provision for family left behind. She was wrong there. Money was in very short supply for missionary workers but George and Harriet, living in hope of being selected, had put a certain amount away each month. George was to arrange with his bank to pay a regular allowance to Anne, and perhaps it was guilt at abandoning their small daughter that the amount was so generous.

Chapter Six

The knock at the front door in mid-afternoon surprised Harriet who was in the kitchen ironing the last but one shirt. She put the iron on its heel and went to answer it. Who could be calling? Then she decided it must be someone from the church.

Harriet wasn't vain, far from it, but just that morning she had washed her hair and being so fine it was flyaway. A quick glance in the kitchen mirror had her patting it in place and hoping it would remain that way. She opened the door and straight away knew who the tall gentleman was. Everyone in Sandyneuk knew Colonel Parker-Munro by sight, but the unexpectedness of seeing him on her own doorstep had Harriet flustered. She hoped it didn't show.

'Good afternoon, Mrs Brown. Do forgive me if this is an inconvenient time to call.' He had a pleasant voice and a nice smile.

'Not at.all, Colonel Parker-Munro, do come in,' Harriet said, opening the door wider.

'Thank you.' He stepped into the narrow lobby and waited until Harriet had closed the door, then she went ahead of him and along to the living-room. The room was reasonably tidy and had a homely, lived-in look. Harriet wasn't too houseproud, she didn't feel bound to put everything back in its rightful place. Books her husband had left lying about remained there until he decided to return them to the book-shelf, and the same went for Beth.

The colonel accepted a chair but remained standing until Harriet was seated. His well-cut tweed suit had seen better days but he wore it with the careless style that only a member of the aristocracy could get away with.

'I'm sorry my husband isn't at home.'

'I am, too. I should have liked to have made his acquaintance but I made a point of choosing a time when Beth would be at school.'

'Then this is about Beth?'

'Yes, Mrs Brown, my visit concerns your daughter and mine. The two girls get on very well together and Caroline is making herself quite ill at the thought of losing her friend.'

'I'm very sorry to hear that,' Harriet said quietly, 'we are not having an easy time with Beth, either.'

'So I gathered.' He was silent for a few moments and Harriet wondered if she should offer to make tea, then decided against it. No doubt the colonel would prefer to say whatever he had to, then depart. 'Beth is to be living with her aunt and uncle in Dundee?'

'Yes, my sister and her husband. They have two boys, older than Beth, but company nevertheless.'

'It must be a worry for you both in case she doesn't settle happily in Dundee?'

'She will in time, I – we – are sure of that.'

'May I make a suggestion?'

She didn't immediately answer but when he raised an eyebrow she nodded.

'Please don't think that you have to give me a reply now. This is something that you and your husband need to consider carefully.'

'I can't answer for my husband but I can answer for myself.'

'Would you consider allowing Beth to live at Inverbrae House under my care, Mrs Brown?'

Harriet was speechless. She didn't know what she had expected but it wasn't this.

'Think about it, Mrs Brown. It would make two little girls very happy.'

'I'm afraid it's out of the question. You see arrangements have already been made and it would be extremely awkward if I were to—'

'Change those arrangements?'

'Yes, it would and my sister would be dreadfully hurt.'

'Is a temporary awkwardness more important than your child's happiness?'

He saw anger in her eyes and hastened in with, 'I'll be completely honest with you, Mrs Brown. Caroline is delicate and highly strung and as a result gets more of her own way than is good for her.' He smiled. 'Beth handles her better than any of us. She doesn't give in to her demands, indeed she doesn't, and I think my daughter quite likes that.' He smiled as though amused. 'Whatever it is I'd say those two are good for one another.'

'Beth can be a determined little monkey and if I am to be honest, too, I know how very much she enjoys the company of your daughter.'

'There is another plus, an important one, I think you'll agree. Beth wouldn't have the upheaval of changing schools, she could continue to attend Sandyneuk Primary and Caroline will, of course, remain with her governess until such time as she goes off to boarding school.'

Harriet nodded. She couldn't deny that it was a big plus. Moving to Dundee and living with virtual strangers would be an ordeal without changing schools as well. Even so she couldn't possibly accept this offer. 'Children adapt very quickly, Colonel Parker-Munro, and Beth would make new friends.'

'No doubt.' He got up. 'May I take it that you and your husband will give the matter some thought?'

'Most certainly, it is very generous of you to make such an offer.' She got up to see her unexpected visitor to the door.

Before departing he held out his hand and she felt the firmness of his grip. 'I do admire you and your husband, it isn't easy to uproot oneself for the unknown.' He paused. 'I know something of that part of India and the difficulties that lie ahead for you. It won't be a picnic.'

'We wouldn't want it to be.' She smiled into his face and the light in her eyes shone out. It was a look the colonel was to remember. 'The dangers have been spelt out to us, and no, colonel, I am not brave, but I do have my faith. He gives his love and protection to those who do His Works.'

He smiled. It was the sort of answer he expected and for a moment he allowed himself to wonder what it would be like to have such faith.

'Perhaps we'll meet again before your departure, Mrs Brown, but in case we don't, let me wish you both a safe journey, good luck – and take the greatest care, won't you?'

'Thank you,' she whispered. The words and the sincerity in his voice touched Harriet and brought an unexpected lump to her throat.

Harriet was in a fever of impatience to tell George about her visitor but managed to wait until Beth was in bed and they were free to talk.

'Sounds wonderful and we would be foolish to turn it down. Indeed, Harriet, I can tell you it is the answer to my prayers.'

She was taken aback. 'You mean—'

'I've been very worried.'

'You didn't trust Anne to look after Beth?'

'On the contrary, she would have looked after her very well but in her own way. You've told me how much you resented the way you were treated as a child and I'm afraid Anne takes after your mother.'

'Perhaps she does, a little, though she doesn't pretend ill health.'

'That's not very Christian, perhaps your mother was genuinely ill.'

'She was eventually,' Harriet said drily.

'Let them have Beth at Inverbrae. She'll be happy and we'll go away with an easier mind, I know I shall.'

'It's more or less settled, then. You're in favour?'

'Absolutely. Aren't you?'

'I suppose so but with some reservations.'

'And what are those?'

'What happens when that child goes to boarding school?'

'That's a long while yet and in the meantime Beth will be well looked after.'

'She'll be neither fish nor fowl as the saying goes. I don't see her accepted as family and I can see Beth becoming very confused.'

'You're looking for difficulties.'

'I'm seeing them. After Inverbrae House how is she going to settle in Sycamore Lane when we come home?'

'She has to adjust now, she'll have to adjust then. Stop worrying.'

'All right for you but I'm the one who has to break it to

Anne and I'm not looking forward to that.'

'Take the coward's way out and write first, then go and see her. And when you do take her a gift, something she'll appreciate.'

'How like a man, but I may just do that.'

On a cold, cheerless late November night, a group of church people stood on the platform at Dundee station to see two of their flock, George and Harriet Brown, leave on the first stage of their journey. Anne and Fred were not at the station, they had said their goodbyes earlier with the coolness that was still there since the change of plans concerning Beth.

In the final weeks Beth had put a brave face on it and kept her tears for her pillow. She was in the bewildering limbo of seeing her parents packing their belongings and of people they hardly knew coming to the house to say goodbye. The initial excitement of hearing that she was going to stay with Caroline at Inverbrae House was fading as Beth thought of the long, long months, even years, without her parents.

Most of all she was dreading the final goodbye and here it was.

As the moment of departure drew near, well-wishers moved back. The last few minutes were for parents and child. One part of Beth's mind noted that her mother wore her old brown coat. She had bought nothing new, declaring that cotton garments were all that she would require in the heat and they could be purchased cheaper out there.

When George lifted her off her feet and held her tight in his arms, she was struggling with her tears.

'You'll be fine, Beth, you'll have a grand time at Inverbrae House.'

Beth gave a muffled 'Yes'.

'Be good, pet.' His voice was rough with emotion. 'Remember us in your prayers as we will remember you in ours.'

'Don't leave me! Please, please, daddy, don't leave me. I want to go with you,' she burst out as she tried to hang on to him.

He shook his head, patted her shoulder, looked helplessly at his wife, then thrust their child into her arms.

Harriet was pale but much more composed.

'Be brave, my dearest Beth. We'll write as often as we can and you must write regularly, each week without fail. We'll be longing for your letters and you must tell us all your news, all you are doing.'

'Oh, mummy!'

'Where's my brave little girl?' She dabbed at Beth's eyes with her handkerchief and wiped a tear from the corner of her own. 'Don't forget to send a little letter, a few lines will do, to your Aunt Anne. She is your nearest relative and it is important to keep in touch. Letters from the villages are sometimes held up for weeks and you'll get a whole batch at one time. When you do tell Aunt Anne and I've asked her to do the same.'

Doors further up the train were slammed as the guard showed his green flag. Her parents got on, a porter clicked the door shut after them. They stood at the window. The others moved forward to wave farewell and a man came from behind to lift Beth up. She glanced down and saw that it was Tommy. Then she was waving until her parents disappeared from sight as the train took the curve. As it did Beth felt a strange premonition and a ripple of fear went through her.

Tommy set her down gently. He saw the state she was in and his own feelings were that people weren't fit to be parents when they could go off and leave their only child with strangers.

Beth clung to his hand as though to a lifeline and he could feel her fear as they left the station and went out into the poorly lit street.

'I'm glad you came, Tommy.'

'The master sent me but I would have come anyway.'

'Would you really, Tommy?'

'Wild horses wouldn't have kept me back. You and me is friends and don't you ever forget it, Beth. If you're ever in trouble you come to me, you come to Tommy. Promise?'

'I promise,' she said solemnly.

They were almost at the parked car. 'Is something wrong, Beth?'

'N–no, just – you won't laugh or anything, or tell anybody?'

'I won't laugh or anything or tell anybody.'

'When the train went away I got a funny feeling that something bad was going to happen.'

'Nothing bad is going to happen, Beth.'

'How can you be sure?'

'I'm just sure that's all.' He opened the car door and she got in the front seat then he went round to the driver's side and started up.

'I wish—'

'What do you wish?'

'That I was going back to Sycamore Lane,' she said brokenly.

He patted her knee. 'Put your hand in my jacket pocket and see what is there.'

She brought out a bar of Fry's Cream.

'Break it in two. No cheating, mind, equal pieces.'

She was smiling and sniffing away her tears. 'Will I

break off a bit and put it in your mouth?'

'Have to since I'm not supposed to take my hand off the steering wheel.'

'Like feeding the ducks,' she said, popping a piece of chocolate into his mouth.

'Cheeky.'

The lamps were on at the gate and Tommy drove up to the front door. The house lights were bright and as Beth stepped out of the car the front door opened.

'It's the master himself, Beth, you're getting a royal welcome. Off you go then, can't keep his Lordship waiting.'

'Thank you, Tommy,' she whispered, then she walked up the stone steps and into the house.

'Come away, Beth, I wanted to be here to meet you. Nanny Rintoul has milk and biscuits waiting for you.'

Her new life had begun.

Chapter Seven

Her eyes were flooding with tears that wouldn't be held back and Beth couldn't find her handkerchief. Giving up the search she wiped at them with the back of her hand.

Nigel Parker-Munro saw the trembling lips, the traces of tears and the misery on the young face and wondered what kind of people could go off to distant lands and leave a child of that age. But, of course, he did know what kind of people they were. He had met them both, and to the colonel, they were a genuinely nice couple, older than he had expected, which made it all the more surprising that the man would give up a steady job and the pair of them forego the joy of seeing that delightful little girl growing up. But then these religious people looked at things in a different way, he supposed.

'Beth, my dear child, come along,' he said, putting an arm round her shoulder. 'Caroline so wanted to stay awake but I'm afraid she fell asleep in the chair and had to be carried to bed.'

'Is it very late?' she asked in a small voice.

'Late for little girls, it's after ten.'

She nodded, suddenly too tired to talk.

'You're dead beat and no wonder, but after a good night's sleep you'll feel very different,' he said kindly.

'Yes.'

He took her hand and together they walked down the

spacious hall, passed a table with brass ornaments that
shone like gold in the light and above it was a stag's head.
Beth had seen it before but now it took on a menacing
appearance. Her cold hand was being warmed in the
comforting heat of the colonel's large hand as they went
up the thickly carpeted stairs to the first floor and then
onwards to the room where Nanny Rintoul, stifling a
yawn, was waiting.

'Here she is, Nanny, here is Beth, and a very tired little
girl almost sleeping on her feet.'

'I can see that, the poor little lamb, but don't you
worry, I'll have her tucked up in bed in no time.'

'Goodnight, Beth, sleep well,' the colonel said patting
her shoulder and, before turning away, nodding to Nanny
Rintoul.

Nanny helped her off with her coat and Beth saw that a
corner of the table had been set with a lace cloth and on it
was a glass of milk and a plate of biscuits.

Beth had eaten a half bar of Fry's Cream with Tommy
and she had no appetite for milk and biscuits. She took a
small sip of the milk that was slightly warm and put down
the glass.

'Don't you want it, Beth?'

'No, thank you, I don't want anything.'

'Just your bed, that's what you want. Come along then.'

Beth got up and it seemed as though they were walking
along an endless corridor before Nanny Rintoul stopped
and opened a door.

'This is your room, Beth.'

The child was too exhausted to notice her surroundings.
She hadn't known where she was to sleep but at this
moment she didn't care where it was. All she wanted was
to get her head down on the pillow.

The choice of bedroom had come as a shock to Nanny

Rintoul but she was informed that it was the one the servants had been instructed to prepare. She couldn't even recall the last time it had been used as a bedroom. At one time she remembered that there had been plans to turn it into a storeroom for surplus furniture but nothing had come of it. The reason for the bedroom remaining largely unused was the tall, very old oak tree which blocked out much of the daylight.

Beth undressed and put on her nightdress which had been folded neatly and placed on the pillow. Then with a small sigh she slipped between the sheets and almost at once the dark lashes fluttered then settled. Nanny Rintoul waited until she heard the steady breathing before tiptoe-ing out and going along to her own room.

Perhaps it was the strange bed, but whatever it was Beth had a disturbed night with confusing dreams. In them she was running alongside the slow-moving train and pleading with her mummy to open the door and let her in. But she wouldn't and just kept on telling Beth to get back. For one brief moment their fingers touched and they were united, then the train gathered speed, tore them apart and in a blackened cloud of smoke it disappeared into the distance leaving Beth alone and frightened in the dark, deserted station.

When Beth opened her eyes it was quite dark with just a faint light coming through the curtains and outlining the heavy Victorian furniture. Why, she wondered, was everything so strange? It wasn't her own bed she was in, this wasn't her bedroom. Where was she? Her fuddled brain could make no sense of it. Perhaps if she closed her eyes then opened them again she would be in her own room in Sycamore Lane. She tried it but when she opened her eyes it was still the same. Then she was brought fully awake by the noise, a swishing, mournful sound followed by a sharp tap! tap! tap! that made her jump and her eyes widen in terror. What was it? There it was again and her flesh crept. Wildly her eyes sought for the door, then she was out of bed and wrenching at the knob until she got herself out and into the passage. Running along the dimly lit passage the sounds seemed to follow her and she opened her mouth to scream but no sound came. When it did it was a thin screech but enough to alert Nanny Rintoul who was a poor sleeper, and she moved with all the speed of which her old limbs were capable.

She wasn't to know it but the sight of that white nightgowned figure coming out of the door so terrified the child that she was close to collapsing.

'Beth! Beth! It's only me, Nanny Rintoul,' the woman said, keeping her voice as calm as she could, but at her approach Beth was flattening herself against the wall, shaking her head from side to side. 'There's nothing to be afraid of.'

The soothing voice eventually got through the terror and Beth let herself be held until the shaking lessened.

'You must have had a bad dream, dear.'

'No, it wasn't! You've got to believe me, it wasn't,' Beth cried as she held tightly to a hand that felt as dry as old parchment. 'I heard it, I know I did.'

'No, Beth,' Nanny Rintoul said in her no-nonsense voice, 'you've had a bad dream.'

'I'm not going back there, I'm not.' Beth was becoming hysterical.

'Hush, dear, or you'll waken the household.'

Another time and the sight of Nanny Rintoul in her night attire, her hair in a long plait down her back, and her mouth all sucked in, would have had Beth giggling. And as if this had just occurred to the woman, she took Beth's arm and guided her along to her own sitting-room and sat her down on a chair. Then with her back to Beth she went over to the bedside table and took something out of a china dish. When she turned round again her mouth was filled with large, very white teeth. The woman hadn't felt the cold until now and she gave a shiver. Her warm, pale pink robe was on the back of the door and she took it down and put it over her nightgown. Her feet were already in pink, fluffy slippers. Beth's feet were bare.

The child was slowly recovering but desperately anxious to have Nanny Rintoul believe her.

'Honestly, it wasn't a dream, nanny,' she said, her eyes imploring to be believed.

'You've certainly had a bad fright and your poor little feet must be cold.'

'They don't feel cold.'

'We'll go along together, and don't worry, you'll be quite safe with me.'

Reluctantly and fearfully Beth allowed herself to be led back to her own room. The door was wide open just as she had left it in her headlong flight but more of the daylight was getting in.

'No! No! Please don't shut the door, leave it open,' Beth cried as her frightened eyes raked the room.

'You can see for yourself, Beth, can't you, that there is nothing, absolutely nothing, to be afraid of,' Nanny Rintoul was saying when Beth clutched at her arm.

'That's it again! Listen!'

They both stood and listened to the gentle taps, then a flurry of more urgent taps. After a moment or two Nanny Rintoul left Beth and, going over to the window, drew back both curtains.

'Look, child, that's all it was, the branches of that tree knocking against the window. The wind must have got up during the night.'

'I'm – is that all it was – I'm very sorry,' Beth said looking shamefaced and feeling very foolish.

'No need to apologise, bairn, anyone hearing that in the middle of the night would have been alarmed.'

'You're not just saying that, are you?'

'No, I am not.' She paused. 'You've no need to feel ashamed.' And to herself she added, it's the one who put you in that bedroom who should be ashamed.

'Did I waken anyone else, do you think?'

'Couldn't have, else they would have been here. I'm a light sleeper, that's why I heard you.'

'I'm glad it was you.'

'So am I,' Nanny Rintoul smiled. 'Now into bed with you and sleep for what is left of the night.'

'What is the time?'

'I couldn't say for sure, probably between half past five and six.'

'Will you manage to sleep? My mummy—' her voice faltered, 'my mummy said she could never get over again if she wakened in the middle of the night.' The tears overflowed. 'I don't like this bedroom and I wish I was back home.'

'Now, now, we'll have no more tears, and didn't you say you liked coming to Inverbrae House?'

'That was when I could go home at night.'

'Well, Beth, my dear, you're here now and you'll just have to make the best of it.' Then, thinking that was rather harsh, she softened it with, 'Once you start getting letters with foreign stamps on them your school friends are going to be very envious.'

Beth smiled at that. It would be nice to show off a little but she decided there and then that she wouldn't give any of the stamps away. She would keep the stamps and envelopes with the letters and when mummy and daddy came back they would be pleased that she had kept their letters. Maybe Colonel Parker-Munro would let her have a big box to keep them in because if she got one every week she'd have a big pile.

Nanny Rintoul checked that Beth was asleep, then got up stiffly from her chair and made her way back to her own room, knowing there was little hope of any further sleep for her. Anger had taken away any chance of that. She couldn't recall a time when she had been so angry. Years in this household had given her the freedom to speak out and she would use it – oh, yes, she would use it.

'Are you trying to tell me that Beth was given that bedroom at the end of the corridor?' the colonel said disbelievingly.

'That is exactly what I am telling you, Colonel Parker-Munro.'

'But why? What was wrong with the spare bedroom beside my daughter's?'

'Nothing that I know of, but apparently the servants were given orders to prepare that room for Beth.'

'Who gave those orders may I ask?'

'The Mistress,' she said, looking him fully in the face.

'Thank you.' The Master of Inverbrae House turned on his heel, his lips set, his eyes furious.

'How could you, Mother? How could you be so cruel to a small child?'

She was sitting in the back sitting-room with the morning sunshine streaming in. There was no heat in it but a log fire gave off plenty of warmth. She wore a long mauve skirt and matching twin-set and on the small table beside her was a cup of tea and the untouched morning papers.

'Do sit down, Nigel, you look quite menacing standing

there with that look on your face. And stop making such a fuss about something so trivial.'

He sat down. 'I wouldn't describe scaring the child half out of her wits as trivial. Had that been Caroline it could have sent her over the edge.'

'Caroline is a nervous, highly-strung child and that girl is most certainly not.'

'That girl as you call her was already distressed after the ordeal of seeing her parents off to India.'

'What right have those people to expect others to shoulder the responsibility for their offspring?' she said in clipped tones.

'That is not the point, though you should remember, Mother, that Beth was to be living with her aunt and uncle and I persuaded, yes I had to use persuasion on them to allow Beth to come here and be a companion for Caroline.'

'If we had all ignored a few tantrums Caroline would have got over the separation.'

'A view not shared by the doctor.'

'What does Dr Grieve know about it? The man panics far too easily.'

'You were concerned yourself.'

'Of course I was. With Caroline it is difficult to know how much is genuine. That young lady knows how to get her own way.'

'You may well be right but personally I wasn't prepared to take the risk.'

She nodded. 'I can understand that. But to get back to what this is all about, the accommodation in question is a guest bedroom, not a servant's room, and I imagine a great deal better than the girl has been accustomed to.'

'When was it last used as a guest room? Everyone knows that it gets precious little daylight with that huge oak blocking the window. Perhaps we should consider having it ruthlessly lopped or taken away altogether.'

She drew herself up. 'Indeed and you will do no such thing, not as long as I am Mistress of this house you won't. The girl must have been over-wrought to imagine something outside the window. Had it been on the ground floor there might have been some excuse.'

'She was in quite a state according to nanny and it is the unknown that frightens us all. Aren't you ever afraid, Mother?'

She didn't answer, just looked at him coldly. In truth she was afraid, afraid of what the advancing years might bring. Her own mother had spent her final years in a wheelchair and now she seemed to have the same symptoms, the pain and the stiffness.

'We all have our secret fears, Mother,' he said gently.

'Even you?'

He laughed. 'Even me.'

It eased the tension and lightened the atmosphere.

'I find that hard to believe.'

He paused. 'Incidentally, you should know that Beth's parents insisted on money coming from their bank account for Beth's clothes and other necessities.'

'A gesture.'

'No, I don't think it was, more like a need to feel that they were making a contribution.'

'Surely you didn't accept—' she laughed, 'this small sum?' She made it sound ridiculous.

'To Mr and Mrs Brown, Mother, that money must have meant a great deal of saving and sacrifice. I happen to know that most missionaries live a hand to mouth existence, money is a very scarce commodity,' he said reprovingly.

She had the grace to look ashamed. 'Yes, I'm sorry,

that was unforgivable of me.'

He stood up. 'I must go. And, mother, I have personally instructed the servants to transfer Beth's belongings
to the bedroom next to Caroline's.'

She inclined her head. 'Hardly your place, but since you
have taken it on yourself there is nothing more to be said.
Before you go, ring that bell if you please. This tea must
be stone cold.'

Chapter Eight

Among the range of emotions Beth went through were a deep sense of shame, and humiliation that her parents could so easily abandon her. Other parents didn't leave their children so hers, she decided, hadn't loved her enough. Then there was the memory of her night of terror when she had made such a fool of herself. She had expected to be embarrassed, instead of which she had received a lot of sympathy and understanding and, most important of all, no one had laughed.

Settling in at Inverbrae House was difficult, it was all so different from what she had been used to, but after a few bewildering weeks she learned to adapt to this new life and began to feel happier. A routine had been established and twice a day Tommy did what came to be known as the school run. Beth took to school with her a packed lunch of sandwiches and fruit prepared by Mrs Noble, the cook. She ate them in the classroom with the other children who lived too far away to get home.

As for school, it was not without its difficulties, and Beth quickly found a change in the attitude of those she had once considered her chums. They weren't exactly unfriendly, just no longer natural with her. She had become different, they imagined a change in her. For one thing no one else had parents who were missionaries in India, a country that conjured up for them all kinds of mysteries. Letting them see her foreign stamps might have helped but she wasn't going to do that now.

What really set her apart was that she should be living at Inverbrae House, that mansion, and living as rumour had it as one of the family. Only occasionally was she asked to join in their play and she was frequently to be seen standing apart and alone, very much as her mother had once stood outside the school waiting for her small daughter.

The arrival of the posh vehicle at the school gate had caused some excitement and there was a rush of children to examine it. Beth would not forget in a hurry that first time she stepped out of the car. When play stopped and curious eyes followed her she went pink with embarrassment. A few shouted, 'Look, it's Beth Brown!' Another voice called out 'swank' and others took up the chant.

'Don't mind them, pay no attention, Beth,' Tommy said when she told him later.

'I don't like being called a swank,' she said unhappily.

'Of course you don't.'

'I'm not one, am I, Tommy?'

'You are not and if any of them bothers you just you tell them that Tommy here will sort them out.'

'You'll give them a good talking to?'

'More than that,' he said darkly. 'Tell you what, Beth—'

When he stopped she said, 'Tell me what?'

'How about if I just come to the gate when it's raining?'

'Where would you wait?'

'In Sea Braes. I'll let you off there in the morning and pick you up at four o'clock.'

'I used to go home to Sycamore Lane by myself.'

'Inverbrae House is a good bit further on, Beth, and I

have my orders to get you to school and back, and that's what I'm going to do.'

With most of her pupils having reached the age of nine, Beth's teacher began giving out homework. Beth did hers in the schoolroom at Inverbrae House and Miss Mathewson offered her help should it be required.

'Do you mind if I see your schoolwork, Beth?' she asked one day.

'No,' said Beth handing the books over.

Turning the pages the governess nodded her head a few times, then looked up.

'Very good, Beth, and extremely neat. Come and see Miss Caroline.'

Caroline made a face but went over and, after looking at the pages of neat figures and the red tick beside each, she turned angrily to her governess.

'Matty, why can she do these sums and I can't when Beth is only at a silly little village school?' she demanded.

'It is not a silly little village school,' Beth said indignantly. 'And anyway, it can't be silly if I can do harder sums than you.'

'Now, now, you two, that is quite enough of your bickering!' the governess said sternly. 'As for you, Miss Caroline, you are perfectly capable of the same standard, but unlike Beth you are not prepared to work.'

'Well I am now, I'm not having her beat me,' she said and burst into tears.

'Caroline, don't cry. You're better at some things than me,' Beth said generously, 'and I'm better at some things than you,' she felt obliged to add.

The crying stopped. 'You are not allowed to be better than me in anything.'

It was all getting too much for the governess and since it was her time off she left them to argue. Actually she was delighted, feeling the victory was hers. Miss Caroline was a spoilt child, a difficult and at times rude pupil, but she was far from stupid. This was what was needed, a bit of rivalry, a bit of competition from Beth. From now on she saw life as being easier, particularly with the old mistress who blamed her for her grand-daughter's lack of progress.

'Why am I not allowed to be better than you in anything?'

'Because you're not.'

'That's not an answer, you've got to give a reason.'

'I don't have to but I will. It's because – because one day I'll be a lady.'

'So will I.'

'No, you won't, you can't ever be one.'

'Why not?'

'Because you're poor.' She paused. 'My grandmama doesn't like you.'

'I don't care, I don't have to like her, she isn't my grandmother.'

'I told her you were my friend and she said you weren't a suitable companion and if you don't know what a companion is I'll tell you. It's something like being a lady's maid.'

'I am not your maid,' Beth said furiously.

'Not that kind of maid, you are a silly thing, Beth. The queen has a lady's maid but she doesn't have to do any housework.'

'What does she do?' Beth was curious to know. Being lady's maid to the queen would be a very important job and you would get to live in a castle. She smiled to herself. A castle would be even bigger and better than Inverbrae House.

Caroline was tiring of the subject, she didn't know much about it anyway.

'I can't remember exactly, but I think she follows the queen about and tells her what to wear. I'll ask my grandmama again and then I'll tell you.'

Beth was finding out things about her friend that she didn't much like. Things that she hadn't known when she was just going back and forward to the Big House. Like how spiteful Caroline could be if she thought that Beth was getting too much attention. But worst of all in Beth's eyes was that Caroline wasn't above cheating at board games.

'Why does Caroline always have to win?' Beth asked Nanny Rintoul one day after her friend had flounced out of the room banging the door behind her.

The old woman sighed. She was getting too old for all this noise and bother and maybe she should think again about making her home with her widowed sister, risk though it was. It wouldn't be easy for either of them, there would be skin and hair flying as her old father used to say after one of their many quarrels. Still, neither of them would have the energy for that now and in the loneliness of old age they would be company for one another. She turned her attention back to the child.

'Did your parents allow you to win at games?'

'Only if I really and truly won, otherwise it wouldn't be winning, would it? I never cheat, nanny. My daddy said that cheating is wrong and that if you do it your – your sins will find you out.'

Quaint little thing, Nanny thought with amusement. Obviously she'd been brought up very strictly with a good understanding of what was right and what was wrong.

'No, I know you wouldn't cheat, Beth, and Miss Caroline doesn't mean to, either.' She felt a need to protect her charge for, difficult though she could be, she had a lot of affection for the motherless girl.

Beth was like a dog with a bone, she wouldn't give up and worried at it until she was satisfied.

'Then why does she? I told her if she didn't stop cheating she would go to a bad place when she died.'

'Oh, dear me, that was a dreadful thing to say and you shouldn't have.' She paused and shook her head. The words spoken so freely had shocked her. 'Miss Caroline's daddy is partly to blame, he always used to let her win.'

'My daddy wouldn't ever do that.'

'No, I'm sure he wouldn't,' Nanny said drily. She didn't like the sound of Beth's father one little bit. 'It's wrong, no denying that, but you have to make allowances for Miss Caroline. You have a mother, Beth, though she isn't with you just now, but Miss Caroline's mother died when she was a tiny baby and she never knew her.'

Beth looked crestfallen. 'I shouldn't have said those nasty things to her but I'll go and tell Caroline that I'm sorry.'

'No, don't do that, better leave well alone. She forgets very quickly.'

'I'll forget too and be especially nice.'

'That's what to do, Beth, forgive and forget. We all make mistakes and Miss Caroline needs a good friend like you. Don't give in to her all the time, that wouldn't be good for her, but be kind.'

'Because she's delicate?'

'She's not so delicate now but she isn't a big strong girl like you.'

'I don't want to be big and strong, I'd rather be small and – and dainty.'

Nanny smiled. Strange how so few of us were satisfied with the looks and figure we were given, but this child beside her had a God-given gift. She was lovely and in a few short years would become a tall, strikingly beautiful young lady with young and not-so-young men beating a path to her door. Caroline would have her admirers, too. She was a pretty little thing, but could she ever be sure of whether her admirer's interest lay in herself or her position and money?

Beth loved her new bedroom. It was next to Caroline's and was a bright room with cream, embossed wallpaper and pretty, flowery curtains. The same material had been used for a bedspread and in place of the heavy Victorian furniture which had added to the gloom in the other bedroom, the furniture here was in a lighter wood. Her clothes hung in the wardrobe and her underwear in the drawers. Gradually new clothes were appearing and some of her older garments were missing.

She asked Caroline about it but she had merely shrugged, saying that she didn't know anything about it. When the colonel came unexpectedly to find out if the bedroom was to her satisfaction she had been overcome with shyness.

'Beth, you don't have to be shy with me. I want you to feel comfortable and be able to tell me if anything is troubling you or making you unhappy.'

She smiled and bit her lip.

'You like your bedroom?'

'Oh, yes,' she breathed, 'it's lovely.'

'As nice as the one in Sycamore Lane?' he teased.

'Better, 'cept for one thing.'

'Oh, dear, then I had better hear where we have fallen down.'

'My daddy made me a bookcase, he made it all by himself out of a box and I kept my books in it.'

'That was very clever of your daddy but I'm afraid my talents don't stretch to that. Do you like reading, Beth?'

'Yes and I like all kinds of stories.'

'Then I'll know to give you books for your birthday and Christmas.'

She blushed with pleasure and decided this was the moment to ask him before she lost her nerve.

'Colonel Parker-Munro, I've got some new clothes and a brush and comb set and I don't know who I have to say thank you to.'

'You don't have to thank anyone, Beth. Your parents left some money with me to buy whatever you needed.' In truth that money was an embarrassment and the colonel had been relieved when the bank manager had suggested transferring the money directly into an account in Beth's name.

Beth looked at him, only half believing. She supposed they must have if the colonel said so, but she was old enough to know that the dresses, petticoats and knickers were much nicer than mummy could afford to buy.

'Missionaries don't get paid a lot of money, they get hardly any,' she said bluntly.

'That is very true,' he said seriously. He would have to go carefully here. 'Beth, your parents did leave money for your requirements but I would be very sad if you denied me the pleasure of buying you the occasional little gift.' He smiled. 'I'm told all little girls like pretty clothes.'

She was standing beside him, looking up and smiling and at the same time going over the side of her shoe.

He pointed. 'If you do that too often you'll have a good shoe and a badly shaped one.'

'I don't even know when I'm doing it.'

'Then I must remind you since you are in my charge.'

Beth liked the sound of that, it made her feel that she belonged.

'I won't let myself forget, and I won't do it, and thank you for buying me things, Colonel Parker-Munro.'

He wished he could do something about the name. She got round it pretty well but it was a mouthful. In the army he had been 'Parky' and had no desire to hear himself called that again. He would have to come up with something, even if it was Uncle Nigel. He thought of his mother's face when she heard it and her reaction, and grinned.

'Before I go, tell me, are your parents well?'

'Yes,' she said eagerly. 'I didn't get a letter for a long time then I got three all at once. Mummy says they are always busy, there is so much to do and they are starting up a Sunday School for the little boys and girls.' She took a deep breath and went on. 'Daddy only adds a little bit at the end. He doesn't mind the heat but he says mummy doesn't like it, it makes her tired.'

He smiled down at her. 'They must long for your letters. Do you write often?'

'Every week. Mummy made me promise to do that even if sometimes it is only a little letter.'

That very next day when she returned from school there was a mahogany bookcase against the wall. It had three shelves and some children's books were already on one of them.

Beth was dancing with excitement and rushed to find Caroline and tell her.

'A bookcase, is that all?'

'Well, I think it is lovely.'

'Those books are old,' she said dismissively, 'daddy had them when he was little. Don't you have any of your own?'

'Yes, I do, that's them on the floor. I haven't had time to put them away.'

'Is that a Bible?'

'Yes.'

'Do you still say your prayers every night?'

They were both remembering when Caroline had barged in and found Beth on her knees beside the bed.

'Yes, I do,' she said defensively. It was true that she did still say them, but only when she was in bed. She felt guilty about it but it was better to feel guilty than have Caroline poke fun at her.

'You only say them because your daddy is a minister.'

'He isn't a minister, he's a lay preacher, and now he and mummy are missionaries.'

'Same thing.'

'No, it isn't.'

'What is the difference, then, and I bet you can't tell me.'

That was a poser for Beth and something she hadn't questioned herself. 'I think, and I only think, it is because ministers are paid and they get a free house called a manse and a lay preacher doesn't get any money and that is why they have to take another job.'

'When you pray what do you say?'

'I ask God to bless mummy and daddy and keep them safe, and I pray for other things, but secret things and I can't tell you them.'

'Do you pray for me?'

'No.'

'Why don't you? I'm your friend.'

'Only sometimes you are. You can pray yourself.'

'I don't want to.'

'You won't go to heaven.'

Caroline seemed scared. 'My mummy's in heaven and I

want to go there when I die. I've got lots of photographs of her so I know what she looks like. Will you tell me what to say?'

'Yes, only you have to think of things yourself.'

'I don't want to now, I'll tell you when.'

But she never did.

Before Beth fell asleep she would sometimes think about her parents and wonder what they were doing. The letters she got were full of the good works they were doing and the great need there was in that vast country for missionaries and helpers. Unfortunately, neither of them had the knack of bringing that faraway land to life. Beth wanted to know about India, not the good works her parents were doing, but what the natives were like and what they did. In her own letters she tried to ask but got no satisfactory answers. If they made the country sound exciting she might want to go out there when she was big, but by that time her mummy and daddy would be very, very old.

In nearly every letter she was asked if she was sticking in at school and being good and she was getting tired of it. They added at the end that they were missing her and she wondered if that were true. She couldn't honestly say that she was missing them – not now. The life she had shared with them in Sycamore Lane was fast fading, and when she tried to remember their faces she couldn't. Sometimes that worried her, but not very much.

Chapter Nine

Beth raised her eyes from the letter she was reading. 'Honestly, my mother's writing is getting absolutely awful, I can hardly read this,' she announced to anyone who was listening.

Caroline's grandmother had dropped the book she was reading, her mouth was half open and she was snoring gently. Caroline was on the couch with her legs tucked under her and flicking over the pages of a magazine which had been left at one time by one of her father's lady friends.

The colonel lowered his paper. 'Maybe your mother is busy, Beth, and just scribbles a few lines when she gets the chance.'

'But she always takes such a pride in her writing and look at it.'

He put out his hand for the flimsy sheet, meaning to do no more than glance at it, but he looked again and was careful to hide his concern. He was remembering Mrs Brown's writing from early correspondence and recalled it as being very neat. This, unless he was very much mistaken, was the writing of someone who could barely hold a pen. The thin scrawl told its own tale.

'Not very clear, Beth, I have to agree. When did you notice a change in the writing?' he asked, keeping his voice casual. He didn't want to alarm her.

'The last few letters weren't very good,' she said after pondering a few moments, 'but not nearly as bad as this.' Then she added spiritedly and with a mischievous grin. 'I'm going to say something about the writing in my next letter because if I had sent writing like that to India there would have been plenty said. I wouldn't have got away with it.'

'Do you hear from your father?'

'Not actually from him, but I hear about him. My mother' – he noticed that she now referred to her parents as mother and father – 'wrote to tell me that he's travelling between the villages, but my mother has decided to stay in one place.'

The girls were now eleven years of age. Caroline had grown but was still small for her age, her health had improved and she was less delicate looking. Beth was a good head taller than her friend, and the long thin legs were becoming shapely. She held herself well and moved with an unconscious grace.

For some months Mrs Parker-Munro had been saying that it was high time that Caroline joined them for dinner in the dining-room. The child, she said, could be excused after the dessert. Her son was in total agreement, and left to him it would have happened sooner. The problem had been, and still was, Beth. The old lady didn't want Beth to dine with them and Nigel refused to exclude her.

'How ridiculous can you get, Nigel! Anyone but you would see how out of place it would be,' his mother said, trying to contain her anger. 'And I am sure the girl would be a lot more comfortable if she were to continue to have her meals with Nanny Rintoul.'

'I've said it before, Mother,' he said patiently, 'and I'll say it again. Beth is a guest in this house and she will be treated as one.'

'And may I ask,' she said sarcastically, 'how long this state of affairs is to continue? Do her parents have any intention of coming home? They must be more than due leave or whatever the term is.'

'I imagine they will be coming home in the near future.'

'What then? Do they go off again and leave their daughter?'

'That I don't know, Mother, we'll just have to wait and see what happens.'

'All highly unsatisfactory.' She played her trump card. 'Miss Mathewson tells me that Caroline has been working extremely hard and, in her opinion, has now reached the entrance standard for Rowanbank. When Caroline goes off to boarding school, what then? Have you asked yourself that?'

'Yes, Mother,' he said wearily, 'it is giving me cause for concern but I'm sure something can be worked out.' He left her and went along to his study. Much as he loved his mother he found her a trial at times.

Behind his desk and comfortably settled in his leather chair he pondered the situation he had got himself into and wondered what could be worked out. His own fault and no one to blame but himself. He had been too anxious to keep his small daughter happy and had given no thought to the problems that might arise in the future. They had arrived and he had to find a solution.

His mother was right. Beth was becoming a problem and would be a bigger problem if and when Caroline left Inverbrae House for boarding school. If the parents were to remain abroad then Beth would have to join them, he was quite sure that arrangements could be made for her education. In the event of it not being possible then Beth would have to take up residence with this aunt and uncle in Dundee. He did feel a fleeting sense of guilt about that, knowing as he did that Beth had little affection for her aunt, but dash it all he was horribly and awkwardly placed.

Beth was looking unhappy and feeling extremely nervous.

'For goodness sake, Beth, what a state to get into about nothing,' Caroline said scornfully. 'My grandmama won't eat you.'

'She would if she could.'

'More likely to spit you out once she'd chewed you to bits.'

At the same moment this struck both girls as enormously funny and they dissolved into fits of laughter.

Nigel, passing on his way out, smiled. It was good to hear Caroline so happy and, though Beth was now causing him problems, he couldn't but bless the day that he had persuaded her parents to allow her to come to Inverbrae House. How much easier it would have been for all concerned if his mother had taken to the girl. Nigel was wrong there. His mother did not dislike the girl, in fact she admired Beth's spirit and her quiet thoughtfulness. When she dropped a book, Beth immediately picked it up whilst Caroline would have stepped over it. If her shawl slipped from her shoulders it was quietly adjusted. It shamed her to think that she seldom said thank you, but it was important to get Beth away from Inverbrae House before it was too late. Thinking herself disliked and unwanted, she would be more inclined to go to those relatives she should have been with in the first place.

Although she would only admit it to herself, the girl had done her grand-daughter a power of good. Miss Mathewson had taken the credit and she supposed some of it was her due. However, the old lady was well aware of the real reason for Caroline's sudden thirst for knowledge as she put it. It was that she couldn't bear to have Beth, her social inferior, shine while she trailed behind. She smiled. Caroline was a Parker-Munro and already showing the family pride.

The reason Mrs Parker-Munro wanted to see the back of Beth was for a reason that would never have occurred to her son, indeed it would not have occurred to the majority of males. She was seeing the situation a few years ahead. Already Beth was blossoming and very soon she would have the figure and striking good looks that would turn heads. Caroline, pretty little thing though she was, would never do that. Far better to separate them now than run the risk of Beth being accepted into the same social circle and spoiling Caroline's chances. In her day the door would have remained firmly shut to anyone of low birth, but in this modern age one could never be sure.

The table was beautifully set, the crystal sparkled and the silver shone. Beth took her place opposite Caroline and wished herself anywhere but where she was. Her hands in her lap were shaking so much that she had to lock her fingers together. Perhaps she would have had more confidence if she had been aware of the attractive picture she made in her pale green dress with its cream lace collar and matching cuffs. Caroline's dress was blue with white tiny flowers on a cream background. It had a wide skirt and a tiny v-neck and had been her own choice. The neckline was wrong and she would have looked so much nicer with a Peter Pan collar.

The colonel in a dark suit sat at one end of the table and his mother, looking very stiff and regal in burgundy and black, at the other. Wine glasses were set in front of the adults and a glass to hold water was in front of the girls.

Beth felt annoyed with herself and, as Caroline had so forcefully said, there was no reason at all for her to be nervous. Certainly her table manners were every bit as good as Caroline's. It was those old, unfriendly eyes that upset her and they would keep resting on her as though willing her to make a mistake.

At a signal from the mistress, the maids began to serve the soup and when they withdrew the colonel and his mother exchanged the day's news. Caroline was occasionally brought into the conversation by her grandmother but Beth hadn't uttered a word and no one had spoken to her. To give the colonel his due he didn't address his daughter either. As a young boy, he had always been silent at the table, as had his brother. Only the parents spoke with occasional remarks about forthcoming events, but largely meals were eaten in silence. The old master had appreciated good food but not idle chatter.

Beth finished her soup and placed her spoon on the empty plate ready for it to be removed. At this point the wine was poured and the girls had their glasses half filled with water from a jug.

Beth was just congratulating herself that she'd got through the soup course without mishap when her cuff caught her fork and sent it to the floor. She had been well taught by Nanny Rintoul and she knew very well that dropped cutlery, or for that matter dropped anything, remained where it fell until the meal was over when it would be picked up by a maid. In her nervousness Beth forgot and bent down to retrieve her fork. The moment her finger touched the silver Beth was aware of her mistake but it was too late, the damage was done. The disapproving silence terrified her and it was only broken by a small giggle from Caroline.

'I'm – I'm so sorry, Mrs Parker-Munro,' Beth stammered, crimson-faced, 'I forgot, I didn't mean to pick it up.'

'But you did,' the old lady said coldly and her meaning was clear. Beth wasn't fit to be at the dining-room table. The old lady signalled to a maid who quickly brought a fork from the sideboard and placed it in its correct position.

'No harm done, Beth,' the colonel muttered, but she felt that she had let him down.

'What a very stupid thing to do,' Caroline said later when they were alone.

'I know, I don't know why I did it,' Beth said wretchedly.

'Neither do I. It's something I would never have done, it simply wouldn't have occurred to me.' She paused. 'That is the difference between us, Beth, I just know what is correct and how to behave and you have had to learn it all.'

Maybe the others had forgotten the incident but it took Beth longer to get over what she thought of as her disgrace and it was several days before she was relaxed enough to enjoy the food placed before her.

Chapter Ten

Beth fingered the letter feeling a curious reluctance to open it. The writing was her father's and she wondered what she was afraid of. Putting a finger under a small unsealed part of the flap she opened it carefully, then took out four sheets of paper in her father's large and well spaced writing. She began to read.

My dear Beth,

Your mother is ill and unable to write to you herself. As you know the heat out here has been a great trial to her, as have the primitive living conditions, although she wouldn't admit to finding it so and has battled on bravely.

Now, I am afraid, she is much too weak to be of assistance here. Everyone has been kind and helpful but nursing an invalid takes up so much time and their talents are desperately needed elsewhere. Your mother recognises this. The doctor says that her condition is worsening and that she must return home. It is out of the question for me to accompany her, my place is here, and the Lord has directed that I remain.

Fortunately, and there is always an answer to our prayers, a Mr and Mrs Deuchars are returning home in a few weeks – I haven't an exact date as yet – and they are to look after your mother on the journey. I personally feel that she will recover her health once she leaves India.

And now to the arrangements, Beth. With your mother returning home always a possibility, I set the wheels in motion in good time. The family occupying our home in Sycamore Lane have been given notice to vacate it. Your Aunt Anne should receive a letter about the same time as you get this. I have asked her to get the house in order for your mother's return and I know that she will be happy to oblige. You, Beth, must give your aunt every assistance.

You will inform Colonel Parker-Munro yourself of the contents of this letter and I know that you will be so happy to return to your own home and welcome your dear mother. She has missed you very much and is longing to see you again.

I trust you, my daughter, to put aside all else and give your love and support to your mother. Of course I am not forgetting your schoolwork and during school hours someone from the church will take over the responsibility.

from
Your loving father.

Beth was glad that she was in her bedroom and alone. She couldn't face questions just yet. She was just too numb with shock and quite unable to take it in at the first reading. This time she read it very slowly. Her mother was ill and she felt dreadful about that, but she wasn't dangerously ill. Didn't her father say that it was mainly the heat and once she was away from India she would quickly recover?

The awful, shameful truth was that she didn't want to go back to Sycamore Lane. She no longer thought of it as her home, yet she would have to return, she had no choice in the matter. How could she fit in there again after life at Inverbrae House? She wanted to weep. She should be so happy yet she had never felt so miserable, so mixed up.

The letter had come with the second post and on her return from school she had picked it up from the hall table. It was now a quarter to five and more than likely the colonel would be in his study. She would go there now. Once she would have been shy to do so but now she was more relaxed with Colonel Parker-Munro. In any case, the sooner he knew the contents of the letter the better. Wistfully she hoped that he would be as unhappy to see her go as she was going to be to leave.

She rapped on the door with her knuckles.

'Come in.'

Beth, still in her school outfit, went in and over to the desk, the letter in her hand.

'It's you, Beth,' he smiled. 'And what is troubling you if trouble it is?'

Suddenly the lump in her throat was too big to swallow and silently she handed him the letter.

'You want me to read it?'

She nodded.

The colonel read the letter and felt an overwhelming relief that his problem should be this easily solved. Of course he was sorry about Mrs Brown's illness, but he'd known others who had had to come home after a few months in that awful heat and Mrs Brown had put up with it for three years.

Her eyes searched his face but she couldn't tell what he was thinking from his expression.

'Don't worry too much about your mother, Beth, because as your father says, once she is on her way home her health should improve.'

'Yes,' she said listlessly, disappointed that he hadn't

97

immediately said how much she would be missed.

'Your aunt lives in Dundee, doesn't she?'

'Yes.'

'Perhaps not too easy for her getting back and forward to the house to get it in order for your mother. Do remind me nearer the time and I'll get Mrs Murdoch to arrange for two of the maids to do what is necessary. That will relieve your aunt and, of course, yourself, of some of the preparations.'

'Thank you.'

Didn't he know or couldn't he guess that after having everything done for her, she wouldn't know where to begin?

Smiling, he handed her the letter, then dropped his eyes to the papers on his desk and picked up a pen. She was dismissed but in the kindest way, or so he would believe it to be. She put the pages back in the envelope, got up and left the study.

On hearing the door click shut the colonel put down his pen and thought about that letter. To him it was clear that Beth's father would be relieved to see his wife depart for these shores. No doubt her illness worried him but not sufficiently to let it interfere with his work. He would put it stronger and say that George Brown was in his element, feeling himself to be indispensable.

Then he thought about Beth. Judging by the look on her face she was none too happy to be going back to her own home. Still, he thought, that was only to be expected. Three years was a long time in a child's life and he could remember the state she was in when her parents had gone off and left her. She had got over that and she would get over this. All it needed was time. Give it that and she would settle back to the life she had once known.

He got up, his concentration gone. Perhaps he should

go and see his mother and give her the news.

'Yes, of course I'm relieved, dear, very relieved and I imagine that you are too?'

'Yes, I am, especially now that we expect Caroline to go to Rowanbank.'

She smiled.

'It also saves a lot of soul searching on my part.'

'Soul searching?' Her brows shot up.

'We have rather made use of Beth and, quite frankly, the thought of sending her to live with an aunt for whom she has so little affection was making me feel decidedly uncomfortable. This, I have to admit, has come at a very opportune time.'

'You dear boy,' she smiled fondly. 'You can live with yourself again?'

'Just about. Actually, I'll quite genuinely miss the child when she goes, which is something you won't.'

She frowned. 'Strange though it may sound to you I shall miss the girl. Having admitted to that, it is better for all concerned that it is the parting of the ways. We have Beth to thank that Caroline is a different girl and I'm sure she'll settle happily and enjoy boarding school. Her cousin Ruth is there after all and—'

'Ruth is two years older, Mother, and I remember enough about boarding school to know that senior pupils are most definitely not interested in taking juniors under their wing.'

'That is as maybe but I am sure that she'll settle.'

'That's absolutely awful, Beth,' Caroline said, close to tears. 'Of course I am sorry about your mother but it'll mean I'll hardly ever see you.'

'Mattie said that you'd be going off to that school—'

'Rowanbank. Some time in the future I may have to, but I don't think Mattie will be in too much of a hurry to see me go. After all she'll be out of a job, won't she?'

'Unless she has something else lined up?'

'Dreadful, these changes,' Caroline said glumly. 'Nanny has been threatening for ages and ages to leave us and go and live with her sister. I never believed her and now it's actually going to happen.'

'Be honest, Caroline, you don't really need a nanny.'

'I know that but it will be strange without her. I mean she has always been here and I suppose she has been a sort of mother to me. Which reminds me of something I was going to talk to you about,' Caroline said in the quick way she had of moving from one subject to another.

'What was it?'

'It was told to me in confidence by my grandmama but I'll tell you.' Her voice dropped. 'She thinks that daddy is serious about a certain lady and she is absolutely delighted.' Caroline kept looking at Beth, waiting for her reaction.

'I hope it is Mrs Cuthbert.'

'It is and I do like her.'

'That makes a change,' Beth said laughing.

'I like Jenny better than the others because she doesn't treat me like a little girl and fawn over me in that sickening way. Keeping in with daddy, that's all it is.'

Beth looked surprised. She had been mistaken about Caroline, she wasn't so easily taken in after all.

'You wouldn't mind if you got Mrs Cuthbert for a step-mother?'

'That really is funny, Beth. I never expected ever to say yes but I think it would be rather fun to have Jenny as my step-mother.'

They were both silent for a few moments, each thinking

of what the future might·hold.

'Sometimes I wish that things would stay the same,' Beth said wistfully.

'Can't, though.'

'No, I know that.'

'Still, I know what you mean,' Caroline said in a small voice. 'We've got used to each other and what I am going to miss most is telling you things that I know won't reach another soul.'

'When I go I'll miss Inverbrae House an awful lot but you most of all, even though sometimes you make me very angry.'

'Do I?'

'You know you do·but I suppose you can't help it, you've always got all your own way.'

'Not now, I don't always get it now. You like my daddy?'

'Yes.'

'You'll miss him?'

Beth nodded.

'Not grandmama, though?'

'Sometimes I nearly like her.'

'Sometimes I think she nearly likes you, too.'

'Because I'm going away.'

'Maybe it is. Grownups are strange.'

Beth couldn't have agreed more. She pondered then said, 'When I'm grown-up and have children I won't be strict with them. I'll let them know that I love them and I'll give them lots of hugs.'

'Didn't you get cuddles from your parents?'

'Hardly ever.'

'Why not?'

'Don't know.'

'My daddy cuddles me because he loves me. Not so

much now because he says I'm getting a big girl which I am not.' She giggled. 'I expect he cuddles and kisses Jenny now.'

Old Mrs Parker-Munro had all but given up hope of seeing her son remarry, and thus it was with a good deal of surprise and pleasure that she saw him look at Jenny Cuthbert in that unmistakable way. The young widow who had recently come to this part of the country had bought and settled into a house a few miles away from Inverbrae House. Discreet enquiries had satisfied the old lady that Jenny was of good family, not quite the equal of the Parker-Munros, but perfectly acceptable.

Attracting women had never given the colonel any trouble but most of them bored him after a while. That he was considered a catch he could not fail to know. A spare man, particularly when he is a handsome widower, is much sought after to make up the numbers at a dinner party. Many a fading beauty who had lost or missed out in the marriage stakes had looked at the colonel with hope in her heart.

In the colonel's case one could add that he was under forty, wealthy and owned an estate. None of this made any impression on Jenny Cuthbert. She was charming and polite when in his company but neither encouraged nor discouraged him, and it was this very indifference that set her apart. She intrigued him as no one else had and aroused feelings that he had not experienced since he lost his beloved Margaret. He had made love to women more beautiful than Jenny, women who had satisfied a physical need. But that was all it was – his feelings weren't involved.

Jenny was quite tall with a slim figure and small, firm breasts. Her eyes were light hazel, her hair, with a hint of a wave, was auburn and cut short in the style of the day. She had a smooth complexion and her face, though it wasn't beautiful, had something compelling about it. Other men saw it, he could tell, and jealousy was a new and not very pleasant experience for Nigel. Often he would find himself wondering about her late husband and what he had been like.

Proposing marriage to Jenny was constantly on his mind but he was desperately afraid of being refused.

'Pay attention, Beth, you'll have to direct me from here,' Tommy said as they approached the Lochee district of Dundee.

Beth had been lost in her own thoughts and looked up quickly.

'Follow the tramcar, that would be best,' she said.

Tommy was amused. 'Fair enough until it stops, what then?'

'I've only ever come by tramcar,' Beth said worriedly, 'go slowly and I'll try to remember where to turn off.'

It wasn't the correct turn-off, she knew it the moment they were in the street and she apologised to Tommy.

'Not to worry, we'll get back on the main road and if we get lost you can always get out of the car and ask.'

She didn't have to, the next turn-off was Walton Street and Tommy stopped the car outside number 6.

'She'll be at home?'

'My aunt? Oh, yes, she doesn't go out a lot.'

'How long will I give you? Half an hour or nearer the hour?'

'Make it about an hour then come up if you want, Tommy. Aunt Anne will give you a cup of tea, she's all right that way.'

'I won't, thanks all the same. Just you come down when

you're ready and you'll find me waiting.'

'How will you pass the time?'

'Take myself for a wee dander. First, though, I'll wait until I'm sure you've got in.'

Beth got out of the car, went in the close and climbed the stairs. Perhaps she should have let her aunt know that she was coming but it had happened so quickly. The colonel's suggestion had just come the previous night that Tommy should drive her to see her aunt and discuss the arrangements for her mother's homecoming. Beth wondered at the haste, it was almost as though he were hurrying her departure. Her mother wouldn't even be on her way home yet and the sea trip took a long time. She was beginning to feel very let down. Apart from Caroline, and sometimes her friend didn't seem too bothered about her going away, she didn't feel that anyone would miss her. Had it something to do with her, was there something wrong, that made people not love her enough? Her parents had left her behind and her mother was only returning home because of poor health. Life at Inverbrae House would go on as before and in a very short time she would be forgotten. Caroline would make friends at her school and those friends would be acceptable to Mrs Parker-Munro. Beth felt very depressed.

Her knock brought hurrying feet and the door was opened.

'Bless my soul, it's you Beth. Come away in.'

'Hello, Aunt Anne.'

'Why didn't you let me know you were coming? Not that I'm often out, I'm not the gadding about type, but this could have been one of the times and then you would have had a wasted journey.' She shut the door and Beth followed her aunt into the kitchen. The ironing cloth was covering the table and the flat iron was on its heel. There was the smell of damp clothes ready to be ironed.

Beth waited to be invited to, before sitting down.

'You've caught me in the middle of ironing, not my usual day, but I didn't want too much for Monday. Take off your coat, no need to act like a stranger, though that is what you are.'

Beth took off her coat with its little fur collar and her aunt took it and put it on the back of a chair.

'Right bonny coat, fine piece of cloth, too.'

Beth nodded. She knew what her aunt was thinking and she was right, her parents could not have afforded to give her a coat like that.

'Managed the journey by yourself?' she said as she prepared to clear the table.

'Please don't stop the ironing, Aunt Anne, we can talk while you do it.'

'No doubt we could but it isn't my way. There's time enough for this when you've gone. I was asking if you managed the journey on your own?'

'No, I got a lift in the car.' She knew that she sounded apologetic.

'Of course, keep forgetting that you're a toff now.'

Beth looked at her quickly but her aunt was smiling.

'Is Uncle Fred well?'

'Nothing coming over him. My, but you're growing into a fine big lass,' she said looking Beth up and down. 'Good to you, are they?'

'Yes.' Beth nodded vigorously, feeling she hadn't sounded sure enough.

The table was cleared, the iron put beside the fire, and the cloth folded. Her aunt did everything very quickly.

'Your Uncle Fred is at the timber merchants looking for bits of wood to make something he has in mind. You won't know but Adam is getting wed and they've managed to get a house. It's not much I'll grant you and I would have liked something better for them. Wanted them to wait awhile but not them, they were in a hurry to get married.' She looked sharply at her niece as though she had said something she shouldn't. 'Not that kind of hurry, she's a nice lass is Morag, a real sensible kind.'

'Have they set a date?'

'Not yet. Morag's folk want to make a splash of it and take St David's rooms for the reception, but it isn't that easy getting a suitable date with it being so well booked in advance.' She smiled. 'I'm happy enough about the delay. It lets them put a wee bit more by them, and more important to me your ma might be home by that time. I'd like it fine if she was well enough to attend, and you too of course.'

'She wouldn't want to miss it.'

'No, she wouldn't and I think that's the kettle boiling. I'll make a pot of tea, you won't be in a hurry to get away?'

'Tommy said an hour.'

'Plenty of time then.'

Beth took the cup of tea and a currant bun. 'Thank you.'

'Still haven't a lot to say for yourself, have you? Thought you would have had with all the posh training.'

'I'm sorry, Aunt Anne, I don't mean to be rude and you've been very kind, it's just – I don't know – I feel so—'

'Unsettled?'

'Yes.'

'Not to be wondered at, feel a bit that way myself. It's the not knowing what to expect. Knowing Harriet I'd say she was in a bad way.'

'You mean very ill?' Beth said, looking anxious.

'No, no, not very ill, that was stupid of me to alarm you. The heat would take it out of her but in her last letters I thought she sounded depressed, as if things hadn't worked out the way she had expected them to. But then that is perhaps just my imagination. What did you think?'

'I just thought that her writing was terrible and I wrote to tell her that.'

Aunt Anne laughed heartily. 'Did you now, Harriet wouldn't take kindly to that. Nice writing she always did, got a few prizes at school for it. I did notice but thought it was your mother in a hurry to get it off, maybe someone waiting to take it to the post. Never mind, once we get her home to her own house we'll nurse her back to health.'

'Yes.'

'You've got mixed feelings because you're going to miss that life you've got used to.' She paused. 'Even so, you've never felt yourself one of them, have you?'

'Is there anything wrong with people trying to better themselves if they want to? And I have been made welcome,' Beth said, stung.

'Bettering yourself is one thing, lass, and good luck to those who try and succeed, but trying to be accepted into another class that's a different matter altogether. Mostly it ends in heartache and resentment. Not that I am suggesting for a moment that those Parker whatever-you-call-them folk haven't been good to you. It has suited them to be. After all, they wanted a companion for their daughter and the lass had taken a liking to you.' She paused to take Beth's cup and put it on the table. 'What is to become of the girl?'

'Caroline will be going to boarding school.'

'There you are then, worked out very nicely for them hasn't it? Very convenient indeed to have your mother coming home at this time. They must be relieved. After all, it stands to reason they wouldn't want you in the house and their daughter away at school.'

What her aunt said made sense and Beth had the horrible feeling that it was all true. She hadn't wanted to accept what must have been clear to everyone else. She had served her purpose and the colonel would be relieved to see her go.

Beth wanted away before her aunt said any more. She got up, anxious to be gone and hoping that Tommy was waiting. 'I'll need to watch my time, Aunt Anne,' she said as she reached for her coat.

'Run downstairs and bring the lad up, he'll be glad of a cup of tea and I'll make fresh.'

'I knew you'd say that, Aunt Anne, and I asked Tommy before I came up but he said no, he had to get back.'

'Doesn't matter. You've got the road now so come again.'

'I'll try.'

'Make it a Sunday and you'll see your Uncle Fred, he'll be fair disappointed at having missed you.'

Chapter Eleven

He had to read it again and yet again. He couldn't believe it, the news was just too awful to take in. How could he tell that child? How could he break such dreadful news to her? Yet somehow he had to find the words to do it. There was the aunt in Dundee, of course, but because Beth was in his care the church authorities had notified him.

The need to tell someone was great and he went along to the sitting-room where he knew his mother would be.

She looked sharply at him. 'Nigel, is something the matter, you look a bit white?'

'Yes, Mother, something is very much the matter, read that.'

'My spectacles – over there on the cabinet.'

He got them for her and she put them on.

Her face was shocked. 'Oh, my dear, this is absolutely dreadful!' She shivered. 'What a wicked world we live in.' From over her spectacles she looked at her son. 'That poor, poor child.' Then she clutched at his hand. 'You must not be the one to tell her, Nigel. This will have to be broken to her gently and it needs a woman to do that.'

'Considering your treatment of Beth, Mother, don't tell me you are suggesting yourself?' he said with mild sarcasm.

She had the grace to look ashamed but even so her eyes were stormy. 'Men can be very stupid and shortsighted on occasion.'

'Explain my stupidity to me.'

'No, Nigel, I won't for the simple reason that you wouldn't understand.'

'Whatever I wouldn't understand, Mother, you are not the person to tell Beth.' He frowned. 'What a pity Nanny Rintoul isn't still with us, they got on so well together, and she could have done it and saved me,' he said as he turned away.

She stopped him at the door. 'If you are determined to take on this responsibility, Nigel, do be careful. Eleven is a very impressionable age.' Her voice grew weary and she closed her eyes.

'I'll be as gentle as I can, Mother, but she must be told at once.'

'Yes, I can see the need for that. The news will soon get out.'

'My relationship with Beth is good. I'll manage.'

'Very well.'

Beth was surprised and a little apprehensive to get a summons to the colonel's study and she went along quickly. She knocked at the door and a voice immediately said, 'Come in.'

Beth went in and closed the door behind her. She smiled, then grew uncertain when he didn't return it. He looked very grave.

'Sit down, Beth,' he said gently. When she did and her dark eyes rested on him he wondered if the study was perhaps the wrong place to break such news. The sitting-room would have been better, less formal, and he could have made sure that they wouldn't be interrupted. Too late for that and he could see that he had already alarmed her.

He was clearing his throat and Beth couldn't wait any longer. She had to ask.

'Is it about my mother, Colonel Parker-Munro, is she worse?' Beth said anxiously. There must be something very wrong when the colonel was taking such a long time to tell her.

He hesitated then said, 'Beth, my dear, it is my painful duty to tell you that I have just now received very bad news—' It was so formal but how else could he say it?

'It is my mother – please tell me, is she very ill?' Then, fearfully, as a terrible thought struck her, 'She's not—' She couldn't bring herself to say more, just looked over at him with frightened eyes.

'There has been a terrible tragedy—' She saw him swallowing before going on and Beth wanted to scream. Why was he taking so long about it? 'A terrible massacre—' He stopped, appalled at himself, he hadn't meant to use that word though that was what it had been.

'A massacre,' Beth repeated the word wonderingly. A massacre was what happened in a war. What was the colonel talking about?

'An uprising is the expression I should have used, Beth, and a number of the missionaries and their helpers have been killed.'

Her mouth went dry. 'My father—'

She saw a look of great sadness cross his face. 'Beth, my dear child, both your parents are dead.'

Her eyes, like saucers, never left his face and Nigel shook his head, took the handkerchief from his pocket and wiped the perspiration from his hands. His mother had been right, it wasn't a job for a man and he was making a mess of it. The minister, now why hadn't he thought of him before? The man was trained for such tasks, he should have been sent for.

Beth felt very strange as though she were floating and everything unreal. What was it the colonel had said? That her parents were dead, but that couldn't be. Her mother was coming home, maybe on her way by now.

'Beth, I can't tell you how sorry I am.'

'They aren't dead, it isn't true. You have made a mistake.'

'Beth, I'm afraid it is true, I have had official word from the church authorities.'

'Why would anyone want to kill them? Who did it?' She had spoken very softly as if to herself.

'Pardon?' He hadn't heard what she said.

'Who killed my mother and father?'

'The very people they were trying to help.'

'But why?'

He raised his hands, then let them fall on the desk. It was a question that would remain unanswered.

'My mother was wrong, she said that God would look after them.'

'Your mother said that to me too.' He remembered the way Mrs Brown's eyes had shone when she said it and hoped that her end had been swift and painless. 'We none of us understand how these things happen, Beth, but we have to believe that it is all for a purpose.'

'Would you like to know what my father would have said?'

'Yes, Beth, I would.'

'He would have said that it was His will.'

'They had their faith, Beth, they wouldn't have been afraid. And they wouldn't have suffered, it would have been very quick.' If only she would cry, scream even, but this calm acceptance, the flat voice, were unnatural and he

112

was growing increasingly concerned.

The strange, floating sensation was going but now the walls seemed to be closing in on her and Beth had a desperate urge to get out of this room. She saw the colonel get up from his chair and come round, and when his arm went round her shoulder she got up and pushed him away.

'Leave me, I don't want anyone,' then before he could stop her she had run from the study. She heard him calling her name but paid no heed. In her haste to reach her own room she almost knocked into old Mrs Parker-Munro. She, too, called out but Beth ignored her and ran on until she was in her own bedroom and the door shut. Then she threw herself on the bed.

Mrs Parker-Munro had been unable to settle and, seeing Beth's fleeing figure, she hurried to the study as fast as her protesting limbs would allow. Her son was at the door.

'Don't scold, Nigel, I was too upset to stay away.'

'I'm not scolding,' he said wearily. 'Come in and sit down, you look all in.' She let him help her into a chair.

'Just tell me.'

'She was very calm, mother, much too calm for my liking. Then suddenly, I wasn't prepared for it, she bolted out of the door. I saw she was heading for her room.' He shook his head and pulled his fingers through his hair, a habit he had when he was bewildered and worried. 'All I was doing was trying to comfort her but she didn't want that.'

'Phone for Dr Grieve, Nigel,' she said urgently, 'I don't like the sound of this at all.'

'I'll phone right away and Caroline will have to be kept away.'

'I've spoken to Caroline and told her that Beth's

parents have been killed in an accident and that the kindest thing would be to leave her alone with her grief.'

'Thank you.'

The middle-aged family doctor came very quickly.

'Just terrible! Unbelievable! I had heard the news before you telephoned. By this time it will be all round Sandyneuk and I think everyone's thoughts will be with that bairn.'

'Will she be all right?' Nigel asked worriedly.

'In time. That is the great healer, and remember she hadn't seen her parents for three years. If I know the lass she'll put a brave face on it.' He paused, closed up his bag, then looked with concern at his elderly patient. 'A tragedy like this affects everybody and I'd suggest, Mrs Parker-Munro, that you try to get a good night's sleep. Take two of your pills.'

'Never mind me, what about Beth?'

'She wants to be left alone and it is better at this stage to give in to her wishes.' He nodded thoughtfully. 'I'd leave her for an hour or so then try her with some food. Come to think about it, it would be better for a maid to take it in, then she won't have to talk unless she wants.'

'Are you leaving something to help her sleep?'

'Yes, but she may not require it. Children are not like us, sleep overtakes them no matter what.'

'One feels so helpless,' the old lady said.

'It's times like these when relatives can give support,' the doctor said. 'There is a need in us all to be able to talk about the dead with someone who knew them.' He smiled sadly. 'That is why grieving relatives, who never see each other from one year's end to the next, gather round at funerals and talk in hushed tones of the dear departed.'

That brought a smile. 'How very sad and how very true,' the old lady said.

'Beth has an aunt in Dundee, she will have been notified,' the colonel said, 'her only close relative as far as I know, but there is no strong bond there.'

'Well, as I say it is just a suggestion.'

The door opened and Beth saw a tray being placed on the table but, before the maid could look over at the bed, Beth had closed her eyes and was feigning sleep.

She couldn't eat, the thought of food made her feel ill. In any case she didn't deserve kindness. This was her punishment. As her father had often said there was no hiding anything from God. He would know that deep down she hadn't wanted her mother to come home. She had wanted them both to stay in India and let her go on living at Inverbrae House. As to boarding school, she didn't believe that Caroline wanted to go and if she made a big enough fuss she wouldn't have to. Caroline always got her own way.

Her thoughts were feverish as she began to toss about on the bed. Because she had these wicked thoughts God had let her parents die and she didn't believe what the colonel said, that they wouldn't have suffered. He couldn't know and he was only saying that to make it easier for her to accept.

Had they been killed together or had one seen the other die? Who would have been the braver? Her mother, she thought, and didn't know why she thought that.

In her mind's eye she began to see black figures with evil eyes and spears in their hands. She saw them stealing towards the camp then – then – the horror was too much for her and she had to get away, had to get out and far away from Inverbrae House. She looked at the clock and her eyes registered that it was well after six. A good time to make her escape and if she was quiet and careful no one would see her go.

From its hanger in the wardrobe Beth got out her school coat and fastened the buttons. Her scarf and gloves were on the shelf but she ignored them. Then she stood for a moment listening before opening the door and checking that no one was about. No one was, all was quiet, and she ran lightly along the passage. In a few minutes she was down the stairs with the only sound the click of the outside door as she let herself out. The cold damp of the November night touched her face but she felt nothing. The grey dark that she so disliked held no fear for her, instead she found it comforting since it would hide her from searching eyes. Keeping well into the side of the drive and brushing against the shrubs, she hurried until she was clear of the gates, then she adopted a steady walking pace. She knew where she was going.

The smell of the sea came to her and she breathed deeply as she made her way along the cobbled path that twisted its way down to the harbour. When she was little it had been her father's favourite walk. Together they would stand and watch the waves crashing against the harbour wall and if the sea was angry, huge mountains of frothy foam would boil over and spray them, forcing them to step back. The shrieking of the gulls as they swooped and dived both terrified and excited her but with her hand held firmly in her father's, she had felt safe.

For three years she hadn't seen them, hadn't greatly missed her parents, but she had known where they were and she had their letters. Now they were gone and she would never see them again. As her aunt had said, those at Inverbrae House had been kind because it had suited them to be. But that couldn't go on much longer, she didn't belong there and Caroline didn't really need her now. Well, perhaps for a little longer, but what after that? What was to become of her? With no money coming from her parents for her keep, Aunt Anne wouldn't be keen to have her, especially since she was so useless. She walked on – down – down – down – towards the sea.

'Daddy, I've looked and looked and Beth isn't anywhere.'

'She has to be somewhere, Caroline.'

'She wouldn't have run away, would she?'

'Don't be silly.' Worry was making him irritable and it showed in his voice. 'Why would she do a thing like that?'

'Well, she isn't anywhere in the house,' Caroline pouted. There was no need for daddy to use that tone of voice to her. 'I've looked, the maids have looked, everybody has looked.' She almost added, 'so there'.

There was no doubt that Caroline was deeply and genuinely concerned for her friend but she was enjoying the excitement, too. It was even worse about Beth's parents than she had thought. Her grandmama had wanted her to believe it was an accident but she knew better. She'd heard two of the maids discussing the tragedy and one had told the other that Beth's mother and father had been murdered by natives with long spears.

A full hour had gone before the search for Beth had got under way. An alarmed maid, coming from Beth's bedroom, had rushed to report Beth's disappearance to the housekeeper. Mrs Murdoch had gone along to check for herself that Beth was, indeed, not in her bedroom and finding it so had straight away reported the matter to the colonel. He in turn ordered a thorough search of house and grounds.

The grey-black November darkness was hampering the

search of the grounds and outhouses but a dogged, determined small band of searchers continued with the task until they were satisfied that the child was not in the grounds of Inverbrae House.

A very worried Tommy saw his employer on the steps of the house and went up to him. The colonel looked at him questioningly and Tommy shook his head.

'Nothing, sir, but could I make a suggestion?'

'Of course, if you have the least idea of where she might be then out with it.'

'Beth and me talked a lot, sir, and she used to tell me about the walks she took with her da. It was always down to the harbour they went.'

'The harbour! Dear God! Not there!' the colonel said as a real, crawling, dreadful fear gripped him. The child had acted strangely and in the state of mind she was in, there was no knowing what she might do. 'Come on,' he said urgently, 'into the car, I'll drive and you keep your eyes skinned.'

The car shot away before Tommy had the door shut. Driving down that road in this weather would be hell and good driver though he was, Tommy was glad it was the colonel who was at the wheel. With the fine mist clinging to the windows the windscreen wipers were of little use, and the car lights didn't give much assistance either. Neither man spoke as the car hurtled round the narrow, steep, twisting road. One concentrated on the driving, the other was looking for a lost, frightened child who could be anywhere.

The colonel was particular about his cars and the tiniest scrape or mark on the bodywork would result in a very severe reprimand. Judging by the scraping noises a great deal of the paintwork must be damaged by now, Tommy thought, but no mention was made of it.

'Sir!' Tommy just stopped himself from grabbing his employer's arm. 'There's something there, I'm sure of it.'

'Where, for God's sake?'

'Down at the bottom. If you could let me out, sir, I'll go and investigate.'

'Stay where you are, I've got us down this far, I'll manage the rest. In any case, I'll need to get to the flat before I can turn.'

'It is her, it's Beth,' Tommy said, trying to keep the excitement out of his voice. He longed to jump out of the moving car and run to Beth but years of obeying orders held him back.

'I'll go to her. You take the car back, Tommy, and watch how you turn it, enough damage has already been done,' he muttered as he put on the brake and got out. Tommy slid over to take the wheel. 'Be as quick as you can and get the news to everyone that Beth has been found, then come back for us.'

'Down here?'

'Good God, no! We'll walk up the Braes and get you there.'

Tommy felt a surge of anger as he watched the tall figure of the colonel walk away. He had wanted to be the one to find Beth and bring her back but typical of that lot to take all the credit, yet he had been the one to think of the harbour.

The shifting of the stones under the colonel's feet made plenty of noise but the figure sitting on the low wall gave no sign that she had heard. So still was she that she could have been fashioned in stone, and the lapping of the water against the harbour wall added an eeriness to the scene.

A damp cold was worse than an icy chill, he thought, and got through to the very bones. The child must be frozen. He would have to be careful how he went about this, the last thing he wished to do was to scare her. If he sat by her for a little – she must be aware that someone was there, he thought, as he sat down on the cold, wet wall and felt the icy cold seep through his heavy coat. He waited for Beth to turn her head but she made no move to see who it was, just kept on staring ahead. Down here it was less dark, he noted, or perhaps it was just his eyes becoming accustomed to the darkness.

'Beth,' he said softly. He wanted to touch her but was afraid to. It was as though the Beth he knew wasn't there and this was a small stranger. He tried again. 'Beth, dear, you must be very cold, come back with me and get a hot drink and then off to a warm bed. You'll feel much better then.'

Had she heard? He didn't know.

'It was my fault,' she said tonelessly.

'What was your fault?'

She turned to him then, a white face with anguished eyes but without a trace of tears. She gave no answer to his question.

'Give me your hand, Beth.'

Obediently, she let him take it. It was icy.

'Come along, dear, we must get back. Everybody is very worried. You shouldn't have run off like that.'

'Is everybody angry with me?' She asked the question but didn't seem concerned.

'No, Beth, no one is angry with you. Everybody was just very worried, but Tommy has gone ahead to let them know that you are all right. By the time we walk to the top of the Braes, he'll be there with the car.'

'Tommy?' she said surprised.

'Yes, it was his suggestion that you might be down here.'

She gave a ghost of a smile. 'Tommy is my friend and I

told him about the walks I used to take with my father.'
She was chatting now and he was glad, though the
sing-song voice wasn't Beth's. 'My mother would never let
me play with my friends at the harbour.'

'Very wise, too, it is dangerous.'

Hand-in-hand the man and the girl walked up the steep
brae. She was calling him 'daddy' now and he was afraid
to correct her.

How strange it was, she thought, that she should be
with her daddy, yet it was Colonel Parker-Munro who was
doing all the talking. Weariness was making her drag one
foot in front of the other and, picking her up, the colonel
carried her the last few yards to where Tommy was
waiting.

Chapter Twelve

Before the car had stopped, the door to Inverbrae House was opened and a blaze of light shone out and down the stone steps. To avoid the sudden influx of cold air into the hallway, Mrs Parker-Munro stood well back and held a restraining hand on Caroline. Behind them was the governess ready to take charge of her pupil once the old lady had satisfied herself that no real harm had come to Beth.

The housekeeper went forward and the colonel, thankful that his part was over, gave Beth into her care. Mrs Murdoch was visibly shocked to see the state Beth was in.

'Poor wee lass, you look frozen to the bone, and is it any wonder and you out on a night like this.' She took Beth's arm. 'Come along with me, dear, I've had two hot water bottles heating your bed and we'll soon have you nice and cosy,' she said soothingly.

'Daddy, why can't I go to Beth, she'll want me, I know she will.' Caroline was just a little bit peeved at all the attention Beth was getting.

'Not just yet, Caroline, Beth isn't well enough.'

'When will she be?'

'Very soon I hope.'

His mother spoke. 'Nigel, you had better change out of your wet clothes, we don't want you down with a chill.'

Nigel laughed. 'Honestly, Mother, you make me feel like a ten-year-old.'

'At that age you had enough sense to do what you were told,' she said tartly. Caroline giggled.

'Don't worry, Mother, I'm just going up and, speaking of chills, you shouldn't be out here.'

'Jenny arrived a short time ago. She heard the news and said she just had to come over.'

'Where is she?'

'In the drawing-room. She said she would prefer to wait there and I'll go along now and keep her company.'

'You do that and I'll be with you shortly,' he said, feeling a warm rush of pleasure at the thought of seeing Jenny.

The brightening of his face didn't go unnoticed, and the old lady was well pleased. She could hear wedding bells.

Wearing a light grey suit and feeling more like himself, Nigel joined the ladies in the drawing-room. There was a roaring fire that gave out a good heat and they each had a glass of sherry in front of them. Jenny was wearing a royal blue, long-waisted dress with large white lapels. She never dressed fussily, he thought, and always managed to achieve a look of elegant simplicity.

As he went forward he had a huge smile on his face. 'Jenny, how very kind of you to come over and enquire about Beth.' But for his mother sitting there, he would have taken her in his arms and kissed her properly, instead of which he had to content himself by touching his lips to her cheek.

'Such tragic news, that poor, poor child,' she said quietly, 'I couldn't stop thinking about her and I wanted to know if there was anything I could do to help.'

Before answering, Nigel poured himself a whisky,

added water then took himself and it to sit next to Jenny. 'I doubt if there is anything anyone can do,' he said stretching out his long legs to the heat. 'I was for getting the doctor but mother wasn't in favour.'

They looked over at the elderly lady sitting very straight in her chair and with her feet on a small padded stool. Jenny's pale-coloured, well-shaped eyebrows were raised in enquiry.

'Jenny, dear, I am afraid I am of the old school and in my opinion Dr Grieve would be of little help at the moment. A good night's sleep can do wonders, and since he comes to see me tomorrow morning he can take a look at Beth then.' She made to get up, feeling that she should leave them together, and Nigel was on his feet quickly to help her.

'Assist me to the door, Nigel, if you please, and I'll manage perfectly well after that. What you can do is tell the maid to have a tray brought to my bedroom. I shan't eat much but I must attempt a little.'

'Won't you wait and have dinner with us?'

'No, Nigel, it's been postponed twice already and it'll be a while yet. I expect it was ruined and they had to start again.' She sounded annoyed. 'Goodnight, Jenny.'

'Goodnight, Mrs Parker-Munro.'

Nigel, closing the door after his mother, showed his relief, and Jenny laughed outright. Drinking the rest of his whisky, he looked to Jenny but she shook her head. 'Mind if I do?'

'You carry on, darling, I'd say you need it.' She paused. 'Before you came in your mother was saying that you haven't been able to replace Rutherford.'

'I haven't. Butlers, my dear Jenny, I am discovering, are a dying breed but Maxwell is standing in and doing rather well. Perhaps I should just let him carry on and have young Tommy take over the driving.'

'Sounds like a good idea,' she said absently. 'Tell me truthfully what condition that child is in?'

'Very confused, worryingly so.' He poured himself a good measure of whisky and sat down. 'Do you know, Jenny, I didn't mention it to mother, but when I had Beth by the hand and we were walking up the Braes to the car, she began to address me as daddy.'

'Did you correct her?'

'No, I didn't.'

'That was sensible, darling,' she said with obvious relief. 'In her confused state she would very naturally connect the harbour and holding your hand with the walks she probably took with her father when she was a small child. I shouldn't worry too much about that.' She paused. 'I didn't bother to say it in front of your mother but I have already eaten.'

'Couldn't you take something and keep me company?'

'I'll have coffee with you, that's all. What I would like to do, Nigel, is go and see Beth. If she's asleep I won't disturb her.'

'She'll be asleep,' he said firmly, 'Mrs Murdoch would have given her something to make her sleep.'

'Let me go to her, Nigel, I may be able to help.'

He was trying to hide his annoyance. In his opinion Beth had caused enough trouble and worry for one day. She wasn't family after all and he had done all that could reasonably be expected of him. 'If you must.'

'Hers is the bedroom next to Caroline's isn't it?'

'Yes. I'll come with you.'

She put her hand on his arm. 'You stay where you are, have your drink, then go and have dinner.' As she finished talking there was a tap at the door and a maid announced that the meal was ready to be served.

★ ★ ★

Beth allowed herself to be undressed and the warmed nightdress to be slipped over her head.

'Into bed with you now,' Mrs Murdoch said.

Beth climbed into bed. Her feet touched the hot water bottle but she felt nothing.

'Don't be putting your feet on the bottle or it's chilblains you'll be getting, and painful things they are. Here, I'll push the bottles to the side,' she said slipping her hand below the bedclothes, 'you keep your feet on the warm patch. No, lass, don't go down, not just yet, you drink this. It'll give you a nice warm feeling inside and make you sleep.'

'I don't want it.'

'Drink it, Beth, it'll do you good.'

'I don't want it, please don't make me take it.'

'Force you? Never. What I'll do, lass, is leave it here on the table beside you and take it when you're ready. The light can stay on for a while.'

'Thank you.'

'Snuggle down like a good girl.'

Beth went under the bedclothes and turned her face to the wall. She was back in Inverbrae House, in her own bed, and she had never felt so frightened in her whole life or so alone. That was strange, she thought, since she wasn't alone.

Jenny gave the lightest of taps on the door before opening it and going in. She saw that the light had been left on and was glad that Mrs Murdoch had had the good sense not to leave the child in darkness.

'Beth, are you sleeping?' she said softly.

It was a strange voice, yet not totally strange, Beth felt sure that she had heard it before. She turned round and looked into Jenny Cuthbert's concerned face.

Jenny saw the dumb misery on the young face and without a word gathered Beth into her arms. Beth felt the comfort of being held in a warm embrace and then at last they came. Hard, painful, retching sobs that seemed to be torn from the small body and all the time Jenny went on holding her and making soothing noises. Only when the racking sobs changed to a soft crying did Jenny lower Beth's head, with its still damp curls, on to the pillow.

'I – I'm sorry,' Beth whispered, using the back of her hand to wipe the tears from her eyes.

An overwhelming feeling of compassion came over Jenny as she looked at the blotched face, the swollen eyelids, and the frightened, haunted expression. The child needed far more than she would get at Inverbrae House. She needed love and understanding and, perhaps most important of all, someone who would listen. She could be that person, she could help Beth, and in her usual impulsive fashion Jenny made up her mind there and then to have Beth stay with her.

'There is absolutely no need to apologise, Beth, dear. There is no shame in crying and we are all the better for a good weep. I've cried myself to sleep and felt a lot better for it.'

'Have you?'

'Yes, and I was a lot older than you.' She paused and took Beth's hand in hers. 'Listen, dear, how would you like to come and stay with me for a few days? Apart from my housekeeper, my treasure I call her,' she smiled as she said it, 'we should be alone. If you want to go for walks, we go for walks, if you don't we do something else or nothing, just as you please.'

Jenny saw the look of interest, then it faded.

'What is it, dear? Don't you like the idea?'

'Oh, I do, I wish I could, Mrs Cuthbert.'

'I'm Jenny to you.'

'I'd like to but I don't think I would be allowed—'

'A few days – a week with me? Can't see how anyone could object to that but, tell you what, I'll have a word with Colonel Parker-Munro, but I don't foresee any difficulty.'

'What about Caroline? I'm her companion.'

'You are her friend and a very good friend, and as for Caroline she can manage very well without you for a few days. Just stop worrying about other people.'

Beth gave a watery smile and Jenny kissed her on the brow. 'Now you can do something for me. You can drink that up, it's to make you sleep.' She handed Beth the glass and Beth took it and drank it all.

'Well done! Close your eyes and you'll be asleep in no time.'

'I love you, Jenny,' she murmured. Already everything was blurring and in less than five minutes Beth was sound asleep. For twelve hours she slept solidly and when she wakened it wasn't the tragedy that came first to her mind, it was the thought of spending some days with Mrs Cuthbert – Jenny as she was being allowed to call her.

'It's kind of you, my darling, but absolutely unnecessary to put yourself to all that trouble.'

'For me it would be a pleasure not a trouble.'

'Beth is my responsibility meantime.'

'Meantime?' she said, picking him up at once on that word.

He frowned, Jenny was becoming a nuisance taking all this interest in Beth. 'It was a temporary arrangement, no more than that. Her mother, poor soul, if only she had left

India sooner, would be living in Sandyneuk in her own house and Beth with her.'

'But the woman and her husband are dead,' she said abruptly.

'Yes,' he said heavily. 'I had met them both, but that first time I went to see Beth's mother she made quite an impression on me.'

'Beth had to get her good looks from somewhere,' Jenny said, amused at the turn the conversation was taking.

'Don't pick me up wrong. She was a pleasant looking woman, Jenny, but it wasn't that, and she was older than I would have expected. Rather it was a kind of innocence—'

'Innocence?' Her brow puckered.

'I'm not explaining this very well, but innocence is the only word that fits. That is what it was, a childlike faith, an absolute and total belief that she and her husband had been called to do God's Work and that no matter what, they would be protected from all harm.'

'Yet this could happen?'

'Makes one question one's beliefs, doesn't it?'

'I prefer not to think about it, but we've rather strayed from the point.'

'What were we talking about?'

'Beth coming to stay with me.'

'You are a very determined woman, Jenny Cuthbert.'

'I can be if something means a great deal to me.'

'Very well, I'll get Mrs Murdoch to arrange what is necessary and I'll drive Beth over to Greystanes.'

'Thank you, darling.'

'What about us? I feel terribly neglected.'

'Poor darling, but as you said yourself, you have a lot of paperwork to get through and not having me around will let you get on with it.'

'I'd rather have you around and blow the work,' he said taking her in his arms and, when their lips met, she returned his kisses but with less passion.

'Dearest,' she said pushing him away, 'I never feel relaxed when there is the possibility of someone coming in.'

'Why don't we get married then? Why keep putting me off? I love you but I'm beginning to wonder about your feelings for me.'

'Then don't wonder. I like you very, very much Nigel, I may even love you, but I do not want marriage.'

'Is it because of your first husband? I would understand, you know, you have nothing to fear. I loved Margaret and, like you, I have my memories but I am ready to love again. I didn't think there would ever be anyone until you came into my life.' He sighed. 'Oh, Jenny, what is it that is truly holding you back? A woman needs a man and I need you.'

'A lot of women need a man, I agree, but not all by any means. I have had marriage. Derek was good to me and I have pleasant memories, but now that I am on my own, I am finding a great deal of enjoyment in my independence.'

'You don't need me,' he said flatly, 'is that it?'

'No, it is not. I do need you.' The look she gave him made her meaning abundantly clear.

'You can't mean—' he said scandalised.

'Why not?' she said, opening her eyes wide, 'I don't imagine you've lived like a monk?'

He flushed. 'That's rather different.'

'Is it? It shouldn't be. Women have needs too, or do you imagine that not to be the case?'

'I don't think I have ever given the matter any consideration,' he said stiffly.

'How like a man.'

'Are you by any chance trying to make fun of me, darling?'

'Far from it. This is a serious conversation.'

'Let me get this right. You are suggesting a relationship rather than marriage?'

'Yes.'

'I can't believe you are saying this.'

'You're shocked at this moment but you'll get over it. Think about it seriously, Nigel. You have been a bachelor for – how long – eleven years?'

'I've told you before that there has been no one in that time whom I wanted to marry until you came along.'

'I'm flattered but not convinced. Had I been like those other women—'

'Not such a large number as you're trying to make out.'

'If you say so,' she smiled. 'The fact is that had I thrown myself at you, you would have quickly tired of me.'

'You would never have done that, you are just not the type.'

'That is perfectly true.' She paused. 'I have really shocked you, haven't I?'

'A little. You are a very remarkable woman, Jenny.'

'I'm honest and I want you to be that too. What we both want and need is companionship and, on occasion, perhaps more, but neither of us wants to lose our independence.'

'I'd still like to marry you.'

'But the alternative has its attractions?'

'I wouldn't deny that.'

'Bang goes your mother's hopes of wedding bells.'

'She's been disappointed before and survived,' he said drily. 'Her real fear is departing this life and leaving Inverbrae House without a mistress.'

132

'She takes good care of herself, I'd say she's likely to live to a ripe old age. As for Caroline she will manage beautifully, she's been brought up to it.'

'Then hopefully my daughter will marry a suitable young man,' he smiled. 'Talking of Caroline, mother and I are extremely pleased with her progress in every way.'

'Much of it I'd say thanks to Beth, even your mother admits to that. Strange that she hasn't taken to the girl, I find her a particularly charming child,' Jenny said musingly.

'Mother doesn't dislike Beth, she just doesn't want her at Inverbrae House. Don't ask me why. When I asked the reason I was told that I wouldn't understand, and that she was only thinking of Caroline. It's the future she is concerned about and I as a mere male wouldn't understand.'

'Ah!'

'What's that supposed to mean?'

'The most likely explanation – first, though, tell me what you see when you look at Beth?'

'What do I see when I look at Beth?' he said mystified. 'I suppose I see a bright, attractive child.'

'And that bright, attractive child in a few years time will turn into a tall, dark-eyed beauty.'

'So?'

'Poor boy, you haven't a clue. Your mother is looking ahead to the time when young men will come a-courting – and she would prefer Beth not to be on the scene.'

'Meaning my daughter won't attract young men?' he said angrily.

'Caroline, my dearest, is a pretty little thing and she will have her share of admirers. Some will love her for herself, others for her money and position. Those who already have money have no need to marry it and they will find

Beth irresistible. That is how I see it, though of course I could be wrong.'

He was thoughtful. 'I see. My mother is afraid that Beth may make a better marriage than her grand-daughter?'

'It shouldn't matter but I rather think it would.'

His smile didn't hide his concern. 'The girls are not yet twelve and long before young men come on the scene they will have gone their separate ways.'

'It's not fair,' Caroline said, two spots of angry colour on her cheeks, 'why can't I go and stay with Jenny as well? I've never been in her house.'

'It'll only be for a week,' her father said, frowning over his newspaper.

She went out, banging the door behind her, and the old lady winced. 'No need for her to get into that state and bang the door, but I can understand the child being annoyed. In my view Beth is getting far too much attention. That said, this separation has my approval.'

'Why?' he said sourly and put down the paper.

'Caroline depends far too much on Beth and this break will help. We must see that she is happily occupied and if I were you, Nigel, I would put Caroline's name down for next term. She badly needs the discipline of boarding school.'

'That's what I'd like, but what do I do about Beth?'

'Obviously we can't have her here without Caroline. You should go along with what Dr Grieve suggested. Didn't he say that after such a tragedy it would be better for the girl to be with her own people?'

'Yes, I recall that.'

'It's where she belongs.' She pursed her thin lips. 'Had she been with this aunt from the beginning the woman would have been receiving an allowance for Beth. That, of course, has ceased with the death of Beth's parents but perhaps if you offered a little money, it needn't be much—'

'Enough to cover her needs until she leaves school and takes up employment? Yes,' he nodded several times, 'that could be the answer.'

Chapter Thirteen

'Almost there, Beth,' the colonel said as the car took the corner. They were in a quiet, tree-lined avenue of detached houses with long, well-kept gardens that sloped down to the road. A few stubborn leaves clung to the branches of the tall trees, and on the lawns were signs of the overnight frost that hadn't lifted.

Strathvale was about eight miles from Sandyneuk and consisted of one long street of shops. The church was at the far end. It was small, had a spire, and was built of weathered stone. To each side of it were a number of headstones partly covered with moss and with much of the writing gone. An old villager made weekly visits throughout the growing season and used a scythe to keep down the grass, and shears for the verges. A rather dreary looking manse was nearby. At the other end of the village was the hall where everything of importance, and a lot besides, took place. The nearby field owned by a kindly farmer was much in use during the summer months for church fêtes, school sports, and various other activities.

Beth wore a cherry-red coat with a black velvet collar and matching buttons. A red beret covered her head and on her feet she had shoes with a strap. Mrs Murdoch was of the opinion that Beth should have been wearing a black armband as a mark of respect to her dead parents but, since it did not appear to have occurred to anyone else, and it was hardly her place to raise the matter, nothing was done.

Beth looked pale and wan. Her appetite was poor, she merely picked at food, and the doctor, informed of the forthcoming short holiday, was sure that the complete change was just the thing and likely to do Beth the world of good.

In a few moments the car slowed down and stopped. Beth saw the front door of the house opening and Jenny waving. Dressed in a calf-length tweed skirt with box pleats and a heavy-knit cream and brown jumper, she ran down the path, avoiding as she did the overhanging branches of trees. The late November day was bright but there was no heat in the sun and it was bitterly cold.

Beth got out first. Then, with a broad smile on his face, the colonel swung his long legs out, shut the door and went to meet Jenny. Beth saw them embrace, then exchange a kiss. She should have looked away but by the time she thought of it, it was too late. The kiss wasn't a casual one on the cheek but one with his mouth on hers that lasted a little while. Beth wondered if that meant that they were going to get engaged but keeping it a secret meantime. If so, Caroline would be getting Jenny for a step-mother and she thought wistfully of how lovely that would be, then immediately she felt a rush of shame and the awful feelings of guilt were back with her. To have thoughts like that was wicked when her own parents had so recently met their death in such a dreadful way.

Beth waited by the car. Her case was in the boot and she would have to stay until the colonel opened it, then she could carry it in. While Jenny and the colonel were talking, Beth took the chance to study her surroundings. Compared with Inverbrae House, Jenny's home was tiny, but compared to the cottage in Sycamore

Lane, Greystanes was huge. It was a substantial, two-storey-high structure of stuccoed stone and over the doorway was a graceful fanlight. On the ground floor were two bow-fronted windows and the long narrow ones above had ivy growing round them.

Beth was enchanted.

'Jenny,' the colonel said sternly, 'will you please get back indoors before you catch your death of cold.' Then he called over his shoulder, 'I'll bring Beth's case. On you go, Beth, with Mrs Cuthbert and I'll follow.'

'I've told Beth to call me Jenny, Mrs Cuthbert is far too formal. Come along, dear, we'll do what we are told for once and get out of this cold,' she said taking Beth's hand and hurrying them both indoors.

'Do you want the case taken upstairs, Jenny?'

'No, thank you, dear, leave it in the hall and come and have a drink.'

'I won't, thanks all the same. I have an appointment and I'm running it rather neat,' he said, depositing the case at the foot of the stairs.

'It was kind of you to bring me, Colonel Parker-Munro, thank you very much,' Beth said politely.

He smiled. 'You get the roses back in your cheeks, Beth.'

'She will if I have anything to do with it. I'll take your coat, dear, and I don't suppose you thought about bringing wellingtons?'

'No, I didn't.'

'Hardly time for those, the real snow doesn't come until after the new year.'

'Miss Harris smells it in the air, Nigel, and she is very often right.'

'Then I hope to goodness that she's wrong this time, I hate an early start to winter,' he growled before sketching a salute and letting himself out.

'I've got heavy shoes with me, Jenny.'

'Not to worry, if we do get a fall I've got a selection of rubbers somewhere and with a thick pair of socks, or a couple of pairs for that matter, we should manage to get you fitted. Oh, here she is, my Miss Harris.'

A pleasant-faced woman in her mid-fifties smiled to Beth and took her coat and beret from Jenny. 'What a lovely shade of red,' she said admiringly. She had a sallow complexion and blue-grey eyes that lit up when she smiled.

Jenny nodded. 'Just what I thought. A Christmas colour, I do love these bright happy shades. Beth, dear, let me introduce you. This is Miss Harris, my treasure, I'd be lost without her. And this is Beth Brown, my very special young friend.' Beth didn't know whether to shake hands or not and waited to see what Miss Harris would do. When she just smiled, Beth did the same.

'I've coffee prepared, Mrs Cuthbert, but I'll bring tea as well if the young lass would prefer that?'

'Yes, please.' Beth had tasted coffee but hadn't as yet acquired a taste for it.

They went through to the sitting-room overlooking the front garden where a log fire burned brightly. Deep blue velvet curtains were at the window and a selection of pot plants were on a table in front of it. Between the two armchairs at either side of the marble hearth was another table covered with an embroidered cloth, and on it were cups and saucers, sugar and cream and a plate of sponge cakes and biscuits. Miss Harris came in with a coffee jug in one hand and a pot of tea in the other.

'Thank you, Miss Harris. Just leave those beside me and I'll pour.'

'If that's all meantime, Mrs Cuthbert, I'll take myself to

the shops. When it comes to butcher meat I do like to see what I'm getting instead of taking what they send.' The door closed softly, then opened again. 'I've taken Beth's case up to her bedroom and I'll unpack it before I go out. That'll save the lass the trouble.'

Beth smiled her thanks and Jenny nodded.

'Are you comfortable there, Beth, or would you like another cushion?'

'No, this is fine, thank you.'

'Once we've finished I'll take you on an inspection of the house,' she laughed. 'That won't take us long, but I want you to know your way around so that you can feel completely at home.'

'We only had a tiny cottage in Sycamore Lane,' Beth's voice wobbled, 'and I think this is the nicest house I have ever been in.'

'Beth, sweetheart, you haven't seen it.'

'But I know, I just know.'

Was this the best time, Jenny was wondering, and decided, since they were on their own, it was.

'There are times, Beth, when it helps to talk to someone. I know in the past it has helped me. I'm a good listener and you can be assured that nothing you tell me will be repeated to another soul. Perhaps I too may tell you things that I wouldn't want others to know.'

Beth looked very solemn. 'Jenny, I would never, ever say anything or tell anybody, honestly I wouldn't.'

'I know that. We are friends and we can trust each other.'

Beth moistened her dry lips. 'I think I must be wicked, Jenny.' She dropped her eyes to the floor.

'That you most certainly are not.'

'I am. You see my father told me, and he must have got it from the Bible, that you don't have to do wrong things to be wicked, thinking them is nearly as bad.'

'In that case there's not much hope for most of us,' Jenny said drily. 'Tell me what bad things you were thinking.'

'I didn't really want my mother to come home from India because it meant I would have to leave Inverbrae House.'

'That wasn't wicked, Beth, it was perfectly natural in the circumstances. Your parents wanted to go to India, it was their wish and they put their wishes first, although it meant leaving you behind. In my book that squares it up. You have nothing to feel guilty about,' she said firmly.

'They wouldn't have gone if they had loved me enough,' Beth burst out. 'You see, Jenny, they never – except for once at the station—' she stopped and struggled with her tears.

'Take your time, dear, we have plenty of it.'

Beth swallowed, dabbed at her eyes with her handkerchief and continued, but in a whisper that Jenny could only just make out. 'Caroline and girls at my school get lots of hugs and kisses, but I only got a hug before they left. My mother never even kissed me at night before I went to sleep.'

'That doesn't mean they didn't love you, I'm sure they loved you very much, they just weren't demonstrative, it wasn't their way. I can understand the hurt, though, probably better than most.' She paused to fill up her cup. 'Come on, dear, have a little sponge, there is only a bite in them. I'm making a beast of myself, this is my third,' she said, picking one up and putting it on her plate.

Beth wasn't the least bit hungry but to please Jenny she took one and bit into it.

'Where was I? Oh, yes, I was pretty much in the same boat, Beth, my parents weren't demonstrative either. I don't even recall them showing affection to each other, but they were happy enough. It wasn't in their nature to show, in a physical way, what they felt, but they both loved me and I have absolutely no doubts that your parents loved you. Am I making myself clear?'

'Yes, you are, but I wish my parents hadn't been like that. You aren't.'

'No, I'm the other way, I'm rather too demonstrative.'

'You aren't and anyway it is much better.'

Jenny smiled and had a faraway look on her face. 'I was lucky to have a grandmother with whom I spent most of my holidays. She was a lovely person, Beth, and I absolutely adored her.' She waved a hand round the room. 'This was all hers and in the Will she left me this house, the contents, and enough to keep me, if not lavishly, then without need for worry. My late husband left me a little, too, and I feel very fortunate to be in the position I am. Independence is a fine thing, Beth.'

'Does that mean you won't want to get married again?' Then she looked worried. 'I shouldn't have said that, should I?'

'I don't mind, and since you are unburdening yourself to me I'll be honest with you. Never is a long time and I can't say for sure that I'll never marry, just that I have no plans to enter into matrimony in the foreseeable future.' She gave a chuckle that made Beth laugh. 'In a few years time I'll be so old and wrinkled that no one will want me and that, I suppose, will serve me right.' She jumped up. 'Good, I've got you laughing, but that is enough of serious talk just now. Come on and I'll show you the house. Will you be warm enough? Upstairs is cold during the day but the bedroom fires go on in the early evening and the rooms are easily heated.'

'This is warm,' Beth said, plucking at the Fair Isle

jumper she was wearing over her navy blue pleated skirt.

'My grandmother used to knit the loveliest Fair Isle jumpers and gloves and she kept me supplied, but sadly my stock is now well past its best.' They crossed the hall to a lounge that looked out on to a landscaped back garden and, beyond that, to trees and shrubs that gave complete privacy to the house. Beth walked over to the window.

'Do you do any gardening, Jenny?'

'In the spring and summer I potter about a bit, but I have a regular gardener who comes and he takes on casual labour when it is needed.'

'My mother was very good, we had the best garden in Sycamore Lane.'

'Perhaps you have green fingers, too?'

'I don't think so.'

'You don't know. Wait until you have your own garden and you may take a great pride in it.'

'This is nice,' Beth said, looking at the Regency striped curtains, the chintz-covered furniture and the water colours on the plain cream walls.

'Yes, I like it myself. Nigel – the colonel is of the opinion that I should get rid of the lot and start again.'

'You wouldn't, though?'

'Probably not. Not for a long time, anyway.'

'Was the furniture your grandmother's?'

'A lot of it. The beds I got rid of, they sagged a bit, and I've added a few pieces of my own but, yes, it is largely as it was in her day. Now we come to the dining-room,' she said going to the next door and opening it. This was a slightly smaller room with an Adam fireplace, a long dining table and high-backed chairs pushed under the table. One picture hung on each wall. The pictures were of country scenes. Miss Harris hadn't as yet returned and they took a peep into the kitchen. There was the appetising smell of recent baking and a fruit cake was cooling on a tray. A cooker and oven occupied one wall and cupboards covered the others. There was a walk-in pantry.

'On the coldest days I envy Miss Harris the warmth of the kitchen, but on hot, sunny days she has my sympathy.' Jenny closed the door and pointed. 'Nothing of interest, just cupboards, and the door at the very end is a toilet. The bathroom is on the half landing,' she said as she went ahead and up the carpeted stairs and stopped. 'That's a bedroom, or could be if required. Miss Harris calls it the lumber room, I refer to it as the glory hole. We won't bother with it but feel free to look around, you never know what you may find there. This is the bathroom,' she added, pushing the door wider. 'Functional but hardly luxurious. One day I've promised myself a whole new bathroom, but the thought of all the upheaval puts me off.'

A further flight of stairs brought them to the three bedrooms. 'This is mine.' Beth saw a double bed with a gold-coloured bedspread, then she was being shown her own where there was a single bed.

'It's lovely, Jenny, and blue is my favourite colour.'

'Good! I'm glad you like it. This was my room when my grandmother was alive. I did have the painters in for this one to freshen it up. And when I was in Perth I saw that blue-sprigged curtain material and couldn't resist it.'

Beth's eyes were shining and Jenny said a silent prayer that she had had the foresight to invite the child to Greystanes, she needed away from Inverbrae House. It wasn't so much grief for her parents that had brought her down to this low, but rather that she didn't feel enough grief. She was very mixed up and Jenny surmised that there was a great deal more worrying her, but all in good time. Beth was beginning to trust her and when she was ready it would all come out.

They went downstairs and could hear Miss Harris singing as she went about her duties.

'She has a good voice, Beth, and with proper training Miss Harris would have been very good. I once said that to her but I couldn't convince her that I wasn't joking. She is totally unaware of her gift.'

'Maybe there are lots of people like that, Jenny?'

'I have no doubt there are and it is such a waste. Come and see this,' she said walking away and opening a door that Beth believed to be a cupboard. It was far from that, it was a studio.

'You paint? You are an artist?' Beth exclaimed as her astonished eyes took in the easel and board, a table cluttered with brushes and paints and a mixture of colours on a palette. A paint-stained smock hung on a hook at the back of the door and a worn rug covered the linoleum beside the easel.

'No, I am not, and more's the pity. My grandmother was the artist and though I know I should, I haven't as yet been able to bring myself to clear the lot out. The paint and stuff won't be much good but some struggling artist could make use of the rest. One day I'll get down to it. The paintings downstairs in the dining-room are my grandmother's work.'

'I didn't get a proper look at them.'

'I showed them to someone knowledgeable and he said there was talent, but what she produced was amateurish because she hadn't had the benefit of tuition.'

'Why didn't she?'

'Money wasn't the problem. My great-grandparents were not wealthy but comfortably off, but in those days it was just not done. Young ladies were not encouraged to have a career and art, in all its forms, was very much a man's world.'

'Then it shouldn't have been,' Beth said indignantly, 'and I bet some women were even better than men.'

'And so say all of us!' She laughed. 'I couldn't agree more, but here we are approaching the 'thirties and things haven't improved all that much, but give it time, Beth, and we may get something approaching equality.'

'Do you really think that?'

'Alas, no, just wishful thinking on my part. Too many women are happy enough with their lot for the others to be taken seriously.'

'One day I hope to have a career.'

'Don't you want to fall madly in love with some handsome young man?'

'And live happily ever after like a princess,' Beth laughed.

'Not all of them are happy. You, my dear, are going to grow up to be a beautiful woman and it may well be that you can have a happy marriage and a career.'

Beth blushed and looked uncomfortable. 'I wanted to be small and slim and graceful when I grew up but I just keep growing.'

'You are to be tall and slim and graceful and believe me, that is very much more desirable. My dear child, you don't know how lucky you are.'

'Caroline is small and pretty,' she said wistfully.

'Yes, she is, and with a little less spoiling she could be a delightful girl.'

'She can't help that though, can she?'

'I think she could, and a dose of boarding school may be just what she needs.'

Beth didn't answer but it brought back all her fears.

'Miss Harris will have tidied up by now, we'll go and see.'

Miss Harris had, the table was back in its own place and logs had been added to the fire. Jenny went over to the fire and stretched out her hands before the warmth. 'Aren't your hands cold?'

'No, they aren't and I'm not in the least cold.'

'Lucky you, my hands go dead. Bring in your chair, dear. No, nearer than that.' Beth brought it forward and sat down and Jenny moved hers even closer to the heat. 'Not desperate to go out of doors, are you?'

'No, I like it here.'

'Fine. For your first day we'll make it a quiet one.'

Beth felt very contented. It was such a novelty for her to be able to talk to an adult the way she could with Jenny.

'We'll have what my old gran used to call a good old chin-wag, and for the rest of your stay we'll have walks in the country and afternoon tea in a darling little tea-room. It's quite a distance from here, but we'll have rested before the return journey.'

'Sounds lovely to me,' Beth smiled.

They were both silent for a few minutes, a comfortable silence, then Jenny touched Beth's hand. 'Forgive me for saying so but you, my dear, are too sensitive for your own good. In this world we have to fight for our own little corner and all of us suffer from guilt feelings at some time in our life.' She paused. 'What I am about to tell you is for your ears only.' She paused again. 'I married Derek for all the wrong reasons. No, don't misunderstand, I had a tremendous affection for him, but I wasn't in love. To my shame I used him to escape from being stifled at home. Mind you, looking back I must have been a trial to my parents, but I longed for freedom and they were old-fashioned and terribly strict. Derek, poor lamb, came along. I saw my chance and took it.'

'Did you regret marrying Derek?'

'No, I didn't, Beth. I never regretted my marriage, only that I had cheated Derek. There you are, you see, my guilt feelings.'

'He must have loved you?'

'Yes, he did,' she said softly, 'and he was very good to me.' She sighed. 'He made no secret of his love, while for me there was a great deal of pretence.'

'Perhaps he never knew that it was pretence?'

'That, my dear Beth, is the nicest thing you could have said and what I have always secretly hoped.'

'Did Derek become ill and die?'

'No, it was an accident. He was a little bit of a show-off, was Derek, ignored the warnings and went too far out. It would have been to impress our friends and he was a strong swimmer. Poor Derek, by the time people realised that he was in difficulties and got help it was too late to save him.'

'That was awful, Jenny.'

'Yes, it was. Had I been there at the time perhaps I might have got help sooner, but I wasn't.' She looked at Beth. 'I'm over it just as you will get over your loss.'

'I think I am getting over it, Jenny, but sometimes I have bad dreams and in them I'm – I'm—'

'Imagining terrible things?'

She nodded and her mouth trembled. 'Colonel Parker-Munro said they wouldn't have suffered, but how could he know that, Jenny?'

'He couldn't, of course.' She paused and looked thoughtful. 'I'm not a particularly religious person, Beth, but occasionally I do go to church and one minister, a visiting minister, said something that stuck with me. He said that no one gets more than they can stand. He was talking about suffering, suffering pain. No one can know for sure but I am of the firm opinion that it would all have happened so quickly that there would have been no time to feel pain. Does that help?' she asked gently.

'Yes, it does.' She gave a deep, shaky sigh. 'Do you know what I wish?'

'No. What do you wish, Beth?'

'That this go on for ever, just us talking like this.'

'You really are a sweet child and you are holding something back, my dear. Remember what I said – a worry shared is a worry halved.'

'It's only that – well, I can't expect to be at Inverbrae House much longer.'

'Why not?'

'Caroline has changed her mind and she doesn't mind going to boarding school now, especially since she would be going as a weekly boarder.'

'You'll see each other at the weekend.'

Beth shook her head. 'No, it won't be like that. Caroline tells me things.'

'What has Caroline been saying that she shouldn't?'

'Only that she overheard her father and grandmother discussing me and they said they could hardly be expected to be responsible for me for much longer, or something like that. They don't want me, Jenny.'

'Caroline may have got it wrong.'

'No, Jenny, it's true,' Beth said miserably. 'Colonel Parker-Munro has been encouraging me to visit my aunt.'

'So that you can go and live with her?'

'Yes.'

Jenny was thoughtful as she lifted the poker, poked at a log, then replaced the poker. What Beth was afraid of could very easily happen.

'Don't worry too much about it, Beth, things have a way of working out.'

They were silent, looking at the fire, then Beth spoke. 'I wonder what will happen to our house in Sycamore Lane?'

'Was it rented?'

'Yes, someone, a family, had the use of it, but they had to get out when—' she swallowed, remembering the letter, 'my father told them to vacate it for—'

'Your mother coming home?' Jenny finished for her.

'Yes.'

'Very likely you and your aunt will have to see to disposing of the furniture and clearing out the house completely.'

'Aunt Anne can have everything.'

'Perhaps some if it could be sold and you would be entitled to whatever it raised.'

'No, I wouldn't want that. Aunt Anne can have it all.'

Beth would look back and remember those wonderful days at Greystanes as being one of the happiest times of her life. Jenny's sympathy and understanding had removed the burden of guilt that had hung so heavily on her. Of course, she still had worries. She couldn't help worrying about what was to become of her when Caroline went off to boarding school. Jenny hadn't been able to help there, Beth thought. In all likelihood she would end up with Aunt Anne and, if she did, perhaps it would have been for the better, as her aunt said, if she had gone there in the first place. Then she wouldn't have had the awful change from Inverbrae House to a tenement in Dundee.

When she awakened on her last day snow was falling steadily beyond the window and a snowy white blanket stretched for as far as the eye could see. Beth dressed quickly.

The small sitting-room was the easiest to heat and, since it had a table, it doubled as a breakfast room and occasionally as a dining-room.

'I like eating in here,' Beth had said on one occasion.

'So do I, but I remember my grandmother saying how easy it was to fall into bad habits, and that rooms in a house should be used for what they were intended. In this case, my dear Beth, it means using the dining-room at least for the evening meal. If I don't I feel guilty.'

'Even when you are eating on your own?'

'Even then, but I hasten to add that I don't dine all that often on my own. I'm either out or have friends in.' They both turned as the door, off the catch, was pushed open and the housekeeper came in carrying a tray and on it plates of fluffy scrambled eggs and a rack of nicely browned toast. 'Is this weather to last, Miss Harris? Beth is hoping it will.'

Miss Harris smiled indulgently. 'Well, Beth, I have it on good authority that this won't last the day. There is a definite change on the way, it'll become milder and all that snow will have disappeared before your head touches the pillow tonight.' She poured tea into the cups and put down the teapot. 'If you want to make the most of it, lass, I'd suggest you get out when you finish your breakfast.'

Beth looked hopefully in Jenny's direction.

'You win, my young friend,' Jenny said in mock surrender. 'I'll look out my wellingtons and then I'll—'

'All done, Mrs Cuthbert,' Miss Harris said smugly, 'I've three old pairs looked out for Beth and some thick socks.'

'Wonderful, isn't she, Beth?'

'I think you both are.'

In her red coat, her beret, a scarf of Jenny's tied round

her neck and her hands in warm gloves, Beth looked cosy and happy. The roses were back in her cheeks, her eyes were clear and bright, and she laughed delightedly at the deep hollows made by her much too large wellington boots. Inside them, over her slim feet, she wore two pairs of thick, hand-knitted socks.

Jenny arrived outside in a bottle green coat with huge pockets and a storm collar. On her head was a woollen cap that covered her hair completely and her boots were shiny black. Looking at the happy eleven-year-old, Jenny felt a deep sense of satisfaction. It just showed what a little loving kindness could do, she thought. Miss Harris had produced meals that looked appetising and would appeal to a child. Small helpings were served with the dish left should either of them want more. No one was more delighted than the housekeeper when Beth's appetite returned and she waited hungrily for the next meal to be served.

'Come on, Beth, we'll take a walk down to the shops and save Miss Harris the trouble.'

'Have you got a list?' Beth said cheekily.

'Meaning I won't remember what to get?'

'Miss Harris says you forget what you are supposed to buy and come back with something totally different.'

'Very true, I'm afraid, but I do have a list this time and a shopping bag which you can carry,' she said handing Beth a crocheted bag that stretched to accommodate a remarkable number of purchases.

The shopkeeper had taken the list, then carefully selected the items before packing them into the bag. Beth giggled as Jenny kept adding whatever took her fancy, and only with difficulty did they all go into the bag.

'It's a mite heavy when you have a fair walk,' the shopkeeper said. 'I could have them delivered to Greystanes once my laddie gets back, but in this weather I wouldn't like to say when that will be.'

'That's kind of you, Mr McGregor, but I'd better say no. Miss Harris is sure to be requiring something straight away, and it is as much as my life is worth to go back emptyhanded.'

'Well, if you put it that way, and you've a helper I see.' He was a red-faced, jovial man with a huge stomach, bristling moustache and keen eyes that missed very little. He needed to have eyes in the back of his head to watch those young scallywags. Take off with an apple or what takes their fancy, they would, if they thought they would get away with it, he told them.

'Let me carry the bag, Jenny,' Beth said eagerly.

'There you are, then. You take it the length of the church, that'll be far enough, and I'll take it from there.'

They set out and after a while Jenny took a bar of chocolate from her coat pocket and broke off two squares. She gave one to Beth and the other to herself.

'Normally I like two squares in my mouth to get the taste, but we'll be dainty today and make it last out.'

When they came in sight of the house Beth stopped talking.

'You're quiet, Beth, and you look sad.'

'I'm sad because this has to end.'

'It has gone quickly, hasn't it?'

'Much too quickly and I wish I had the right words to tell you – to tell you—' she broke off, too choked to go on.

'Beth, dear, I have enjoyed it too and I know that Miss Harris has loved having you. You'll come back when the better days arrive.'

'You mean that?'

'Beth, you should know me well enough to know I don't say things out of politeness. Of course I mean it.'

★ ★ ★

'Jenny, what time is Colonel Parker-Munro expected?'

'He didn't say, but I imagine late morning or early afternoon, and as patience isn't his strong point you had better be packed and ready.'

'I'll go and get my case packed this very minute,' Beth said, making to get up from the breakfast table. She had finished hers but Jenny took a long time over her second cup of tea. Beth could please herself, she could either wait or excuse herself from the table. Jenny didn't stand on ceremony.

'No, Beth, dear, leave the packing to Miss Harris,' Jenny said stifling a yawn. She was in her dressing-gown but Beth was dressed.

'I can easily do it myself,' Beth protested.

'I daresay you could but it would be a waste of time since it would end up being unpacked. Miss Harris has a special way of arranging everything neatly into the smallest possible space. Left to me I usually have to sit on the case to get the wretched thing to close.'

'I'd better leave it then.'

'Sit still and tell me something I keep forgetting to ask.' She drained the last of her tea. 'Has the colonel ever suggested some other way of addressing him?'

'No.'

'Colonel Parker-Munro is such a mouthful.'

'That's what my mother once said.'

'Did she?' Jenny pursed her lips. 'Not an easy one, it's difficult to know what would be acceptable.' She flicked a crumb across the table and grinned. 'Don't tell him or anyone else for that matter, or he'll kill me, but in the army, among his fellow officers, he was known as Parky.'

Beth looked shocked. She couldn't imagine anyone being sufficiently disrespectful to shorten the colonel's name like that. 'He doesn't look like someone you could call Parky,' she said.

'I have to agree there, but apparently they did and he hated it.' Jenny wiped her mouth with her napkin. 'To call him colonel is a bit too casual and I doubt he would approve. Personally, I see nothing wrong with Uncle Nigel, not after three years in his household, but the old lady would have something to say about that I'm afraid.'

'I could never call him Uncle Nigel,' Beth said firmly. She knew that Mrs Parker-Munro would be horrified and she rather thought that Caroline wouldn't be too happy about it either.

'Sorry, love, but you appear to be stuck with that mouthful.'

'I don't mind, I'm used to it.'

As forecast by Miss Harris and the villagers the snow quickly disappeared and by afternoon it had turned to slush and a dreary dampness was in the air. Lunch over, Beth was at a loose end and with the colonel due to arrive at any time she couldn't venture far. After a last look in at all the rooms, Beth went along to see Miss Harris. She wanted to say thank you for all the kindness shown to her.

'Was that the car, Beth?'

'No, not yet, but when it does I won't have the chance to thank you properly.'

'Nothing to thank me for, lass,' the housekeeper smiled as she emptied the water from the basin where she had been scraping and peeling the vegetables. After carefully holding back the scrapings from going down the sink and choking it, she dried her red roughened hands on a towel and gave her whole attention to Beth.

'You've been very kind and I wish I didn't have to go,' she said wistfully, then, afraid to have given the wrong impression, she hastened in with, 'I don't mean I'm unhappy at Inverbrae House, I'm not, but this has been special.'

'You're looking a lot better. Mrs Cuthbert has been a comfort to you and from time to time we all need a bit of that and a shoulder to cry on.'

'Jenny is the only grown-up I've been able to talk to – to – about—'

'What's been worrying you.'

'She told you!' Beth felt an overwhelming disappointment. She had been so sure that Jenny would keep her promise and not repeat a word of what she had said.

Miss Harris was watching the young face. Beth wasn't old or experienced enough to hide her feelings.

'All Mrs Cuthbert told me, Beth, was that you had your own private worries but you were getting to grips with them. She is not a lady to break her promise but I didn't need to be told, I could see that you were sorely troubled. Mind this, lass, worrying doesn't do any good.'

'Jenny said that.'

'Easier said than done, but you're a bit easier now?'

'Yes, and I feel a lot better.'

She smiled. 'I'm glad. At your age you shouldn't have worries.'

'Have I been much trouble?'

'Anything but. What you have been is a very nice, well-behaved young lady.'

'I never did anything to help.'

'And do me out of a job? Now I wouldn't want that, would I?'

'My aunt thinks all girls should do some housework, but my mother never made me. She said I would get plenty of it when I was older.'

'A lot of folk are like your aunt but I would say with your mother, and if I had been blessed with a daughter I hope I would have allowed her to enjoy her childhood with just the occasional wee help. Something tells me that you are going to grow up to be a very lovely lady.'

'Caroline, she's Colonel Parker-Munro's daughter, says I can't ever be a lady because I was born poor. But that is not true, Miss Harris, we were never poor, we just didn't have a lot of money.'

Miss Harris burst out laughing. 'Beth, you are a caution, and as to being a lady, to my mind it has nothing to do with wealth or position. A lady is someone who is kind and gentle and good inside.'

'Like Jenny?'

'Yes, like Mrs Cuthbert.'

'Is that my name I hear—'

'Miss Harris was telling me what a real lady is like and you are one, we both said that.'

'And I am going to say something else. Will you both kindly leave my kitchen and let me get on?'

'Come on, Beth, we know when we are not wanted.'

Lunch was over and cleared away before the colonel arrived. Jenny went out to meet him. Beth stayed indoors, she wanted to keep out of the way until they had greeted each other.

The colonel was bare-headed and wore a heavy tweed suit, one that Jenny, in her outspoken way, had said was only fit for a beggar and one who wasn't too particular. They were arm-in-arm when they came into the house.

'I hope Beth is ready.'

'She is and has been since morning,' Jenny said tartly.

'Don't blame me, it wasn't my fault, I got held up and couldn't get over any earlier.'

'Didn't matter, I was in no hurry to part with my guest.'

'No problems with her?'

'None.'

'Mother said to be sure to tell you how grateful she is for you taking Beth for a few days.'

'It was a pleasure, I assure you, and be sure to tell Mrs Parker-Munro that.' There was a small frown on Jenny's face. Were they trying to make out that Beth was a burden when nothing could be further from the truth? Then again she could be wrong and it was kindly meant. It didn't do to jump to conclusions.

'Yes, I'll give mother the message.' They were now in the sitting-room with the colonel standing until Jenny had seated herself. She saw that he looked well satisfied. 'Just shows how quickly children adapt to change. I expected Caroline to have missed Beth, be lost without her, but it wasn't the case.'

'Perhaps the break from each other did them both good.'

'Could be. Certainly Caroline didn't weary.' With the arrival of Beth they broke off their conversation. 'Ready, Beth?'

'Yes, I'm ready, Colonel Parker-Munro.'

'Good! Go and wait in the car and I'll be out directly.'

Her case was by the door and as she made to pick it up, Jenny gave a small shake of her head.

'A week is a long time, Jenny, and I've missed you.'

'Have you, darling?'

'You know I have.' He paused and just wished that Jenny would say that she had missed him too. 'Since you didn't enjoy the last play I didn't get tickets for this one,' he said.

'It was poor, you have to admit that. The players are so wooden Nigel, or am I being over critical?'

'No, Jenny, you aren't. Attendances are falling. It wasn't a full house when we were there but I blame the choice of plays rather than the players.'

'You may be right. I do wish we had an Opera House close by.'

He raised his eyebrows. 'Nothing to hinder us having a weekend in Edinburgh and enjoying what is on offer, is there?'

She smiled. 'Nothing that I can think of.'

'As regards this evening – dinner at the Majestic, I thought?'

Her eyes lit up like a child promised a treat. 'Wonderful, for want of a better word,' she said. Jenny made no secret of what pleased her and what didn't. Her total lack of pretence was one of the things Nigel loved about her.

The newly built luxury Majestic Hotel, with its commanding view of the snow-peaked hills and a glimpse of the sea, had opened its doors only the previous week and those who had wined and dined there were loud in their praise.

'Come early, Nigel, and I promise to be ready. It'll give us time for a talk before setting out.'

'Should manage that, and the talk, is it about anything in particular?'

'Something I would prefer to discuss here rather than over a meal. In any case I want to give my complete attention to the food.' She got up. 'Nigel, that poor child is waiting in the car.'

'Sorry, I forgot. Being with you puts everything else out of my mind,' he said, getting to his feet and picking up the case.

'Off you go, darling, I won't come out. I'll watch you leave from the window.' She blew him a kiss.

When the car had disappeared from sight, Jenny was still deep in thought. All that talk about Caroline not missing Beth, had it more significance than just a casual remark? She was uneasy and Beth could be right about her days at Inverbrae House drawing to an end. Surely, though, Nigel wouldn't be so cruel? He wasn't by nature uncaring yet where his mother was concerned he was inclined to give in to her. And the old lady was determined to be rid of Beth.

In his well-cut dinner suit the colonel looked very handsome and Jenny's heart gave a lurch. He really was a charming and attractive man.

'Darling, you look very handsome.'

'And you look enchanting.'

'Rubbish! Quite the wrong word, I couldn't look enchanting no matter how much I tried. Elegant and attractive, I'll settle for those.'

'Elegant and attractive and so much more,' he laughed.

'Tell me what you think of my gown, then pour yourself a drink and I'll have a sherry.' She stood quite still waiting for his approval.

Looking at her his eyes softened. The deep blue gown hugged her figure then fell in soft folds. The low neckline showed off the long stem of her neck and was bare.

'Quite perfect, my dearest, and you are the only woman I know who can resist jewellery, and how right you are to do so.'

'Thank you and now we can relax with a drink.' She sank back on the cushions with her sherry and Nigel, whisky in hand, joined her. A table was at hand.

'This talk, I'm curious.'

'It's about Beth.'

She saw that he was annoyed. 'Beth is getting rather too much attention.'

'Losing her parents in such horrifying circumstances I think she should be getting a great deal of attention,

Nigel. More than attention, loving care.'

'You seem to forget she isn't family.'

'And that holds you back?'

'Obviously it makes a difference.' He lifted his glass and Jenny put hers down on the table.

'Why should it, Beth is in your care?'

'She is and has been very well looked after.' He moved the amber liquid in the glass and studied it. 'Forgive me, Jenny, but Beth is hardly your business. As a matter of fact our family doctor was of the opinion that Beth would be better with her own relatives. Tragedy draws families together.'

'Which in Beth's case means an aunt for whom she has little affection.'

He shrugged. 'The woman is still family and Beth likes her uncle.'

'All this is because you want rid of her,' she said quietly.

'I don't care for the expression but I do think the time is right for Beth to make her home with her relatives.'

'In other words, she has served her purpose and it is time to go.' Jenny turned sideways to look him straight in the eyes and, under her scrutiny, he shifted in his chair and looked both annoyed and uncomfortable.

'I can't for the life of me understand why we are having this conversation at all,' he said stiffly, 'and isn't it about time we were setting off?'

'Not really, it is early enough. Nigel,' she said softly, 'I'm not quarrelling with you or at least I don't want to, but I've grown very fond of Beth and in a funny sort of way I feel responsible for her.'

'That, my darling, is simply ridiculous.'

'Ridiculous or not it is how I feel.' She paused. 'You know, Nigel, I can't help remembering you saying that you had a hard time persuading Mrs Brown to let you have Beth. That is true, isn't it?'

'Yes,' he said reluctantly.

'If she had refused to let you have her child, Beth would have been living with this aunt and uncle and by now have accepted that way of life.'

'Exactly my point and that is what will happen. Give it time, that is all it needs.'

'You honestly believe that, or do you just want to make yourself believe it?'

'I do believe it.'

'You can say that,' she said incredulously. 'For heaven's sake, Nigel, the change from a cottage to a tenement is very, very different to a change from Inverbrae House to a tenement, and remember she's had three years of it, a very large slice of a child's life.'

'She will adapt I tell you,' he snapped. 'Now can we kindly end this conversation?'

'In a few minutes.'

'I have nothing further to say.'

'But I have. You are being very cruel and I won't have Beth treated like this.'

'What, pray, do you intend doing about it?' he said sarcastically.

'Beth can come and live with me,' she said quietly.

She saw by his expression that she had shocked him. 'With you?' he said, then gave a half laugh. 'For a moment I thought you meant it.'

'I do mean it. Miss Harris will be more than delighted to help look after her, and Beth can attend a good day school.'

'Out of the question, I won't allow it.'

'Are you her legal guardian?'

'No.'

'Then you have no say in the matter. The choice will be

Beth's. Her aunt or Greystanes and I know which one she will choose.'

For a long time he was silent, not looking at her, then with a sigh he got up to refill his empty glass. Jenny had hardly touched her sherry.

'I can't have you doing this, Jenny,' he said at last, 'but you must see that having Beth at Inverbrae House with Caroline away at school—'

'Why can't Beth go to Rowanbank with Caroline? I can't believe the expense would upset you?'

'The expense – no, of course not,' he said dismissively, 'but even if I were to entertain your suggestion it would never come to pass.'

'Your mother would object?'

'Too true she would, but it was of the school I was thinking.'

'Meaning Beth wouldn't be accepted?'

'She wouldn't.'

'Nonsense. Your position, not forgetting your charm.'

'Flattery will get you nowhere,' he said lightly, the anger leaving him.

'She's a bright girl and you have her to thank that Caroline has reached the entrance standard.'

'Pity I tell you everything, I must watch in future,' he said glumly. 'Remember, though, that Caroline has been introduced to subjects that are not taught at Beth's village school.'

'No great problem. Beth will soon pick up what she needs.'

He leaned back. 'You have precisely two minutes to state your case, Jenny, and then we either go to the Majestic or it will be too late and we'll have to forget about it.'

'Two minutes will do.' She took a deep breath. 'Take

Beth away from her school now and let her share lessons with Caroline's governess.'

'You have it all worked out, haven't you?'

'Nigel, you owe it to Beth and I think if you did abandon her you'd feel horribly guilty and you would deserve to be.' She jumped up. 'I'll get my cloak,' and when he got to his feet she put her arms round his neck. 'Thank you, darling.'

'For what?'

'For doing the right thing.'

He held her close but didn't answer. He hadn't promised anything. Jenny, he thought fondly, got so easily carried away, the dear girl was so impetuous. By tomorrow she would be regretting her offer to give Beth a home, and with Beth away from Greystanes, it would all be forgotten.

As to the future, he would get in touch with this aunt and make the necessary arrangements.

Chapter Fourteen

'I didn't miss you, at least not very much,' Caroline said when Beth joined her. They had moved on from the playroom to their own sitting-room, leaving behind all childish things except books and a few favourite games. The square-shaped room had a fire burning brightly and a guard in front of it in case of sparks flying. At first Caroline had strongly disapproved and had removed the offending fireguard. When this had been discovered by the colonel and Mrs Parker-Munro, there had been a stormy scene with Caroline stamping her foot in a rage, but all to no avail. The fireguard would remain in place or it was a return to the playroom. Caroline was discovering that throwing a tantrum did not get her her own way as it once had.

Beth was turning the pages of a book showing pictures of the beautiful Swiss Alps. Usually the scenes gave her a lot of pleasure and she would imagine herself ski-ing down those slopes. Not that it was ever likely to happen, it was a sport for the privileged few, but there was a lot of pleasure to be derived from dreaming.

'I'm glad, I didn't want you to be lonely,' Beth said quietly.

'I was anything but that.'

'What did you do?' Beth closed the book and sat back in her chair. Caroline was stretched out on the sofa with a selection of glossy magazines.

'Mrs Watson invited me over,' she touched the magazines, 'that's where these came from. Most of them are about fashion and Mrs Watson says it is never too early for young girls to be interested in clothes.'

'Was Emma there?'

'Of course.' Emma was coming up for ten, a podgy, sweet-tempered child who had been teased mercilessly by her brothers, Leonard and Ralph, until boarding school claimed them and peace reigned between the holidays. 'Mrs Watson took us shopping and we had tea and lovely cream cakes and there was an orchestra playing.' She looked to see if Beth was impressed and was disappointed that she didn't seem to be. 'Then I spent another day with Aunt Gwen,' she continued, 'and she said I must come when Ruth is there so that she can tell me about Rowanbank.'

'Do you know when you will be going?'

'To Rowanbank? No, I don't, daddy hasn't mentioned it for a while. I expect he's wondering what to do about you when I do go.'

Beth felt the breathlessness that was the beginning of panic. With Jenny beside her she hadn't felt like this. Jenny had been able to smooth away her fears but with those words Caroline had brought them back.

'You're not saying anything,' Caroline said accusingly.

'What do you want me to say?'

'Don't you care what happens to you?'

'Of course I do but Jenny said worrying about things won't change them.'

'Jenny this, Jenny that,' Caroline said nastily, 'she just took you away to please daddy, and grandmama was pleased about it too. You'll have to go and live with that aunt of yours and you'll be poor again like you used to be.'

Then, seeing Beth's stricken face, she hesitated. She hadn't really meant to be nasty and in truth she didn't think she wanted Beth to go away. Being with Emma Watson and the other day with her Aunt Gwen had been all right, it put in the time, but Beth was much more fun. Sometimes she couldn't understand herself. She wanted Beth, then she didn't. 'I'm sorry, I didn't mean to say that and truly I did miss you.'

Beth smiled. 'I'm glad, it's nice to be missed.'

'What did you do when you were with Jenny?'

'Went for walks mostly.'

'Is that all, how dull.'

'It wasn't, it was fun.'

'I suppose Jenny is your most favourite person.'

'Yes, she is.'

'I wonder when daddy will marry her,' she said, letting the magazines slide off her knees to the floor and bending down to get them.

Beth remembered what Jenny had told her, that she enjoyed her independence and had said in confidence that she had no plans to remarry and perhaps she never would. Beth hugged this knowledge to herself and, though she liked the colonel very much, she preferred to think of Jenny and Miss Harris together at Greystanes. She was saved an answer by a maid giving a knock and popping her head in the door.

'What do you want?' Caroline asked, putting on her mistress of the house voice.

The maid ignored her. 'The master wants you, Beth. He said you are to go to his study at once.'

Beth looked shattered. This was it and much sooner than she had expected. The maid withdrew.

'Better go, Beth, then come back here and tell me what it is all about. It'll save me asking daddy if you tell me.'

Beth nodded.

She closed the door on Caroline but Beth didn't hurry to the study. Bad news was something you put off hearing for as long as possible. She took her time and tried to let her mind go blank. The maid who had brought the summons passed her as she reached the stairs, and stared curiously at Beth. She certainly wasn't hurrying herself and the master could be a crabbit devil if folk didn't jump to do his bidding.

'Come in.'

Beth opened the door and went in. The colonel's smile was to put her at ease, she thought, or maybe it was just to soften the blow before it came. He indicated the chair with a movement of his hand and she sat down on the very edge of it.

'Usually I manage to open my mail early on but with a busier than usual morning and having to collect you from Greystanes, I've only just worked my way through it.'

Beth nodded. She wondered what that had to do with her. Was he blaming her because he had to collect her from Greystanes? She thought he would have been pleased, after all it gave him a chance to see Jenny.

He fingered a letter. 'It appears that there is some urgency about clearing out the furniture in your old home. This is to allow new tenants to take possession. I, of course, have nothing to do with it, Beth, other than to inform you that the authorities have also contacted your aunt on this matter.'

Beth wished the colonel wouldn't talk in that business-like manner, but relief was flooding through her that it wasn't the news she had feared.

'You do understand what I am saying, Beth?'

'Yes. The house in Sycamore Lane has to be emptied.' Why couldn't she bring herself to say her parents' house or even her old home? The colonel had been speaking and she hadn't heard. 'I'm sorry, I didn't hear—'

'Pay attention, Beth.' He sounded irritable as if already he had spent too much time with her. 'What I was saying was that you and your aunt must get together to arrange for the house to be emptied.'

'Yes.'

'And, Beth?'

She looked at him enquiringly.

'I feel that you should spend more time with your aunt and her family, get to know them better. They are, after all, the only family you have. Perhaps a weekly visit, Tommy can take you if he is not otherwise engaged but you are of an age now to be able to travel by public transport.'

'Tommy doesn't need to take me at all,' she said spiritedly. Anger was driving out the fear and she was beginning to see this family, the much respected Parker-Munros, in a less flattering light. Their generosity, she was discovering, only extended to those who were of use to them. She had been a companion for Caroline, his delicate daughter, and mistakenly she had thought of herself, not as family, she wouldn't presume that, but as a sort of extended family.

'Very well, you can take public transport and I must remember to give you a little money.' He smiled. 'In your situation it is important to learn to be independent.'

'Yes.'

'Oh, I'd better mention this now in case I forget. Your parents insisted on leaving a little money—'

'Yes, you've already told me that,' she interrupted.

The colonel frowned heavily. He was not in the habit of being interrupted.

'As I was saying,' he continued in clipped tones that

showed his annoyance, 'the money, needless to say, was not touched by me and it is in an account at the bank in your name.'

'Thank you, Colonel Parker-Munro.'

Beth wanted to weep. To weep for her parents who had been so anxious to support their own daughter. They hadn't wanted her to be totally dependent on the Parker-Munros. That her mother and father had gone to India and left her behind, Beth had forgiven them that. She was older now and perhaps her parents had been singled out as very special people to do the kind of work that was required. They had known the dangers before they went and had been prepared to risk their own lives but not the life of their young daughter. She would never know if that were true, but she wanted to believe it.

Her mind kept wandering but she really must keep her attention on the colonel and his voice was droning on.

'—a very small sum, but a start. Once you leave school, Beth, and take up employment you should be able to add to it.' He wasn't an unkind man, she knew that, but he couldn't completely hide his amusement. To him the sum was so paltry, yet for her parents it had been a lot of saving. Just to provide for their daughter they would have considered it no hardship to do without all but the basic necessities. At this moment she felt very proud of them.

'That's it, you may go now, Beth.'

'Thank you.'

'Well, what was it all about?' Caroline was very curious and didn't bother to hide it.

'I've to arrange with my aunt to have my old home cleared out.'

'What for?'

'So that another family can live there.'

'That was all?' She sounded disappointed.

'Yes, what did you expect?'

'Something more interesting than clearing out a lot of rubbish.'

'It is not rubbish.'

'Well, maybe not exactly rubbish but since you were poor the furniture can't be up to much.'

'I do wish, Caroline, that you had the good manners to stop calling me poor. My father was in a good job and we always had proper clothes and my mother cooked nice meals.'

'Not as good as you get here.'

'Sometimes they were better.'

'I'm going to tell my grandmama what you said.'

'Go and tell her then and see if I care. Sometimes, Caroline, you can be hateful.'

'I am not hateful.'

'Yes, you are.' Beth made for the door.

'Where are you going?'

'Out.'

'That is no way to speak to me,' Caroline began haughtily. She had been precariously near to the edge of the sofa and, with her legs in the air and a splendid show of underwear, she toppled over and landed on the floor in an undignified heap.

Beth had her hand on the door knob but turned and came back. Caroline's face was a picture of wounded pride and in spite of her anger and hurt, Beth burst out laughing.

'I have seldom witnessed such unladylike behaviour,' Beth said sounding, though she didn't know it, remarkably like Caroline's grandmother.

As so often happened the quarrel ended in laughter.

'If I am hateful you are worse, Beth Brown, a real lady

would have turned her eyes away.'

'And missed that spectacle?'

Caroline got herself back on the sofa. 'Friends again?' she asked.

'Until the next time,' Beth grinned. Caroline could be infuriating, the absolute limit, but she was still her friend.

The December day was cold and raw as Beth, well wrapped up against the chilly air, waited for her aunt. In her coat pocket was the key to 3 Sycamore Lane but she had no intention of opening that door. She wanted to be with someone when she did. Although it was just two o'clock in the afternoon, already the day was darkening. Beth shivered, not from cold, just from a dread that she couldn't explain. Her aunt would probably say that she should have gone inside to get out of the cold wind but the chilly dampness of an unheated house could be worse than standing outside.

Her own suggestion had been that she should meet her aunt off the bus but for some reason this hadn't been acceptable. Meeting at the house would be better, she had said, and that way there would be no danger of missing one another. Since the Dundee bus made only one stop in the village, Beth, for the life of her, couldn't imagine how they could possibly miss each other but it was always better to fall in with Aunt Anne's wishes.

She didn't stand directly outside the house; Beth did not want neighbours coming out to talk to her. Her mother had never had much coming and going with them, just passing the time of day unless there was illness and then she would enquire. And in her own case, with Tommy transporting her to and from school, there had been no need for her to go anywhere near her old home.

The end of the lane was the best place to stand and from

there she would be able to see her aunt climbing the hill. Her wrist watch told Beth that the bus was due and after five more minutes a straggle of passengers began the climb. Ahead of them was Aunt Anne. Beth set off to meet her.

'Hello, Aunt Anne. Coming to meet you was better than standing waiting.'

'I daresay,' said her aunt. There was no physical contact, no kiss on the cheek, no hug. 'You're colder here than Dundee, that's what I always told Harriet.' They had fallen into step. 'I'm still not taking it in, Beth, and the little faith I had I'm in danger of losing.' She was out of breath. 'Slow down, lass, once I could have run up this brae but those days are gone.'

Beth didn't think she had been hurrying but she reduced her pace.

'How could a God in heaven let that happen to folk doing His work, I keep asking myself?'

Beth shook her head. 'My father would have answered that it was His will.'

'So he would and meaningless words they are to my way of thinking. Why does God take good living folk like Harriet and her man, not forgetting those others who died with them, and spare murderers and robbers?'

'I know, I wonder those things too, Aunt Anne.'

'Do you? Aye, I suppose you do.' There was a weariness in her voice.

'Yes, I do and I feel angry, then I'm afraid to be angry.'

'Stands to reason, you are their bairn.' She gave a half smile. 'Some of it must have rubbed off.'

Beth smiled at that as they walked to the top of the hill. Now that she was looking at her aunt properly, Beth thought that she looked poorly and there were dark shadows under her eyes. Like her mother had, Aunt Anne wore a lot of drab colours. Something brighter and she might have looked better, Beth thought, then she remembered that her aunt was in mourning and she didn't know for how long that went on.

'Are you keeping well, Aunt Anne?'

'Well enough, I have my worries but they'll keep for the now anyway.'

Did that mean that she was going to hear about them? Beth wondered.

'Is the house clean?' she asked abruptly.

'Should be, two of the maids spent a whole day in it.'

'That's not to say they were working. Without supervision I doubt they would do all that much.'

'I think they are quite dependable, Aunt Anne.'

'Doesn't matter all that much. It would have if your mother had been coming home. Still it's easier and nicer to handle stuff not thick in dust.'

In silence they reached 3 Sycamore Lane and walked up to the front door.

'Gives you a peculiar feeling.'

'Yes,' Beth said fighting a lump in her throat. It was far worse than she had expected. If only her aunt would take the key from her and open the door but she made no move.

'Just given the front door key, were you?'

'Yes.'

'Not many got to come in this way, just those and such as those. For the rest of us it was the back door. Of course, you'll be minding all that?'

'Yes.' She was remembering it clearly, the shining brass door knob and letter box. So dull now, no shine at all on them.

'Come on, lass, open up and get it over.'

Beth inserted the key, surprised to find that it turned so

easily when before she recalled it being stiff to turn. Those who had followed her mother must have come in and out this way.

The door opened on to a small, narrow passage with enough light getting in to let them see to go about. Beth went ahead. The door to the living-room was slightly ajar and she pushed it wide. There was a box of matches on the mantelpiece and Beth picked them up, meaning to light the mantle, but she was stopped.

'No, lass, never take chances with gas, we'll manage well enough.'

It was a strange feeling returning to a house that had once been home and Beth shivered.

'Upsetting you, is it?'

'Yes, a little. It looks familiar and strange at the same time. That sounds silly, I know. I remembered it as being so much bigger and surely it wasn't as shabby?'

'Told you, didn't I, that no one looks after a house the way you would yourself?'

'Yes, you did.' The chair that her father had once sat in looked sad and lost as did the smaller one that had been her mother's. Daft to think like that but she couldn't help it. Aunt Anne was watching her face. 'It's more than shabby, Aunt Anne, it looks so neglected.' She wanted to weep.

'Worse for you after that posh place you've been living in. It's clean enough, there isn't a lot of dust in here.' She rubbed her finger over the surface of the sideboard. She paused and then sat down, not in either armchair but on a hard wooden chair beside the table. 'Have you thought of what you are to do with everything? It's all yours now.'

'There is nothing I want. Oh, yes, there is, just one thing and I hope it is still there.' They had both been talking in low voices, just above a whisper, but Beth raised hers.

'What is it?'

'A picture.' Beth went quickly into the room that she had slept in for nine years. How pokey it was, she thought, looking about her and comparing it with her bedroom in Inverbrae House. Her eyes went to the bookcase, the one her father had lovingly made from an old orange box, perhaps two orange boxes. It was stacked in a corner, the shelves broken and now only fit for firewood. The lump in her throat returned but she would fight her tears, Aunt Anne wouldn't like her to break down.

The picture was there, on the wall above the bed and was just as she remembered it. The bedcover was stained and tatty looking and there was no one to scold her for standing on the bed in heavy outdoor shoes. Carefully she removed the painting from the hook on the wall and got down from the bed. Then she went through to her aunt who had got up and was examining the sideboard.

'Look, Aunt Anne, my father bought it for me.'

'That's the harbour! Good likeness, I'd say, but I'm no expert on paintings.'

'Take whatever you want, Aunt Anne, I'd like you to and the rest will just have to be disposed of somehow.' She looked about for something to wrap the picture in but there was nothing, nothing in the kitchen either. It didn't matter, she would carry it under her arm.

'Pity to throw out what could be of use to someone. Not me, lass, I've enough to do me all my days but Adam and Morag are just starting out and what is here would be a grand start to them, tide them over nicely until they can afford to replace them with new. Not the sideboard, though, I was with your mother when she bought that.

Cost a bit it did but as I always say you get what you pay for. A good polish and it'll take pride of place in Adam's house.'

'I'm so glad,' Beth smiled and she was glad. It was nice to think of her parents' furniture still being in the family. 'How will they manage to get all this to Dundee?'

'Adam knows a lad with a van. Mebbe need two journeys but you don't need to worry yourself about it. The pair of them will clear the lot and Morag will give it a good brush out.' She paused. 'Gone through the cupboards and drawers, have you?'

'No.'

'Neither have I, better do it though.'

They went round the house checking on everything.

'Nothing much just some china and cutlery and other odds and ends. Morag might find some of it useful.'

'Sure to and, of course, your mother had away with her what she valued. The pity of it is you'll never see any of it.'

They were both silent. They knew that everything that Harriet and George had possessed would have long gone and that there would be no money. What little they had would have been spent on those they considered less fortunate than themselves. That was their way.

'Sit yourself down, lass, I've something to tell you,' she said abruptly.

Beth sat down on a wooden chair and looked expectantly at her mother's sister and wondered what was coming.

'I'll not beat about the bush, Beth, your Uncle Fred has been put on short time.'

'Oh, I am sorry to hear that.'

The woman sighed and straightened her back. 'Aye, it's come as a shock. Bad though it is, there are some who have been harder hit and lost their jobs. Luke's working but for all he brings in it doesn't keep him or anything like it. Adam was a help, or becoming one, but he'll be away from the house before long. Which brings me to the wedding. I don't suppose you would want to go?'

Beth would very much have liked to attend and meet the cousins she hardly knew and be introduced to Morag but it didn't sound as though Aunt Anne wanted her there. She wondered about that, it wasn't like her aunt, then she thought that she understood. Aunt Anne had hoped her sister would be home from India and able to join in the festivities whereas Beth, on her own, would be a constant reminder of the tragedy. A tragedy that needed to be forgotten on that special day.

'I would have liked to be at Adam's wedding but it would be awkward – I mean, getting back to Inverbrae House could cause problems and I wouldn't like to be a nuisance,' she ended lamely.

'Who said anything about being a nuisance? You wouldn't be that but, as you say, transport could be difficult. You could hardly expect your folk to send a car for you.'

The 'your folk' had a false sound. 'No, I wouldn't expect it of them.'

Her aunt smiled. Beth thought it was of relief. 'These affairs can go on long enough when folk get cheery.'

Beth nodded. 'I suppose so. You'll give Adam and Morag my very best wishes, won't you?'

'I'll do that, lass.'

'Poor Uncle Fred, he'll be miserable about being on short time.'

'Miserable and worried like myself. Yon's a good house we have but it's a steep rent and that has to be paid before anything else.' She paused. 'I'm just that glad to know that you are happy with those Parker folk. You are, aren't you?'

'Yes.' Beth wondered if that were strictly true. It wasn't easy to be happy when you felt yourself to be unwanted but that was her own worry and by the sound of it her aunt had enough of her own.

'Well, now, that's a big load off my mind because, lass, I couldn't take you now, I couldn't afford to. You've still two years to go before you can leave school and whatever job you managed to get it would only pay a pittance.' She smiled sadly. 'You do understand, Beth?'

'Yes, of course I do, Aunt Anne.' Not wanting her face to betray her, Beth spoke quickly. 'But before we go I would like a look out the back.'

'On you go, then, but don't be long.'

'I won't.'

Now that it was sinking in the shock was devastating and with it came a feeling of unreality. This couldn't be happening to her, it couldn't. Blindly she went through to the kitchen. The key was in the back door, she turned it and went outside. A greyness added to the gloom and after seeing the condition of the house, Beth had no great hopes for the garden. Fortunately the semi-darkness hid most of the neglect but in any case did she really care? She had cared but not any more. The new occupants could deal with the neglected house and garden and lucky they were if that was all they had to worry about. Her own position, her uncertain future, could hardly be worse.

Standing just outside the door, her eyes went down to the foot of the garden where once had been the chicken coop. Her mother had had it removed and that corner tidied before they had set out for India. That chicken coop, she thought, had been the means of altering her life. Had it not been for taking the eggs to Inverbrae House she would not have met Caroline and she would not be facing this crisis that loomed ever more threatening. Instead she would have been living with her aunt and uncle in Dundee and by this time considered part of the family. Changed circumstances would not have meant her being shown the door. They wouldn't have put her out or rather put her into an orphanage when times got hard. She would have shared those hard times with them.

She must go inside now. Beth forced a smile to her face and rejoined her aunt.

'Well?'

'Much as I expected, Aunt Anne. Whoever gets the house will have a lot to do.'

'Hard work never killed anyone and I'm getting anxious about that bus,' she said, getting to her feet and picking up her handbag. 'Is it due soon, do you know? I wouldn't want just to miss one and have a long, cold wait for the next.'

Beth consulted her watch. 'If we leave now you should be all right.'

'No need for you to come.'

'Of course I'll see you off and about the key—' Beth began as she locked up.

'Give it here, good job you reminded me.'

'It has to be handed in—' Beth began anxiously.

'I know, Beth, I have the address, it was on the letter I got. Rest assured the key will be handed in once the house has been cleared out and the place swept clean.'

'That's fine then.' She handed over the key and her aunt opened her bag and dropped it to the bottom.

They had almost reached the square when the bus arrived and three people got out. A few were waiting and they quickly got on.

'Better hurry, Aunt Anne, it just turns and leaves.'

'Not without me, it doesn't,' but she hurried all the same and got herself on to the step of the bus. 'Look after yourself, Beth,' she said, turning briefly to her niece before going forward to a seat.

'Goodbye, Aunt Anne.'

'Goodbye, lass.'

The bus moved away and Beth felt a lump in her throat. Her hand went up to wave but her aunt was already looking for her fare. She let her hand fall and turned to walk back the way she had come. At least she had been able to hide her shock from her aunt and she was thankful for that. It was certainly true that she had never wanted to go to Dundee and live with her aunt and uncle, indeed she had dreaded the thought, but now that the offer was no longer there Beth realised that, at the back of her mind, she had always thought of it as a home if the worst came to the worst. And it had, and she had no place to go.

No one cared about her. No one cared what happened to her. She was about to be alone, an orphan in a frightening world. Fear made her stomach knot. She had never felt so utterly and completely alone.

With her painting under her arm, her head down, she trudged the road back to Inverbrae House. Almost without realising it she was at the gates of the house and ahead of her a gardener raked smooth the gravel on the drive. Beth didn't feel ready to talk, she needed time to calm herself and still the panicky fluttering in her stomach. Leaving the main drive she took one of the winding paths that circled the landscaped gardens. The bleakness of winter was all around, the trees were bare and the gardens without colour. Only very infrequently did Caroline and Beth venture far from the summer house and the smooth velvety lawn where once two six-year-olds had met. In the cold weather Caroline was unwilling to leave the warmth of the house unless it was to be driven to a house party or some other entertainment.

Calmer now, remembering that Caroline would be having her music lesson, she went in through the servants' entrance and unseen slipped up to her bedroom. Looking about her for a suitable hiding place for the picture, her first thought was of the floor of the wardrobe with something covering it. She decided that the drawer where she kept her underwear would be better. She couldn't bear it if someone ridiculed the picture and she knew that she would not be permitted to hang it on the wall in her bedroom.

Beth would have loved to master the piano and had secretly hoped that she would receive lessons but in this the colonel and his mother were in total agreement. Young ladies in Caroline's position were expected to have mastered the piano and be able to give a reasonable performance to invited guests. Beth would have no need of such an accomplishment.

Her head ached and for a little while she sat on the bed refusing to let herself think. She tried to let her mind wander to happier times and for a short while she succeeded. Feeling better, she went to their own sitting-room and found Caroline already there.

'Hello, I thought you would still be having your music lesson.'

'My dear Beth,' she said haughtily. 'I have had my lesson and if I have to do another scale for that stupid teacher I'll go mad.'

'You should be grateful for the opportunity to learn.' Beth knew what was going to follow but it was helping her to act normally.

'I – do – not – have to be grateful for anything.'

'Lucky you.'

'And poor you, always having to be grateful for every little thing. If I were you, I'd be sick of the word "grateful".'

'I am sick of the word. And if I have children, that word will never be used to them.'

'How did it go?'

'All right.'

'Not very forthcoming, are you?'

'Didn't expect you to be interested.'

'Well, I am. Did you get all your stuff disposed of?'

'Disposed of, yes I did. My cousin, Adam, is getting married very soon and my aunt suggested it would start them off.'

'Will you be going to the wedding?'

'No.'

'Why not?'

'I don't want to,' she lied.

'Because it is too soon after – you know—?'

Beth was surprised and a little touched. Caroline could be thoughtful at times.

'Yes, that is the reason.'

'You'll have to give your cousin a gift and how do you do that when you have no money?'

'That's where you're wrong,' Beth said lifting her head high. 'I do have an account in my own name at the bank. Your father told me about it, it was money my parents sent towards my – my upkeep.'

'Wouldn't be very much.'

'A little to you is a lot to me.'

'You sound very sorry for yourself all of a sudden.'

'I don't mean to.'

'Ask daddy, he'll give you money to buy a gift and we can go together and choose something.'

'Adam and Morag are getting plenty from me. I'm just

185

about furnishing their home.'

Caroline giggled.

'What's so funny?'

'You and me. We are poles apart but we still manage to laugh together.'

Beth nodded. It was true.

Chapter Fifteen

On Christmas eve and again on Christmas day there were flurries of snow and the forecast was for snow after the new year. In preparation for a heavy fall, and in case the village was cut off, folk took the precaution of getting in emergency supplies. At Inverbrae House the fires burned brightly. Stocks of fuel and food were plentiful and there was an abundance of everything, enough to last for a number of weeks in the unlikely event that the roads remained impassable for that length of time.

There had been the usual festivities at Inverbrae House with the exchange of Christmas gifts. Below the tree in the drawing-room the gifts were piled up. Caroline's pile was by far the largest and her presents the most expensive. From the colonel, Beth had been given a sum of money to choose her own books. Her other gifts were small, mostly boxes of handkerchiefs or gloves with only Jenny treating them alike. She had given both girls beautiful silk squares, Caroline's in shades of pink and Beth's in shades of blue.

By the middle of January most of the snow had disappeared and the hazard had changed to icy roads. The road to Sandyneuk School was particularly dangerous for the car and Beth insisted that Tommy took her only part of the way. She didn't mind slithering and sliding to school, others did it.

In preparation for Rowanbank, Caroline was being

taught French and a little Latin and she was particularly proud of her progress in French.

'You don't get taught languages in your village school,' she said, preening herself. 'When I go on holiday to Paris I'll be able to use my French.'

'You mean you hope they'll understand you?'

'Of course they will understand me. Mattie is a fluent French speaker and she is teaching me how to raise my voice at the end, as though everything were a question.'

'I wish we got to learn French but when I go up to the secondary, I'll get it there.'

'If I taught you, you'd know some before you went.'

'Would you really teach me?'

'I could try and, Beth Brown, if I decide to give you homework, I would expect you to do it.'

'Yes, Miss Parker-Munro,' Beth said meekly. She wanted very much to learn another language and wondered if Caroline meant it. 'This isn't a joke? You would really teach me?'

'Haven't I just said so and it could be fun. When you reach the stage that I am, it will be easier, you'll just be one lesson behind me.' She paused. 'Not Latin though, it's horrible, all those ghastly verbs. Mattie says it is a dead language and all I say to that is that I wish to goodness it could be well and truly buried.'

Beth laughed. Caroline was such a mixture. Here she was being kind and helpful but in a few short minutes that could change and she would become rude, difficult and impossible to please.

As the dullness of winter changed to the delicate colours of spring, boarding school was seldom mentioned. But it was always at the back of Beth's mind, a nagging worry that wouldn't go away. Only to Jenny could she have poured out her worries but it was as though they were deliberately keeping them apart. On those occasions when Jenny was at Inverbrae House, Beth would be sure to be sent on some errand that kept her away and only at the dinner table did they set eyes on one another. Then Jenny would smile across to her in that special way she had and make some remark that Beth would answer. Quickly the colonel or Mrs Parker-Munro would claim Jenny's attention and occasionally bring Caroline into the conversation. Beth never spoke unless she was spoken to. It didn't upset her being left out, she had become used to it.

On one occasion Jenny and Beth did meet. Caroline had left that morning to spend the day with her aunt and her cousin who was home for half term. The invitation had not included Beth. Jenny was coming out of the study on her way to the drawing-room, intending to sit with the old lady until the colonel had attended to work that required his immediate attention.

'Beth, wait!' she called as she caught sight of her.

Beth swung round. 'Jenny! I didn't see you,' she said smiling broadly.

'I know you didn't. We never do seem to get the opportunity to have a talk.' She laughed. 'You are not by any chance trying to avoid me?'

Beth looked wounded. 'I would never do that. You didn't really think that did you, Jenny?'

'Of course not, you silly goose. Where are you making for?'

'Our sitting-room, Caroline's and mine.'

'We could be interrupted there, what about your bedroom?' She raised her eyebrows. 'Caroline, I believe, is taken care of and I don't imagine anyone else would barge in?'

'No, they wouldn't.'

'Lead on. I can't stay long or there will be a search party sent out.'

Beth giggled. A few minutes in Jenny's company and she forgot her worries. Once inside the bedroom with the door shut, Beth said, 'There is something I want to show you, Jenny. It's a painting my father bought for me and I went over and got it from the house.'

'A jolly good job you did, someone might have taken a fancy to it.'

Beth shook her head. 'No, Jenny, the people who lived in my house were careless but honest. I don't think they took anything that didn't belong to them.'

Jenny was sitting on the bed looking bandbox fresh in a long black skirt and primrose yellow blouse with a frilled neckline and matching cuffs. From where she was she watched Beth open a drawer and bring out a framed picture.

'Why keep it hidden? It should be hanging up on the wall where you can see it.' Taking the small painting from Beth, she began to study it.

'Beth, dear, this is very good. Mind you, I wouldn't call myself an expert but I would say that the artist has a lot of talent. This is Sandyneuk harbour and he has captured it exactly.' She smiled at Beth with her eyes sparkling. 'Who knows, one day it might be worth quite a lot of money.'

'I would never sell it, no matter how much it was worth.' Beth's voice faltered. 'It's all I have to remind me of my parents.'

'You must have photographs?'

'A few. I wish I had more.'

'You have your memories, no one can take those away from you,' Jenny said gently.

Beth looked down at her hands. 'I find it harder and harder to remember them.'

'That is the way of the world, my dear,' Jenny said, giving the picture back to Beth. 'We are meant to forget the pain and heartbreak of losing those nearest and dearest to us but from time to time you will be given glimpses of your old life, special moments that will never leave you.'

'I'd like to think that.'

'Then you must.' She watched Beth take another look at the harbour scene then prepare to put it back in the drawer.

'Would you like it hung on the wall?'

Beth shook her head. 'No,' she said firmly.

'What would you like?'

Beth's dark blue eyes looked into hazel eyes that were full of understanding. 'Would you take it and keep it for me?'

'If that is what you want?'

'It is. You don't have to hang it up unless you want.'

'I do want. I shall hang it up in the hallway for all to see. Would you mind very much, Beth, if I got another frame for it? That one is—'

'A bit awful,' Beth finished for her. 'My father said that one day he would get a new frame for it only – only—'

'Only he never managed it. Talk about your parents, Beth. Believe me, it is better to do so and each time it will get a little easier. Regarding the frame, I'll get a friend of mine to see to it and since this is to be our secret we have to find a way of getting it from here to my home. Any suggestions?' She began whispering as though they were conspirators.

'I can't think of one.'

'I can,' she said. 'Listen to this. On my way here Colonel Parker-Munro very kindly stopped the car so that I could collect a dress from the dress-maker. It is in a box on the back seat and you, my child, must find something to wrap the painting in then take it out to the car, it won't be locked, and tuck it under the box.'

'Won't Colonel Parker-Munro wonder how it got there?'

'Not him. Men don't notice these things, Beth, and even if he did I'd think of something.'

Beth didn't doubt it for a moment. 'I can get paper and string from the kitchen,' she said eagerly.

'Good, we've got that settled and now before I fly, tell me is all well or is something worrying you?'

Beth hesitated. It didn't seem fair to burden Jenny with her worries.

'Come on, there is something so out with it.'

'It's only that I am almost sure that Caroline is going to Rowanbank and I think it might be soon. When she goes I won't be able to stay here and I don't know what is going to happen to me.'

'You are right that she is going, that is definite enough, but as to when I wouldn't know.'

Beth nodded miserably.

'It is the thought of living with your aunt and uncle in Dundee that is making you unhappy?'

Beth looked at Jenny but said nothing. How could she tell Jenny that she was no longer welcome in her aunt's home, that the door was closed?

Jenny misunderstood the silence. The poor child was dreading the thought of life in a tenement and who could blame her? There could hardly be a bigger contrast to this life and the life she would be going to.

Jenny gave her a quick hug before leaving. 'Try not to worry. Things will work out, you'll see.'

Beth forced a smile. It was easy to say not to worry but Jenny didn't know just how bad it was. Right now she would have given a lot to have her Uncle Fred in full employment and the door once again open to her.

On her way to the drawing-room, Jenny was thoughtful. That poor child was making herself ill with worry and Jenny was getting angrier by the minute. It was monstrous to treat a child the way they were doing and unless she herself did something about it, Beth's fate was sealed. She was still thinking what she could do when she joined the old lady who had wakened with a start when Jenny entered.

'Never in all my born days have I heard anything so ridiculous. Have you gone completely mad, Nigel?'

'No, Mother, but I am in danger of losing my patience.'

'Then kindly listen to me—'

'No, Mother, I am doing the talking for a change.' He saw her colour was high and her breathing harsh but this time he was ignoring the signs. Heartless and unlike him though it was, he had just about had all he could take. 'Like it or not, Beth is going to Rowanbank with Caroline because I have no choice in the matter,' he said slowly and distinctly.

'Who may I ask is holding a gun to your head?' she said sarcastically.

'Jenny, if you must know.'

'What has Jenny to do with it?'

'The answer to that should be nothing but unfortunately Jenny is making Beth her business.'

'And you are allowing her to dictate to you?' The eyebrows shot up and she glared.

'As I have already told you, Mother, I have no choice in the matter.'

'Kindly explain yourself.'

'Should I not agree, Jenny is to take Beth to live with

her and her housekeeper and enrol Beth at a good day school.'

'I wouldn't have believed this of Jenny.'

'Neither would I, but apparently she and Beth had grown very close in the week they were together at Greystanes.' He looked closely at his mother, at her angry face. 'And if you recall, Mother dear, you were very much in favour of Beth going there.'

'Yes, I was. I saw it as a way of separating Caroline and that girl. I see my mistake when it is too late but there is no use dwelling on that.'

'I agree with you there,' he said wearily.

'Jenny doesn't mean it and you should realise that, Nigel.' She took out her handkerchief and dabbed at the corner of her mouth. 'She has no intention of saddling herself with Beth. It is no more than a threat to get her own way. Scheming woman that she is,' she said viciously. 'How wrong we can be about people.'

'Jenny does mean it, every word of it. If we are to keep our good name, we cannot afford to go against her.'

'Keep our good name? What on earth are you talking about?'

'The tragedy in India made the headlines throughout the country not just here. Our friends and acquaintances got to know that Beth was living here as a companion for Caroline and she came in for a lot of sympathy.'

'Of course such a gruesome tragedy was on everyone's lips. We have all been very sympathetic and understanding. No one could have been kinder than you during that difficult time when she disappeared and had us so worried. We were all very supportive, we couldn't have done more for her even if she had been family.' She paused and said forcefully, 'We have nothing at all with which to reproach ourselves.'

'True, but our friends are going to have something to say if Beth goes to live with Jenny and she will tell them the reason that we no longer want her.'

'You are convinced that Jenny is serious?'

'I have no doubts whatsoever.'

Mrs Parker-Munro was thoughtful for a long time and Nigel drummed his fingers on the spindly-legged table beside him.

'Do stop that, it is getting on my nerves.'

'Sorry.'

Suddenly she smiled. 'How silly we are to be worried about something that won't happen. Rowanbank would never accept Beth.'

'At one time that would have been true.'

'Still is.'

'No, Mother, times are changing I'm afraid. More people are going abroad and firms anxious to entice the best are offering perks. One is to have their children's fees paid at a good boarding school and to meet that demand new schools are opening up and offering a first-class education together with all the extras that would appeal to parents forced to make a painful separation.'

'Even so, Rowanbank is very exclusive. It always has been and they wouldn't want to lower their standards.'

'I'm sure you are right, Mother. They won't want to lower their standards, no one does, but if they have vacancies they can't afford not to fill them.'

She threw up her hands. 'This is a world gone mad and I can't say I'll be reluctant to leave it.' It wasn't true, of course, the will to live was stronger than ever. She was needed at Inverbrae House since marriage between Nigel and that woman, a union she had once encouraged, would never happen. Her son had had a narrow escape.

Inverbrae House needed a woman and that woman in a

few years time would be Caroline. She would see to it, if God spared her, that her grand-daughter made a suitable marriage and not to take too long about it either. She was in favour of girls marrying young. Beth must be kept out of sight. It could be done, it would have to be done.

Caroline, she knew, would not be returning home until after the evening meal and the old lady had no intention of eating with Beth present. Her reluctant admiration for this quiet-spoken girl had changed to a bitter resentment. It wasn't the girl's fault, she accepted that, but nevertheless she had caused nothing but trouble.

Attending the village school, Beth was a nobody but once she was accepted at Rowanbank, and Nigel thought it more than probable, she would have the kind of school behind her that would open all doors. With her appearance and all the signs of respectability that Inverbrae House had given her, eligible males seeking a wife would be queuing up and poor, pretty little Caroline would have to take a back seat.

Pressing the bell brought the maid.

'Yes, m'am?'

'The master and I will be dining at the usual time but Beth will have her meal in the girls' sitting-room. See to that.'

'Very good m'am.'

'Just the two of us, Mother?'

'Yes.'

He nodded. It was a relief. At the moment, the less he saw of Beth the better he would be pleased. It was all getting completely out of hand and he cursed the day, instead of blessing it, when Beth Brown had captivated his daughter and he, too, had been charmed.

Left to dine on her own, Beth had a book propped up in front of her and couldn't have been more pleased. The very thought of sitting at the dining-room table without Caroline had terrified her. Once it had been the old lady who had made her feel uncomfortable but now it was both of them. The colonel was always perfectly polite but there was a coldness that hadn't been there before.

'Who is your letter from?'

Beth had picked it up from the hall table, an envelope addressed to herself in a large school hand.

'Don't know.'

Caroline glanced at it. 'Cheap envelope and from someone not very well educated. I could write better than that even before I was nine years of age.'

'But you are a real clever clogs and think of the opportunities you've had.'

'Oh, come on, open it or aren't you going to?' she said impatiently.

'I'll open it when I feel like it and you know what curiosity did?'

'Killed the cat. Go on open it, I'm dying to know who is writing to you.'

'I don't ask about your letters.'

'You could hardly since I never get any unless on my birthday. I don't have secrets from you.'

'Yes you do, lots of them. How often do you go and leave me on my own?'

'That's not my fault or are you blaming me?'

'No.'

'I can hardly force Aunt Gwen to invite you to her house since she doesn't like you, now can I?'

'No.' She had been looking at the envelope but raised her eyes. 'I wouldn't want to go.' Beth didn't much care for Caroline's mother's sister. Her Uncle Robert was all right and his appearance had come as a bit of a surprise.

She had expected someone more like the colonel for Mrs Esslemont. Robert Esslemont was a stout, bald-headed man with a pleasant manner and much given to wearing plus-fours. Ruth, the cousin at Rowanbank, took after her father in appearance and nature. She was an ungainly, plain girl with a lovely nature that was sorely tried by her mother's constant reference to her bulging figure and she was the despair of her small, neat mother who secretly wished that Caroline were her daughter. Her niece, though two years younger, was already interested in fashion and, being so pretty and dainty, was a joy to dress.

'Ruth was asking for you.'

'That was nice.'

'She wondered why you weren't with me.'

'Did you tell her?'

'I didn't have to. Aunt Gwen overheard her and said that now that I was growing up, I would be mixing with other young people. She said it wouldn't be possible to include you, Beth, that it was different when we were small children. Oh, well, if you aren't going to open that wretched letter, don't,' she said tossing her head and turning away.

Beth left her and went to her bedroom. Opening the letter she drew out the pages of lined paper that had been taken from a jotter. Both sides of them were filled with the large writing. Beth could tell that the sender was not in the habit of writing letters but that a great deal of care had been taken in the writing of it. She began to read.

> 19 Broomfield Road,
> Dundee

Dear Beth,

Adam's mother said that she had thanked you for all the furniture you let us have but I wanted to write to you myself. Adam and me could hardly believe it. We expected to wait for a long time to get furniture except for what we couldn't do without, of course. Adam's mother is a very good worker, well you would know that and we have polished everything until you can nearly see your face in it.

Adam says he only remembers you as a little bairn. The wedding went off well. I was in a white dress with a veil, it was my cousin's but we are about the same size so it didn't need much alteration. Only when it was nearly the end did my Uncle Joe make a fool of himself. He isn't used to the drink and I don't know who got him into that state. Adam thought he was funny but his mother did not and she wasn't very pleased. Still it was a wedding after all and my mother said it was to be expected and she thought our side behaved themselves quite well.

Thank you very much again and if you want to come and see me and Adam we'll be very pleased.
Your cousin-in-law
Morag

Beth read it over again and again and found herself smiling. It was such a nice letter, a genuinely friendly letter and she wanted very much to meet Morag and Adam too. She was smiling when she went to join Caroline.

'The letter was from my cousin's wife, thanking me for the furniture and inviting me to their house.'

'Will you go?'

'Yes, I'm looking forward to it.'

Chapter Sixteen

She closed the door and the colonel looked up briefly.

'Sit down, Beth,' he said curtly.

A shaft of sunlight came through the window and showed up the hairs on the back of his hand. Beth pulled out the chair and sat down with her hands folded in her lap. She had on a grey flannel skirt, white blouse and a grey cardigan that was unbuttoned. For so long she had dreaded this summons and now that it had come she was curiously relieved. There was no doubt in her mind about what she was to hear. Bad news was something she had come to associate with a summons to the colonel's study.

Her eye followed his pen as it raced over the headed paper then stopped while he read over what he had written. It must have satisfied him because he scrawled his signature at the foot of the page and returned the pen to the marble stand. That done he looked across at Beth, subjecting her to a lengthy and unsmiling scrutiny. Once she would have hung her head in confusion wondering what she had done to displease but no longer. Her dark eyes held his gaze.

'What I am about to say, Beth, will come as a surprise to you,' he said making an arc of his fingers. She had begun to notice that it was something he did when he was either thoughtful or annoyed.

With his eyes still on her, Beth wondered if he was waiting for her to speak. Or could it be that he was just postponing the moment, searching perhaps for words to soften the blow?

'I am arranging for you to go to Rowanbank with Caroline.'

Beth stared at him stupidly. What was he saying?

'Well?'

'I am to go to Rowanbank?' she squeaked.

'I believe that is what I have just said.'

'I don't know what to say, Colonel. I never thought – I never expected—'

He screwed up his face in annoyance and cut her off. 'The reason for you going to Rowanbank need not concern you. However, no pressure will be put upon you to accept. Indeed it would be better for you and understandable—'

'Oh, please, I would like to go, I—'

'Kindly do not interrupt. The one thing you must understand is that in no circumstances can you continue to live at Inverbrae House once Caroline is away at school.'

'I do understand that,' she said quietly.

'An ordinary secondary school would be more suitable for a girl in your position who must earn her own living. Your education in such an establishment would prepare you for suitable employment.' He smiled. 'Rowanbank is for young ladies—'

'Who don't have to earn their living,' she added without thinking.

'Precisely – and I do wish you would get out of that deplorable habit of interrupting. It is the mark of bad manners.'

'I'm very sorry. I didn't mean to be rude and I

appreciate all you've said but I would still very much like to go to Rowanbank with Caroline.' She stopped breathless but she just had to get that in.

'One day you may regret the choice.'

'I'll work very hard, Colonel, I promise you that,' she said earnestly, 'and I am very grateful.'

'Your academic progress is of no interest to me,' he said cruelly, 'and as to being grateful so you should.' He paused and spoke in a resigned voice. 'Since you have set your mind on going to Rowanbank I would expect, indeed I insist that you help Caroline at all times and put her interests before your own.'

'I can promise that.' Beth was bewildered. There was a lot she didn't understand but her relief was so great that she wasn't to be homeless after all, that she had no wish to question her good fortune.

The colonel saw the relief and bewilderment on Beth's expressive face and felt a rush of shame. Why was he taking it out on the child? She was in no way to blame for this mess. He it was who had brought her to this house expecting it to be for a short period but fate had dealt them all a bitter blow. The death of Beth's parents was having unforeseen repercussions. He gave a wry smile. The real culprit was Jenny. Not many dictated to him and he deplored his weakness but Jenny had become necessary to his happiness. He had never known anyone like her. No matter the bitterness of the disagreement, she never let it spoil their relationship, declaring that the two were quite separate. If anything, their relationship had improved. She had become more loving and as a result even more desirable.

Jenny could forgive and forget, she wasn't petty and never vindictive. Pity, he thought, that his Mother wouldn't take a leaf out of her book but alas she was not the forgiving kind and Mrs Cuthbert, as she had now become, was no longer welcome at Inverbrae House. It made it dashed awkward for him.

Beth waited while the colonel appeared to be lost in thought. She pondered often at the change in him. Not that he was ever unkind, just distant, as though he didn't have a great deal of time for her. Yet how could that be? Having her educated at Rowanbank would cost a great lot of money and he hadn't wanted her to accept. Why offer her the chance then?

Was he under some kind of pressure, but if so by whom? Count out Mrs Parker-Munro, most certainly count her out, Beth thought grimly. That only left Caroline. Had she demanded it as being the only way to get her to go to Rowanbank? Mentally she shook her head. That wouldn't do, Caroline wasn't too concerned about going on her own to boarding school. Then she smiled to herself as something just occurred to her. Of course it was Caroline, she could be quite the actress when she chose. She'd had it planned all along. Those lessons in French were to keep her from being too far behind. Her friend had done this for her. Beth felt a surge of pure happiness. If Caroline wanted to keep it a secret then she would be happy to go along with it.

'You have a very unfortunate habit of letting your attention wander,' the colonel said testily.

'I am sorry, I do apologise.'

'A display of bad manners such as that will not be tolerated at Rowanbank.'

Beth hung her head.

'Persuading the headmistress to accept you was difficult in the extreme but, since she has now consented to have you as a pupil, it is essential that you work hard to reach the necessary standard.'

'Yes. When do I—?'

'The school year starts at the end of September. It will be necessary for you to leave the village school immediately and from now on to share lessons with Caroline.'

Beth wouldn't shed any tears over leaving her school. She had been happy enough there but had no close friends.

He smiled, the cold unfriendliness gone. 'This has come as a shock to you but remember that school for Caroline will be a much greater ordeal than it will be for you.'

'I'll look after her.'

'Yes, you must do that.' He stood up. 'That is all, Beth, off you go.'

'Thank you, Colonel.' She got up and closed the door quietly behind her. Then she let out a long, shaky breath, hardly able to take it in. It was just too wonderful to be true. She just managed to stop herself from jumping for joy and hurried along to her bedroom. Once inside she shut the door and dashed to the mirror. Her face was flushed, her eyes sparkling and turning away she danced round the room before collapsing on to the bed. With her hands behind her head, she thought back to those scenes in the study and the wonderful opportunity that had come her way.

When she did go along to the sitting-room her heart was singing with happiness.

'Where have you been?' Caroline demanded. 'It is very nearly lunch time.'

'I was in the study, your father wanted to see me.'

'What about?'

'As if you didn't know.'

'I don't and I won't until you tell me.'

Beth smiled happily. 'Caroline, you could make a name for yourself on the stage.'

'I am that good?'

'You are and I'm over the moon about going with you to Rowanbank.'

Caroline looked puzzled. 'What on earth has that got to do with the stage?'

'Nothing at all but thank you for teaching me French.'

'I'm a good teacher?'

'Oh, yes, you are and it will make it so much easier. Mattie won't have to start at the beginning.'

'That's what you think. She'll say I haven't taught you properly and the reason for that is she won't want to admit how good I am.' She looked very pleased with herself.

'You can take it from me that you are good. Now, we are going for lunch, aren't we?'

'Yes, come on,' Caroline said jumping to her feet.

'A walk after it, it is such a lovely day.'

'We'll see.'

'Caroline, you need fresh air. It isn't good to be cooped up indoors.'

'A short walk then, no further than the village.'

'That'll do me,' Beth said as both girls went along to the breakfast room where a light meal awaited them.

'Remember this, I am not allowed to go to the harbour. For one thing it is too far and for another it is dangerous. I told my grandmama about being there with you and she was very angry. She said it was perfectly all right for you but not for me. I suppose she thought that I might go too near the edge or something and fall in and drown.'

'Wouldn't matter if I did, though?'

'She would be sorry but not half as sorry as she would be if it was me.'

'Incidentally, that day you are talking about, Caroline, you suggested the harbour yourself. You said you had only ever seen it from the car.'

'Did I? I don't remember.' They had reached the breakfast room. 'I hope Mrs Noble has produced something decent for a change.'

Beth's appetite was good and she ate hungrily. Caroline picked at hers, but in the end had eaten a reasonable amount.

The signs of spring were everywhere and the gardeners were busy tending the flower beds and hoeing the ground. Clumps of long trumpeted daffodils surrounded the tree trunks and, with the blues and pinks of the crocuses, made a glorious splash of colour. Together the girls walked down the drive, past the thick bushes with their buds just opening and on to the road. Behind the sun there was a coldish wind and both of them wore warm coats. Caroline wore a scarf and her hands were inside lined gloves. She always said that her hands were the coldest part of her. Beth, delighting to be outside, breathed in the clear fresh air and raised her face to the sun. She needed neither scarf nor gloves.

'Did I tell you that grandmama is absolutely livid, I've never seen her so angry?'

'What about?'

'You, of course. And I have to say it came as a complete shock to me – don't look so dim, of course I mean you going to Rowanbank.'

'Oh, that,' Beth said offhand. If Caroline wanted to carry on with the joke she wouldn't spoil it.

'She says it will be very difficult for you at Rowanbank.'

'Why should that be? I'm not stupid.'

'That has nothing to do with it. It's being born into the

right family, that sort of thing, and you weren't.'

'Unless you tell them they won't know.'

'I won't but I'm afraid you'll have to be prepared. Miss Critchley, she's the Head, has to know everything about her pupils so daddy, whether he wanted to or not, would have had to tell her.'

'Everything? What do you mean by everything?'

'Your humble beginnings, your parents being poor—'

'Not that again,' Beth said furiously.

'Poor to her and poor to you don't mean the same thing.'

'If I am so unsuitable why has Miss—'

'Critchley.'

'Miss Critchley condescended to accept me?'

'You want to know what I really think?'

'Yes, I would.'

'Daddy wants me to be happy at Rowanbank and he thinks that it might be a bit much – you know, separating us and me going off to school.'

'You were coming round to it.'

'Yes, I was. I was prepared to put on a brave face because I thought I had no choice. Daddy can be quite grumpy at times and I don't always get my own way now.'

They had reached the village shops. 'Do you want anything?' Beth asked. 'No use deciding you do when we are half way home.'

'I am not giving in to temptation and buying chocolate. Aunt Gwen says it makes one fat and she blames Ruth's weight problem on eating too much of it when she was younger. And you, Beth Brown, are not going to buy any either.'

'Can't, I haven't any money with me.'

'What were we talking about?'

'School. Caroline, are you really glad that I'm going with you to Rowanbank?'

'Of course, you ninny. You'll be there to look after me,' she said smugly, 'but enough about boring school. Have you noticed how grumpy daddy is these days?'

'Could be he's worried about something.'

'Can't think what.' Then she giggled. 'Yes, I can. I think he has had a tiff, a lover's quarrel, with Jenny.'

'What makes you think that?'

'Well you must have noticed that she hasn't been at Inverbrae House for two whole weeks?'

Beth had noticed and wondered if Jenny had tired of the colonel. She wasn't in love with him after all, or so she said. Maybe she had met someone she liked better. 'Perhaps she has gone off on holiday or something.'

'No, it won't be that. I think daddy must still be seeing Jenny but it will have to be in her house and that's making him mad.'

'Why?'

'Because of grandmama,' she said opening her eyes wide. 'I just happened to mention Jenny's name to her and that I hadn't seen her and she got all starchy.'

'What do you mean by starchy?'

'Stiff, that's what it means. What she said to me was, kindly do not mention Mrs Cuthbert's name in my presence. Her lips were pursed in that disapproving way.'

'Sounds as though your grandmother and Jenny have had words.'

She nodded. 'Pity, I liked it when Jenny came here.'

'Me too, she's the very nicest person I know.' It was in that moment that Beth made up her mind to write to Jenny and tell her about Rowanbank. She was certainly going to be surprised about that. Beth felt wonderfully happy and a little sorry for Caroline. Being the much-loved daughter of the house, she was denied freedom and couldn't go where she wished. No such restrictions were put on her.

They were indoors, their coats off and back in the sitting-room.

'Put that book down, you are not going to read. I want to talk,' Caroline said flinging herself on the sofa.

'What about?' Reluctantly, Beth put down her book and gave her attention to Caroline.

'For a start when are you going to visit your cousin and his wife?'

'Soon, I hope. Sunday is best if I am to see both of them.'

'Do you know how to get to their house?'

'Aunt Anne gave me directions. I know the tramcar to get and the stop to get off at. I'll manage perfectly well.'

'I've never been on a tramcar,' Caroline said wistfully.

'I don't expect you ever will.'

'Why not?'

'There is always a car at your disposal.'

'You could get Tommy to take you.'

'No, thanks, I quite enjoy the bus run then catching the tram.'

'Would you take me to meet your cousin and Morag, that's her name isn't it?'

'Yes, that is her name and no, I wouldn't.'

'Why not?'

'My Aunt Anne lives in what is considered a good neighbourhood but you wouldn't think so. Adam and Morag are in a run-down area, I haven't seen it yet but I know you would be horrified and turn up your nose.'

'You think I am a snob,' Caroline said indignantly.

'I know you are,' Beth grinned.

'Maybe I was but I'm not like that now.'

'You'll never change.'

'That isn't the word of a friend. I thought you liked me.'

'I do, but it is the way you've been brought up, Caroline. You can't help it.'

'Which is just a way of saying that you don't want me to meet your cousin and his wife?'

'That's right, I don't.'

'If I demand to be taken?'

'Demand all you like but I won't take you.'

'You've been with me to see my relatives.'

'Exactly,' Beth said grimly, 'and they made sure I felt out of it.'

'Not really. They aren't like that, the fault was yours.'

'Because I didn't fit in? I didn't, I knew it and that's the way it would be if you met my relatives. They would try to make you welcome but all they would do would be to make you feel uncomfortable. We would all be glad when the visit was over.'

Beth could have stayed in bed longer but she couldn't, she wanted up, she was too wide awake. Padding across the room in her bare feet, she drew back the curtains. The window was open top and bottom and the welcome cool air coming in was pleasant. The sun shone out of a cloudless sky to welcome this very special day. Beth dressed in her usual school clothes, navy skirt and white blouse, and went down for breakfast. A maid was always on duty to replenish the dishes and those who wanted breakfast helped themselves.

Beth was alone in the breakfast room. Caroline didn't get up until the last minute. The colonel was an early riser and ate a hearty breakfast of bacon, eggs and sausage, before setting out. He had long gone. Mrs Parker-Munro had a tray taken to her room.

She helped herself to porridge and followed it with a rasher of bacon and scrambled eggs. After that she had toast and marmalade. Excitement hadn't taken away her appetite. She felt very proud that she, Beth Brown, was to be taught by a governess. Even yet she had difficulty in believing it.

What was lifting was the nagging fear that she would be made to feel inferior. No one need know that she had been educated at the local school, there was no need for it to be mentioned. She could with perfect honesty, say that she had shared lessons with Caroline.

When told of the changes, Tommy had been glad for her but disappointed that the school run was to cease. Theirs had been an easy friendship with plenty to talk about. Not a lot happened to her but Tommy had a fund of stories that he swore blind were true. Beth knew that they were exaggerated, sometimes, she guessed, made up but she didn't mind, they were amusing and made her laugh. Six months previously Tommy had married his sweetheart and now Mabel's name was constantly on his lips.

She remembered that his dream had once been to have his own taxi service but since becoming chauffeur to the colonel, it had lost its appeal. No one, that is no one with any sense, would throw up a steady job with a reasonable wage, uniform provided and a tied house with a nominal rent, in exchange for a dream.

The schoolroom at Inverbrae House was a large airy room with a fireplace, a scuttle of coal at one side and a filled log basket at the other. Miss Mathewson saw to the fire herself but other hands cleaned it out and checked that there was always plenty of fuel. Two desks and seats, similar to the ones in the village school were set well apart. There was a blackboard and a box of chalk at the far end of the room and this was seldom used. Miss Mathewson had her own table and chair, a large cupboard for school books and a very old-looking cabinet that held jotters, pencils and rulers.

Beth had gone back to the breakfast room to collect Caroline so that they could go along to the schoolroom together. Caroline was drinking the last of her tea.

'Why didn't you wait for me, you know I dislike eating alone?'

'You've always done it before. By now I would have been half way to Sandyneuk School.'

'Well, you don't go there now so in future wait for me.'

'If you are late I won't. Come on, Caroline, I don't want to be late and get a bad mark on my first morning.'

'It doesn't bother me one little bit if I am late.'

'It bothers me so hurry up.'

'Good morning, Miss Caroline,' the governess said giving her tight little smile.

'Good morning, Mattie.' Caroline yawned and sat down at her desk.

'Good morning, Beth.'

'Good morning, Miss Mathewson,' Beth said shyly.

'You take that desk.'

Beth sat down and looked at the jotter on the desk. In the groove were a pencil and ruler. She made to lift the lid of the desk and stopped herself.

'It's empty. Your teacher kindly let me have some of your work, Beth. She said she was sorry to lose you, that you were one of her best pupils.'

Beth blushed. 'Thank you.'

'Why are our desks so far apart?' Caroline demanded to know.

'I prefer it that way.'

'In case Beth copies from me?'

'No, in case you copy from Beth,' Miss Mathewson said swiftly but with a smile.

'As if I would. I don't need to.'

'Neither of you needs to.'

'I've been teaching French to Beth.'

'She has, Miss Mathewson.'

'Indeed!'

'Beth won't have to start at the beginning now.'

'She most certainly will.'

'Why?'

'Miss Caroline, you make mistakes which I have to correct.'

'Not many.'

'One is too many. Nevertheless it was nice of you and I am sure Beth appreciated that.'

'I did, Miss Mathewson.'

'Enough of this, we cannot waste any more time. Miss Caroline, while I am with Beth you will do some calculations. You are weak in mathematics and that won't do.'

'I won't ever need maths so why bother about it? It's a waste of time teaching me.'

'That may well be true but it is my duty to get you to the required standard and that, Miss Caroline, is what I intend doing. Kindly get on with your work,' she said firmly. 'Neat figures if you please and all workings at the side.'

Caroline looked at Beth, raised her eyes to heaven then got her head down.

Miss Mathewson brought her chair over beside Beth.

'Je suis—' Caroline said softly.

'Miss Caroline, are you going to behave?'

'Yes, sorry, couldn't resist it.'

There was no more trouble. Beth could see that Caroline was wary of going too far.

Chapter Seventeen

On a hot windless afternoon in May, Beth set out for Broomfield Road. It wasn't the best day to be going to the town with its smoke-filled air, and those who could would be heading for the beach.

For her visit she had decided on a cap-sleeved green and white patterned cotton dress with a narrow black patent belt. On her feet she wore white ankle socks and brown sandals and over her arm she carried a white cardigan. In her purse was enough money for her fares and a bit over. Since it had been the colonel's wish that Beth visit her relatives, he had arranged for her to receive a weekly sum to cover her expenses.

Beth was feeling very grown-up and she was enjoying the experience of making these trips on her own. This was her first visit to her cousin and his wife but she had already paid two visits to Aunt Anne and Uncle Fred.

After getting off the bus in Dundee she walked smartly to the tram stop only to see one disappearing into the distance. During the week the wait would have been of only five minutes but this was Sunday and there were ten minutes between trams. No one else was at the stop and when the tram arrived Beth got on and sat down on the wooden seat that stretched down one side. A few people sat opposite. The conductor came for her fare and gave her a ticket. Two passengers got up and were standing ready to get off when the tram trundled noisily to the next stop. After they alighted three women and a child got on. Near to the stop was a cluster of shops and since it was a Sunday all but the newsagents had their shutters up. From her seat Beth could see that the window was festooned with advertisements and a few youths and one girl were studying them. The next stop but one was hers and she got up in plenty of time. The conductor said a smiling cheerio and she smiled. For a moment Beth stood looking about her, then having got her bearings she continued for a few yards to a side street, went down it and running across the foot of it was the sign saying Broomfield Road.

Here the tenements stretched uniformly on either side and Beth, used to space, felt hemmed in. It was a shabby, depressing area and much as her aunt had described it. Dirty-faced, snotty children played happily in the road. The boys were shouting and kicking a tin can about and the girls had bits of rope and were skipping. One girl in a clean dress had a proper skipping rope with handles and was holding tightly to it. An older child, or perhaps a parent, had used white chalk to make neat squares on the pavement. Beth knew the game and slowed down to watch a small stone being thrown to land in one of the squares. Then a girl in a torn dress made complicated movements as she jumped about. Beth moved away and quickened her pace.

She checked the numbers where they still existed and fortunately the number nineteen was quite clear. The close was clean from a recent washing and the smell of disinfectant mingled with the cooking smell of cabbage coming from upstairs. The door to the left was the one she wanted and a piece of white cardboard held on by two drawing pins told her that she had come to the right house. Printed on it was the name A. FARQUHARSON.

Beth knocked and after a few moments it opened. A girl in a thin beige skirt and a blue hand-knitted, short-sleeved, string jumper gave a welcoming smile. She was smallish with an elfin face, even white teeth and straight fair hair with a fringe. Beth thought her very pretty.

'You are Beth, aren't you?'

'Yes, and you're Morag?'

'Come in, you managed to find us then?'

'Without any trouble,' Beth smiled as she stepped into the lobby with its floor covered in faded linoleum. 'Aunt Anne gave me very detailed directions.'

'So she would. Still, better that than directions you couldn't follow.' Morag went ahead and into the front room and immediately she was in it her eyes went to her mother's sideboard which graced one wall, and graced was the correct word, Beth thought. In Sycamore Lane she couldn't recall it ever shining this bright. An embroidered cover hung over both ends and on it was a marble clock with a spotted china dog on either side. The clock was broken or it hadn't been wound up. The hands pointed to half past ten.

'That doesn't go, that's why we got it. My mother said we could have it if we got it mended.'

'You will, won't you?'

'Sometime. Adam is going to hunt around to see who will do it cheapest. He'll be here in a minute, Adam I mean, he was just getting ready when you knocked.' She laughed. 'Speak of the devil.'

Adam was slightly above average height with broad shoulders, good features, dark brown springy hair and blue eyes.

'Hello, Beth.' His grip was firm. 'Glad you managed to make it and give us the chance to thank you properly. You could have got a tidy bit for the furniture and we know that.'

'I wanted you to have it and I'm sure it would have been my mother's wish,' Beth said quietly.

'Are you over that awful tragedy?' His blue eyes were concerned.

'I think so, Adam. It was difficult but I'm over the worst now.'

'Why are we all standing?' Morag wanted to know.

'Because you haven't invited our guest to be seated,' Adam teased.

'Beth, sit down. I'm not very good at this – we haven't had much practice. Isn't that right, Adam?'

'Not counting our folks and a couple of my pals and one of Morag's friends, you are our first real visitor, Beth.'

'Adam, are you going to or—?'

'That's my wife's broad hint to put the kettle on,' he said as he made to go.

'Remember, the water must be boiling,' she called after him.

She waited until the door closed before saying, 'Adam is really very helpful, Beth. He sees to the fire before he leaves for work and he's not like some I know who won't lift a hand because they think all housework is woman's work.'

Beth was sitting in what had been her mother's chair and Morag on the sofa. There was none of the strangeness that is common at a first meeting and they were talking about the furniture.

'We hardly have anything that is new, Beth, only the bed and a basket chair,' she grinned.

Beth smiled and saw Morag looking anxiously at the door. 'You won't mind if I leave you a minute? You see, I've only one set of china and the odd bits we use ourselves and I'd rather carry the good ones through myself.'

Just then Adam put his head round the door. 'Everything is ready, tea infused and pancakes buttered. See what a hen-pecked husband I am?'

'You don't look it and incidentally, Adam, I have a bone to pick with you. Why did you and Luke always disappear when we visited Dundee?'

'Did they?' Morag stopped to hear the answer.

'Beth, you were just a wee bairn and we were two strapping laddies – or rather I was a strapping laddie and Luke a bean pole.'

'All right, I forgive you.'

The small table, Uncle Fred's handiwork, was pulled forward so that they could set their cups and saucers on it.

'Morag, how did you manage to get that shine on the sideboard? My mother never did, I'm sure.'

Morag drank some tea then put down her cup. 'I can't take the credit. Honestly, Beth, I do not know where that woman gets her energy. My mother thinks herself a good worker but she says Adam's mother puts her to shame. Not just polishing either. This house was pretty mucky, wasn't it, Adam?'

'Filthy.'

'That's true. I don't think it had ever had a proper clean in years. Adam and me didn't know where to begin.'

'Until ma took us in hand.'

She giggled. 'Talk about being organised. Adam's ma got her sleeves up.'

Adam took over the story. 'Out came the buckets and scrubbing brushes and the three of us set to like nobody's business,' he recalled.

Morag nodded. 'Even when we were more than half

dead she kept us at it. We're laughing, Beth, but I was very grateful. Maybe she works everybody until they are on the point of dropping but she doesn't spare herself.'

'At one time I was scared of Aunt Anne, not Uncle Fred—'

'He's a lamb,' Morag said.

'I remember I was just coming up for nine and Aunt Anne was horrified that my mother didn't make me do housework but my mother said that I would get enough of that when I was older. She didn't want me to work the way she had to when she was little.' Beth swallowed remembering. 'She was all for me enjoying my childhood.'

'I like the sound of your mother, Beth. Mind you, I haven't much to grumble about. We did have to help but my mother did all the hard jobs herself.' She turned to her husband. 'You had to do your stint, didn't you?'

'Certainly did but you shouldn't complain, Morag, it's thanks to ma that I can just about turn my hand to anything.'

'Your mother, Adam, told mine that I would grow up to be useless and she's right. I don't know a thing about housework.'

Adam groaned. 'No help with the dishes, I can see that, and it'll be yours truly as usual.'

'Thinks himself hard done by that one. Don't mind him, Beth.'

'Seriously, ma's bark is worse than her bite, Beth,' Adam defended his mother. 'She means well but like my da says, she's just naturally bossy. She can't help it.'

'I do understand her better now, Adam.' Beth had eaten a pancake and was accepting another. 'These are very good, Morag, did you make them?'

Adam choked over his tea and his wife glared.

'I had hoped to get away with you thinking they were

222

mine but I might have known better. No, Beth, my mother made them this morning and came over in the tram with them still warm and wrapped in a tea towel. She never has a baking failure and I hardy ever have a success.'

'That I do not believe.'

'It is true but supposing I say it myself, I'm a good cook.'

'She is, Beth, makes a grand steak and kidney pie does our Morag.'

'That's what you are getting for your tea.'

'Lovely. Steak pie is my favourite.'

Morag looked pleased.

Beth had been shown round the house by a proud new housewife with Adam hovering nearby. In the kitchen where they were to eat, the table was set with a white tablecloth with a yellow border. The pepper and salt pots – vaguely familiar to Beth – sat in the middle. Four places were set with cutlery. The wallpaper had a flowery pattern and the cream painted ceiling showed a number of cracks. The linoleum was new and in brown and gold and the curtains picked up the colours. Beth thought it all very pleasing and said so.

'Out the back is awful,' Morag said apologetically.

And it was. Beth looked out of the window to a row of cellars, one for each house. They were in a dilapidated state, one had no door at all.

'Never mind, we'll get something better in a year or two, won't we, Adam?'

'Long before then,' Adam said firmly. 'It's just a case of keeping eyes and ears open and being first there when someone moves.'

'Before that, Adam, you've to be there when someone

is just thinking about moving,' Morag laughed. She opened a door. 'Our bedroom.'

Beth stood at the door, she could see it all from there. The flooring was of linoleum so threadbare that the original pattern and colours were long gone. There was a double bed with a pretty blue cover and two pairs of slippers sat side by side between the wardrobe and the basket chair.

Adam moved away and Morag whispered, 'The "you know" is in the close, that's the real drawback to living here. My mother was more concerned that we might have bad neighbours but we haven't, they are all quite nice in this close. The woman upstairs from us,' she pointed to the ceiling, 'said she had a bonny house like ours when she got married but between losing her man—'

'You mean he's dead?' Beth asked.

'That or he walked out. You don't ask questions like that, Beth, not hereabout. They'll tell you what they want you to know. Anyway between losing her man, three bairns in three years, and poor health because of it, she lost heart. I feel sorry for her but Adam's mother says she could do more for herself if she tried. She looks so old yet she's a lot younger than my mother.'

The "you know" was worrying Beth since she would have to make use of it sometime. Then she thought how foolish she was. It was a toilet in the close instead of one in the house, that was all. Adam had been used to a bathroom, very likely Morag had too, but they must have been so anxious to get married that they had been prepared to put up with any inconvenience. The real problem, she imagined, would be having to get up in the middle of the night. She never had to and perhaps it was only very old people who were troubled that way.

'Does it give you a strange feeling to see your parents' things here?'

'No, it doesn't,' Beth said truthfully. 'It's a nice feeling and the furniture suits the house.'

'That is what everybody says.'

Beth gave a start when there was a sharp knock at the door and she saw husband and wife exchange smiles.

'No prizes for guessing who that is. You answer it, Adam.'

They heard him say, 'It's you. You don't live here, you know.'

A very tall, painfully thin youth came in. He had reddish fair hair, a healthy complexion and a crop of freckles on his forehead and across the bridge of his nose.

'This lad just can't stay away.'

'Morag likes me coming.'

'Of course I do, Luke, you know you are always welcome.'

'Came specially to see my wee cousin, ma said she'd be here.'

'She's not so wee,' Morag said.

'No, I'm not, I just keep growing and growing. Hello, Luke.'

She expected them to shake hands but Luke bent down from his great height and kissed her cheek. 'I'm allowed that since you're family.'

Beth blushed but she was pleased.

'That's a liberty I didn't take,' Adam said and promptly touched his lips to Beth's brow.

'The pair of them are awful teases, Beth. You'll get used to them, I've had to.'

'I hope they are looking after you,' Luke said as he began to unbutton his jacket.

'Oh, they are.'

225

'Let me take your jacket, Luke, and I'll put it in the bedroom.' Luke gave it to her. He had on a pale blue open-necked shirt.

'Don't tell me you were allowed to come out without a tie and this a Sunday?'

'I'm a big lad now, Morag, and I do what I like.' For a split second he scowled and Adam, raising an eyebrow, glanced at his wife. Beth wondered what had brought on the scowl or perhaps she had imagined it. Luke was all smiles again.

'You staying for tea?' Adam asked his brother.

'Is there enough, Morag?'

'Plenty, I had a feeling you would come.'

'Any tea in that pot?' he asked hopefully.

'No, but I'll make a fresh pot.'

'Don't do that. I'll have a couple of pancakes and that'll do me until I get my tea. What's for it?'

'Steak and kidney pie.'

'Great! She can make a good steak pie, Beth.'

'I know.' Beth was loving it. This was family life and already she felt herself being drawn into their circle.

It was five o'clock and they were seated round the table in the kitchen. With no scullery, the gas cooker, their most expensive buy, was next to the window. The bunker used to keep the coal was covered with a cloth and the ashet was balanced on a square of thin wood to take the heat. Morag was cutting up the pie with its nicely browned flaky pastry and sharing it between the four plates. Adam had the task of carrying them to the table. Morag, flushed from the heat and her efforts, emptied the mashed potatoes from the pot and into a large tureen. It went to the centre of the table with a big spoon so that they could help themselves.

'That's the only serving dish—'

'Tureen, sweetheart.'

'Tureen then, I couldn't think of the word.'

'Didn't know it, be truthful.'

'Hit him over the head with something, Morag.'

'I'm coming very close to it, Luke.' She went back to the cooker. 'Excuse the pots,' she said as she dished the vegetables straight from the pot on to the plates.

Beth was hungry, the steak pie was very good and she ate heartily. There was no ceremony here, just plenty of laughter and good-natured teasing. How different from the dining-room at Inverbrae House, where there was little laughter and only a low hum of conversation, to which she contributed nothing.

Luke dropped his fork and immediately bent down to get it, and for a moment Beth was back in time. How dreadful she had felt, and had been made to feel, when she had broken the rules and did what Luke had done.

'Beth, come on and tell us what it is like to live with the toffs and have servants to do all the work.'

'Maybe she doesn't want to, Adam, and Luke, you greedy scamp, that's enough potatoes, leave some for the rest of us.'

'Sorry, can't resist them. Ma says I'll turn into a tattie if I don't cut down.' He looked at his cousin. 'Come on, Beth, you're the nearest we've come to gentry.'

'I was just wondering where to begin. For one thing there is never any hilarity at the table.'

'Not done in the best of circles?'

'Not done at Inverbrae House anyway but there is another house I go to. After – after they died I went to stay with Jenny and she was wonderful to me. She's a real lady and we were always laughing in her house.'

'Are you happy with those people, Beth?'

'They have been good to me, Morag,' Beth said quietly, 'so I shouldn't complain.'

Morag nodded. 'Like Adam's mother said, they are good to you because you keep that lass of theirs happy.'

'I suppose that's true. When I was younger I felt myself the same as Caroline because her Nanny treated us alike. Then when I was a bit older I could tell that they were relieved because my mother was coming home.'

'Then the tragedy?'

'Yes. I caused them a lot of worry at that time and they were kind. Even so, I don't know how to describe it. It all seemed to be on the surface and that I had become an embarrassment. Honestly, I'd never felt so miserable and alone.'

'Some people make me sick,' Morag looked on the verge of tears. 'You wanted a lot of loving and understanding and anybody with any decency would have known that.'

'I got some from Jenny but no one else. I've always felt starved of love—' She stopped, embarrassed.

'Your parents, surely—?'

Beth looked sad. 'They loved me in their own way but they were quite incapable of showing it.'

'No hugs or kisses?' Luke had been silent until then. 'A family thing, Beth. I mind when I was a bairn and coming in with a bloody nose or scraped knees and just getting cleaned and bandaged and a raging. The others, my pals, got a good telling off and a hug. I just got the telling off.'

'Was that the way it was with you, Adam?'

'Yes, but it didn't worry me, I wasn't bothered.'

'I tell you here and now, Adam Farquharson, that our bairns will get plenty of love. And don't look at me like that, we all need it.'

'Help! What have I done to deserve this?'

'You mean what have I started?' Beth laughed.

'Shut up you two I want to hear Beth's story.'

'Jenny was a friend of Colonel Parker-Munro—'

'You didn't have to call the old fellow that, did you?'

'Yes, I did, at first anyway.'

Morag giggled. 'Heavens! I would never have got my tongue round it.'

'I got used to it. Jenny was marvellous to me and after a week with her I felt much better.'

'I bet you have to be meek and grateful,' Luke said.

'Not meek, I could never be that. Having to be grateful is bad enough.'

Morag got up to collect the dishes and Adam helped her. They exchanged smiles. Luke and Beth were hitting it off well.

'I bet.'

'Something inside me won't let me feel grateful for what others, like Caroline, take for granted. That's wrong, I suppose. Caroline was born into this family and she has the right to feel superior.'

'You don't really believe that?'

'No, but I should.'

'No, you shouldn't, you are every bit as good as them.'

'Oh, I almost forgot to tell you, I am being sent away to school.'

Morag stopped what she was doing. 'Sent away where?'

'Caroline is going to Rowanbank after the holidays and I've just been told that I'll be going with her.'

'Boarding school you mean?' Morag said with awe in her voice.

'We'll be weekly boarders.'

'Will you still manage to come and see us?' Morag

asked and then, more slowly, 'Maybe you won't want to come here.'

Beth looked hurt. 'If I'm invited I'll come and it'll be because I want to.'

'She'll always be welcome, won't she, Adam?'

'Beth knows that. She might be living with the toffs but we are her family. Better keep it to a Sunday.'

'That won't be easy, Adam. We've got to be back in school by seven at the latest.'

'Are you looking forward to going?'

'Yes, I am, Luke. I'll get a good education and I'm going to work hard to get qualifications. When I have those I'll hopefully get a good job and be independent.'

'Until you get married?'

'I won't be in a hurry, I want to taste independence.' She glanced at her wrist watch. 'Goodness, it is time I was on my way.'

Adam got up but Luke said hastily, 'No need for you to leave Morag on her own. I'll see Beth to the bus.'

'No, please, I can manage on my own,' Beth protested.

'Maybe, but you're not going on your own. Is someone meeting you at Sandyneuk?' He paused and added, 'Or is it not very far?'

'It's quite a bit but I don't mind and nobody knows where I am.'

'Then they should,' Adam said angrily. 'You're just a bairn and someone should be concerned about you.'

But Beth was already at the door. 'Thank you both for a lovely day,' she said.

'When will you manage to come again?'

'It might have to be in the holidays, Morag, but I'll write and let you know how I'm getting on at school.'

Morag nodded. 'Yon letter I sent you was the first I'd ever written. Didn't ever need to before.'

'It was a lovely letter.'

She got a hug and a kiss from Morag and Adam before she left. The streets were quiet as they set out, the children all indoors.

'I must be taking you a lot out of your way, Luke?'

'Not much.'

The tram was just moving away and they both sprinted. Beth jumped on and Luke followed. The conductor shook his head. 'You'll do that once too often, that's the way accidents happen.'

'Surefooted,' Luke laughed as he handed over the money for the fares. Beth wanted to pay her own but he wouldn't hear of it.

'Surefooted until you fall,' came the sour reply.

'Where do you work, Luke?'

'The foundry.'

'Adam still in the shipyard?'

'Yes, he's doing all right. Ma keeps on at him to try and get me in.'

'Would he manage that?'

'Possible and it's better than the foundry, better money.'

'But not what you want?'

'No, Beth, not what I want but my wishes don't seem to be important,' he said bitterly.

'What do you want to do?'

'Go off to sea. It's all I've ever wanted and I'd take any job going.'

'What's holding you back?'

'Ma, she goes on at great length about me being too young – I'm nearly nineteen – to know what I want and that I would live to regret it. Just a lot of tripe, she doesn't want me to go that's the sum total of it.'

'She's afraid for you.'

'That's stupid. Danger is everywhere, you just have to look out for yourself.' He glanced out. 'Come on, it's our stop.'

'So it is,' Beth said, springing to her feet. 'It's a good job someone was paying attention.' They were walking when she said, 'What has Uncle Fred to say?'

'Da doesn't say much but he isn't keen. The reason for that is he had a brother lost at sea.'

'Understandable then?'

'Suppose so.'

In a companionable silence they walked to the bus station. The Sandyneuk bus, though not due to leave for eight minutes, was already in the station. The driver was leaning against the bonnet and smoking a cigarette.

'Thank you, Luke, and good luck.'

'Same to you, I'll be thinking of you in that posh school and don't let them push you around.'

'I won't.'

He gave her shoulder a squeeze just like a brother, she thought, and she got on the bus and took a seat at the front. He turned once and waved then he was lost to sight.

Beth sat and thought about her day. It had been hugely enjoyable. She liked her cousins and Morag very much but she didn't think she could ever live in such conditions. Perhaps being in love made the discomforts bearable. It must. Adam and Morag had made a choice, either wait until a better house was available or take what was on offer and get married right away.

Beth didn't hurry when she got off the bus. It was a balmy night and it was pleasant to breathe deeply of the fresh air that smelt of flowers. In the distance was Inverbrae House, aloof and proud like its owner. They had a privileged status in life, the colonel and Mrs Parker-Munro, but were they happy? She supposed they were – it was the only life they knew. As to herself, she was about to be given the benefit of an education at a top school and that was something for which she would be grateful.

Caroline was in their sitting-room, drooping like a wilting lily.

'You've got back? Mrs Watson came over for me and I'm absolutely exhausted. Leonard and Ralph are home and you won't believe the difference in those two. Remember how rough they used to be?'

'I haven't seen them more than twice.'

'Neither you have, then take my word for it. They have become so nice and polite and we played the gramophone. Imagine what grandmama would have said about playing it on a Sunday! Beth, I've come to the conclusion that I quite like boys. I always said I didn't but I've changed my mind. Was your day awful?'

'Why should it have been?'

'I don't know that is why I am asking.'

'I had a perfectly lovely day.'

Chapter Eighteen

The postal van was never late. Folk could very nearly set their watches by it, because business and other institutions depended on the mail being delivered on time and now the post office had let them down. It just wasn't good enough. Muttering his annoyance, the colonel left Inverbrae House without having seen the mail. Damn it! he thought. More than likely there would be a letter requiring his immediate attention.

One mile from Inverbrae House, the post office van was parked at the side of the narrow country road with its bonnet up. A mechanic was half inside it and a worried looking postman, a cup of tea in his hand, stood nearby and watched. The tea had come from the young woman who lived in one of the farm cottages. A toddler and an older boy arrived to see what was going on.

'Will it no' go?' the older boy, who would be about five, wanted to know.

'No.'

'Is it broken?'

'Yes.'

'Are you a different postie?'

The postman sighed. He couldn't be bothered with bairns, not right now, but it was their ma's tea he was drinking so he'd better not ignore them. 'Your own postie's on holiday.'

'Where's he gone?'

'Don't know.'

'We never go a holiday.' The woman was back. 'We never go a holiday do we ma?'

'Hold your sheesht, Bobby, and take Herbert inside.'

'Don't want to, I want to watch.'

'Inside I said.' Her hand shot out and pointed to the open door.

Taking his wee brother's hand they walked away, with Bobby turning round once to see if his mother had had a change of heart. She hadn't.

The mechanic's head appeared. 'Try it now.'

'I'll keep my fingers crossed,' the woman said as she took his cup.

'Ta, that was fine,' the postman said. He got behind the wheel, turned on the ignition and the engine spluttered into life. 'Thank the Lord for that.'

'Let it run for a wee while to make sure.'

They listened. There was a slight hiccup when they looked at each other anxiously then came the sound for which they had been waiting.

Before moving off the postman called out, 'Thanks, lad, what was the trouble?'

The mechanic scratched his head with his oily hands. 'Can't rightly say, just one of those things I suppose.'

The postman nodded. It was the answer he had expected.

'Thanks again for the tea.'

'You're welcome.' She smiled and waved. It made a nice break in her day.

The van shot off with the first stop Longacre Farm then it was on to Inverbrae House. There would be complaints, he thought bitterly, and the blame would be his. Not the van's fault, not sloppy maintenance, no one else's fault just his. That was life and silence, he had discovered, was the best policy if he wanted to keep his job. It didn't do to lose your rag.

Mrs Parker-Munro was annoyed. She usually read her letters in bed. They arrived with the breakfast tray but not this morning. It was too bad and it upset the routine of her day.

When the van did eventually arrive the maid collected the mail, carried it through to the hall table and placed the letters on the silver tray left there for the purpose. A few minutes later Mrs Parker-Munro's stick could be heard on the parquet floor, and seeing the pile she went over. Sitting down on the tapestry covered chair she took her spectacles from her cardigan pocket, put them on and prepared to go through the letters. Most were for her son. Two were marked 'Urgent' and underlined in red ink. Her frown deepened. Not good enough. Nigel would have something to say and with good reason. There could be no excuse, this wasn't the winter after all, and even then the greatest effort had to be made. Wasn't it their boast that no matter what the post got through?

She fingered one, a pink envelope and spidery writing, that would be from Leonora. Her letters were always a delight, so full of news and gossip, pity it wasn't easier to read. That one she would keep to the end. She put it aside along with another two from friends and several accounts that required settling. What was this? She looked at it closely, examining the stamp and the postmark. Australia? Who did she know in Australia? No one. She checked that it was addressed to her. It was. Written very clearly on the envelope was Mrs Euphemia Parker-Munro. Who could be writing to her? At her age she didn't like shocks, they quickened her heartbeat and that could be dangerous. Perhaps she should wait until evening when Nigel would be here. He would read it first then break it to her whatever it was.

Gathering up her letters and leaving the rest in an untidy pile, the old lady picked up her stick and went slowly along to the sitting-room. She would ring for tea, even though it was just an hour since she'd had breakfast. Tea was one of her greatest comforts.

By midday Mrs Parker-Munro had done fingering the letter. She was being ridiculous, she told herself, acting as though she were in her dotage. The letter could be from a friend of a friend, for goodness sake. But she knew it wasn't. Something told her that it was important, important to her.

Using her letter opener she slit the envelope and drew out several flimsy sheets. She looked at the address in the right hand corner and then began to read. As she read, her eyes widened in shock and her face lost the little colour it had. After coming to the end of the first page she went back to the beginning to go over it again before turning to the next.

Dear Mrs Parker-Munro,

This is a very difficult letter to write and I don't quite know where to begin. Perhaps it would be best to tell you who I am, that I am your daughter-in-law. I was married to your son, James, for sixteen years, and sadly he died six months ago from a brain haemorrhage. He was a good husband and father and our three children are finding it hard to accept his death. For me it was a devastating blow but life must go on and ours is a close and loving family. My children and I are being well looked after.

James spoke little of his early life but I knew there were times when he regretted losing touch. On these occasions I would plead with him to write to his family but he said

*that he had left it too late. Though I didn't agree with that
I had to respect his wishes but I did feel he was wrong in
depriving his children of grandparents and you and your
late husband of knowing about your Australian grandchildren.*

*Shall I now tell you about our family? Robert is fifteen
and there is a resemblance to James. I think so but others
think he takes after our side of the family. People see
what they want, don't they? William is thirteen and
resembles neither of us but he has the look of his
grandfather Reid. Emily, the baby, is nine. She is a
lovely sweet child and James adored her. He loved his
sons dearly but when Emily was born it was as though I
had given him the greatest gift of all.*

*My thoughts are wandering and the letter is getting a
bit disjointed. How did I get your address? Going
through James's papers I found letters dating from far
back, long before I knew him. Not knowing the position
at Inverbrae House I got our solicitor to make enquiries
and I learned from him that James's father had died.*

*I met James when he came to work for my father. We
have a very large sheep farm and all the family are
involved in it in one way or another. Robert and William
are both away at school and are happy enough although
they would much rather be at home. Emily is taught by a
governess who is very good but in a year or two Emily
too will have to go away. I try not to think of it.*

*Robert, our eldest, is fascinated to learn about his
Scottish family. Unlike William who has no wish ever to
leave Australia, Robert would like to see a bit of the
world, and once his education is completed, he intends to
do just that. Most of all he would like to see where his
father grew up and to meet you all. Perhaps one day this
will happen.*

*I feel sure that you would like to have photographs of
James and the family and once I hear from you I'll sort
out the best and post them on. Would you be kind
enough to send on one or two photographs of James as a
boy? I would so love to have them for myself to see the
little boy that was James, and for the children to treasure
and add to the family album.*

*I'm so sorry that I failed to persuade James to write to
you and I can only imagine as a mother myself, what you
have been going through.*

*We have a large ranch-style house and three smaller
homes nearby. This gives us the privacy needed in all
families and yet the nearness to work together which is so
essential out here. My grandfather, who is ninety on his
next birthday, lives with my parents. He is still active and
takes an interest in everything as well as keeping us all in
order! He loves nothing better than a good argument and
he always said that James was the only one who could
hold his own. Such happy times.*

*The news of your son's death will sadden and distress
you, and my heart goes out to you and your son, Nigel. I
hope that I have managed to convey in this letter the
happiness we all enjoyed. Your son got on well with
everyone, Mrs Parker-Munro, and was a much-loved
member of our family. We all miss him so much.*

*Before I end this very difficult letter I had better tell
you that James called himself Munro not Parker-Munro.
Out here they would have shortened it anyway!*
Very sincerely,
Your daughter-in-law,
Dorothy Munro.

Euphemia Parker-Munro kept the pages between her
fingers. How often had she read it? The tears, unheeded,

rolled down her cheeks and lodged for a moment in the deep crevices round the mouth. Her son was dead. She would never see James again, not in this life. For years his name had been barely mentioned but always there had been hope in her heart that one day he would return to Inverbrae House. Now all hope was gone. Just lately it had been easier to remember the past than what had taken place a few short weeks ago. A sure sign of age.

James so different from Nigel. He had been such a naughty little boy, unable to keep out of mischief but so lovable. Certainly he had been a trial to everyone, especially to his father who was bewildered and angered by such behaviour. If only they hadn't taken such drastic action and believed mistakenly that the army would be the making of him. A little more time, a little more understanding, and he might well have outgrown his rebelliousness. The letter was proof of that, James had settled down to be a responsible family man.

She moved in the chair and winced at the pain, sharp for a few moments then dulling to the usual ache that she had learned to live with. Her husband was gone and so was her son James but James's children were very much alive and he had called his first born Robert, after his own father. She smiled.

Robert Munro. Robert Munro he might be in Australia but when he came to Scotland that would change. Time was ticking away for her and she tried to calculate how long it would be before her grandson, Robert, would be old enough to travel to Scotland and come to Inverbrae House. Eighteen would likely be the school leaving age unless, of course, he wanted to go on to university or college. His father had not wanted that but his son might be different. She was tired in body but her mind was working feverishly.

Robert could come to Scotland when he left school and attend a Scottish university if that was what he wanted. Perhaps St Andrews, where Nigel had gone? That could be easily arranged. What was important was Robert coming to Inverbrae House. She would have liked to see her other two grandchildren but that seemed unlikely.

If only Nigel would come. She kept looking at the clock and willing the hands to go round. In a fever of impatience, unable to eat, but drinking endless cups of tea and between them giving the maids frequent and strict instructions that the master was to come and see her the moment he arrived.

The master, thus informed as he stepped inside his home, was irritated and showed it. He marched along, knocked out of habit and went in.

'Mother, what is it that can't wait? I don't have much time with the mail not turning up and having to be dealt with now.'

'You can deal with that later.' There were times, she thought, when her son annoyed her and this was one. She wasn't in the habit of demanding his attention on frivolous matters, she thought indignantly. He should know that it was important.

Something in her face, perhaps its greyness alarmed him and he regretted his brusqueness. 'What is it, Mother?' he said gently. 'What is troubling you?'

'I've had a letter about James,' she said shakily.

'James! You've had a letter from James,' he said disbelievingly.

She shook her head. 'If only that were so. James is dead, Nigel.' The letter was on the table and she put her hand over it. He saw that it shook.

Nigel was shocked and upset and he sat down abruptly

as though his legs had given way.

'James dead – I can't believe it!'

'His wife – his widow has written a long letter, such a nice brave letter. Read it, Nigel, read it for yourself. I think I know it almost off by heart.'

He read it through quickly then read it again.

'My poor, poor James,' his mother said brokenly.

'He had a happy life, Mother, that leaps off the pages.'

'But so young to die?'

'Yes. I like the sound of my sister-in-law very much, I think she must be a very remarkable woman.'

'Her letter moved me deeply. She has taken such care to break the news as gently as possible and at the same time to bring the family to us.'

'A very carefully worded letter. Mother, you'll have to get used to the idea of having four grandchildren,' he smiled.

'I find that quite wonderful and I only wish there weren't so many miles between us.' She paused and looked at Nigel. 'Fancy James settling so far away, right at the other end of the world.'

'Father made a mistake thinking the army would be the making of James.'

'I seem to recall you agreeing with him,' his mother said drily.

'If I did then I was wrong. I remember James telling me once that he felt trapped here. I suppose he thought of the army as another trap. He yearned for the open spaces and Australia offered him that.'

'How anyone could feel trapped in Inverbrae House is beyond me.'

'From all accounts he landed on his feet. There is plenty of money there and if the son wants to travel, I don't imagine anything would be put in his way.'

'The boy must come here,' she said firmly, 'and you, Nigel, must go and see to that urgent business of yours.'

He got up. 'Indeed I must.'

'You aren't going out this evening?' She looked wistful.

'No, and had I been it would have been cancelled.'

'You are a dear boy.'

'Shall I send Caroline in?'

'No, I don't want the child's chatter just at present. What I do need is to talk about James.'

He kissed her cheek. 'Directly I finish, we shall talk of James and tomorrow Caroline will be told of her Australian cousins.'

'She will be thrilled and perhaps the teeniest bit jealous,' the old lady smiled.

'No, just thrilled, I think.'

'You'll never guess, the most exciting thing ever has happened.'

Beth, used to Caroline's exaggeration, looked up briefly. She was on the floor sitting on a cushion and trying to concentrate on her French reader. 'Mmm,' was all she said.

'Kindly stop reading that and listen to me. Beth, I am talking to you.'

'All right! All right! Hurry up and say what you are going to, I'm not even half way through this.'

'You don't have to work as hard as all that. You heard what Mattie said that we are well up in what we are supposed to know. You, Beth Brown, are in danger of turning into a horrible little swot.'

'Not a chance since you never stop chattering.'

'I'll let that pass and now listen. Grandmama has had a letter from Australia.'

'So your grandmother has had a letter from Australia?'

'Telling her that she has grandchildren. I've got three cousins I didn't know existed.'

She had Beth's attention now.

'Daddy's brother, James. I think he was a rebel. Isn't that exciting? Apparently he ran away from home, from Inverbrae House, and for a while he sent postcards from different parts of the world then that stopped and nothing was heard of my Uncle James.' Her pale blue eyes grew round.

'Until now?'

She nodded. 'Uncle James is dead and his wife, she's called Dorothy, that means I have an Aunt Dorothy—'

'I managed to gather that.'

'She wrote to my grandmama to let her know that she has three grand-children, that makes four counting me.' She grew very serious. 'Robert is fifteen, William is thirteen and Emily, she's just nine.'

'You'll have to start writing to them.'

'Sometime. I'll wait until I see the photographs when they come. Grandmama says Robert is supposed to be a little like his father and she says that Uncle James was quite nice looking so I expect this Robert will be too. He is to be invited to come here when he leaves school, that'll be when he is eighteen. He's three years older than me, than us.' She said all this barely stopping for breath.

'That's a long time and maybe he won't want to come to Scotland.'

Caroline looked scornful. 'He does want to come, he wants to see where his father lived and that's only natural.'

'I saw my cousins and Morag in Dundee. You never asked about them?'

'Forgot all about your visit to Dundee. Anyway it's much, much more exciting having cousins in Australia than boring old ones in Dundee.'

Beth let that pass. 'I had a lovely, lovely day and I'll be going back to see them.' Beth was determined to get her cousins a mention.

'That may not be possible since you are going off to school. Oh, I nearly forgot, Aunt Gwen is taking us both to Perth on Tuesday to get our uniform and all the other dreary things on the list.'

Beth felt excited at the thought of the uniform but wished it hadn't been Caroline's Aunt Gwen who was to take them. She wasn't exactly rude, that would never do, but the woman had a habit of ignoring Beth almost as though she weren't there. Beth thought if it wasn't rude it was certainly bad manners.

'What is the uniform like?'

'Haven't you seen Ruth in hers?'

'No.'

'Well, it's grey and red.'

'That should be nice.'

'Glad you think so, I find all talk about uniform and everything else utterly boring.'

'Boring seems to be your favourite word just now.'

Caroline grinned. 'One ordeal we are going to miss.'

'Oh!'

'Ruth says it is normal to visit the school, be shown around then introduced to the Head but for some unknown reason the Critchley female won't be available and instead she is to meet the new girls when they arrive.' She made a face. 'Thank goodness you are coming with me, Beth. Now that it's getting near the time I'm getting butterflies in my stomach when I think about it.'

'You shouldn't. Ruth likes it so it can't be too bad.'

'Oh, her! Aunt Gwen says she is so easy going that nothing ever bothers her.'

246

'That's the best way to be.'

'Not according to Aunt Gwen, she gets very annoyed at Ruth. It is easy enough for you, Beth Brown, not to be worried. You know what school is like, I've only ever been taught by Mattie.'

'You'll be all right, I'll look after you.'

'You'll have to, that's why you are getting to go to Rowanbank.'

'Something you are going to remind me of constantly.'

'For your own good. In case you haven't noticed, I look after you too. One learns by example,' she said haughtily, 'and I've been your model. You used to watch me before you did anything.'

'Maybe I did but I don't have to now.'

'My cousins in Australia are very wealthy, even better off than we are or so daddy says. They have a huge sheep farm.'

'One day you might go to Australia to visit them.'

'No, Beth, I wish I could but grandmama has been reading about Australia, the climate and everything. She says the dry heat wouldn't do with me.'

Chapter Nineteen

On the day the school broke up for the Christmas holidays, there was a lot of noise and excitement from the full boarders but less from the weekly boarders. The classroom windows were open and there was the smell of chalk and polish as cleaning got under way. Outside it was crisp and cold. Cars began to arrive with parents or chauffeurs to take the girls back home for the two-week break. Tommy, smart in his uniform, stood outside the colonel's car waiting to drive his boss's daughter and Beth to Inverbrae House.

On several occasions Caroline had made it clear that she did not approve of any familiarity with the chauffeur. She frowned on Beth for engaging Tommy in conversation. Tommy was aware of this and, fearful of losing his job, contented himself with a wink to Beth when the young madam wasn't looking.

Tommy dealt with the trunks when they arrived back in Inverbrae House. Both girls ran up the steps and into the house.

'The decorations look a bit dull,' Caroline said with critical eyes as she looked about the hall. 'These same ones appear each year.'

'Look all right to me and there is plenty of holly.'

Caroline shrugged and went over to the silver tray. 'No letters for me.'

'Were you expecting some?'

'One anyway. I wrote to Aunt Dorothy in Australia.'

'Takes ages for letters to get there and the reply to come.'

'Suppose so.' She began to unbutton her coat and Beth did the same. 'Come on, leave our coats here and show ourselves to grandmama.'

Mrs Parker-Munro was sitting by the fire when they went in. It was stiflingly hot but even so she had a shawl round her shoulders.

'You've arrived then?'

'Yes, grandmama,' Caroline said going over and giving her a kiss.

'Nice to have you home, dear.'

'We are both glad to be home, aren't we, Beth?' There were times like now when Caroline tried to include her friend.

As though just aware of another presence she inclined her head but gave no word of greeting.

'You are happy at school, Caroline?'

'It isn't too bad, could be worse.'

Her grandmother smiled. 'That means you have settled down as I knew you would.'

Beth remained standing. She would have liked to go and leave them together but required permission to do so and she wasn't going to ask. Caroline had gone to sit beside her grandmother.

'Those decorations in the hall have seen better days. Who is supposed to see to having them renewed?'

'That would be my responsibility, dear. Mrs Murdoch arranges for them to be put up and after the new year they go back into the attic. You, my dear child, can see to that come another year. It will be a beginning for the time when you will have the responsibility for this house. A very great responsibility, Caroline.'

'Surely the servants see to that,' she said carelessly.

'They do but the orders must come from you.'

'Not daddy?'

'His duty is to the estate and yours will be to the house.'

'Unless daddy gets married and that would make a difference.'

'I think we can rule that out.' She frowned as though just remembering that she and her grand-daughter weren't alone. 'Beth?'

Beth was startled out of her day-dreaming. 'Yes, Mrs Parker-Munro?'

'I had forgotten you were there. Go along to the kitchen if you please, and have tea for two sent to the sitting-room.' She smiled to Caroline. 'You and I, my dear, have things to talk about.'

It was a dismissal and Beth went along to the kitchen. The journey she knew to be unnecessary since ringing the bell would have brought the maid. Beth gave the order and went back to the hall. The coats were still where they had left them and Beth put hers on. She would go outside and have a chat with Tommy if he was cleaning the car.

He looked up. 'Safe to talk now? How are you getting on at that posh school?'

'All right.'

'Better than the secondary where you would have gone?'

'Different.'

He laughed. 'Understatement of the year.'

'How are things with you, Tommy?'

'Can't complain. Life's pretty good. I reckon it's what you make it.'

'I reckon you're right.'

'What do you plan to do when you finish school?' He

stopped the polishing and looked at her.

'Get a job.'

'And live here?'

'I wouldn't want to do that. I want to be independent.'

'That'll be all right for a wee while. Know what I see for you?'

'I'm listening.'

'You're going to have a lot of admirers, me among them if I hadn't been caught.'

'Pull the other one. You wouldn't change Mabel for the world and don't try and tell me otherwise.'

'That's true enough but, kidding apart, Beth, there are going to be a few after you. Know it or not, you're going to be a smasher.'

'What about those few after me,' she laughed.

'Take care and choose carefully. The nobs,' he jerked his head, 'set more store on suitable marriages than a love match. Don't you make that mistake, Beth. What me and Mabel have is special and money can't buy that.' He stopped and grinned. 'Sound soppy, don't I?'

'No, you don't, Tommy, and one day if and when I marry I hope we'll be as happy as you and Mabel.'

'No ifs about it.'

She went away laughing.

Caroline's coat was still in the hall and Beth picked it up and took it to the cloakroom along with her own. With being so near Christmas the mail had been late and there were letters on the silver tray. Beth went through them to see if there was one for Caroline from Australia. There wasn't, but there was one addressed to Miss Beth Brown. The address was printed and Beth put the letter in her pocket and went along to her room to read it. Opening it she smiled, it was from Jenny. A short scrawled note.

My dearest Beth,

In the unlikely event of you being alone on Christmas day do please take an early bus and come to Greystanes for luncheon. I am to be with friends in the evening and we shall drop you off at Inverbrae House.

Don't bother to reply. If you don't come I'll know that you are being entertained. If you do decide to come Miss Harris and I will be so delighted.
In haste,
love
Jenny.

There was nothing she would enjoy more than being with Jenny on Christmas day but she couldn't accept. She would be expected to have the meal at Inverbrae House. There wouldn't be much celebrating in Dundee, Christmas day wasn't a holiday in Scotland. New Year's day was. For some lucky children there would be a trip to the pantomime and in the morning they would rush to see what Santa Claus had left in their stocking. Others would get an apple and an orange and perhaps a new penny. For the very large number where the breadwinner was unemployed there would be nothing. Did these children question why Santa Claus always forgot them or were they so used to poverty and want that they had lost the ability to wonder?

Beth sat in her usual place in the dining-room. Earlier in the day the colonel had spoken briefly to her and then, with Caroline hanging on to his arm, they had gone to join Mrs Parker-Munro. How very stiff and formal the meals were and how different from that meal with Adam and Morag where there had been laughter and good-natured banter. Jenny had brought laughter to Inverbrae House but now her name was never mentioned.

253

Caroline chatted about school and from time to time brought Beth into the conversation. Beth responded then ate what was before her and drifted into her own thoughts.

After the maid had removed the plates Mrs Parker-Munro touched her lips with her napkin and began to speak.

'Caroline, dear, there is a change of plan for Christmas day.'

'Why, what is happening?'

'Your Aunt Gwen has very kindly invited us to spend Christmas day with them. It is to be a family gathering.' She turned her head to look at Beth. 'Since it is family only, you will understand, Beth, that the invitation does not include you but I'm sure the kitchen will put on something special. You can take your meals with Mrs Murdoch, who is quite agreeable to this, or you can have them on your own, just as you please.'

Beth felt the colour rush to her face. She felt humiliated and wished, oh, how she wished, that she could get up from the table and never have to eat there again. Then she remembered the invitation from Jenny and a little of the devil was in her.

'How very, very kind of you, Mrs Parker-Munro, to put yourself to all that trouble on my behalf,' Beth said sweetly.

The old lady looked at her sharply. Had there been a hint of impertinence in that answer? But the girl's expression gave nothing away.

Caroline looked displeased and was frowning. She knew it was going to be dull and boring at Aunt Gwen's. Everybody old except Ruth and they never had a lot to say to one another. Beth and she could have had a giggle and really it was too bad the way they were treating her friend

It hadn't always been like that and she wondered what had brought it on.

'I think it is too bad of Aunt Gwen not to invite Beth. Don't you agree, daddy?'

The colonel raised his eyes and avoided looking at Beth. 'Your Aunt Gwen is kindly arranging a family party and since she has emphasised that it is to be family only and Beth isn't family, there is no reason why she should have been included in the invitation.'

The old lady nodded her approval.

'I still think it is too bad and I know someone who is going to agree with me.'

'Caroline!' Her father said warningly.

'Thank you, Caroline, but it is all right.' Beth smiled across at her friend. Her eyes were bright and she was going to enjoy the next few minutes. 'Even had I been invited I would not have accepted.'

There was a gasp of outrage from the old lady. Beth smiled and carried on. 'You see, I have already had an invitation for Christmas day so no one need worry about me.'

Caroline opened her mouth to say something then thought better of it.

'How very suitable, Beth, I am very pleased.' Indeed the colonel seemed to be inordinately pleased. 'It is a time for family and your place is with yours.'

Beth saw no reason to correct him.

On Christmas eve there had been a few flurries of snow but to the disappointment of many, mostly children, it wasn't to be a white Christmas. Instead the morning dawned bright and cold and was pleasant for getting about. With breakfast over there was a movement to the drawing-room where the gifts were set beside the

Christmas tree. It all looked very festive and the four people were smiling as they awaited the exchange of gifts. Caroline had appointed herself to be the one to read the names on the gift cards.

As always both girls had been given a modest sum of money to buy small inexpensive gifts for the tree. After a good deal of thought, Beth had purchased a bottle of eau de cologne for Mrs Parker-Munro and a leather bookmark for the colonel. Her gift to Caroline was the same as Caroline's gift to her. Unwrapping them they thanked each other effusively for their very first box of make-up. The old lady frowned heavily.

'Good skin needs nothing but soap and water,' she said severely. 'That cheap rubbish can only do harm.'

The girls paid no attention and the colonel chuckled and shook his head.

Beth's gift from Caroline's grandmother was a box of lace-edged handkerchiefs and from the colonel she had been given money to buy books. Since there were a great many books at Inverbrae House to suit all ages, Beth had begun to save the money she got for birthdays and Christmas. She had her account at the bank and knew the procedure for making deposits. Seeing her savings grow was giving Beth a great deal of satisfaction.

Her father and grandmother gave Caroline jewellery, a beautiful necklace and bracelet that had cost a great deal of money. After a quick glance at them she kissed her father and grandmother, said a dutiful thank you, and returned to the box of make-up which was giving her the greatest amount of pleasure.

On Christmas eve Beth had gone into the village for two last-minute gifts. There wasn't much choice but a small glass ornament of a horse took her fancy and she bought it for Jenny.

'Would you like me to wrap it for you?' the woman assistant asked.

'Yes, please,' Beth answered with such a dazzling smile that the woman, after wrapping it, added a bow of red and gold ribbon.

'That should give someone a lot of pleasure,' she smiled.

'I'm sure of it and thank you for being so kind.'

Beth left the shop and went to look at the other windows. She would like to take something to Jenny's housekeeper but what could she get for Miss Harris? It was a problem. In the end she settled for a box of chocolate gingers and had to ask for it to be wrapped in Christmas paper. There was no ribbon for this one. The girl behind the counter looked tired and dispirited, and Beth thought that perhaps she didn't have much to look forward to. She sympathised, knowing that she could well have been in the same boat.

Since the buying of the school uniforms, Caroline's Aunt Gwen had taken on the responsibility for her niece's wardrobe. A fashionable figure herself, she was delighting in Caroline's interest in clothes, more especially since her own daughter had to be dragged protesting to the shops. Only when a spurt of growing demanded new clothes did Beth accompany them.

Mrs Esslemont picked out a chocolate brown pinafore dress with a lighter brown blouse. 'Is that her size?' she asked the saleslady.

She looked at the label. 'Yes, it is.'

'Then that should do you nicely, Beth.'

That Beth was not taken with the outfit was obvious but it was ignored.

The head saleslady who always attended to Mrs

Esslemont felt sorry for this tall, quiet girl and wondered about the relationship. The fair-haired girl was
the daughter of Colonel Parker-Munro and a niece of
Mrs Esslemont. The dark-haired girl must be a poor
relation, judging by the way she was being treated.

'Excuse me, Mrs Esslemont, I'll take the young lady to
one of the cubicles.'

'Since it is the correct size, is that necessary?'

'A fitting would make sure.'

'Very well but, before you do so, have you anything else
to show my niece?'

'I'm afraid not.'

'We'll consider these again, Caroline.'

'I do like the pink one with the shawl collar.'

'Do you, dear? I thought the style a little old for you.'
Caroline made a face.

'All right, dear,' she said fondly, 'we'll take it and the
peach one which is quite perfect with your colouring.'

The assistant left them to it and hurried to where Beth
was waiting. She was in her petticoat and looking glumly
at the pinafore dress.

'Doesn't look much on a coat hanger but really it is very
nice on.' The saleslady touched the cloth. 'A good material like this always hangs well.'

Beth wasn't convinced. 'It is dull though, isn't it?'

'With that blouse, yes, I agree but slip this one on and
see the difference.' She handed Beth a cream satin blouse
with a delicately embroidered collar.

Beth's eyes brightened as she put on the outfit. 'Don't
the two have to go together?'

'Supposed to but, to my mind cream and brown, coffee
and cream, are made for each other.'

Looking in the mirror and turning to see herself at
different angles, Beth couldn't hide her delight. The

slightly flared skirt suited her girlish figure and the cream shade was perfect with her lovely colouring.

'I didn't expect to like it and now I love it,' Beth said happily.

The saleslady smiled, she was well pleased. The fair-haired little madam, no matter what she eventually chose, would not look as well as this dark-eyed, graceful girl.

'Do you want to ask Mrs Esslemont if you can see something else?'

'Oh, no, I want this, please, but is the blouse more expensive than the other?' she said anxiously.

It was double the price but the account was going to Colonel Parker-Munro and, in any case, Mrs Esslemont would consider it vulgar to discuss the cost.

'Not by very much.' She waited until Beth was dressed and then they joined Caroline and her aunt.

'Was it all right for you, Beth?' Caroline looked up briefly from examining the dresses draped over the chairs.

'Yes, a perfect fit, thank you.'

'The blouse was rather too wide at the neckline, Mrs Esslemont, but I managed to get one that is a better fit.'

'Very well. Have them all sent to Inverbrae House.' She got up in a cloud of perfume. 'Come along, Caroline and you too Beth, we'll have afternoon tea before thinking about shoes. A small dainty heel for you, Caroline.'

Caroline smiled. 'With straps?'

'If that is what you want.' She turned to Beth and frowned. 'You're such a big girl, you can only wear flat shoes.'

Beth was furious but said nothing. She was being made to feel that she was a big heavily-built girl when in fact she was tall and slim. She used to want to be smaller but now she wasn't so sure.

For her visit to Greystanes, Beth wore a herring-bone,

belted coat. Her head was bare and at her neck was a small colourful scarf. Her gloves were in her pocket in case she needed them. Under her coat she had on her pinafore dress and the cream satin, long-sleeved blouse. Her gifts she carried in her hand.

The ten o'clock bus, surprisingly busy, left punctually and an hour later Beth was being ushered in and hugged by a delighted Jenny. Jenny had on a very fine knitted suit in a pale peach and a matching blouse and looked her usual bandbox-fresh self.

'You look wonderful, Beth. Happy Christmas, dear.' She kissed her on both cheeks.

'A happy Christmas to you too, Jenny,' Beth said shyly. 'It was very kind of you to ask me.'

'And nice of you to come. No standing on ceremony, you know your way about the house so just make yourself at home. Hang your coat up in the cloakroom.'

Beth did so then handed Jenny the gift.

'For me? Oh, Beth, my dear, how lovely of you and so beautifully wrapped too.'

'The shop lady did that. It isn't very much, Jenny, but I hope you like it.'

'Darling, I know I'm going to love it but you must never, never apologise for a gift.' She smiled as she said it. 'I have something for you and we'll open them together and in the proper spirit.' She laughed and took Beth's hand. 'Miss Harris made her famous ginger cordial since you are too young for sherry.'

'That's funny, ginger cordial I mean, I bought chocolate gingers for Miss Harris.'

'You darling girl, she'll be so pleased and what a very nice thought. But before we go to the sitting-room come and see this.'

'My picture! It looks much better now.'

260

'The frame sets it off and, my dear, it is a good painting and has been much admired. Now let me look at you. You've grown, Beth, and in that pinafore dress and the lovely blouse you look a very attractive young lady.'

'When I saw it first I didn't like it. This isn't the blouse that should go with it.' She began to tell Jenny about the shopping expedition. Hearing about it, Jenny was seething with anger. Beth wasn't telling all but she could imagine the rest. Silently she blessed the kindly saleslady.

The sitting-room was warm but not stuffy and there was a Christmas tree at the window. Jenny poured cordial for Beth and sherry for herself and set them on a table between them.

'Now we shall open our gifts,' she said as she handed Beth a small, neatly packaged box. Jenny had hers open first. 'Charming, simply charming, Beth, thank you so much and see how it sparkles in the light from the fire. I wonder – I wonder – where shall I put it? On the cabinet, I think, but not before I show it to Miss Harris.'

Beth had unwrapped her gift. Lying on a velvet pad was a brooch in the shape of a butterfly studded with tiny stones in every shade of blue.

Beth caught her breath. 'Jenny, I've never had anything so pretty and I'll be afraid to wear it in case anything happened to the catch and I lost it.'

'No fear of that, it has a safety catch and you are to wear it, Beth, not stick it in a drawer. It really wasn't so very expensive and it won't bankrupt me.' Taking it from the pad she pinned it on to Beth's dress. 'There now.'

'Thank you,' she whispered, 'thank you very much.'

When they went along to the kitchen Miss Harris was putting the finishing touches to the trifle.

'There's Christmas pudding too, Beth, but I thought you might prefer this.'

'Take some of each, Beth, or I'll be eating them until the new year.'

Jenny produced her gift from Beth. 'Look what I got from my young friend.'

'That's pretty and something else for me to dust,' she smiled as she moved the trifle and wiped her hands on a towel.

'That's for you, Miss Harris, it isn't very—' then stopped as Jenny coughed delicately. 'I mean, I do hope you like them.'

Miss Harris went a rosy pink. 'How very kind of you, lass,' she said as she undid the wrapping. 'Chocolate gingers that's a treat for me.'

'You like them?'

'Too much. I'll have to ration myself. That was a very nice surprise.' Her eyes were suspiciously moist and Jenny took Beth's arm. 'We'll let Miss Harris get on.'

They were back in the sitting-room and Beth took rather too much cordial. It caught at her throat and sent her into a paroxysm of coughing.

'Easy does it, Beth. I should have warned you that Miss Harris's brew is quite strong.'

'I like it but I took too much at one time,' Beth said as she recovered and wiped her eyes.

'Satisfy my curiosity if you will. How did you get away from Inverbrae House?'

'The Christmas luncheon was to be at Caroline's aunt's house and it was for the family only.'

'Don't tell me you weren't invited? You are practically family.'

'I wasn't but I was so glad when I got your letter, Jenny.' She dimpled prettily. 'I was a bit naughty,' she added.

'This I want to hear.'

'Mrs Parker-Munro said that the invitation didn't include me but that the kitchen would put on something special and I could have mine with Mrs Murdoch.'

'What had you to say to that? I know what I would have been tempted to say but go on tell me.'

'Well, Jenny, I thanked her for all the trouble she had put herself to—'

'Naughty! Naughty!'

'I know,' Beth grinned. 'I said I couldn't have accepted even if I had been invited because I was going somewhere else for Christmas luncheon.'

'Taken aback, was she?'

'Oh, yes, she didn't say anything.'

'That would make a change.'

'The colonel said that he was delighted to hear that I was to spend Christmas with my family in Dundee and I just let him go on thinking that.'

'Very wise in the circumstances.' She took a sip of her sherry. 'What is life like at Rowanbank? Are you happy?'

'I did write.'

'You did and nothing could be as perfect as you made out.'

'Oh, dear.'

'Is that all you are going to say?'

'Honestly, Jenny, everything is fine. I'm very grateful to be getting such a good education.'

She smiled. 'I won't question you further. I have enough confidence in you to know that you will deal with any difficulties in your own way. Remember, too, that you will come out of it all the stronger.'

Chapter Twenty

Beth knew by Caroline's face that she was bursting to tell her something but the opportunity for confidences didn't come until the morning of Boxing day. A friend of Jenny's had driven Beth back to Inverbrae House. He was a married man with charming manners and the brother of the hostess who had been grateful to have him chauffeur any unescorted ladies. Asked by Jenny if he would drop Beth off at Inverbrae House, he had declared himself only too willing to do so and dismissed as nothing the extra few miles involved.

Nine o'clock had already chimed when Beth let herself in by the side door. Before going up to her room, she decided it would be wise to tell Mrs Murdoch that she had returned.

'Did you have a nice Christmas, Beth?' the house-keeper smiled. She was quite flushed and Beth thought with amusement that she must have been quite free with the sherry or perhaps it had been wine. She was glad. Her own day had been so very enjoyable that she wanted everyone else to be happy.

'I had a lovely time, Mrs Murdoch.'

'Glad to hear it. With everybody away we took advantage and had a bit of a party.' She gave a small hiccup followed by a giggle. 'Mrs Noble did us proud, and the men folk produced two bottles of wine. Normally I wouldn't approve of such carryings on but well, what's the harm when it's only once a year?'

'No harm at all, Mrs Murdoch.' She paused. 'If Miss Caroline asks for me, please tell her that I've gone to bed.'

'I don't blame you, all that excitement fair tires you out.' She yawned. 'I'll be making tracks myself in a wee while.'

Before going to bed Beth put her brooch back in the box and into her drawer. She would have to be going to some very special occasion before she wore it. Caroline already had a social life and her day would come.

'What time did you get home, Beth?' They had eaten breakfast and were in their own sitting-room.

'About nine o'clock. You were well after me.'

'I know. I don't remember the actual time but I know I almost fell asleep in the car coming home. Grandmama snored in the chair all afternoon then when she did waken up she said she was as fresh as a daisy. Then, of course, everybody just talked and talked and the gentlemen disappeared with Uncle Robert. I am quite sure a lot of drink must have been consumed because they were all very happy and as you know Uncle Robert and daddy don't usually have much to say to one another.' She paused. 'Better ask did you have a good day with your cousins?'

'I had a marvellous day but I wasn't with—' Beth had been about to tell Caroline that she hadn't been with her cousins but with Jenny, and that she should keep the information to herself. But she didn't get the chance. Caroline cut her off, so anxious was she to have her say. Beth thought it would be safer to say nothing about Greystanes unless it couldn't be avoided.

'Wait until I tell you, you just have to hear this.' Her

eyes were dancing. 'When Ruth said what she said I think Aunt Gwen could have willingly strangled her.'

'Poor Ruth, she does tend to put her foot in it,' Beth laughed.

'Both feet more like. But listen, this is serious and you were the cause of it.'

Beth looked annoyed. 'Since I wasn't there I find that difficult to believe.'

'That was why, silly. Oh, do stop interrupting and let me tell it in my own way.'

'Knowing the time you take to tell anything I'll get myself into a more comfortable chair,' Beth said as she dropped herself into one of the armchairs.

'There we all were sitting round the table and I had better tell you it was beautiful but then you know with Aunt Gwen that everything has to be just perfect.'

'How many were round the table?'

'Just ourselves and Uncle Robert's two unmarried sisters. What a pair!' Caroline rolled her eyes. 'One is as deaf as a door post and the other yelled in her ear to keep her up with the conversation but that is just by the way. Ruth came in wearing a navy and white dress and I think it made her look slimmer. Aunt Gwen was already annoyed with her because Ruth was the last to come to the table and then when she sat down and looked around she asked me where you were and before I got a chance to say that you were in Dundee, Aunt Gwen looked daggers at Ruth and said that since it was a family party, you had not been invited. Ruth said that was ridiculous and since you lived at Inverbrae House as family, then you were practically family and you should have been invited.'

Beth looked uncomfortable. 'I do wish Ruth hadn't said that.'

'I'm not finished,' Caroline glared, 'so do be quiet.

267

Grandmama, I could see, was about to put in her bit to support Aunt Gwen when Uncle Robert, who as you know likes a quiet life and seldom crosses Aunt Gwen, announced that he thought it was just terrible, and he absolutely agreed with Ruth, and what was his wife thinking of? Wasn't this Christmas and a time of goodwill to all? Well by this time Aunt Gwen was glaring at husband and daughter and everyone was feeling very uncomfortable and glad when the maids arrived to serve the meal.' Caroline giggled. 'The funniest bit for me was those two old dears. Uncle Robert, I'm positive, must have been a late baby, because they looked ancient. The deaf one felt she was missing out on the fun and demanded to be told what was going on.'

'It didn't spoil the day, did it?'

'Of course not, Beth Brown, you are not that important.'

'Never suggested I was. I just didn't like the thought of being the cause of any unpleasantness.'

'You weren't, at least not after the food arrived and daddy was at his most entertaining. The same funny stories come out year after year but no one seems to notice but me.'

'The others are probably too polite to say so.'

'Could be, I suppose. Grandmama was talking about the Australian side of the family and Ruth said she wished she was there, in Australia she meant. She winked at me but I knew what she meant. After we'd gone she would be in for a good talking to from Aunt Gwen.'

'Poor Ruth.' Beth got up and wandered over to the window. 'I think it is going to stay fair so how about a walk?'

Caroline swithered. 'Perhaps I should, all that food yesterday and today will be just about as bad. Being small I can't afford to put on weight.'

'You won't.'

'How do you know?'

'Someone said if both your parents are thin then you will be too or it is true most of the time.'

'Oh, good, that means I can eat as many chocolates as I like and not get fat.'

'Make yourself sick, that's all. Are you coming or not? I'm going anyway.'

Caroline sighed. 'Anything for a quiet life but not too far remember!'

'Just a short brisk walk.'

The wind whipped the colour into their cheeks and both girls were enjoying being outside. Caroline was a lot less delicate now, particularly since starting school. She was excused games but just occasionally Beth thought there was a wistful longing in her face as if she would like to join in but was afraid to in case her health suffered.

'Beth, I hope you know that it was no fault of mine that – that—'

'I got left out? No, and I honestly don't mind.'

'You know, Beth, I had a thought in bed last night. Poor you, you're not going to meet anyone special, you never get the chance, but wouldn't it be funny and nice too, if my cousin came over from Australia and he liked you and you liked him.'

Beth laughed.

'It could happen. If you got married one day, then you would be really part of the family.'

'You can forget that, Caroline. I don't want to get married for ages and ages and only if I fell in love.'

Caroline didn't look convinced. 'Tell me honestly, Beth, if you had the choice of marrying a boy you loved who had no money and a boy who was wealthy, whom would you choose?'

'Love and poverty,' she said immediately, 'but we wouldn't need to be all that poor because I would take a job and earn money.'

'Not after you were married, surely?'

'Yes, I see no wrong in that.'

'What about when the children arrive?'

'Then, of course, I wouldn't be able to work.'

'What would you do for money?'

'Wait until we could afford to have children.'

'Can you do that? Choose your own time I mean?'

'I don't know.'

'You see, Beth,' Caroline said seriously, 'sometimes I get very frightened.'

'What about?'

'Having babies. My mother died having me,' she whispered.

'Caroline, you mustn't worry about that. No two persons are alike, not even mother and daughter. In any case, doctors are much cleverer now and know far more than they did when you were born.'

'I'll try to remember that.'

With Caroline spending so many of her Saturdays with her Aunt Gwen, Beth felt very alone. She decided to visit Dundee more often. She would go and see Aunt Anne and Uncle Fred this very day and another Saturday she would visit Adam and Morag.

The day was pleasant with no sign of rain when Beth set off to catch the bus. Once she would have asked permission, or at least stated where she was going, since the colonel approved of her having closer links with her family. She didn't bother this time, for the very good reason that no one cared, no one was the least concerned where she went or what she did. She had all the freedom she could want yet deep down she was unhappy about that. Having to account for where she went would have shown that someone had her welfare at heart. Knowing no one did made her feel very isolated.

Her aunt's face beamed with pleasure and Beth felt a glow at her welcome.

'Now this is a nice surprise, come away in, Beth.'

'Hello, Aunt Anne,' Beth smiled as she went in. 'Is this you on your own or is Uncle Fred at home?'

'He's got a wee job on a Saturday and that helps to fill in his time. You'll mind he's handy with a saw and he's cutting up lengths of wood over at McGregors. Doesn't get much for his labours but it's something for his pocket. Hang your coat in the lobby. I take it you're staying awhile?'

'If you aren't going out?'

'Not me, I don't venture far and I've got the messages in. Sit yourself down, lass.'

Beth sat down. 'Aunt Anne, could I ask a favour?'

'Well you could ask. But as to whether I grant it, that's another matter.' She was smiling as she said it. 'Let's hear it then.'

'Would you teach me to cook?'

'Mercy me! Am I hearing right? And what's given you this notion?'

'I don't know what I'll be doing when I leave school and I think it might be useful to be able to cook. Just simple cooking, nothing complicated.'

'No complicated dishes in this house, just good whole-some food,' she said, shaking her head. 'All that expensive schooling, filling your head with a lot of stuff you'll never need.' She tut-tutted. 'I doubt if you're capable of making yourself a pot of tea.'

'Don't make me out to be worse than I am,' Beth

laughed. 'I can just about manage that. Pouring boiling water over the tea leaves is all there is to it.'

'That's where you're wrong. There's a lot more to it, as you'll find out before I'm finished with you.'

'You're going to take me on?'

'That I am. Away and get yourself a pinny from that top drawer in the sideboard. I'll do the stew now instead of later. First though we'll prepare the vegetables.'

Beth got an apron from the drawer and put it on over her skirt. She hadn't expected to start this early but, as her aunt would say, there is no time like the present. She went over to the sink to await instructions.

'That's the best knife, you take it and scrape those carrots. I've topped and tailed them and mind a thin scraping.'

Beth put her hands in the water and gasped. 'Aunt Anne, this water is absolutely freezing.'

'You didn't expect hot water did you?'

'I'm not saying another word,' Beth laughed.

'No, just you concentrate on the job you're doing. Get that done and the meat browned then we'll have ourselves a cup of tea.'

By the time Beth had finished the carrots Aunt Anne had peeled a pot of potatoes. 'Will that do?' Beth asked.

'Not too bad, we'd all to crawl before we could walk.'

'How is Luke? I suppose I'll be away before he gets home?'

'More than likely.' Her lips pursed. 'Never a moment's worry with Adam but Luke,' she shook her head, 'right from the time he started school he's been in some kind of trouble.'

'Not serious trouble though?'

'Serious enough, skipping school when the wee devil felt like it.'

Beth smiled. 'That was a long time ago.'

'Time to have mended his ways but he hasn't. Oh, he turns up for work, if he didn't he would be out on his ear. No, lass, it's more than that. He's that moody, your uncle says it's just a phase and he'll grow out of it but that is all he ever says.' She paused and went to see to the meat. 'Men don't worry the same as we women and of course mothers are worst of all, as you'll no doubt find out one day. If I just knew what was bothering him—'

'Have you asked Luke?'

'Have I asked him? Time without number and I could have saved my breath. Nothing is wrong is all I ever get.'

'Probably because nothing is and you are worrying yourself needlessly.'

'I don't look for trouble, lass, I don't have to.' She brought down the biscuit tin. 'Here, put some of those on a plate. Where was I? Oh, yes, moods I expect from young lads and lasses too, all part of growing up, but his have gone on too long.' The kettle boiled and she went over to it. Come along and make your first decent pot of tea.'

Beth waited.

'Heat the teapot by putting in some boiling water, leave it a second or two then pour it out.'

Beth did that. 'There's the caddy, two good spoons of tea then fill up with boiling water and make sure it hasn't gone off the boil. Now leave that until it draws, a good three or four minutes.' She smiled. 'That should give us a good cup of tea.'

Beth returned to Inverbrae House feeling well satisfied with her day. How wrong she had been about Aunt Anne. It was only that abrupt manner that made her seem unapproachable. Underneath it was a genuinely kind and caring woman.

★ ★ ★

Back in school, Caroline was telling Beth about the photographs that had arrived from Queensland.

'I've seen them but grandmama won't let them out of her sight.'

'What are they like?'

'Very good. Uncle James isn't, or I should say wasn't, as nice looking as daddy but quite nice all the same. Robert looks a bit like him but not so tall but then maybe he hadn't stopped growing when they were taken. William is two years younger but you can see by his loose build that he is going to be tall. Grandmama was a bit annoyed with me for saying so and I can't think why—'

'Saying what?'

'Only that William is nicer looking than Robert. She said they were both good looking boys and that photographs weren't always a true likeness.'

'True, I suppose.'

'Aunt Dorothy looks nice and friendly just the way she writes if that makes sense. Emily looks all right too. The house, Beth, is huge or looks to be but not a bit like Inverbrae House. Daddy says it is ranch style and there are a few others but smaller homes nearby for the rest of the family.'

'Is your cousin, Robert, coming over?'

'Yes, but no date is fixed. Aunt Dorothy says both boys will be given a year to travel where they want. William doesn't want, at least that is what he is saying at the moment, but Robert intends doing the capitals of Europe or some of them. Doesn't that sound wonderful?'

'Certainly does. Will he be on his own?'

'Yes. Aunt Dorothy says it is good for them, character building and had Uncle James lived, he would have been all for it.'

★ ★ ★

Another weekend and they were back in Inverbrae House.

'I told daddy and he is all for you doing business studies.'

'I rather thought he would approve.'

'Approves of it because it'll help you to get a job. But he agrees with Miss Critchley that it is bad for the school's image and if the Board of Governors aren't careful, he says Rowanbank will cease to be an exclusive school. Another thing he said, before I forget. He said he could do with some clerical assistance and it will be good experience until you get fixed up.'

'That suits me.'

'See this,' Caroline said holding up a large brown envelope. 'Guess what is in it.'

'Photographs.'

Caroline's face fell. 'How did you know?'

'Educated guess,' Beth grinned. 'Thought it probable since you have spoken of little else since they arrived.'

'I couldn't get them earlier because grandmama would hardly let them out of her sight.'

'You managed?'

'Nipped them when she was snoring her head off. Funny how she snores worse than ever now. When I told her she snored, she almost took my head off. "Ladies do not snore and you would do well to remember that, Caroline," her grand-daughter mimicked. Then she returned to her normal voice. 'Bring your chair nearer mine,' she said, 'and I can hand them over and explain who everyone is.'

One by one Caroline brought out the photographs of her Australian relations, making some remark about each. What struck Beth first was how happy they looked, their very ordinariness. They couldn't have been more different from the Parker-Munros of Inverbrae House, with their stiffness and formality, especially in the dining-room. Beth thought those on the photograph would have quite happily sat down at the kitchen table.

'That is Uncle James, one of the last taken before he died. Take note of the large brimmed hat, that is the badge of the true Aussie,' she grinned.

'Maybe your uncle was more at home in his adopted country than he was when he was here.'

'That's probably true. Robert looks a little like him. I'm a teeny bit disappointed, he's quite ordinary looking isn't he?'

'I think he looks nice.'

'But not handsome. William might be when he is a bit older, pity he wasn't the elder brother, he looks rather fun – see that mischievous grin on his face?'

'The little girl Emily is pretty.'

'Not bad.' She handed over another photograph 'That's a good one of Aunt Dorothy.'

'She didn't know it was being taken and those always turn out best.'

Caroline jumped up. 'That'll have to do and I'll pop along before she wakens but don't you go – I have something else to tell you.'

'What about?'

'Ruth, but I'll tell you when I get back.'

Beth waited for Caroline's return. She wanted to hear about Ruth. Caroline's cousin had always been kind to her. Once she had confided in Beth her wish to take up nursing but knew there would be stiff opposition from her mother who was desperately looking for a young man, or failing that a not-so-young man of good family, who would marry Ruth and take her off her hands. An unmarried clumsy daughter at home was something she could do without.

As had been predicted, Mrs Esslemont was both shocked and horrified. Nursing was perfectly acceptable for a working- or even middle-class girl but most certainly not for her daughter. It was a hard life, she pointed out, with unspeakable tasks to perform, and never, never would she give her consent.

Ruth sulked, refused to have her wardrobe renewed, would not accompany her mother on social rounds and in general made life miserable for everyone herself included. Ruth's father had reservations himself. His daughter was stubborn and of strong character but he rather doubted that she would last the course. After much discussion Mr Esslemont won over his wife by saying that their daughter would be unlikely to complete the course and after a few months would be only too willing to return home. A further inducement was that Ruth could train at Edinburgh Infirmary and during that time live with an acquaintance of his, a senior doctor and his wife who had their home in Morningside.

Caroline flung herself in the door. 'Just made it, she was just stirring.'

'Come on, what is the news about Ruth? Done exceptionally well in her exams, is that it?'

'No, it is not, though actually she has done well but I would hardly call that exciting. My cousin, believe it or not, has got herself engaged. Engaged to be married,' she added unnecessarily.

'But that is wonderful,' Beth exclaimed, 'and I only hope he is worthy of her.'

Caroline shrugged. 'He's a doctor, five years older than Ruth and his name is Ian Melville. Aunt Gwen and Uncle Robert have met him.'

'Did he pass the test?' Beth said drily.

'With Uncle Robert, yes and his doctor friend is high in his praise. A clever lad who could go far in his profession was his opinion.'

'Couldn't fault that, surely?'

'Not his profession but he comes from a working-class background and like you his parents are dead.'

'His working-class background is against him as far as your aunt is concerned,' Beth said sarcastically.

'Beth, you have been very slow to understand this but one's background, the family one is born into, is very important. Much more important than money, I may say, and I think it is extremely generous of Aunt Gwen to accept this engagement without having to rejoice in it.'

Beth laughed. 'You really are a pompous little madam and I think you and your aunt are well matched. You, not Ruth, should have been her daughter.'

'The pompous bit I shall ignore but the rest I accept. Aunt Gwen has never made a secret of the fact that she would have liked to have me as a daughter.'

'What does he look like?'

'Ian? Tall and skinny.' She giggled. 'Actually—'

'Do you have to say actually quite so often?'

'I don't know when I'm saying it. But, actually, Ruth has lost quite a lot of weight and needless to say is happy about it. She says it is the result of being so happy. When she was miserable, which was a lot of the time when she was at home, she used to stuff herself with sweet things.'

'All that running about the wards will help too.'

'Do they have to run?' Caroline asked.

'They run because they are in a hurry. Nurses never walk. Next question. Have they fixed a date for the wedding?'

'No. Battle two commences before that.'

'Won one, good chance of them winning the next.'

'My daddy says it will end in a compromise.'

'Why?'

'Ruth and Ian want a quiet wedding and you must remember that Ian has no close family. He is all for tying the knot in the Registry Office and Ruth wouldn't mind. But to please her mother she would be married in church, but quietly and with only close relatives.'

'Ruth should stick out for that.'

'Probably will. Uncle Robert offered to buy them a house in Edinburgh and Aunt Gwen favoured that. Her daughter and son-in-law in a good practice and living in a desirable residence, she could just about live with that.'

'All satisfactory then?'

'No, it isn't. The wretched Ian wants to work with the poor and needy and, as he says, not sit in some posh surgery listening to imaginary ailments. The cheek of him, as though we couldn't be ill the same as everybody else.'

'I know what he means and I admire him.'

'Well you would, wouldn't you? Actually – yes I know I am saying it again – Ian would have been a good match for you.'

'He happens to be in love with Ruth.'

'Enough about my cousin. I am not going to Aunt Gwen's next Saturday so we can go somewhere together.'

'Sorry I can't.'

'Can't or won't?' Caroline said huffily.

'Take your pick. For goodness sake don't go off in one of your huffs. This is serious. Morag wrote to tell me that my aunt is in a terrible state. Luke has run away to sea.'

'How exciting! Did he leave a message for them to find?'

'Yes, saying he couldn't stick it any longer and since

they wouldn't let him go to sea he is doing it this way but not to worry.'

'As a sailor?'

'An extra hand he called it but same thing I suppose.'

'Shades of Uncle James.'

'I hope not. Your uncle never came back but I think Luke will. He did say he would write as soon as he could. My uncle told them that he would most likely be on a boat going to India since they leave from Dundee. He said they are always short of hands and glad of anyone and Luke is a strong, healthy lad.'

Aunt Anne had shed her tears but her eyes were anguished.

'Good of you to come, lass.'

'I wanted to as soon as I heard.' Hardly aware of what she was doing, Beth put her arms round her aunt. 'Try not to worry, Aunt Anne. Luke will be all right and in a few weeks you'll be getting letters and postcards from different countries.'

Her aunt didn't immediately push her away and seemed to get comfort from the embrace. She gave a little smile then patted Beth's shoulder. 'You're a good lass, Beth. You've turned out better than I ever expected.'

'That's a relief,' Beth said trying to hide her amusement. 'You sit down and I'll make you a good strong cup of tea the way you like it. Uncle Fred, you're not going out, are you?'

'Not the day, lass, so you can make that two cups, no three counting yourself.'

Beth had put down a shopping bag on the floor and her aunt picked it up.

'Fair weight in that.'

'Open it.'

She did. 'Grand looking potatoes and fine vegetables you have there.'

'For you.'

She bristled. 'I don't accept charity from those posh folk of yours.'

'You are not being asked to,' Beth said quietly, knowing she would have to go carefully. 'How often do you complain about waste? The gardeners have too much and the surplus is just left to rot.'

'Sinful that would be. In that case, thanks. I can make good use of it.'

Beth sighed with relief. She hadn't been honest. Nothing went to waste at Inverbrae House. What wasn't required in the kitchens went to any of the staff who would take the trouble to carry it home.

Beth made the tea and they had it with buttered scones.

'Why would he do that to us, Beth? He would know I'd be worried out of my mind.'

'He left a note, Aunt Anne, and it would have been far worse if he hadn't.'

'Just what I've been trying to get into her head, lass,' Uncle Fred said as he clattered his cup down. 'We can blame ourselves, Anne. The lad told us often enough that he hankered after a life at sea. We should have given him his head. If we'd let him do what he wanted, we would have been spared this.'

His wife shivered. 'I have a horror when I think about a wee boat being—' her voice broke.

'Lass,' her husband said patiently, 'he'll no' be on a wee boat that I can promise you. It'll be a sturdy, sea-worthy vessel.'

'So you say,' she sniffed, 'and you with a brother that was drowned at sea.'

'Aye, that's true enough, Danny got a watery grave but

281

others lose their lives in accidents at work or get run over in the streets. Too many cars on the road with idiots inside them. They'll mow down a few, you mark my words.'

'Is that supposed to comfort me?'

'Just my way of telling you that the sea doesn't claim any more than any other occupation.'

She turned to her niece. 'Still doing well at that school?'

'Yes, thank you. Another year and I'll be job hunting.'

'And what had you in mind?'

'Probably an office job.'

'Wouldn't hold out much hope for you there. At seventeen you'll be a bit old, the lasses hereabout have office jobs, taken on at fifteen when they left school. No boss is going to pay a seventeen-year-old when he can get a fifteen-year-old to do the same work.'

'A proper ray of sunshine your aunt is.' Uncle Fred shook his head. 'Don't you worry, Beth, your good education won't be lost but you'll maybe need to wait a while until the right job comes along.'

For the first time Beth felt less confident. Her aunt, after all, was only stating what Miss McAndrew, the English teacher, had said. Far from being an asset, her expensive education could well be a drawback.

Chapter Twenty-One

Her schooldays were over. As the colonel was driving the car down the drive and through the gates for the last time, Beth could not bring herself to turn round for that final look at Rowanbank School for Young Ladies. She wondered how, in the years to come, she would look back on her schooldays at Rowanbank. Would she manage to forget the bad times and only remember the good days, or would it be the other way round? A bit of both, she decided.

Father and daughter were not concerned with her, they were talking and she was in the back seat with her own thoughts and they were taking her back to what had happened a short time ago. Where on earth had she found the courage?

The other girls had behaved properly, saying what was expected. Goodbye, Miss Critchley, I shall miss Rowanbank and all the happy times or some such words but they would have stuck in Beth's throat.

Somehow she had managed to say and in a voice loud enough to carry, 'I have no wish to shake your hand, Miss Critchley, and I certainly have nothing for which to thank you.'

There were gasps, shocked looks. Someone had giggled. She had walked out of the hall with her head held high.

★ ★ ★

The car stopped in the drive and the three of them went up the steps and into the house.

An hour later the colonel approached Beth. 'I want you to come to my study in half an hour, Beth.'

'Yes.' She wasn't surprised – this was only to be expected. She was to be asked to go but she was older now, she was seventeen and she rather thought she wouldn't be left homeless. She had her savings and they had grown to a sizeable sum. Not that it would last long if she had to pay for lodgings while she looked for a job but Aunt Anne had softened and she thought she would be welcome to stay in her house for a short time. Then there was Jenny who had made it clear that she would always be welcome at Greystanes. It was a comforting thought but most of all Beth wanted to be independent. That was the way to self respect.

She knocked and wondered if this might be the last time she would enter this study. His voice: 'Come in.'

Closing the door behind her, she did not wait to be invited to do so but sat in the chair facing him. His elbows were on the desk and his fingers pressed together.

'This commercial course you have completed, what qualifications has it given you?'

'My shorthand is about a hundred words a minute and my typing is good. I have a certificate to prove—'

He stopped her. 'That is of no interest to me.' He paused. 'What I have in mind, Beth, is for you to assist Mr Blair. He manages the estate, as you know, and fulfils that position to my satisfaction. Sadly, he is very slipshod regarding the paperwork and though he says he has a filing system, I am at a loss to understand it.'

Beth smiled with relief. 'You would like me to take over the filing and put it in order?'

'That and other things. Blair can spend more time seeing to his other duties if he doesn't have to worry about the paperwork. Come along,' he said getting up, 'and I'll show you where you will be working.' Beth followed him. Outside the sun was shining and there was the merest whisper of a breeze as they walked together to the office building. She knew it, of course, but she had never been inside. The colonel unlocked the door and went in, leaving her to follow. Once it had been home to a family, a cottage with three rooms, a tiny scullery and a toilet. The wall between two of the rooms had been knocked down and this was the office. There were two windows that gave plenty of light and both were curtained in brown and gold material. The walls were painted cream but in need of a freshen up. A desk with a chair behind it was over at one of the windows. There was an Underwood typewriter on a table. The cover was on and there was a lot of dust. Filing cabinets against one wall were only partly filled and bundles of papers were piled on the floor. The fireplace was empty, Beth supposed for the summer months, and there was a brass scuttle for coal or logs.

The colonel was over at the desk examining papers and Beth wandered through the rest of the office. The small room where she stood was obviously where the manager made himself a meal. There was an old dresser containing crockery and cutlery, a table and two chairs. In the scullery just off it was a rather ancient cooker. There was also a kettle and two pans. The toilet was tiny and she was glad to see that it had a lock.

'Have you seen all you wish?' He was behind her.

She turned. 'Yes, thank you.'

'Better sit down while we discuss one or two things.' She did and he went to the chair behind the desk. 'You must have realised, Beth, that you cannot continue to live at Inverbrae House.'

'I'm prepared to leave now or as soon as I have accommodation arranged,' she said coldly.

'Kindly listen to what I have to say and don't be so prickly,' he frowned. 'You would agree, I hope, that you owe me some repayment for all that has been done for you?'

'Yes.'

'Until such time as you find suitable employment, I want you to take over the office here.'

'What about Mr—?'

'Blair won't trouble you. He will have his meals at home and, apart from calling in occasionally, you won't see much of him.'

'What are my duties to be?'

'Normal office work. You will type my letters.'

'I can take them down in shorthand.'

'I prefer to write them out in longhand.' He cleared his throat. 'First and foremost, you must get a good filing system going and then see that accounts are paid before the final date. Remember to file the receipts. You are following me?'

'Very easily.'

'This is to be a business arrangement, Beth. You will work office hours 9 am to 5 pm with the whole of Saturday off. As to your meal times,' he paused and avoided looking at her, 'you will continue to have your meals up at the house but you will not dine with the family. Instead you will take yours in the breakfast room.'

'That will suit me very well.'

'That is all, I think.'

'Not quite, Colonel Parker-Munro,' Beth said quietly. 'Since this is to be a business arrangement and I am to be working office hours, there is the matter of remuneration.'

He looked startled. 'I – I—'

'I would expect the going rate for the job,' she said boldly, 'with a deduction for board and lodging.'

She had angered him but he was trying not to show it. 'I'll see to it,' he said stiffly.

'Thank you.' Her eyes were suspiciously bright and there was a tremor in her voice. 'When do I begin?'

'Immediately.' He smiled. 'Caroline's life and yours will be very different from now on. Now that you are a working girl, you will see a lot less of each other. Start tomorrow. This will be good experience for you.' He dangled the keys. 'You had better have these. You can stay as long as you wish but remember to lock up.'

'Yes.'

He went. Beth waited until the door closed and the sound of his footsteps had died away. Then she sat down to do some thinking. She wouldn't stay in Inverbrae House a day longer than necessary and from now on she was going to look after herself. Newspapers came to the house including the *Courier & Advertiser* which was the newspaper for the area. Apart from *The Times*, many of the papers remained unread and by evening were seized on by the staff. She would get the 'situations vacant' pages and begin to apply for jobs straight away. If she was lucky enough to get an interview, she would go with or without permission and whenever they wanted her to start she would be happy to oblige. On the other hand, if no job came along as had been hinted by Aunt Anne, she would continue to work for the colonel and get valuable experience which should help her to get a position in the future.

Caroline was avoiding her, that was obvious. But Beth didn't blame her. It couldn't be easy for Caroline and it was likely that she had been told to keep her distance.

With her now an employee she was not a suitable companion. It was hurtful but she had a lot of experience of being hurt.

She knew Mr Blair by sight only but he proved to be a pleasant man of middle age who was clearly delighted to be rid of the paperwork. Beth had a free hand but it was a daunting task to start a new filing system. Nevertheless it had to be done and the quicker she got the papers off the floor the better. The colonel had his own keys and he made use of them because quite often in the morning she would find letters on her desk waiting to be typed.

She was neither happy nor unhappy. The work filled her day and most weekends she spent in Dundee, even staying overnight and sleeping in Luke's bed. As yet no letter had arrived but there had been a postcard from Calcutta. Not much on it. He was well. He was happy. But it was enough to take away the anguished look from Aunt Anne's face.

'You can stop worrying, that is great news,' Beth said when told.

'Surely he could have taken the trouble to write a proper letter,' Aunt Anne grumbled.

'He may have and the letter hasn't arrived.'

'No address, I can't even write to him and give him a piece of my mind.'

'He won't have an address,' Uncle Fred said from behind his paper. 'Just be content with what you've got and change the subject. Tell Beth the good news.'

'I was going to if you'd give me time. What I would give to have you back working full time and out from under my feet,' she said irritably.

'And me I wish I was away from that tongue of yours.'

Beth knew that it was the worry about Luke that had them at each other's throats. Worry and sleepless nights could strain even the best marriage.

'What's the news, Aunt Anne?'

'Adam and Morag have got another house after spending all that time and money on the one they are in.'

'Where is it?'

'Ten minutes' walk from where they are. A better district or a bit better anyway and there is an inside toilet which is the main attraction.' She smiled. 'Morag has put her foot down and says there will be no more flittings until they get the key to a corporation house and that will be a long while, the waiting list is as long as your arm.'

'Tell them I am delighted.'

'I'll do that, and happy though I am to see you, I'm thinking you're not spending much time with those Parker folk. You and the lass fallen out, have you?'

'No, we haven't, but Caroline has a busy social life.'

'Which does not include you?'

'No reason why it should.'

'That's as maybe. They'll be looking for a good match for the lass.' She shook her head. 'Times I'm sorry for the family of gentry.'

'Why? They have it made as far as I can see,' Beth said a little sourly.

'All that talk about arranged marriages in those foreign countries but to my mind it is the same with the nobs. Nobody is going to choose your husband for you, Beth.'

'You're right there, but wrong about Caroline. Provided she doesn't choose someone totally unsuitable, she will marry whom she wants.'

With each passing month Beth was becoming increasingly disheartened. She had written numerous applications for clerical vacancies in Perth and Dundee and had, as requested, enclosed a stamped, addressed envelope. In due course the envelope came back and inside it a small typed note thanking her for her interest and informing her that the post was now filled. Her experience hadn't improved her chances since there were fewer jobs for seventeen-year-olds and those that did appear from time to time demanded more in qualifications than she could offer. The trouble was that she was over-educated in subjects that were of little use in her present circumstances and when asked to state the school she had attended, Beth was reluctant to do so. Far from being an advantage, it merely hastened her application into the wastepaper basket.

One person was extremely pleased with her and the arrangements were very much to his satisfaction. Beth had proved to be a good and conscientious worker with a real grasp of what was required. What was more she was on the spot and willing to do work outside the stipulated hours. The filing system she had introduced was simple and efficient and the office had changed out of all recognition. Beth had made her own small demands and had the maids come in regularly to clean out the premises and wash the windows. New curtains had replaced those that were badly faded with the sun and a rug of good quality had been brought down from the attic and was on the floor beside the desk. During the cold winter months a fire blazed and Beth thought of the office almost as her home. Here she was king of her castle. There was tea and a bottle of Camp coffee and in the mornings she made herself a cup of coffee and in the afternoon she had tea. The biscuits and the occasional bar of chocolate she bought in the village shop.

Most days Tommy called for the mail and took it to the post office but on others she posted the letters herself and enjoyed the walk. Speaking nicely to the gardeners meant she was given choice blooms or flowering plants for the window sills.

'This is all very attractive,' the colonel said approvingly as he prepared to sign his letters.

'I work better in pleasant surroundings.'

He nodded. 'You are doing a good job for me, Beth, and I am well pleased.'

'Thank you.'

He smiled. 'In a month or two we must reconsider your salary or should I call it wages?'

'Wages since I am paid weekly,' she said quietly.

'Would you prefer to be paid monthly?'

'No, the present arrangements suit me quite well.'

'As long as you are happy—' He signed the letters, the final one with a flourish. 'By the way has Blair been in about those repairs to the dyke, the one dividing the north fields?'

'Yes, it is being dealt with and he wants your attention drawn to the roofs of two of the cottages. They are in a bad condition and urgently require new roofing before the next heavy rainfall.'

The colonel gave an exaggerated sigh. 'A nominal rent is all they are charged and for that they expect a palace. Some people don't know when they are well off.'

Beth didn't answer. She was getting her eyes opened. Doing this job meant she was getting to know a great deal about the estate and the way it was run. The colonel was quick enough to have workmen see to any fault, major or minor, at Inverbrae House but there was absolutely no urgency about work being carried out on leaking roofs. Pails were constantly in place to collect the drips and a long wet spell was a nightmare and an ever-increasing worry.

The colonel was thoughtful as he left the office. Beth was very quiet and distant and that should please him but it didn't. It was a tricky situation trying to keep her at Inverbrae House and at the same time distancing her from Caroline.

Once she was an employee, Beth's sleeping arrangements had been changed. Her bedroom would be required for guests, she was told, and her belongings had been transferred to a much smaller bedroom in the little-used wing nearest to the servants' quarters. Caroline had been apologetic and embarrassed about the move but as she said there was nothing she could do about it. That could well be true Beth thought but she didn't much care. This family had lost the power to hurt her – or so she thought.

No one is irreplaceable but when she did leave, the girl who succeeded her would need training and that would have to come from the colonel or his manager, neither of whom would relish the task.

To be independent was Beth's goal and she longed to be free of Inverbrae House. But she had to be sensible. Staying where she was had a lot of advantages for, apart from buying clothes and other personal items, the money was found and she was able to save. Entertainment took little of her money and only occasionally did she meet up with girls she had known in the village school to accompany them to a cinema or a local dance. Boys asked her out but she didn't accept and this amazed the other girls. After all, they were nice boys and it didn't do to be too choosy and get a name for yourself. A date was a date and a way of keeping in circulation until someone more exciting came along.

Over at Inverbrae House mother and son were together in the drawing-room. It was the end of January and outside a blizzard was blowing. Inside the house the fire gave out a good heat. Nigel finding it too much for him moved his chair back. His mother leaned forward and held her hands out to the blaze.

'Hard to believe that our little Caroline will be eighteen next month,' she smiled.

'Shouldn't be, Mother,' he smiled back at her, 'since you've talked of little else but her eighteenth birthday.'

'Such an important day, dear, and I'm very grateful to Gwen for offering to see to all the arrangements.'

'Very good of her and a relief to me. A ball, even with modest numbers, takes a bit of arranging.'

'Oh, but I were younger,' she sighed. Then she brightened. 'Gwen has it from me that no expense is to be spared and I am to pay for Caroline's gown. She must get something extra special.'

'She will, I'm sure.'

'What is making it perfect for me is having Robert with us. It couldn't have been better timed.' She paused. 'How long does Robert intend staying in London before travelling up, or don't you know?'

'I do as it happens. I have written to Robert and his mother to say that I'll meet Robert in London and he can spend a few days there if he wishes or travel up here and visit London on another occasion. In either event I'll accompany him on the journey and that will give us an opportunity to get to know one another before he meets the family.'

'Gwen is in her element and I rather think she is looking on Caroline as her daughter. Do you mind?'

'No, why should I?' He laughed. 'Caroline is the daughter she would have liked, Ruth is what she got.'

'Ruth's wedding won't take any arranging. The affair is to be as quiet as possible. Her intended has no one of his own. Rather sad really.'

'Yes.'

The old lady sniffed or as near as elegance would allow. 'Poor family background, I believe, and that is so important. One has to think of the children of the marriage and how they would turn out.'

'Which brings us to Beth.'

'I had hoped we had finally got rid of that girl.'

'Beth does a very good job for me, Mother, in fact I would go as far as say I would be lost without her. We have come to depend on her.'

'Nonsense, any girl from a business college could meet your requirements.'

'I am afraid you are wrong there but we'll let the matter rest. Incidentally, Caroline feels that she cannot leave Beth out of the guest list and in any case she wants her there. No, don't say what you were going to: that Beth is a working girl and no longer a threat to Caroline. To be honest, I feel very offended that you should think so little of your grand-daughter's charms that you would consider Beth a threat.'

'I do consider that, I always have. You, my dear, are blinded by love of your daughter and her resemblance to Margaret. I am not, I see what is there. Caroline is pretty, Beth is beautiful. Take it from me there will be no invitation going to Beth Brown and you can leave Caroline to me.'

Chapter Twenty-Two

On a bitterly cold February day when the wind was at its strongest, Robert Munro, with a fellow traveller, stepped on to British soil and shivered. The two young men got on so well that they had decided to enjoy what London had to offer before going their separate ways. They booked in at a cheap boarding house which supplied a comfortable bed at night and a hearty breakfast in the morning. Robert was not short of funds and neither, as it turned out, was his companion but, being unaware of the other's circumstances, they settled for inexpensive accommodation.

Uncle and nephew had arranged to meet in the small private lounge reserved for residents of the Grand Hotel in Tottenham Court Road. Nigel had booked two nights for himself and one night for Robert.

Both were a little anxious, a little apprehensive. The exchange of letters was one thing, but meeting face to face was quite another. In the event it went off very well.

Nigel sat in a large, leather armchair, a drink to hand. Each time the door opened, though it was not yet the appointed time, he lowered his newspaper to see if the incomer was his nephew. Robert was punctual, however, and immediately he entered and looked about him, Nigel sprang to his feet, dropped the paper, and with a welcoming smile extended his hand.

'Robert, my boy, you have the look of James without

resembling him,' he said. 'Make of that what you will,' he said, laughing.

The handshake between uncle and nephew was firm and each was weighing up the other.

'Great to meet you, sir, and I do know what you mean,' he said and grinned. 'My Mother says much the same thing only she is a little more direct and says my dad was better looking.'

Nigel laughed. 'Now that I did not say. Come on, Robert, sit down, we'll talk better over a drink.' He pushed the bell on the wall and in a few moments it was answered.

'What will yours be, Robert?'

'A beer if that is all right,' he said in a voice that held only the faintest suggestion of a drawl.

Nigel glanced up at the waiter. 'A beer and bring me another whisky.'

'Very good, sir.'

'For an Australian born and bred you don't have a pronounced drawl.'

'Mine got ironed out. Dad loved his adopted country and its people but not the way they speak.' He paused. 'I miss him,' he said simply and for a moment his eyes were bleak.

'I'm sure you do,' Nigel said quietly, 'and we will be forever grateful to your mother for getting in touch. She wrote such a wonderful letter, Robert, and your grandmother has read it so often that she has it off by heart.'

'It wasn't for want of trying. Mum tried hard to get dad to write and maybe if he had been spared longer she might have succeeded.' He shrugged. 'Who knows?'

The drinks arrived. Robert's luggage had been taken to his bedroom and his short leather coat was over a nearby chair.

'Judging by the photos sent out to us, you have a very pretty daughter.'

'Yes, Caroline is a pretty girl,' his uncle said proudly. 'As a young child she was very delicate but her health has improved though she can't do anything strenuous.' He paused to drink the remainder of his first drink and move the glass aside. 'I have to confess that, being an only child and motherless, Caroline has had a lot of her own way.'

'Like my sister, she gets away with murder.'

'Girls do. I gather you and your brother were made to toe the line.'

'You could say that but, if dad was firm with us, he was always fair.'

They talked for an hour and then decided to go for a walk to stretch their legs.

Nigel was all but a head taller than his nephew. He wore a dark, double-breasted suit and over it a Crombie coat. The military style looked well on him. Robert, at his mother's insistence, had packed a dark suit and this he wore with a blue shirt and a rather gaudy tie in blues and reds. Over the suit and to keep out the cold, he had on a leather coat with a fleecy-lined collar. As they left the hotel, older women turned to look at the colonel but Robert got barely a glance from their daughters. For all that he was a pleasant looking young man of average height with thick light brown hair, a tanned skin, grey eyes and an open, friendly face.

Tommy was at the station to meet the train which was ten minutes late. Nigel would have hailed a porter to deal with the luggage until Tommy took charge of it but Robert waved away assistance and carried his own baggage to the car, leaving Tommy to pack it all into the very large boot.

The London streets had been wet with slushy snow

swept to the side. Here the countryside was blanketed in white. 'Take a good look, Robert,' said the colonel. 'You are seeing snow at its best before it turns into filthy slush. Add to that severe overnight frost and driving becomes a nightmare. Black ice can take one unawares and spin the car out of control.'

'How do you manage?' Robert brought Tommy into the conversation, much to his uncle's annoyance.

'By keeping down my speed and putting up a prayer,' Tommy answered. Nice bloke this Australian, no side with him, must tell Beth, he promised himself.

It was late afternoon by the time they reached Inverbrae House and already darkness was falling. The gloaming they called it. The lamps to either side of the house were lit and as the car travelled up the long drive, Robert got his first look at the house which had been home to his father. What he had expected he couldn't rightly have said but the photographs hadn't prepared him for this magnificence. Perhaps it was due to the semi-darkness and the flood of lights coming from the house that gave it a fairyland appearance.

'Here we are,' Nigel got out to go ahead and Robert followed him up the stone steps that had been swept clean of snow earlier on but already had a fresh covering. The heavy door opened and the wind sent a shower of dry snow inside and on to the floor of the hall. Then they were inside and the door hastily shut against a further onslaught.

Here I am in Inverbrae House, Robert thought. He had the strangest feeling that he had come home.

Mrs Murdoch was waiting with a maid beside her to take their coats. Then Caroline came in, her face pink with excitement. She had taken care over her appearance and wore a warm dress in a shade of burnt orange. The

colour suited her and the style emphasised her tiny waist.
On her feet she wore black patent shoes with straps and a
medium heel. High heels would have been her choice but
she lacked the confidence to wear them. Not to worry, her
aunt said, that would come.

'Caroline, dear,' her father said kissing her brow and
giving her a hug, 'this is your cousin, Robert.'

They smiled to each other. Caroline wondered if he
would kiss her cheek or just shake hands. Robert wondered that too. Back home it was all so easy and natural,
and his mother's parting advice hadn't been especially
helpful.

'Be yourself,' she had said.

Caroline put out a small, slim hand and he took it in his.
Solemnly they shook hands until his cousin, with a hint of
mischief in her eyes, said mockingly, 'Being a relative you
are permitted to kiss me on the cheek. Or don't they do
that in Australia?'

'Stop teasing, Caroline.'

Robert was about to kiss his cousin when a noise made
them all turn. Mrs Parker-Munro stood at the open door,
leaning on her stick.

'You were taking your time and I couldn't wait a
moment longer to meet my grandson.'

Robert went forward with a big smile on his face.
'Hello, grandma.'

She winced at being addressed as grandma and this
would be conveyed to him at a later time but nothing must
be allowed to spoil this moment. Putting her stick against
the door post she held out both hands.

'Robert,' she said and her eyes were moist.

Her grandson took her hands in his and kissed her on
both cheeks. He was used to old people and good with
them. Her appearance had surprised him, knowing as he

did that she was just in her mid seventies. She looked so old and wrinkled but haughty too and very much the lady of the manor. This was only to be expected, he supposed, since she was mistress of Inverbrae House. Could be her health wasn't too good. His great-grandad never gave in to age, indeed he said the minute you did you were finished. His recipe for a long life was to look after the body, take an interest in life, be concerned with what was going on in the world and keep the brain active. And, at the end of the day, never to forget to count your blessings.

She was subjecting him to a long, steady look from those faded blue eyes.

'A little of James there but you must take after the other side of the family.'

'They don't see it, but I must take after someone,' he grinned.

'You are a Parker-Munro, no doubt about that.'

'Begging your pardon, grandma, but I'm Robert Munro or Bob Munro to my friends.'

'Whatever you call yourself, young man, you are a Parker-Munro,' she said firmly, 'and very, very welcome in Inverbrae House.'

Nigel moved forward. 'Mother, you are standing too long, we should go along to the drawing-room and you had better take my arm.'

'No, Nigel, my grandson will help me.'

'Delighted to,' Robert said quickly and with a gentleness that surprised them, he took his grandmother's arm and together they went through the spacious hall and along to the drawing-room.

'Thank you, my dear, I shall manage now,' Mrs Parker-Munro said as she crossed to her usual chair. Robert stood in the centre of the room and looked up at the high frescoed ceiling and then to the solid, old-fashioned furniture and the cabinets that held priceless ornaments.

'This is going to take some describing when I write home. Our house is considered pretty good and it is but nothing remotely like this.'

His grandmother nodded. Caroline said, 'Have you seen a fire before or is it always too hot to need one?'

'We have coolish nights when we do light a fire but, far from dominating the room, it is tucked away in a corner and not much noticed.'

'Are you going to like Scotland?'

'Caroline, give your cousin a chance,' her father laughed, 'Robert has only just got here.'

'Sure to and you'll have to forgive me if I ask a lot of questions.'

'Ask as many as you like.'

'Thanks. I've had strict instructions to write home at least twice a month and tell them about you all and this house. A tall order, how can I do justice to it? To me it is magnificent and I wonder how dad could have turned his back on it.' He stopped, 'Or is that something that isn't spoken about?'

'Not at all, Robert, but this isn't quite the time,' his grandmother said. 'Once you have settled we'll have a talk, you and I, and I'll tell you about your father. He was a rascal, James was, a lovable rascal who couldn't keep out of mischief. But that is all I am going to say just now.' She paused, took a breath and smiled to him. 'What I will say, however, is that we are all just so happy that you are to be with us for Caroline's eighteenth birthday.'

'Having a big splash?' he asked, turning to Caroline and thinking that she really was a very pretty girl but too delicate for his liking. Not like Gemma back home. That had been the worst part about leaving Australia, having to leave Gemma behind. Since small children they had played together, quarrelled and made it up. Pals they were until the night before he had to set sail and neither of them knew how it had happened. Just that they were in one another's arms, clinging to each other. He had tasted the salt of her tears when their lips met in a long kiss that left them both shaken.

Would she wait for him? Nothing had been said, no promises made. Gemma was a fun-loving, attractive girl with no shortage of admirers. He would write but would she reply? He thought not. He couldn't imagine her sitting down to write a letter. Riding, swimming, any outdoor activity and dark-haired Gemma would be taking part.

They were talking to him and his mind had wandered.

'Robert?'

'Sorry,' he apologised, 'what were you saying, Caroline?'

'Only that my birthday is being celebrated here and for the first time in years the ballroom is to be opened up—'

'A ballroom!' He stretched his eyes.

'It isn't huge, just big enough for family and friends,' she said primly.

'Sounds to me like a dress affair and I had better warn you what I stand in is the only formal suit I possess.'

'Of course it is a dress affair,' Caroline said, outraged. She was becoming just the teeniest bit annoyed with this Australian cousin. For heaven's sake, they were wealthy and must surely attend some functions that demanded the correct clothes.

'Robert, we didn't expect you to bring your entire wardrobe,' Nigel said laughing. 'It will be my pleasure to take you along to my tailor to have you measured for a dress suit and anything else you require.'

'Good of you, Uncle Nigel, but I couldn't possibly accept, I mean I can—' he floundered to a stop. He was about to say that he had money and more would follow when it was needed.

'That could be James talking,' the old lady came in swiftly to avoid any awkwardness. 'He had absolutely no interest in clothes and your Uncle Nigel wasn't all that keen either. Often my son wears clothes that are shabbier than the ones his workers wear.'

'Not the cut though, Mother, and that is what counts.'

'I wouldn't deny that.' She frowned. 'When is that wretched maid coming with the tea? Caroline, give that bell a pull and see what is going on. Where was I? Oh, clothes, I remember now. Robert, my dear, do accept your Uncle Nigel's offer and get what is required. I imagine that you have lightweight suits that are totally unsuited to this climate of ours.'

There was a tap at the door then a maid, looking flustered, came in with a tray and went over to put it on a table. Another maid followed with plates of daintily cut sandwiches.

The mistress examined the food and nodded. It would do until the evening meal.

'The weather is colder than I expected. Thanks, Uncle Nigel, your offer is accepted and I'll accompany you to your tailor's and not disgrace the family,' he grinned.

'Good! Good!' Nigel nodded his head a few times. 'Seeing round the estate will be of more interest I imagine?'

'Much more.'

'Weather permitting, I'll show you around tomorrow.'

The maids poured the tea and handed round the cups and, at a nod from the mistress, departed. Caroline got up to hand round the plate of sandwiches.

'Robert, I simply must hear about Queensland,' she said as he took a sandwich.

'Great country but why don't you come back with me and see it for yourself?'

His grandmother and her son exchanged looks. 'Caroline couldn't stand the heat, I'm afraid. Extremes of temperature are bad for her and she is better to remain indoors in the coldest weather.'

'I understand.' He looked sympathetically at his cousin who was pulling a face.

'Have another sandwich, Robert,' Nigel said taking the plate from Caroline.

'Thanks.'

'Take two, hardly a bite in them.'

Robert agreed and reached for another. The kitchen at home never produced anything this small.

'Did your family make their money out of sheep?'

'Caroline, that was rude,' her grandmother said sharply.

'I don't mind answering that, grandma. Yes, the money comes from sheep, Caroline – don't you ever get called Carrie?'

'Never.'

'The real hard work was done by my great-great-grandfather. He sweated it out and against all the odds it began to show a profit. The sons followed him, did their bit, and now,' he said proudly, 'ours is the biggest and best sheep farm in the whole of Queensland.'

'A family concern?' Nigel asked.

'Very much so and not just close family either, there is enough work for everybody.'

Next morning the weather was bright and cold. The overnight frost had not been as severe as expected and, in heavy footwear, Nigel and Robert set out. They would go on foot, the colonel said, and take it in easy stages. The farm cottages interested Robert, and he was amazed at the smallness of them. How, he wondered, did they manage to bring up a family in such cramped conditions? He asked the question of the colonel.

'They manage because it is what they are used to. Like everything else, Robert, one accepts what one has and makes the best of it.'

'How about ambition?'

'That doesn't enter into their lives.'

'Surely they would want to better themselves for the sake of their children?'

'They have a roof over their head, food for their stomach and enough sense to know when they are well off,' Nigel said shortly.

Robert said no more. This, then, was the class system of which his father had spoken on those rare occasions when he had mentioned his homeland. Had that been the reason for his turning his back on his own country? Remembering the man his father had been, the way he judged people for themselves and not their possessions, he rather thought it possible. Being the younger brother, the ties would be less since Inverbrae House and all it stood for would never be his.

They left the row of cottages and came to one well apart from the others. Smoke was coming out of the chimney and a girl was sitting at what could be a table or a desk. His uncle surprised him by saying, 'This is the manager's office, but I have a girl in doing the paperwork. She may have letters for me to sign so we'll pop in for a minute or two.'

With a turn of the knob the door opened into a small passageway that took them to where the girl was working. Robert saw a good-sized room fitted out as an office, with everything neat and tidy. A fire burned in the grate and there was the crackle of logs. The girl had stopped typing when her visitors entered.

'Anything for me to sign, Beth?'

'Two, Colonel Parker-Munro. You can have this other if you wait a few minutes.'

'No, these two will do, I'll sign them.' He took out his fountain pen, uncapped it and after reading them, signed his name. Then he smiled. 'Come along, Robert, there is much to see.'

Robert was appalled and embarrassed at what he took to be a display of bad manners. There had been no attempt made to introduce them. Was this the way they behaved to all employees? If it was, give him Australia any day. They had their snobs but very few. Before following his uncle, Robert smiled and she did too and he rather thought the eyes held amusement.

She was a looker, as they would say back home, and there was a quiet dignity about the girl that made him wonder why she worked in such a lowly position. He would have expected someone like her to be in a streamlined office, as secretary to some prominent businessman. On the other hand, maybe that didn't appeal to her and this was just to fill in time until she got married. He laughed at himself for taking so much interest in the girl but even so he was already promising himself that one day, on his own, he would come this way again.

'Carrie?'

'I do not answer to that, Robert.'

'Carrie is nice and you can call me Bob.'

'No, thank you, we'll keep to our proper names if you don't mind.' She pursed her lips. 'Bad enough that you call yourself Munro when your surname is Parker-Munro.

Grandmama is going to keep on at you until you agree to use your full name.'

'Not a chance.' He saw her give a small shiver. 'You're cold, do you want that fire attended to?'

'I was about to ring for the maid.'

'No need, I'll see to it.' He lifted the shovel, put on coal and added a log. 'That please your ladyship?'

'No, it does not. Our maids are employed to do that and you are a guest as well as being family.'

'Know something?' he said as he sprawled in the easy chair.

'Quite a lot, I should hope.'

'Smart girl! Touch of Gemma there.'

'Who is Gemma?'

'A girl back home.'

'Your sweetheart?'

'Hope so.'

'Don't you know?'

'No, it just hit us when I was leaving.'

'Robert, can't you be serious for a minute?'

'I am serious, Caroline, and it is just as I said.'

'Then for goodness sake write and tell the poor girl how you feel.'

'That would sound better coming from your grandma.'

'What do you mean by that?' she said indignantly.

'Just that you are a sweet, little, old-fashioned girl,' he teased.

'I am not old-fashioned.'

'It was intended as a compliment.'

'Telling a young lady that she is old-fashioned is anything but. It seems to me, Robert Parker-Munro, you have a great deal to learn.'

'Meaning I lack polish?'

'Would you be very angry if I said yes?'

'No, since you mean it.'

She laughed. 'Robert, I do like having you here. It is almost like having a brother and being able to insult each other without either of us taking offence. Let's get back to Gemma. Are you really serious about her?'

'I am dead serious, but I am not at all sure that Gemma is. Until our final goodbye, we were just good pals.'

'Poor you. You're afraid to tell her in case you embarrass the girl and you lose the easy friendship you had.'

'Quite a bit of sense in that little head of yours and yes, you've just about got it right.'

'Want my advice?'

'Yes, but no guarantee I'll take it.'

'Write and tell her all you are doing and say how much you are missing her. Then add, as a sort of afterthought, that you are going to my ball, tell her it is my eighteenth and it is to be a very grand occasion.'

'So?'

'So, silly boy, she'll know that there are bound to be a lot of young ladies invited and that you might fall for one. It could make her jealous.'

'Some hope.'

'Nonsense,' Caroline said sharply. 'You want to know where you stand, don't you?'

'I suppose so and, speaking of young ladies, I met one in your manager's office.'

'Oh!'

'Uncle Nigel went in to sign letters.'

'Does she interest you?'

'Not in the way that look suggests.' He smiled. 'I steer clear of tall girls but she certainly is easy on the eyes and wasted, I thought, in a small office like that.'

'Obviously she doesn't think so.'

'Do you know Beth?'

'You were introduced?'

'No, her name came up that's all. Does she live around here?'

'Yes.'

'In one of the cottages?'

'No.'

'Not very forthcoming, are you?'

'What is your interest in Beth or is it curiosity?'

'Bit of both. Where does she live?'

'At present she is living here in Inverbrae House but you are unlikely to see her.'

'Don't tell me servants' quarters!'

'Of course not. Beth is not a servant, she is in charge of the clerical duties for the estate or something like that,' she said vaguely. 'It was grandmama's suggestion that she ate her meals with Mrs Murdoch and she has a pleasant bedroom which, Robert, isn't bad and much better than she would get elsewhere.'

'Board and lodgings thrown in?' he said sarcastically and wondered why he felt so annoyed.

'Exactly.' Caroline felt a twinge of conscience. It would have been far better for all concerned if Beth had taken employment in the town and made a complete break instead of this unsatisfactory state of affairs. It was her father's fault, she knew that, she was useful to him and he was holding on to her. She wondered what Beth thought and how she had taken to being told she could no longer have her meals in the breakfast room.

Beth was not too concerned. In fact, it suited her quite well. She had no desire to meet any of them, not even Caroline, and had taken to using, not the servants' entrance, but the little-used side door. She would put up with anything until she could afford to walk out.

The vacancies columns had yielded nothing suitable and she wondered if Jenny would be able to help. There was an open invitation to Greystanes but, even so, she had to check that it was convenient before taking the bus over.

Jenny was her usual charming self and embraced Beth warmly.

'Miss Harris and I were just talking about you the other day and hoping you would put in an appearance and here you are. Take your coat off and we'll go through.' Miss Harris had heard the voices and came to take Beth's coat.

'Picture of health and bonnier every time I see her, don't you agree, Mrs Cuthbert?'

'I do indeed.'

Beth blushed.

On their way to the sitting-room Beth took a long look at her picture hanging on the wall.

'I'm going to miss that when it goes,' Jenny smiled.

'That won't be for a long time.'

'We'll exchange our news first then tea, does that suit you?'

'Yes, but I'm afraid I'm about to ask another favour.'

'Ask away and don't sound so apologetic.'

'You know I've been applying for jobs but I can't get one that pays enough to cover a rented room somewhere. That is the only reason I stay where I am.'

'Tell me about the position at Inverbrae House. Not too comfortable?'

'I don't see any of them except the colonel when he comes in to sign his letters or he wants me to do something.'

'Don't you see Caroline? You must, you sleep next door to each other.'

'Not now. I'm over at the other end of the house and I have my meals with Mrs Murdoch.' She saw Jenny's face and rushed in with, 'Honestly, Jenny, I don't mind, in fact I actually prefer it.'

'That may well be but I think it is dreadful. Sadly I can't help since Nigel and I decided to part as good friends.'

'Oh, I didn't know.'

'Far better since the poor dear was horribly embarrassed not to be able to invite me to his home. I made him angry by saying that he gave in to the old lady far too much.'

'You've done such a lot for me, Jenny, and I only discovered by chance that I owe my education at Rowanbank to you.'

'A mixed blessing, as it turned out.' She began to laugh.

'Don't I get to share the joke?'

'My dear Beth, you have become quite famous. That waspish Miss Critchley has few friends but what is said is usually behind her back. You, my brave girl, told her to her face just what you thought of her and I am so proud.' She took Beth's face in her hands and kissed her brow. 'Now tell me about this favour you want.'

'Do you know of anyone who needs secretarial help? Or if you hear of something, please let me know. I also need a room to rent.'

'My dear girl, you are welcome to stay here.'

'I know and I am grateful but I remember what you once told me.'

'What was that? I seem to have told you a lot of things.'

'That independence is something to be treasured. I want to make my own way, Jenny, but,' and here she smiled, 'I need a bit of help to get started.'

'Be sure I'll keep my ears open. As it happens, I do know of one vacancy but I hardly think it would appeal to you.'

'Try me. You never know.'

'Does the name Anna Martin ring a bell?'

Beth shook her head.

'Hardly thought it would. She is an elderly, rather eccentric woman who writes historical books. Her home is between here and Sandyneuk.'

'She wants someone to do her typing?'

'Yes, she wants her manuscripts typed and from what I gather they are none too easy to make out.'

'Very bad?'

'Apparently her writing is atrocious.'

'Could be a challenge, if nothing else.'

'The only plus as far as you are concerned is that accommodation goes with the job if wanted.'

'She wants someone to live in?'

'She would prefer it.'

'Like a companion?' Beth said dismissively.

'Far from it. Our Anna Martin keeps herself to herself but she likes the thought of someone else in the house.'

'She sounds a bit weird.'

'I like her, as it happens, but it is not what you are looking for. As I said, I'll keep my ears open—'

The tea arrived and the conversation was general until Miss Harris left.

'Tell me about the Parker-Munros. I confess to still being interested.'

'There is to be a ball for Caroline's eighteenth birthday, a very grand affair. Mrs Murdoch says the ballroom has been taken out of mothballs and freshened up for the occasion.'

'I see the fair hand of Mrs Esslemont in this!'

'She is seeing to all the arrangements and the nephew from Australia, Caroline's cousin, has arrived in time to attend.'

Jenny's eyes opened wide. 'This I want to hear. What is he like?'

'Very pleasant.'

'Your heart didn't miss a beat?'

'No, absolutely not.'

'How did you two come to meet?'

'The colonel was taking him over the estate and they dropped in.'

'To introduce you?'

'No, to sign letters.'

'And what did this Australian say?'

'Nothing. He smiled and I smiled and they departed.'

'From that I gather you were not introduced?'

'That's correct but it didn't upset me. After all I am just an employee. Robert seemed surprised, though.'

'Being an Australian, he would. They are a friendly bunch and don't stand on ceremony. I like them.' She paused. 'Cinderella isn't going to the ball?'

'Cinderella wasn't invited but even had I been I would have refused.'

'Why?'

'Because a gown for such an occasion would not only make a dip in my savings, it would clean me out.'

Chapter Twenty-Three

Robert had not forgotten Beth but there were few occasions when he was left alone. Today, surprisingly, he was. Caroline was having the final fitting for the much spoken-of gown. Her excitement, with only eight days to go, was bordering on the feverish and Robert wished that they would stop going on and on about the forthcoming event. He was sick of hearing about it but had gone to be measured for an evening suit and a dinner jacket. Being honest with himself, he had been pleasantly surprised. The young man in the mirror looked passably handsome.

The suggestion had come from Mrs Parker-Munro that Robert should accompany his uncle to Edinburgh but he had managed to get out of that. It was a business meeting and Nigel freely admitted that there was no saying how long it would last. In truth, the colonel hadn't been too disappointed at Robert's reluctance to join him. He was rather looking forward to meeting his friends and, with Robert to be considered, he would have had to leave before the customary drinks in the private bar.

When Robert set out a pale wintry sun was bravely peeping out from between the clouds. In a short time he was knocking at the door of the office. Expecting it to be Tommy, Beth shouted, 'It's open,' and didn't immediately turn round but finished what she was doing. When she did turn she was flustered.

'I'm so very sorry,' she said, 'I thought it was someone else or I would have gone to the door.'

He smiled. 'No apology necessary. Is this an awkward time to barge in and are you very busy?'

'No to both questions. Is there something I can do for you?' she asked politely.

'For a start you could sit down, then I would be able to do likewise.'

Beth went over to sit behind the typewriter and Robert sat down in the nearest chair.

'We weren't introduced. I'm afraid it was an oversight on my uncle's part but let me put that right. I'm Robert Munro.'

She liked the sound of his voice and she liked this Robert Munro. Not Parker-Munro, she noted. The colonel not introducing them had been no oversight but it was nice of his nephew to suggest it had been.

'I'm Beth Brown,' she said.

'I know it is short notice but may I ask if you are doing anything special this evening?'

Beth was taken aback. 'Why?' she asked at last.

'If you aren't, I wondered if you would take pity on a lonely Australian and have dinner with me?'

'The bit about being lonely doesn't impress me in the least since I don't believe you.'

'Then would you believe it if I said I would like a change of company?'

Beth thought she could believe that. 'It's kind of you, but I won't accept, thank you all the same.'

His face fell and he looked genuinely disappointed. 'I do wish you would. Let me say that this is friendship pure and simple. I have a girl back home.'

She shook her head and he sighed.

'I suppose I should have known that a nice-looking girl

316

like you wouldn't be likely to have a free evening.'

Why shouldn't she accept? Beth thought. It would be very pleasant to have a night out and she appreciated his honesty. She would be honest too.

'I'm not doing anything this evening.'

'Then you'll change your mind?'

Beth laughed. 'I have changed it and I'll be happy to accept, thank you.'

'You choose where we should go and make it somewhere nice.'

'But not too far away,' she said thoughtfully.

'That doesn't matter I can borrow a car.'

'No,' she said firmly. She wouldn't feel comfortable in a vehicle belonging to the colonel.

'A taxi then?'

'What is wrong with the bus?'

'Nothing as far as I am concerned but, for the return journey, I must insist on a taxi.'

'May I ask why?'

'Hanging around in this freezing weather waiting for a bus would be a poor end to what I hope will be a very pleasant evening.'

Beth smiled and looked apologetic. 'I'm sorry. That was thoughtless of me. You must be taking bad with this cold.'

'Takes a bit of getting used to I have to admit.' Then he grinned. 'No problem seeing you home.'

'How do you know that?'

'Caroline told me.'

'Ah!' Beth wondered just how much Caroline had told her cousin, and was reasonably confident it had been very little.

'Have you made up your mind where we should go?'

'The choice is limited unless we go much further afield and I'd rather not.'

'As I said, you choose.'

'There is a rather old-fashioned hotel' – Jenny had called it quaint – 'just beyond Strathvale and I can recommend the food. It has another advantage, someone runs a taxi service close by.'

'Sounds perfect. Better book,' he pointed to the phone.

'I don't make use of it for private calls.'

'Then get the number for me and I'll make the booking.'

'Probably wouldn't be necessary.'

'Better to be sure.'

Beth found the number for him and Robert got up.

'A table for two for this evening, please,' he said into the phone. 'Time? Oh, about eightish.' He looked at Beth for confirmation and she nodded. 'The name is Robert Munro of Inverbrae House. You've got that? Thank you, goodbye.' He replaced the receiver. 'Charming lady, she said she would look forward to seeing us.'

Beth wound a sheet of paper into the typewriter and Robert, taking the hint, began to walk towards the door.

'When do we leave?'

'Seven-thirty should do.'

'And where do we meet?'

'At the side entrance,' Beth said firmly.

He seemed about to object. 'That's where I'll be,' she said.

'Your wish is my command.' He sketched a salute and went out closing the door quietly behind him.

After he had gone Beth sat thinking and made no attempt to type. Perhaps she had been wrong to accept but she was in a rebellious mood, born out of anger and frustration against the humiliating position in which she found herself. Why should she deny herself a social life? She wasn't answerable to anyone. Stupid though, when she considered it. Here she was just waiting her time to be free of the Parker-Munros and accepting an invitation from the Australian nephew. Would she never learn?

If they found out, the Parker-Munros would be none too pleased. They might even go as far as suggest to Robert that he had made an unfortunate choice. The Australian would have his answer to that, she felt sure, but it made her more anxious than ever to get away. And that brought her thoughts to the eccentric woman writer of whom Jenny had spoken. Maybe it was worth serious consideration and, if it came to anything, and the woman wanted her to start right away, then she would oblige. Since she was paid weekly, the legal entitlement was for one week's notice. If it upset the smooth running of the estate, which she uncharitably hoped it would, then so be it. She would feel no guilt.

As he walked away from the cottage, Robert whistled happily. Instead of the dull evening he had been contemplating, he was to be in the company of a very lovely young lady. Very soon now he would be packing his bags and setting out on his travels. Paris and Rome were a must and after that he would just go where the mood took him. The final week or two he would spend at Inverbrae House. He had an affection for his relatives but he wouldn't be heartbroken to leave them. Poor Caroline didn't have much of a life, he thought, and as far as he could see had absolutely no freedom. Everything was arranged and she just had to fall in with the plans made for her. Beth, now, where did she come in? There was a mystery here and perhaps tonight he would learn something.

His lounge suit had not been in need of sponging and

pressing but it had been taken away and duly brought back ready for him to put on. Making work for themselves, that's all it was. Back home no one looked for work – there was always plenty of it.

The bus rattled its way along the country roads and let them off at the far end of Strathvale near to a garage that advertised a taxi service. A short distance from that was the Halfway Hotel. It was a lovely old building that had started life as a coaching inn, and the atmosphere inside was warm and inviting. The dining-room had an open fire set into an alcove and it gave out a good heat. A lighted candle in a holder was on each table. Two of the tables were taken and at one there was an animated conversation going on between two couples, punctuated by peals of laughter.

The table Beth and Robert were shown to was some distance away and, as if the other diners were suddenly aware of them, the noise grew less and the laughter more subdued. Beth wore a dress in duck-egg blue with a matching embroidered bolero. Having stopped growing when she was in her final year at school meant that she still had a reasonable wardrobe of clothes. Those she bought from now on would be from the inexpensive stores.

'You suit that colour, in fact you look delightful,' Robert said admiringly.

'And you look very nice too,' she laughed.

'I'm glad about that. Compliments on my appearance don't come flying this way all that often.'

'Mostly casual wear back home, is it?'

'Don't forget the big hat,' he grinned.

'Tell me about Australia, Robert, I'm interested.'

'I wouldn't know where to begin and, presumably, you

would have got some of it from your geography lessons at school.'

'Not all that much, I think we were short-changed on Australia and New Zealand.'

'That was disgraceful.' They looked up and accepted menus but didn't immediately study them. Robert was leaning across the table. 'Did you know that Australia is the largest island in the world?'

'I'm not sure but if you are telling me then, of course, I believe you.'

He opened the menu. 'Better study this and get the order in.'

For her main course Beth decided on roast beef and Yorkshire pudding. Robert swithered between that and steak, eventually settling for the same as Beth. The waitress arrived in her stiffly starched apron and Robert gave the order.

'Where were we?'

'Improving my education.'

'Ah, yes, so we were. Australia, my dear girl, has everything. Wide open spaces, spectacular scenery, and miles and miles of soft white sands. And as to culture we are not starved of that either nor city life.'

'Sounds perfect,' Beth sighed.

'Although I say it myself it is pretty good.' He paused when the meal arrived and watched the wine bottle being opened then left on the table. 'For your information this is summer time back home and it will be very, very hot and my folk will be sweltering.' As they ate he spoke of his family with such warmth that he brought them alive for Beth.

'Does Scotland come up to your expectations?' she asked.

'It does. I love what I have seen of it. My dad didn't talk

a great deal about his homeland but when he did there was a lot of pride in his voice. Much as he loved Australia, Beth, he never thought of himself as an Australian.'

'You do?'

'Of course I do, that's where I was born and brought up and I'm proud to call myself an Australian.'

'Could you settle here or would you always be homesick for Queensland?' She took a sip of her wine while waiting for his reply.

'Difficult one that,' he said thoughtfully, 'because Inverbrae House pulls me in a way I find difficult to describe. When I arrived I had the strangest feeling that I had come home.'

'Inverbrae House is very beautiful,' she said softly. 'I have always thought so.'

He leaned back. 'That is my turn over and now I await the story of your life.'

'Not a great deal to tell.' And that was far from the truth, she thought.

'I rather think there is,' he said gently.

Just then the waitress came to collect the dessert plates.

'Would you like coffee served at the table or would you prefer a more comfortable seat at the fire?'

'That sounds like a good idea.'

Beth laughed. 'He means he would like a comfortable seat at the fire.'

They moved to sit in the chintz-covered armchairs and partly facing each other. A small table was pulled over. The coffee arrived together with a plate of tiny triangles of shortbread.

Beth drank some coffee and hoped Robert had forgotten and they would talk of something else but no such luck, she thought. He was looking at her with his eyebrows raised.

'I'm waiting, Beth.'

'That was a lovely meal, Robert,' she said playing for time. 'I think the wine has gone to my head. I feel deliciously drowsy.'

'Don't fall asleep on me and if that is an excuse—'

'No, it isn't but, before I begin, I need your promise that you won't repeat any of what I tell you.'

'You have my promise,' he said solemnly, 'that not a word of it will be repeated.'

She gave a deep sigh. 'It all began when I was six years of age—'

Beth had not intended to tell Robert very much but it was as though she couldn't stop herself. To this man, the nephew of the colonel, she poured out her miseries, especially those after the tragic death of her parents. The lighter moments came when she told of her speech on the final day of school.

'Good for you,' he said admiringly, 'and the girls rushing over to the car to congratulate you must have made you proud?'

'I didn't feel proud, Robert, and Caroline was very shocked.'

'What about uncle?'

'He was disgusted with me and with good cause, since he had paid my fees.'

'Not willingly, I gather, but I'm glad this Jenny has your interests at heart. You need someone to look after you.'

She frowned. 'I don't, Robert. I can look after myself.'

'You won't need to. Someone else will want to do that. A lovely girl like you should have plenty of admirers and you would if you didn't keep yourself hidden away.'

'I'm doing something about another job.'

'That's the spirit. Beth,' he took her hand. 'I wish you all the luck in the world, you deserve it.'

323

'You do believe what I've told you?'

'Every word. As you know, Beth, my father walked ou['] on this family and according to my grandma he was a bit o['] a handful, a difficult boy to control and a worry to everybody. Probably all true, dad never gave his reasons for running away to pastures new.'

Beth was showing distress. 'Robert, don't think badly o['] your uncle and grandmother on my account. They truly believed they had done their duty by me and many would agree they had.'

'I'm not one of them.'

'I'm not family so it was understandable.'

'Back home you would have been one of the family from day one.'

'To begin with they were very kind—'

'Exactly,' Robert said grimly. 'They used you and when you ceased to be necessary to them they wanted rid o['] you. That in my book is despicable.'

'We'll stop there. That is quite enough about my problems. I don't usually talk this freely and I blame the wine.'

'What you told me was in confidence but I'm glad you did.'

To get off the subject, she said, 'Tell me about the preparations for Caroline's big day.'

He groaned. 'Absolutely not, that's all they ever talk about.'

'Mrs Parker-Munro will be so delighted to have you here for Caroline's ball. You'll be expected to partner her.'

'So I gather but I make myself scarce when someone more interesting comes along. This elaborate do is just an exercise to find a suitable husband for Caroline.'

'You think so?'

'I know so. Wealth isn't all that important, family is and a younger son would be more acceptable.'

Beth looked puzzled.

'Should have worked that one out, Beth. Caroline's husband-to-be must be willing to live at Inverbrae House and assist in the running of the estate.'

'You could be right.'

'My little cousin is a spoilt brat but I like her and I just hope she has some say in whom she is to marry.'

'Don't worry, Caroline always gets her own way.'

'In things that don't matter all that much, yes she does. But this concerns the future of Inverbrae House. I just hope that the chosen one will bring Caroline happiness.'

'I hope so too.' Beth gave a start when she saw how late it was. 'Robert, look at the time, I had no idea!'

'Neither had I, but there is no danger of us being locked out.' He smiled as Beth reached for her coat and he helped her into it. 'Don't panic, I'll get the bill and the taxi is taken care of, I thought to mention it when we arrived.'

The waitress brought the bill. 'Did you enjoy the meal?' she asked with a tired smile.

'Very much and apologies for the lateness of the hour.' He settled the bill and added a tip that had her protesting.

'You've more than earned it.'

'Thank you very much, sir and I took the liberty of calling your taxi. It should be here by now but I'll check.' She came back. 'Yes, it is.'

They left the warmth and got into the taxi. The engine was running and there was a little heat in the car.

'Are you and Caroline the same age?'

'I'm a little younger, my birthday, my eighteenth isn't until the fifteenth of next month.'

'Too bad I'll be on my travels by then or we could have celebrated it.'

The taxi drew up and when it had gone Robert opened the side door to Inverbrae House. 'Thank you, Beth, for an evening I shall long remember.'

'And thank you for an unforgettable evening.'

Robert kissed her lightly on the cheek as he turned the key in the lock. Together they walked quietly along the passageway. At the end they separated, one going to the right, the other to the left. There was no sound, nobody was astir.

Beth took the bus into Perth. There was no invitation for her to the birthday ball but even so she couldn't let the day pass without a small gift. Going from shop to shop she despaired of finding something that would appeal to Caroline. What did one give a girl who had everything? In the end she bought a glass ornament similar to the one she had given Jenny. Caroline could put it on her dressing-table and when the light touched it the glass would sparkle. She found a suitable card and returned satisfied. She would wrap up the gift and give it to one of the maids to put on the hall table. There were moments when Beth was wistful, imagining the glitter of the occasion and thinking how wonderful it would be. Perhaps the music would reach her bedroom and with an imaginary partner she would dance round the room. Dreams! Dreams! But what would life be without them?

Replenishing the postage stamps was Beth's responsibility and she chose a time when her work was well advanced. She had letters to post and set off for the village. The weather was cold and frosty but she was warmly clad. After popping the letters in the pillarbox she went inside the post office for stamps. Daydreaming was still a failing of Beth's and, coming out of the door, it was entirely her fault that she collided with someone.

'Sorry! Sorry! Sorry!' said a male voice as he steadied her.

'My fault – I wasn't watching where I was going.'

Laughing blue eyes were looking into hers and Beth felt the colour rush to her face. He was the most handsome man she had ever met and her heart was doing a somersault. Becoming aware that she was still in the stranger's arms and feeling desperately embarrassed, Beth broke away and as she did a sheet of stamps fluttered from her hand and on to the pavement. He was there before her to pick it up.

'Someone is going to be very busy,' he smiled as he handed the stamps over.

She smiled back. 'Thank you.'

'Which way are you going?'

She pointed.

'May I walk with you?'

'Yes, if you wish.' Beth felt breathless as though she had been running. The young man, whom she took to be about twenty-five, was having a most disturbing effect on her. Could it – was it possible that what she was experiencing was love at first sight? Not so long ago she had ridiculed the idea but now she wasn't so sure. Then she tried to talk sense to herself. He was an exceptionally handsome young man and there weren't too many of those around Sandyneuk. Tall and well built with thick, dark brown hair, blue eyes and a face that, were he a film star, would have women swooning. Was it possible for a man to be too handsome? When she was unobserved, she searched his face for some fault and found one. The chin could have been firmer.

As they walked they spoke mainly of the invigorating

weather and other generalities until they reached the gates to Inverbrae House.

'This is where I leave you.' She saw his start of surprise.

'You live here?'

'Yes.'

'Don't go, please, not just yet.' He held out his hand. 'I'm Adrian Scott-Hamilton.'

'Beth Brown,' she said. It was time to move away but she couldn't bring herself to and he was in no hurry either.

'Would it be possible for us to meet? I'm staying at Rockville Manor.' His hand went vaguely in its direction. 'Leonard Watson and I were at school together.'

She nodded then shook her head. 'I don't know—' she began hesitantly.

'Tomorrow evening? Could you manage that?'

Very easily, she thought but would it be wise to accept? The Watsons were close friends of the Parker-Munros—

'Well—?'

'Perhaps for a short time,' she said weakening.

'Tell you what, I'll slip away after dinner and meet you here at eight-thirty. You'll find me parked round the corner. A drink somewhere, a place where we can talk.'

He was so sure of himself, so sophisticated but she wasn't certain what going out for a drink meant.

'I don't drink.'

She saw the amusement in his eyes, they were dancing with merriment, and she felt foolish but she would stick to her guns.

'You don't have to drink. There is a charming little inn that Leonard introduced me to and if you would prefer a soft drink or a coffee for that matter—'

'Yes, all right, thank you.'

'Had this been the summer we could have walked and talked but in this weather we could either sit and shiver in the car and talk, or be comfortable beside a fire.'

Her face felt hot and she wanted away to hide her confusion. There had been none of this when she had accepted an invitation from Robert Munro. The difference was that she saw Robert as a friend and no more, whereas she didn't know what to think about Adrian Scott-Hamilton.

He saw her confusion and had a quiet smile to himself. His charm never failed.

'Until this evening,' he said softly.

'Yes,' she smiled and, in a daze, walked up the drive to Inverbrae House.

'Leonard?'

'What?' The Watsons kept open house and the boys had been encouraged to invite their friends for the school holidays. Adrian Scott-Hamilton had taken full advantage and was a frequent visitor to Rockville Manor.

'I met a smashing-looking girl in the village.'

'Did you now?' Leonard didn't take his eyes from his paper.

'The name Beth Brown mean anything to you?'

The paper was dropped and there was a look of surprise on his friend's face. 'Where did you see Beth?'

'Coming out of the post office,' he laughed. 'We bumped into each other. It was her fault, I hasten to add, but being the gentleman I am, I took the blame.'

'Made a date?'

'This evening.'

Once Leonard had thought Adrian could do no wrong but now he was actually beginning to dislike him.

'We parted company at the gate to Inverbrae House. Is she a relative of the Parker-Munros?'

'No.' He showed his annoyance as Adrian got up to

help himself to a drink. 'Better go easy on that stuff. The old man is beginning to notice. He complained the other day that he had never known whisky to evaporate before.'

'You wouldn't deny me a small one, would you?'

'It's going out of sight and that is hardly a small one.'

'What's got into you?'

'Nothing.'

'No love life, that is your problem.'

'Shut up, Adrian.'

Leonard Watson was of medium height and plump. He was a good-natured, shy young man who longed to have a steady girl friend but few spared him more than a glance when Adrian was around. Of late he was wishing that Adrian wouldn't visit so often but his mother, who thought him charming, told him to come when he wished. There was always a welcome for him.

There was never an invitation to Adrian's home in Stirling and the reason given was that his mother did not enjoy good health and was troubled with her nerves.

'Tell me about Beth.' Adrian eyed the amber liquid and drank it down.

'Wasting your time there. Beth is as poor as the proverbial church mouse.'

'With her speech and manner I would say—'

'Beth's parents moved to India and, as Beth and Caroline got on so well, Beth was invited to live in Inverbrae House until the parents returned.'

'Only they didn't.'

'Exactly. Since they could hardly throw the child out she continued to live at Inverbrae House.'

'One of the family?'

'No, never like that. She works in the colonel's office and I believe she has her meals with the housekeeper. So you see, she is not for you, old boy.'

'Pity she wasn't the daughter of the house. I fancy her, I fancy her like mad.'

'Don't play around with Beth,' Leonard said sharply.

'Any chance of her being at this birthday "do"?'

'I think it unlikely.'

Beth left the office punctually and had her meal alone. This was Mrs Murdoch's day off and she always spent it with her sister and her family.

A bath, a long, leisurely bath, then she would take her time over dressing. She wanted to look her best but not in something too dressy. Her hair, never a problem, was cut short and needed only a brush to shape it the way she wanted. A pleated skirt in a soft shade of green was her eventual choice. It was mid-calf length and the fine woollen jumper in the same colour made it look like one garment. She swithered about shoes, her newest ones were quite high but she didn't want them ruined and there might be a bit to walk from the car to the inn. Better to be safe than sorry and wear her medium heels.

A dab of perfume behind her ears and on her wrists and she was ready.

Beth smiled at her reflection in the mirror and felt a surge of pure excitement at what lay ahead. She took a deep breath, knowing that she must keep calm. Someone like Adrian Scott-Hamilton would expect a small show of sophistication and she didn't want to let herself down. Happily, her appearance pleased her. Her long black coat with its astrakhan collar suited her figure and had been the last garment to be charged to the colonel's account. There had been mild opposition from Caroline's Aunt Gwen who thought it much too old for her but she hadn't been all that interested and the coat became Beth's.

In the semi-darkness the car was not easy to see and

Beth approached carefully. She started slightly when the door opened.

'Beth?'

'Yes,' she whispered and heard the laughter in his voice.

'In you get.'

Beth went round and got herself in. She felt flustered and a little ridiculous. 'I couldn't be sure it was you.'

'I know and a girl can't be too careful. Think how awful it would have been to find yourself in someone else's car.'

'It doesn't bear thinking about,' she laughed.

'Comfortable?' he asked turning to her briefly before starting up the engine.

'Yes, thank you.'

Not until he had negotiated the double bend did he speak again. 'Dangerous bit of the road this, particularly at night and it doesn't do to take chances.' He smiled to himself as he said it. The only reason he was taking extra care was because his own car was off the road meantime and this was borrowed from the Watsons.

'I'm sure it doesn't.' She wished she could think of something to say instead of just answering but her brain seemed to have stopped working.

In a short time they turned into a narrow road full of pot-holes that had Beth hanging on to her seat.

'Sorry about that,' he apologised.

'Why doesn't someone fill them up?'

'You may well ask. One reason given me was that it acted as a warning and slowed down a getaway. The inn is very isolated, Beth.'

'Tell them of a car approaching and anyone up to no good would be hampered making their escape.' She paused to peer out of the window. 'Makes sense I suppose.'

'Yes, it does but it is damned hard on the car.'

Beth was out before Adrian got round and together they went up to the entrance. Lights shone from a few of the windows and a lamp was at each side of the door. It looked welcoming. Adrian's arm went round her shoulders and Beth felt the thrill of his nearness.

The door pinged when it was opened and a roar of men's laughter came from nearby. Adrian took hold of her arm.

'Don't be alarmed, that's coming from the bar. It'll be quiet where—' he broke off as a man in a white apron and carrying a tray stopped.

'It's all right, I know the way,' Adrian said pleasantly.

'You do? There's a good fire burning and I'll be coming for your order just as soon as I get rid of this.'

The room they found themselves in was warm and welcoming after the cold of outside. There were a number of small tables, one with empty glasses. Four people got on their feet and were preparing to go.

'The table beside the fire, Beth, or would it get uncomfortably hot?'

'It might.' The flames were leaping high and there was a pile of logs ready to go on when necessary.

'The corner one then.' He pulled out a chair for her and, after loosening her coat, she sat down. The man arrived to take their order.

Adrian looked enquiringly at Beth.

'A glass of orange, please.'

'Whisky and bring water.'

'Very good, sir.' He used a cloth to wipe the surface of the table and brought over a glass ashtray which he placed in the middle. Then, with a smile to Beth, he left.

The room fascinated Beth. It was so unusual and could have been a small library in a private house. From floor to ceiling books lined every wall. Most of them were huge volumes and very old. Some had broken spines, others had tattered covers and the lettering was faded and difficult to read. Only a very few looked in good condition.

'Pure show,' Adrian smiled.

'Nice, like being in a library.'

'A reference library. On one occasion Leonard and I had a good look round and we were of the opinion that the lot had been picked up very cheaply at an auction sale hoping it would bring a touch of class to the place.'

'Which it does and full marks to whoever it was.'

Their drinks arrived and the orange set before Beth.

'The young lady was admiring the books.' Adrian smiled lazily, moving his long legs to a more comfortable position.

The man put down the whisky. 'For myself I like a good thriller but there's no accounting for taste, is there? Still it's a talking point and if it keeps the customers happy who is complaining? My old lady wouldn't give them house room, I can tell you.' He went away chuckling.

The small exchange had relaxed Beth and she drank some of her orange. The logs crackled and burned and she thought this was so much nicer than sitting in a hotel.

'Cosy, isn't it?' he said. 'And all to ourselves.'

'You chose well.'

'Oh, I have excellent taste and not only in this.'

She couldn't mistake his meaning. She blushed, and lowered her eyes to hide her confusion.

'Tell me about yourself, Beth,' he said softly.

'There isn't much to tell.' Not so long ago she had been asked the same question. For a moment she remembered Robert and how easy it had been to tell him about herself. That was different, though. Robert was a Parker-Munro

334

he had been sympathetic and understanding and the outpouring had done her a lot of good. Adrian was only being polite. He didn't want her life story just a little about herself.

'For a start, what is your connection with Inverbrae House?'

What a strange question she thought. She must have looked surprised.

'I have to confess I did ask Leonard Watson about you.'

'He hardly knows me.'

'Not the impression I got, most certainly it is not. Poor old Leonard doesn't have much success with girls and I suppose he admires you from afar.' He paused and lifted his glass. 'All he told me, Beth, was that you and the daughter—'

'Caroline.'

'Yes, Caroline, were childhood friends and that you now work for the colonel.'

'You know it all then.'

'Far be it for me to pry.' He was looking across and holding her gaze. 'Beth, you are very lovely but no doubt many have told you that.'

She shook her head. No one who mattered had told her that.

'Leonard called you a lovely girl but that isn't how I would describe you.'

'It isn't?'

'No.' His voice was like a caress. 'To me you are a beautiful young woman who has completely bewitched me. I hope I am not alone in thinking that this is the start of something very special.' Leaning forward he gently touched his lips to hers. 'Tell me it is the same for you, that is what I want to hear.'

Her heart sang. She wanted to shout it from the roof

tops. Yes, Yes, Yes, I feel it and it is wonderful, wonderful. She wanted to tell him that he was the handsomest, most exciting man she had ever met. One day she would but not yet.

'Your shining eyes are answer enough – or at least I am taking that as an encouraging sign.' He had been holding her hands but let them go. 'Drink up your orange and later you must let me introduce you to the delights of something a bit stronger – nothing to go to your head—'

'But more acceptable than orange?' Suddenly she didn't want to drink any more of it.

'Yes, my darling. You are no longer a schoolgirl and I have a great urge no, wrong word, a great wish to introduce you to a whole new world.'

Beth felt thrilled but disappointed too. 'Do I seem so very naïve?'

'A little but I find that utterly charming. My joy and pleasure will come as each day that passes makes you more beautiful and more desirable.'

Beth reached for her glass for another drink and shivered. It wasn't from the cold drink, the shiver had come from a strange new feeling that both alarmed and excited her.

'Your turn now, Adrian,' she said shakily. 'I know nothing about you.'

He shrugged. 'My second home is with the Watsons and I am grateful to them for making me so welcome. My home, or rather my parents' home, is in Stirling.'

'Do you have a large house in Stirling?' she found herself asking.

'Yes. Once it was a house to be proud of,' he began, but she heard the bitterness creep into his voice. 'Sadly it is now in poor condition but since the family fortunes have gone not a lot can be done about it.'

'Perhaps your fortunes will change,' she said gently.

'That is in our nightly prayers,' he said flippantly. 'So you see, my dear Beth, I am poor.'

Beth wondered about the degrees of poverty. She had seen real poverty in the poorer quarters of Dundee and Adrian saying he was poor was just laughable. He couldn't want for much when he drove a car, ordered drinks and spoke of taking her out to dinner.

'You must do something, have some kind of job?'

'If you could call it that,' he said looking at her with amusement. 'I have business interests which require my attention from time to time.'

'Yes, yes,' she nodded but she thought it could hardly be called hard work. Still, that was the way the upper classes lived. Come to think about it, the Watson boys didn't appear to do anything but then again they would be involved in the family business.

'I'm sorry I don't understand these things,' she murmured, anxious to get off the subject.

'Women, particularly beautiful young women, are not expected to. But back to you – tell me, what really is your position at Inverbrae House?'

'I told you. I do clerical work for the estate and meantime I have accommodation in the house.'

'Part of the family?' he asked though he already knew the answer.

'No, not family and not servant. Just something between.'

'Don't you have anyone of your own, Beth?'

'Not here but I do have relatives in Dundee and I visit them occasionally.'

'An independent young woman who can do much as she pleases. No checking up on when you get in at night.' Or even if you get in at all, he added to himself.

'No one checks on me, that is true, but there is no reason why they should. I keep respectable hours and that's the way it stays,' she said firmly.

'I should think so too, I am all for keeping respectable hours but it does mean that there is no need to panic if by chance you were delayed.'

'That's true.'

Adrian ordered another whisky but Beth wanted nothing more. He drank his quickly then glanced at his watch.

'Ah! Time we were getting on our way. I don't want to keep you late on this our first date.' He smiled as he said it then drained his glass.

Beth was relieved that she hadn't had to remind him of the time. He was a real gentleman and she could trust him absolutely.

When they reached the gates of Inverbrae House he switched off the engine and turned to face her.

'Beth, I come and go a lot, I have to.'

'Yes.'

'How do I get in touch with you? What are your hours in that office?'

'Usual office hours, though sometimes I work later.'

'Then I can pop in to see you! Honestly,' he said with his disarming smile, 'I wouldn't keep you off your work, it would just be to make arrangements to meet.'

'No problem, Adrian,' she said eagerly. 'I'm on my own for most of the time so you can come into the office.'

'Or tap at the window and have you come out?'

'If you prefer.'

'Whereabouts in the grounds is this office?'

She told him.

He leaned over and kissed her on the cheek and she thanked him for the evening.

'My pleasure and I hope the first of many.' This time he

gently turned her face towards him and pressed his lips against hers.

Beth felt herself slip into a world of warmth and excitement as he took her into his arms and, unable to stop herself, she put her arms round his neck and returned his kisses.

'I must let you go, my darling,' he said huskily.

She could only nod. Her voice seemed to have deserted her and her eyes were gazing at him adoringly. She got out, still in a daze, and watched him drive away.

Adrian Scott-Hamilton was well satisfied. Beth was very different from his usual women, which made her all the more desirable. He knew how to handle women and Beth was so young and trusting that she was going to be a walkover.

As for Beth, in those following days, she was experiencing first love with all its pain and wonder. And Adrian discovered to his relief that the estate office was well away from the workers' cottages and out of sight of the Big House. He took to calling on her and though she invited him in, he didn't do so, preferring that she came out. The back of the office had the benefit of trees and shrubs and no one was likely to see them.

Chapter Twenty-Four

Smiling warmly, Jenny welcomed her guests and gave a special smile to the new faces. It was a warmish night and none of the men, who were in the majority, wore coats. They were ushered through the hall and into the drawing-room. Food and liquid refreshments, including some of the hard stuff as Jenny called it, were set out in the dining-room which was being used as a buffet. There was the low murmur of voices from those who had just arrived, and were at the polite, not-quite-at-ease stage with strangers. That would change before long as groups with similar interests gathered round to hear and discuss what was happening in their own small world.

A ring at the door and Jenny excused herself and went to answer it.

'David! Lovely to see you,' Jenny said as his lips brushed her cheek.

'Looking lovely as ever, my darling, and I know you won't mind that I have brought a friend with me.'

Jenny turned her attention from the heavily-built, middle-aged man to the younger one who was standing a little apart and clearly not happy at the situation in which he found himself.

'Jenny, this is Peter Nicholson and Peter, your hostess, Mrs Cuthbert.'

They shook hands. 'Peter is a talented artist and already

making a name for himself. Let me add that I almost had to drag him here.'

'Now why was that, Peter?' Jenny looked amused. 'Not many have to be forced to attend.'

'I'm sure they don't, Mrs Cuthbert, but I feel this is an imposition landing on you like this.'

'Nonsense, a new face is always welcome. Next time, I hope you will want to come and not have to be dragged!' She smiled into his face as she ushered them both indoors.

David closed the door behind him, beamed at them both then went ahead to where the laughter and talk was coming. Jenny looked at Peter and they both laughed. 'Like a homing pigeon,' she whispered.

Together they went along the well-lit hall until Peter stopped abruptly.

'How on earth do you come to have that? Where did you get it?'

Jenny was taken aback at the brusqueness of his manner but she saw that he was unaware of it, that genuine amazement had caused it. The look on his face was almost comical.

'If you are referring to the picture it does not belong to me. Why, may I ask, does it interest you so much?'

He went nearer. 'Not easy to make out the signature but I remember I was so shocked to get a sale that when it was pointed out to me that I hadn't signed it, I just scrawled my name.'

Jenny was all smiles. 'Now aren't you just glad you came?'

'Most certainly I am.'

'I've always thought it very good.'

'Thank you. It's not bad,' he said modestly, 'but hopefully I've improved since then.' He paused then turned away from the picture to face Jenny. 'If it isn't yours, would you mind telling me to whom it does belong?'

'A young friend of mine,' Jenny said carefully.

'Would your friend sell it back to me, do you think?'

'I doubt it. Are you very anxious to have it?'

'Only because selling it was the turning point in my life. I was very young and impatient, Mrs Cuthbert, and hope was dying. In fact I had reached the stage when I was agreeing with my parents that this should be kept as a hobby and that it was time I found myself a proper job.'

'Peter, I do understand your wish to have the painting but then again I can understand my friend's wish to keep it.' Her eyes went to the clock. 'Should be any time now if she is coming and if she does, I'll introduce you. Meantime do circulate Peter.'

He smiled and Jenny left him looking at the painting.

Beth had been in two minds as to whether it was worthwhile going to Greystanes since it was so late, but then she decided it was. She didn't want to miss it. She changed quickly into a long-waisted dress in a strawberry shade, pulled a comb through her hair, a touch of colour to her lips, and she was ready.

Miss Harris answered her ring.

'Just about giving you up, Beth,' she smiled as Beth walked in.

'Nearly didn't come, thought it was too late.'

'Just warming up by the sound of it. I'll take your coat and you go right through.'

The door was half open and groups of people, a glass in hand, were engaged in animated conversation. Beth saw Jenny trying to get her attention and went over.

'Hello, dear, and don't you look charming? In fact,' she said, 'I would go as far as saying you look blooming. Is there a special reason for the happiness shining out of your eyes?'

'Oh, Jenny, is it so obvious? I've met the most wonderful man—'

'Tall, dark and handsome, a perfect specimen of manhood and you've fallen very, very badly,' she said softly.

'Yes, I have,' she said just a little put out and Jenny saw it.

'I'm a tease but truly I'm happy for you. But I won't say more until I hear about him and that will have to wait until later. Meantime there is someone here who is very anxious to meet you. A young man, tall, fair and utterly charming.'

Beth looked mystified and Jenny took her by the hand and over to where a young man had moved away from a group to join them.

'Beth, dear, this is Peter – sorry, Peter, I've forgotten your other name.'

'Nicholson, Peter Nicholson.'

'Beth Brown, the young friend of whom I spoke.'

They shook hands.

'Now come along and see what this is all about.' She had them each by the hand like children and led them into the hall. Stopping beside the picture of the harbour at Sandyneuk she let go of them. 'I'm going to leave you, and Beth, when you get over the shock do see that Peter gets some food. I do love the lean, hungry look but it worries me too.'

Peter laughed and his eyes crinkled. 'It used to worry my mother as well but I do eat like a horse, Mrs Cuthbert.'

'Peter isn't going to tell you but I will. I have it from David that he is a very talented artist with a bright future.'

'Spare my blushes, please, and David exaggerates. I've

had a few lucky breaks that's all.'

'Which wouldn't have come your way unless you had that extra special something.' She pointed to the picture. 'Beth, meet the artist in the flesh.' She gave them a mischievous smile and walked away.

'You – you painted it?' Beth said incredulously.

'Guilty, and if you look very closely you will just about make out my signature.'

She nodded and he saw the hint of tears. 'I was with my father when he bought it for me.'

'I know. You were the little dark-eyed girl and long ago though it was, I remember you both very well.'

'He died,' she said quietly. 'Both of my parents are dead.'

'I'm sorry,' he said gently. 'Is this distressing for you?'

'No, it isn't, far from it. It's just that I can't get over it. Please tell me why, after all these years, you should remember us?'

'Because that sale shaped my life. Without it my life would have been very different.'

'In what way?'

'Because I had reached the end and was about to return to my parents' home to admit that they had been right and art should be kept as a hobby.'

'You were going to look for a job that brought in a regular wage?'

'Yes.'

'That would have been such a waste.'

'Thank you.' They smiled, both a little shy and Beth, remembering her instructions said, 'Peter, food, we'd better go and see what is left.'

Miss Harris piled sandwiches on a plate. 'That should start you off.'

'Lovely.' Beth said looking and finding a place apart

from the others. 'This do, Peter?'

'Perfect.' They used a corner of the table for their cups and ate the sandwiches in a companionable silence. Peter broke it. 'Would it upset you to talk about your parents?'

'No, it was a long time ago, I can talk about it now. They went out to India as missionaries and were killed – murdered by the very people they were trying to help. I didn't go with them, they left me behind.'

'And a good thing.'

'Yes.'

He looked shocked, stricken almost. 'That was dreadful, just awful.' He shook his head. 'I feel an almost personal loss. I can't explain it but because your father had a small but important part in my life it somehow makes it so much worse. Are you an only child?'

'Yes. I was looked after and in many ways I was fortunate. Jenny, Mrs Cuthbert, has been marvellous to me.'

'I've just met her but she strikes me as being a good friend to have.'

'She's kind, helpful and completely honest.' She looked up at him. 'Not too many people are, honest I mean, have you noticed that?'

'Well—'

'No, I'm explaining it badly. What I mean is that she would never lie, no matter what it cost her to tell the truth.'

'The truth, the whole truth and nothing but the truth.' He shook his head. 'Not in complete agreement with you there. A white lie can often save a great deal of distress and I'm sure Mrs Cuthbert has told one or two but who is to know?'

She laughed. 'I suppose you are right. Where do you live, Peter?'

'If you mean where do I belong it is in Edinburgh. My parents' home is there as I think I mentioned. I have a younger brother, Alex, and a married sister. Ruby and Norman have a two-year-old boy, a bundle of mischief. Foolishly I agreed to do a portrait of their offspring.' He clapped a hand to his brow. 'The wee monkey couldn't or wouldn't keep still for more than a minute but happily I caught enough of his expression to please his doting parents and grandparents.'

'Are you specialising?'

'Yes and no to that. Portraits are what I want to concentrate on and I've had a few good commissions. Even so, I like to keep my hand in with landscapes and coastal scenes, mostly from around here.'

'You must live nearby.'

'Number five Summer Street.'

'I know it.'

'This is an evening I am going to remember and to think I was reluctant to come.' She blushed under his scrutiny. 'Don't mind me, Beth, when I see a face that interests me, good manners fly out of the window.'

'Why does my face interest you?'

'The bone structure. I see a perfect oval with high cheekbones, delicate features and a warm mouth with its hint of a smile as though from some inner happiness.'

I'm in love, she wanted to tell him. Had he experienced love, did he know what it was like? She could tell him. She only had to think of Adrian and the sun shone on the darkest day.

'One day perhaps you will sit for me?'

'I would like that.'

'Don't be passing Summer Street without coming in to see me or I would feel very hurt.'

'Don't worry. I had no intention of passing. I wanted an

excuse to see you at work and now I don't need one. I'll accept your invitation.'

'Knock and come in, the door is always open.'

'Terribly sorry to break this up, you two. Hello, Beth,' David said as he put on his coat. 'Problem is it is always difficult to tear ourselves away from Greystanes – oh, dear me, have I spoilt something, Peter, were you going to see Beth home?'

'No, he wasn't, I'm staying overnight with Jenny. There is a lot of clearing up to do—'

'Which we shall leave until tomorrow,' Jenny said appearing at their side.

Goodnights were said and Peter's parting words were. 'Don't leave it too long before you come.'

'I won't.'

'What a very nice, charming young man, not all that young, he must be in his late twenties.'

'Yes, he must,' Beth said doing a quick calculation and ignoring Jenny's amused expression. 'He has invited me to see his studio.'

'I hope you accepted.'

'Of course I did, I've never seen an artist at work, not in a studio.'

'Don't you find him attractive? I know I do. Not disgustingly handsome, I do hate very handsome men they are all so sure of themselves—' Then, seeing Beth's face, she began to apologise. 'Why don't I think before I speak? Of course, there are always exceptions to every rule and this young man of yours is one.'

'Yes, he is, Jenny, and he can't help being handsome.'

'Of course he can't. Come along into the kitchen. I've made a fresh pot of tea and we'll have it and a postmortem of the evening. Someone once said that and I thought it apt and amusing.'

348

Beth giggled and took the cup handed to her.

'Is this wonderful young man local?'

'No, his home is in Stirling but he spends a lot of time with friends who live nearby.'

'May I ask his name?'

'Adrian Scott-Hamilton.'

'A very impressive name and what does this Adrian do? Or is he one of the idle rich?'

'He isn't rich, far from it, and he doesn't actually work but he has business interests.' It sounded a bit lame but it was all she could say.

Jenny nodded her head but said nothing. Scott-Hamiltons of Stirling, it shouldn't be difficult to find out about them if she ever thought it necessary.

'I love him, Jenny.'

'And needless to say he loves you?'

'I hope he does. He says he does and he wouldn't say it if it wasn't true. What would be the point? Jenny, he could have any woman and yet he wants me,' she said shakily.

'This is serious then?'

'For me it is. I'll never love anyone the way I love Adrian but I worry sometimes—'

'What about? Do eat up. Have another sandwich and I'll have one as well since I didn't eat much earlier on.'

'I shouldn't, but to please you—' She took one and put it on her plate. 'Jenny, he's so marvellous and sophisticated, what can he see in me?'

'Someone very lovely and completely unaware of her own charms. That must make a change for this sophisticated young man.' She didn't know why, she hadn't met this Adrian but already she disliked him and that wasn't like her.

Beth didn't answer. She hardly heard.

'Darling, you'll be falling asleep in the chair. Off you go

to bed for what is left of the night.'

She got up and yawned. 'Goodnight, Jenny.'

Jenny sat nursing her cup for a while. This Adrian wasn't for Beth but there wasn't much she could do about it and of course she could be wrong and he could be a thoroughly nice young man. Peter, now, had it been Peter – she was very taken with the young artist and if she wasn't very much mistaken, Peter was attracted to Beth.

That first dinner she had with Adrian had been perfect, quite, quite delightful. How handsome he had looked in his dinner jacket and how proud she had been to be with him. Heads had turned to look at him but other heads had turned to look at the handsome young couple being shown to their table. Beth had worn a long black skirt with a lovely pale green chiffon blouse. Jenny had come to her rescue when she complained of having nothing suitable to wear and that she would have to go and buy herself a new gown.

'Nonsense, dear,' she had said. 'That would be an unnecessary extravagance and after two or three times you wouldn't be able to wear it again. Take my tip and buy yourself a couple of long skirts, one of them black. Teamed up with different blouses you will get away with it again and again. Have different necklines too so that you can dress it up with jewellery for a special occasion, and on another go for simplicity and wear no jewellery of any kind.'

It had been good advice and Beth was glad now that she had followed it.

'My darling, you do have very good dress sense,' Adrian remarked. He had said as much on more than one occasion and she had been so pleased.

True to his promise, he had introduced her to various

wines and other drinks, sherry among them. To please him she had tried to like them. Occasionally she failed and made a face and she had expected him to laugh but he hadn't and she had felt miserable. Much as she loved him, she didn't always understand him.

Another niggling worry was the amount Adrian drank. Admittedly it didn't seem to affect his driving but she was beginning to have to fight him off when he would pass beyond kissing and go too far for her liking. No, that wasn't true and that was the worry. Still Adrian always took no for an answer and was most apologetic afterwards.

'Sorry, my darling, but it gets harder and harder to resist you.'

'I'm sorry, Adrian, it's difficult for me too. I do love you but I would never give myself before marriage and deep down you wouldn't want me to.'

He had almost choked keeping in the laughter. Did the silly girl really think that marriage was on the cards? But she must. He would break down her resistance when the time was right. Strangely enough, he was enjoying the situation, finding it a novelty. Not many resisted his charms; most of them were only too happy to oblige. Good God! he wasn't in love with the girl, was he? He couldn't afford to be but on the other hand he had no intention of letting her go. He had to marry money and that couldn't be put off much longer.

Why Peter Nicholson should come into her thoughts this particular morning Beth had no idea but suddenly she wanted to visit Summer Street and this very evening, she decided, she would go and surprise him.

It was only a fifteen-minute walk from Inverbrae House or a short bus run. She arrived at the stop with minutes to spare but since no one was waiting there was a good chance that the bus had gone before its scheduled time. She didn't mind too much since it was pleasantly cool and dry and her feet were in flat-heeled shoes.

Perhaps he wasn't at home or too busy to welcome a visitor – these were her thoughts as she knocked at the door. She didn't like to open it and walk in. Beth knocked again and was on the point of leaving, feeling more disappointed than was reasonable, when the door was thrown open. A startled but clearly delighted Peter stood there and Beth couldn't but think of the contrast between the artist and her Adrian. Even in casual clothes, Adrian always managed to look immaculate. But now Beth had a sudden urge to giggle. Peter wore a pair of paint-stained baggy flannels and a loose cotton jacket with huge pockets. A rag protruded from one pocket and Beth thought he had used it to wipe his hands before answering the door. The jacket had started life as charcoal grey but now sported cheerful streaks and blobs of various colours. The thick blond hair had fallen over his forehead and Beth had a silly wish to push it back.

'Beth! by all that's wonderful, I'd all but given you up. Come in! Come in!'

What a lovely welcome! Beth was smiling as he closed the door then led her along a narrow corridor and into a room that had a coal fire burning in the grate.

'This is where I eat and sleep and through there' – the rooms were connected by a door which was open – 'is where I work.'

'Have I interrupted something, Peter? I don't know but I imagine artists don't like to be disturbed when they are working.'

'Depends,' he grinned. 'Go on, take off your jacket and

352

put it over a chair or on the bed. You are staying for a while?'

'I'd like to.' She took off her jacket and he was about to take it then drew back.

'Better not, can't guarantee that my hands are paint free.'

Beth put it on the back of a chair and began to look about her.

'This is nice, Peter, cosy too.'

'Suits me.' He smiled. 'I don't have far to walk for anything.'

There was a table and two chairs tucked under it. A single bed was against the wall and a woven bedcover kept it looking tidy. Two shabby but comfortable-looking armchairs were at either side of the fireplace which had a fender and a brass stand. Hanging on the stand were a poker and a pair of tongs. Small rugs covered most of the linoleum but what surprised her was the total absence of pictures. There were plenty of picture hooks but no pictures.

Peter must have anticipated the question. 'The craft shop took the lot. Most of them were small and of local scenes.'

'To display and sell?'

He smiled. 'Apparently they do bring people into the shop. Not necessarily to buy a painting, more to browse. Then they end up buying some ornament.'

'That doesn't tie up with what Jenny said. She says your paintings are much in demand.'

'Can't grumble,' he said, walking away and into the other room. Beth felt honoured to be invited into Peter's world and it *was* like stepping into another universe. The room, a twin of the other, was a happy, friendly clutter of artist's tools, canvases, paints and brushes. Paintings were stacked against the walls, some awaiting frames and a few unfinished and sad, looking as though the painter had lost interest and withdrawn from them disheartened. Perhaps he hadn't quite captured what he had seen with the eye.

She went over to the easel to see what Peter had been working on when he'd had to leave it to answer the door. There was enough done for Beth to call out delightedly, 'Peter, the white house—'

'Good! You recognised it?'

'Of course. It brings my childhood back. I used to worry myself sick that it would topple and end up in the sea and it took my father to show me the house before I was convinced it was safe.'

'What an imaginative child you must have been. It's the angle, of course.'

'Is it commissioned or are you just doing it because it appeals to you?'

'Only because it appeals. To live in such a house is an artist's dream. Can you imagine, Beth, the sheer delight of getting up each morning and looking out at a different scene. The sea is forever changing— Oh, listen to me going on and not remembering to offer hospitality. Sadly there isn't much to offer, just tea and biscuits. Tomorrow is my day for stocking up and I'm afraid even the coffee jar is empty.'

'I don't need anything.'

'Tea and biscuits, you must.'

'All right. Let me help.'

'Never refuse help.' The scullery was smaller than her Aunt Anne's, she thought, and remarkably tidy. It had an uncurtained window with a white sink under it. There was a geyser that gave hot water and a cooker crowded one corner. Shelves covered the remaining spaces.

'Very compact.'

'Tight fit for two but not of our build.' He filled the kettle, got down a biscuit tin and a plate and put them down on the board beside the sink. 'You see to that and if you're lucky you'll find two cups and saucers that match.'

'A nearly match, Peter,' she said as she leaned over to get them from the shelf. 'One odd saucer.'

The gas was turned fully up and before long Peter had the tea made. Beth was amazed at how comfortable they were. It was as though they had known each other all their lives and even when they bumped into each other there was no awkwardness. Beside the fire, dunking ginger snaps, they talked of everything that came to mind.

'Beth?'

She looked up and studied his face. Not a handsome face, the features were irregular and the face rather long but it was an interesting face, full of character and something else was there – kindness. It was in the eyes, a caring person. He would be attractive to women, some would want to mother him. 'Beth, I can squeeze another cup or make fresh?'

'No, no thank you, Peter. That was lovely but I must go.'

'Must you?'

'I'm afraid so, I have a bus to catch and I don't want to be late.'

He didn't argue. 'I'll see you on the bus but before you go would you do me the honour of having dinner with me? Any evening that suits you.'

'Peter,' she said getting up for her jacket, 'it is very kind of you but I'm afraid I can't—'

'There is someone and he would object?'

'Yes. You do understand?'

He nodded. 'Someone very special?'

Her face softened. 'Very, very special.'

355

'Lucky fellow, I hope he appreciates his good fortune but I'm sure he does. Sorry I haven't time to change but a mac and the darkness will cover my shabbiness.' He took her hand and, with a show of olde worlde charm, kissed it. 'Thank you for coming.'

'I've really enjoyed it.'

'Then you'll come again?'

'If you want me to?'

'I do. Beth, we are friends and I want you to promise me that if you should need help in any form you will come to me. I do mean it, Beth.'

'I know you do and thank you.' She wondered what had made him say that but it was nice to have Peter for a friend.

In the end there was a rush to catch the bus and no time for further talk.

Going back, Peter was thoughtful and strangely depressed. Mrs Cuthbert, or Jenny as she had become, didn't believe that this Adrian Scott-Hamilton had serious intentions and was afraid that Beth was going to be badly hurt. He hadn't asked how she knew and in all likelihood she wouldn't have divulged that information but she would have her own method of finding out what she wanted.

Peter wasn't a violent person, quite the opposite, but he knew he would cheerfully strangle the person who brought unhappiness to Beth. In her short life she had had more than her share.

Chapter Twenty-Five

When she was with Peter everything was so easy, Beth thought, but then that was because they were friends. With him she could be herself and not give a thought to her appearance. He certainly didn't give a thought to his, though he could dress smartly when the occasion demanded.

Refusing Peter's invitation to dinner hadn't been easy. She had wanted to accept because he was such fun and they seemed to have so much to say to each other. But she was right to refuse, she had done the right thing.

Adrian was waiting in the car at the usual place. He always arrived punctually and so did she and that meant that the car was never parked for any length of time beside Inverbrae House. Beth saw no need for this, no need for secrecy, and wondered at Adrian thinking there was. He said it was for her sake, and he said it so firmly that she hadn't pursued the matter.

When it was to be a dress affair Adrian always told her, even suggesting what she should wear. She didn't mind, welcomed it really, and it saved any unfortunate mistakes.

She missed him dreadfully when he was home in Stirling and lived for that tap on the office window, the signal for her to rush out to the back of the premises and for a few precious moments be in his arms.

Dinner this evening was to be at a small hotel, somewhere new where they hadn't been before. Beth was spending more than she wanted to on clothes but she had to be smart for Adrian. The latest buy was a navy blue fine-knitted suit with brass buttons and to complete the outfit she wore navy court shoes and a navy handbag.

'Very nice,' he said approvingly then seeing she was settled and the door shut he moved off. 'How did you spend your time when I wasn't here?'

He often asked that and expected the usual answer that she had done nothing much.

'Nothing much apart from going to see a friend of mine.'

'Male or female?' he smiled.

'Peter is an artist. We met in a friend's house and strangely enough he met my father—'

'Old, getting on a bit, nothing for me to be worried about,' he smiled.

'Late twenties,' she said and then added mischievously, 'He's talented and charming and one day I think he may well become famous.'

'What were you doing with – this artist?'

'What's that supposed to mean? What would I be doing with him?' she said angrily.

'That is what I am asking you. I understood that you were my—'

'Of course I am yours. I belong to you, Adrian, but there is such a thing as trust.'

'I'm sorry, Beth,' he said softly, 'I can't bear to think of you with someone else, that is all. Forgiven?'

'Adrian, of course you are forgiven, if there is anything to forgive and you have nothing to fear. I love you and only you.'

'Thank you, darling, I shouldn't want anything to spoil this evening.'

They arrived at the Grange Hotel. It was a small, rather shabby hotel but according to Adrian it had a good reputation for food and offered a fine selection of wines. Adrian always took a long time over the choosing of a wine and had been known, to Beth's embarrassment, to have tasted one and sent it back.

Beth had her usual sherry before the meal and allowed her wine glass to be topped up more than once. It pleased Adrian and it was a small price to pay. A sweeter wine and she might have liked it but Adrian preferred a dry wine and he was the expert.

The dining-room was warm and getting warmer. A number of people were dining though no one known to them. Beth began to feel pleasantly drowsy, not enough to want to sleep, just to lean back in the chair and let the murmur of voices drift by.

'More coffee?' The waitress was over with the coffee pot.

'Beth?'

Beth roused herself. 'No, thank you.' The waitress went away and Adrian excused himself. She didn't think anything of it, for in a short time she too would be asking to be excused. The minutes ticked away. Surely this was a very long time? Perhaps he was unwell but, if she asked someone to find out and he suddenly appeared, she would feel all kinds of a fool. Just as she was seriously thinking of asking a waiter Adrian appeared and was looking very apologetic.

'Sorry, darling. Did you think I'd got lost or something?'

'I did. Another few minutes and I was to ask the waiter to check and see if you were all right.'

'Good God! You wouldn't have done that, surely?'

'What else was there for me to do?'

'True. The truth is, Beth, that something very unfortunate has happened.'

She looked startled. 'What?'

'You remember the car was playing up on the way here?'

She didn't, everything had seemed normal to her but obviously something had been wrong. 'Yes, I think so.'

'No use explaining to you the mechanical fault that has developed but—'

'You mean you can't drive, something's broken?'

'Yes.'

'Can't you get a mechanic to see to it?'

'At this time of night?'

No, she supposed not. 'Then someone will have to drive us back.' She did feel light-headed but her brain was still functioning and better than Adrian's by the sound of it.

'That's what I was taking so long about. No one is available but not to worry, we can stay here overnight and a mechanic will look at the car first thing in the morning and you'll be in the office at your usual time. Should you be a little later no one will bother?'

'No.' It was true she wouldn't be missed, not for a while.

'You're tired?' He sounded concerned.

'I am a bit.' She saw that he had keys in his hand, not his car keys, she would have recognised them by the lucky charm on the ring. They went upstairs and he opened a door.

'Is this yours or mine?'

He didn't answer and she followed him in. It was a large room and nicely furnished but all Beth saw was the double bed.

'Plenty of room for you,' she said with an attempt at humour but really she was dreadfully tired. She yawned. 'I didn't get much sleep last night and I am hopeless without sleep. Do you mind if I go to my bedroom now?'

'This is the only room available.'

'The only room available,' she said stupidly.

'Afraid so.'

'What happens now?'

'What do you think?' He was smiling.

The lightheadness was beginning to go. She didn't know why, but she was suddenly very frightened. Was this a trick? No, it wasn't, Adrian wouldn't do this to her or would he? She swung round to face him. 'You did try, didn't you?'

He looked hurt. 'Darling, don't you trust me?'

'I – I don't know, I think so but I am not going to sleep with you. I'm not sharing this room.'

'Not even if I sleep in the chair?'

Beth thought about that. Where was the harm? Then she pictured it. Adrian in the chair and she in the double bed. What if – no she couldn't risk it, there had to be another way. She would go to the desk and ask, the hotel didn't seem busy.

'I'm sure there must be a spare room, I'm not fussy just provided it has a bed and I'll make do with anything.'

He turned away to hide the scowl. Worth one more try.

'Beth, look at me.'

She did.

'You love me don't you?'

'Yes, you know that but—'

'And I love you very, very much. I want you and I think if you are honest with yourself you want me. Beth,' she could feel his breath on her face, 'when two people love each other the way we do it can't be wrong.'

'I'm sorry, Adrian, I think it wrong and I won't change my mind.'

'If you won't then come on and I'll drive you home.'

She stared. 'This was all – the car isn't—'

'If I tell you I'm deeply ashamed would you believe me?'

'Yes, I suppose so, Adrian, but why – why go to all this—' She looked at him helplessly.

'I need you Beth, and now I've spoilt everything.'

He did look genuinely upset and in a way he was paying her a compliment.

'No, we'll just forget all about it.' She went to him and put her arms round his neck. After a moment he put her aside.

'If you want home we'd better be on our way.'

'Yes.' She thought about the room, would he have to pay for it? 'Adrian, what about—'

'The room? Since I've booked it it'll have to be paid. I'll come back and sleep in my lonely bed and think of you in yours.'

She giggled. 'Adrian, you're hopeless.'

Yes, I am, he thought. It would have taken time but he could have seduced her. Why hadn't he? He couldn't understand himself.

It didn't come as a surprise, she had expected it since Adrian was such a regular visitor of the Watsons but it upset Beth more than she was prepared to admit. She wondered what would have happened if the invitation to Caroline's birthday ball had included a partner but it hadn't.

'A shortage of young males that's why I was included in the invitation,' Adrian said. 'Unfortunately I was not in a position to suggest I bring you.'

'I know that and you can tell me all about it.'

'Won't be much to tell. You don't expect me to describe the gowns, do you?'

'Not in detail.'

Alone in her room on the evening of the ball, Beth tried not to imagine the scene but it kept coming before her eyes. The dimmed lights, the haunting music of the waltz, the lovely gowns and beautiful women all eager for Adrian's arms to hold them as they danced the evening away.

Trying desperately to sound off-hand, Beth had asked Adrian if he had enjoyed himself.

'How could I not, since nothing was spared to make the evening a success? With you there, darling, it would have been quite, quite perfect.'

She smiled into his eyes. 'Did Caroline look very lovely?'

'Yes, very nice, pretty little thing but far too excitable for my liking. You aren't, you cannot be jealous?' One eyebrow lifted in that special way he had.

'I don't want to be but I am,' she said with complete honesty.

'Foolish girl, you have no need. Not one woman there could hold a candle to you. Satisfied now?'

She nodded feeling the tears sting the back of her eyes. He was a dear and those were the words she had wanted to hear. Where they were, behind the office and in the shelter of the trees, she fell into his arms. Adrian loved her and if he was slow to mention marriage then he must have his reasons and she would be content to wait. He would propose in his own time.

'Darling, I have to go away,' he murmured, nibbling at her ear.

'Oh, no, not again,' she said moving back to look into

his face. 'I've hardly seen you,' she whispered.

'The Watsons will be getting sick and tired of me and I must go home. I have things to see to, you know.' She thought she detected the faintest touch of irritability in his voice.

She couldn't hide her misery. 'Sorry, I know I'm being unreasonable but I'm lost without you.'

'Nonsense. You've managed before. Just be a good girl and I promise to come back as soon as possible.' He took out his cigarettes, put one in his mouth and lit it with a gold cigarette lighter.

Beth was completely under his spell, he thought smugly. Adrian enjoyed his power over women but only a very few earned his respect. Beth was one. A wife with money was essential and he needed Beth. Having both would take a little arranging but it could be done.

It was only very rarely that Beth and Caroline set eyes on one another and when they did there was a slight awkwardness. To Beth's knowledge, Caroline had never set foot in the office so it came as a surprise when, two days after her birthday, she tapped at the door and entered.

'Hello!' Beth said startled.

'Not bad in here,' Caroline said glancing around.

'I've added the homely touches. Have a seat.'

'Haven't time, Beth, just popped in to thank you for the gift.'

'That's all right, did you like it?'

Caroline looked vague. 'Ye – es, I got so many—'

'It was a small ornament for your dressing table.'

'So it was, I remember now, sweet little thing.'

'Did everything go well?'

'Everything was absolutely perfect, it couldn't have been better.' She did sit down. 'My gown was heavenly, everyone said so and told me that I was looking lovely. One person,' she blushed, 'said I looked enchanting.'

'What colour was your gown?'

'Peach, my favourite colour.'

'Yes, I remember.'

'Wish you had been there to see me.' Her eyes grew dreamy. 'It was the most wonderful night of my life, Beth, and I'll just whisper it.' She dropped her voice and gave a small giggle. 'Someone very, very special was there.'

'Caroline, you've fallen in love?'

'I have and don't you dare laugh, it happened the moment I saw him and this is absolutely true, Beth, he said it had been the same for him. I don't expect you to understand—'

'I think I can, Caroline,' Beth said softly. 'It's—'

'Magic?'

'Yes, that is it exactly.'

They were laughing together like they once had. Caroline got quickly to her feet. 'There is so much going on, so much excitement, that I don't know whether I'm coming or going. Robert leaves for London tonight, then it is Paris and dear knows where after that. Grandmama is quite pleased to have him travel and see places of interest just so long as he spends some time with us before he goes back to Australia.' She walked to the door. 'Must go and let you get on with whatever you are supposed to be doing. 'Bye.'

'Goodbye, Caroline, thanks for calling.'

The days went in, empty days that seemed endless and the nights when she couldn't sleep were worse. Each morning she looked for a letter and each morning she was disappointed. Adrian knew when her birthday was, it had come up in conversation, but would he remember?

The morning of her eighteenth birthday came and she

wondered if anyone would remember. Not many knew the date. Aunt Anne wasn't one for remembering birthdays. There was only one gift she longed for or even a card, just something to show that Adrian hadn't forgotten her.

Mrs Murdoch fetched the letters and any for Beth were put on a table. Today there were three. Three small packets addressed to Beth. Two had come by post. The one without a stamp was in Caroline's writing, the other from Jenny. The third one had her heart racing, the postmark was smudged but she didn't need to examine it, it could only be from Adrian.

Shaking with excitement she took the packages to her room. Adrian's she would keep until last. She fingered it lovingly then put it aside. Caroline's gift was a pretty string of beads and Jenny's a bottle of perfume, a heavenly choice. Adrian liked a whiff of expensive perfume. Now to open his gift – carefully she undid the wrapping and then tissue paper and she was looking at a slim box. Opening it she found a lovely silver bracelet. She slipped it on and her eyes were shining. There was a card and she turned it over and read the words. To Beth on her eighteenth birthday with my very best wishes. Perhaps we'll meet again when I return from my travels – Robert.

How long did she stand there? From the heights to the depths. She wondered how she was going to cope with the disappointment. Fancy Robert remembering? How very very kind of him but if only – if only – it had been from Adrian.

He came when she had all but given up. The small tap on the window had her on her feet and running out to fling herself into his arms. In her joy at seeing him she gave no thought to them being seen. Someone had, however someone who was too shocked to move as she stared at the couple locked in each other's arms. For several disbelieving moments she stared at them and then, her feet making no noise on the grass, she ran towards Inverbrae House. Once there she was panting for breath and had to lie down until she could breathe normally.

When he left Beth, Adrian was whistling happily. He went out and returned by a different entrance. One had to be careful. He had been back living with the Watsons for a week, much of it spent in Caroline's company. Everything was going well and according to plan. The girl was besotted with him, he thought smugly. The old woman, bless her heart, was completely won over and the colonel had accepted him. And why not? The Scott-Hamiltons were county, their name much respected by all but those who had suffered financially, their bills unpaid and likely to remain that way. Adrian smiled grimly. Gambling was a mug's game and not a weakness of his but it had been the ruin of his family.

It was no crime for the gentry to be in debt but it made living conditions difficult. A skeleton staff was all they could afford and only a wing of Bankhead House was used. The thought disgusted him as he compared it to the lavish living at Inverbrae House.

He had missed Beth, missed her more than he would have believed possible but Caroline was the catch. If he played his cards right he could have marriage to Caroline and Beth as the love of his life.

Chapter Twenty-Six

Her face a frozen mask of fury and her hands clenching and unclenching, Caroline barged into the office.

'How dare you, Beth Brown! How dare you embarrass Adrian with your unwanted attention. He was disgusted and so am I.' She almost spat the words.

Sheer disbelief held Beth silent and she could only stare at Caroline.

'You stupid, stupid creature. To think you had a chance with Adrian! Did you really believe he would have anything to do with the likes of you, a nobody? Adrian happens to come from a good family and is a perfect gentleman.'

Beth was pale and shocked but she had found her voice.

'It is simply not true to suggest that I—'

Caroline cut her off. 'Useless to deny it. I saw you with my own eyes.'

'Saw what?'

'You tearing out of the office and throwing yourself at Adrian.' Her lips curled.

Beth was about to hotly deny it when she remembered that it was partly true. She had rushed out to see Adrian, she had been so happy to see him. But surely it couldn't be true what Caroline was saying? Surely the arms that held her were willing arms? Desperately she searched for some explanation. Adrian wouldn't do this to her? He wouldn't, he couldn't, not after – not after— After what? she asked herself dully. The endearments, his kisses, how much had they meant to him? Nothing if what Caroline said was true.

'Caroline, it wasn't quite what it appeared to be,' Beth said unsteadily.

'Adrian had just come back and—'

She gave a self satisfied smirk. 'For your information, Adrian has been back in Sandyneuk for the last seven days—'

'But that is impossible, he couldn't have, he told me—'

'Of course he did. To be rid of you was worth a white lie,' Caroline said smugly. She had relaxed a little but her eyes were hard. 'Adrian came with the Watsons to my birthday ball and hardly left my side all night.'

Caroline was telling the truth, Beth was sure of that now. Adrian had been amusing himself with her and she had been fool enough to read more into it. Her face burned at the thought but she wasn't alone in being taken in. Adrian wasn't in love with Caroline, had she been a nobody he would not have spared her a second glance.

Beth was sickened and shattered at her own naïvety but she was the lucky one. Her eyes were opened and she was seeing Adrian for what he was. She was probably setting herself an impossible task but she must try to warn Caroline.

'Caroline?'

'Yes?' she said haughtily. 'If this is a belated apology you can save your breath.'

'It is far from an apology. The fact is, Caroline, Adrian has made a fool of me and yes I am humiliated and hurt but I'll recover. We have both been taken in by a handsome face and a great deal of charm.'

'So that is it! You just can't accept that Adrian is in love with me because you want him for yourself. This time, you have gone too far.' Her pale blue eyes showed outrage and her face hardened. 'Daddy isn't here but in his absence I am ordering you out of Inverbrae House and what is more I wish never to see you or speak to you again.'

Beth gave her a long, steady look. Then she got up from her chair where she had been sitting all this time while Caroline stood. Without hurrying herself, she took her coat from the coat-stand, put it on, fastened the buttons, drew the belt round her slim waist and buckled it. That done she collected her handbag and made to walk to the door.

'Where do you think you are going?'

'Obeying instructions – yours.'

'I said to remove yourself from Inverbrae House. No doubt daddy will terminate your employment as soon as he gets a replacement.'

'As far as I am concerned the job and the accommodation go together,' Beth said quietly. She touched the keys. 'I'll leave them with you.' She turned the knob. 'Goodbye, Caroline. Perhaps the day will come when you wished you had taken my warning seriously.'

She left Caroline looking uncertain and a little afraid.

Somehow Beth got herself to her bedroom at Inverbrae House, though she had no recollection of what she did after leaving the office. Throwing her coat on to a chair, seeing it falling off and doing nothing about it, Beth sat down, put her hands over her face and tried to think. Her whole world had collapsed, lay in ruins at her feet and how was she ever to pick up the pieces? Did one get extra strength at a time like this? She tried to picture life without Adrian and couldn't. For so long she had just lived for the times they were together but that was over. She let out a shuddering breath. This couldn't be happening to her! She must be dreaming? But it was no dream.

How could he be so cruel? And it was the spark of anger, faint though it was, that gave her the courage to go on. She had been in deep despair before and had come through it. Now she was older and it should be easier to hide her hurt and humiliation. Only it wasn't.

Other more pressing worries were surfacing in her mind. What am I to do? she thought in panic. She had no home, she had no job. The luxury of grieving over Adrian would have to take a back seat while she thought of her position.

Jenny was always there and she was tempted to phone only she wouldn't. The time had come for her to stand on her own two feet. It was then that she remembered Anna Martin though, after all this time, it was very unlikely that the writer would still be seeking a typist.

Once, out of curiosity, she had gone to see Lilac Lodge and found it to be an attractive house and bigger than she had expected.

No time like the present – she would go now. Beth walked to the bus stop and after a few minutes a bus came along. She got off at the foot of the brae, went along to the house and up to the door. Taking a deep breath she tugged at the bell-pull. She heard footsteps and the door opened. The woman was tall and thin with a pleasant face free of make-up and she wore her short grey hair with a fringe. Round her neck was a double string of wooden beads and Beth thought she looked charmingly Bohemian. Her long shapeless garment was in silver grey and over it was a loose black cardigan.

'Are you Miss Anna Martin?' Beth asked.

'I am.'

'I'm Beth Brown, Miss Martin. Perhaps Mrs Cuthbert, Mrs Jenny Cuthbert, mentioned my name?'

'Not that I recall.'

'Oh!' Beth swallowed and wondered what to say next. 'I – I do typing and I'm looking for a position but perhaps you don't require anyone,' she said in a defeated voice.

'That all depends but we'll talk better indoors. Do come in.'

Beth entered a modest hall, square-shaped, with a polished wood floor on which were two fringed rugs. Against one wall stood a grandfather clock and in a corner was a coat-stand with an umbrella, a collection of walking sticks, and an ancient raincoat hanging on one of the pegs. A stairway curved upwards, and to the right was a room, quite large, with a bow-window. There was an Adam fireplace and the fire was set ready to light with curled up paper, sticks, and a few pieces of coal. A gas fire stood in front of it and Miss Martin lit it.

'Instant heat and so handy to take the chill off the room.' Beth was standing. 'Please sit down.' She gestured to an armchair.

'Thank you.'

A cat was curled up in another chair and Miss Martin lifted it and sat there herself. With a look of outrage at having been disturbed the cat padded round the chair, then jumped up on its mistress's knees and curled up into a ball.

Beth laughed.

'Likes his home comforts but then don't we all?' Her hand gently smoothed the fur. 'My apologies, my dear. Thinking about it, I do seem to remember Jenny mentioning a young friend who might be interested in typing my manuscripts. I don't think she mentioned your name and, of course, it was a long time ago.'

'Yes, and you must have engaged someone by now.'

'Yes and no to that. My typing is done by an agency that charges the earth and refuses to have the mistakes corrected unless they receive further payment. I am not mean but I hate to feel I have been cheated.'

'Miss Martin, I'll be honest, until this afternoon I did clerical work including a lot of typing for Colonel Parker-Munro—'

'Ah!' A look of understanding crossed her face. 'I see the connection with Jenny but do go on.'

'I had a disagreement with his daughter, an unpleasant scene and because of that I am without a job and with nowhere to live.'

'Jobless and homeless, you poor thing.'

Beth had believed herself to be in control but without warning she gave a gulp and the tears began to flow. 'I'm so – so very, very sorry—' she sobbed, 'I can't help it but I'll be all right in a minute.'

Anna Martin touched her arm gently. 'The kindest thing I can do is leave you alone. Cry your heart out, my dear, you'll feel the better of it. I'll go and put the kettle on – come on, puss.'

'No, please—'

'My usual time for having a cup of tea and making two cups is as easy as making one.'

Beth was feeling all kinds of a fool. Why did she let herself get so upset? Heaven knows, she had plenty of practice of getting hurt and humiliated. She should be used to it. It wasn't Adrian's shameful behaviour but the look on Caroline's face that stuck with her. The look had been one of hatred.

She was composed and shamefaced when Anna Martin came in with a tray. On it was a teapot, two white china cups and saucers, sugar and milk and, on a plate, slices of Madeira cake.

'Very plain fare with me, I'm afraid.'

'Miss Martin—' Beth bit her lip.

'No apologies, my dear, it's totally unnecessary. A good weep is like a refreshing shower of rain. Just tell me, are you feeling better?'

'Yes, I am, much better, thank you.'

'Good! You owe me no explanation, we shall talk of other things such as your reason for coming here. You have secretarial skills and let me point out that those will be wasted here—' she put up her hand as Beth made to interrupt. 'Let me acquaint you with my requirements. First I need someone to type my manuscripts and my writing has been described as atrocious. It isn't, of course, and I'm sure you would master it in no time. Like most writers I make a great many changes but again you will get used to that.'

'May I ask what you write, Miss Martin?'

'Obviously you are not a fan of mine,' she sighed, then laughed as Beth looked uncomfortable. 'I am a historian with a great love of the past and do a lot of research into the lives of people who have shaped this country of ours. My following is small but genuinely interested and I ask no more. Fortunately my parents left me this house and enough for its upkeep. If not I would have been unable to indulge in what I find to be a fascinating hobby.' She paused to take a drink of the tea and to insist that Beth take another piece of Madeira cake.

'Thank you, it is very good.'

'Now where was I? Oh, yes, from time to time you

would be required to do some research for me and that would mean a trip to town and a lengthy spell in the library. The staff are helpful.'

'I would enjoy that.'

She smiled. 'Should you wish to remain in town to do shopping or whatever feel free to do so. No set hours here Miss—'

'Brown, Beth Brown.'

'You are much too young and pretty to be Miss anything – how old are you?'

'I've just turned eighteen.'

'Neither child nor woman, a difficult age but in your case I'd say a mature eighteen. Life hasn't always been kind to you, my dear, that much I have gathered. It is obvious, really, when you are looking for a home. You never know but this could be the turning point in your life I hope so.'

'I hope so too, Miss Martin,' Beth said quietly.

'More tea?'

'No, thank you.'

Miss Martin took the cup from Beth and put it on the tray. 'I shall call you Beth, a pretty name. Is it short for Elizabeth?'

'Yes.'

'Provided the work is done, Beth, you can do it when it suits you. By the way, can you cook?'

'Just about,' Beth smiled. She was blessing Aunt Anne for having taught her.

'Just about should do it. I eat when I feel like it, have no set meal times and I cook to suit myself. You must do the same. A Mrs McLeod comes in to do the housework and the laundry, sheets and towels – your personal laundry you would see to yourself. Am I making sense?'

'Yes.'

'My thoughts take off and I'm inclined to wander but you'll get used to my peculiar little ways.' She glanced round her. 'This is my sitting-room or the parlour as it was called in my parents' day. Mrs McLeod is very thorough and cannot bear to see anything out of place which is why she is on pain of death to enter my sanctuary. Come along and I'll show it to you.' They crossed the hall and Beth tried to hide her surprise when the door was opened. It was quite large, the ceilings were high, and a very large desk dominated the room. Two of its drawers were pulled out and papers were strewn over the floor. On the desk were books, many of them open and pages and pages of handwritten notes. A child's mug held a quantity of sharpened pencils and beside it was a pencil sharpener. There was a glass ashtray half filled with cigarette stubs. 'I only smoke when I am waiting for inspiration so you'll be able to tell from the state of the ashtray whether or not I am having a good day.'

Beth looked at the stubs and laughed. 'Not too good?'

Miss Martin laughed ruefully. 'As you say, not too good. Incidentally, let me make this point, believe it or not I can straightaway put my hand on what I want.' She waited a moment or two. 'We'll now go to the back of the house where you would be working. The reason for you being so far away is because the constant tapping of the typewriter keys would drive me mad.'

This room had flowery curtains at the window and the view was of a well-kept garden. There was a desk, a filing cabinet and a covered typewriter sitting on the table.

'That's a Royal. Is that the make you are used to?'

'No, but it is very similar.'

'Now to where you would sleep. Oh, by the way there are gas fires in all the rooms to save work but I've kept the fireplaces and occasionally I have a coal fire in my sitting-room. To work well one must be comfortably warm, Beth, and I don't grudge heat. What I do object to is waste and by that I mean a fire on and no one in the room.'

'I would be very careful.'

The bedroom was small with a single bed, a wardrobe, and a dressing-table. There were two chairs, one with arms and both had cushions. The curtains and bedcover were matching in a pleasing pattern of yellows and blues.

'Suit you?'

'Perfectly,' Beth said beginning to feel excited at the prospect of working and living here.

They went into the room next to the bedroom. It was larger and was furnished as a sitting-room. 'When I was a young girl these two rooms were mine. No doubt you will have a few possessions of your own, Beth, so please change things around to suit yourself. If this is to be your home you must feel comfortable in your surroundings.'

'You are very kind.'

'Method in my madness. If I can leave everything to you, the payment of accounts and all the day-to-day trivia, I shall be free to concentrate on my own work.'

Beth followed the flowing skirt down the carpeted stairs. 'There is a bathroom upstairs and a cloakroom with a toilet and wash-hand basin downstairs. The kitchen,' she waved vaguely in its direction, 'is your average kitchen with a fairly new cooker which works very well.' They were downstairs and back in Miss Martin's sitting-room.

'What do you think?'

'Am I being offered the job?'

'Would I have shown you over my home otherwise? Of course I am offering you the job.'

'Thank you very, very much and I accept.' Beth's eyes were shining.

'Sit down and tell me when you can start.'

'Now if you want.'

Miss Martin raised her eyebrows. 'You do need to give notice to your employer.'

'His daughter told me to leave the house at once and since job and accommodation go together—'

'Now, my dear, don't be hasty, a very common fault of the young. The daughter would have no authority over your employment. You must give notice to your employer—'

Beth looked stubborn. 'I was told to go so I wouldn't think that necessary.'

'Nevertheless it is. Don't put yourself in the wrong, Beth. Only your employer can dispense with your services and not his daughter.'

'In that case, Miss Martin, it would be one week since I am paid weekly.'

'A week will pass very quickly. You must first arrange for your belongings to be brought here.'

'When should I do that?'

'Would you like to move in now?'

'Yes, please, and I am really very grateful. Tommy, he's the chauffeur, he would help me. I'm friendly with him.'

She shook her head. 'Not a good idea, it could get this Tommy into trouble. I have someone who sees to transport when I require it. How long would it take you to pack?'

'Not long.'

'What about cases?'

'I have two.'

'Harry can take an extra case or boxes. Excuse me and I'll see when he could be available.'

'Miss Martin, it would have to be the side entrance.' Beth was becoming more bewildered by the minute at the speed of events.

'All this speed is alarming you but I am someone who likes to get things done immediately then I can forget about them.'

'I am only too happy to have you take over because frankly I'm in a daze.'

Miss Martin went away and came back five minutes later. 'All arranged. I've just remembered one important omission – we haven't discussed salary.'

'I wouldn't expect much, not with living here.'

'May I ask what your present salary is?'

Beth told her.

'Including board and lodgings?'

'Yes.'

'Well, Beth, I'll match the salary but you will have to buy in your own food and cook it so you will be worse off.'

'I shouldn't mind that. In fact I'm going to enjoy doing something for myself.'

Anna Martin smiled. 'As I said all arranged. Harry is to be at the side entrance to Inverbrae House at seven o'clock.'

'In a minute I am going to waken up.'

'Poor child, you shouldn't be going through this ordeal at your age. If you want my advice, I would suggest you go now and do your packing then I would—' she stopped and chewed at her lip.

Beth waited for her to go on.

'Your letter of resignation, I'd write that out, and make

it clear that you are giving the legal requirement of seven days' notice. That should take the wind out of his sails for I doubt that he would expect you to know that.'

Beth nodded eagerly. 'I'll do that and I'll get the work as far forward as possible to make it easier for whoever takes over.'

'Good girl. Just this once I'll have a meal ready for you when Harry brings you and your belongings. After that I'll show you where to get sheets and pillowcases for the bed.'

When Beth returned to Inverbrae House she went straight to the office. There was the possibility that it would be locked but it wasn't. Mr Blair, the manager, was there and looking glum.

'Beth, tell me it isn't true, you aren't going?'

'Yes, Mr Blair, I am. As a matter of fact I was told to go.'

'Not by the boss, you weren't. That Miss Caroline, was it?'

'Same thing.'

'No, it isn't. You two had a row and Miss Caroline lost her temper—'

Beth stopped him. 'A lot more to it than that but as it happens she did me a good turn. I've got another job and accommodation.'

'Just like that?'

'Just like that,' she smiled.

'You'll stay until he gets someone else,' he said anxiously.

Beth knew he was thinking of himself and felt sorry for him. 'I'm giving one week's notice, Mr Blair, but I'll get everything as far forward as I can.'

'You'll be difficult to replace.' He cheered up. 'Maybe you'll be offered a rise to stay on?'

'I won't change my mind.'

The manager grunted and went out, leaving the keys behind. Once he'd gone Beth put paper in the typewriter and typed out her resignation. She signed it and put it in an enveloped addressed to the colonel. That small bu important job done, she placed it in a prominent place on the table. Satisfied, she left the office and went to the house to do her packing.

Coats and jackets could be carried over her arm and the rest of her clothes would go in the cases. Boxes would be required, since her worldly possessions proved to be more than she thought. Over the years she had received gift and all these would go with her. Jenny could keep he picture, meantime.

She was as ready as she could be and at five to seven she was downstairs carrying one case and two coats over he arm. A car slowed down and a voice called, 'Would you be Miss Brown?'

'Yes.'

He smiled. 'Harry at your service. Give me that cas and I'll put it in the boot. Put your coats on the bac seat.'

She did that. 'I'll be as quick as I can and I'll take two c these boxes.'

'I'll come up with you, then the one journey will do.'

Beth looked uncertain. 'I'm only an employee—'

'And me the removal man,' he grinned. 'I don't see m meeting much opposition, do you?'

She had to laugh. He was a very large, well-buil middle-aged man. 'No, I don't.'

For all his bulk, Harry was quick on his feet and in short time everything was in the car. Beth didn't loo back and she just wished that the next seven days wer over.

The remainder of that eventful day passed with Beth not quite sure if she was coming or going. Anna Martin had busied herself preparing a tasty meal but Beth was too choked to do justice to it. When she tried to apologise, her expressions of regret were waved away.

'It has been a traumatic experience and it takes a day or two to recover. Get the next seven days behind you and you'll feel very different.'

Next morning on the dot of nine, Beth was at her desk. The colonel had been in, the letter was gone and there was a pile of letters waiting to be typed. Beth was glad, it would keep her occupied and her mind off what was ahead. Perhaps there would be no unpleasantness and the colonel would be glad to see the back of her. He came in just before four o'clock. She looked up from her typing.

'Good afternoon, Colonel Parker-Munro,' Beth said quietly. She was nervous and her heart was racing.

'Good afternoon,' he said coldly.

He hadn't used her name and abruptly he turned away to pick up the letters that were ready for his signature. He sat down to read them and scrawled his signature.

'Stop typing, if you please.'

Beth took her fingers off the keys and sat back.

'Your disgraceful behaviour has greatly upset my daughter.'

'May I ask what I am supposed to have done?'

His eyes were icy, like blue pebbles and she heard the anger in his voice, 'You are a selfish, ungrateful girl. You tried to ruin my daughter's happiness.'

'Far from it.' Beth was calm now, she had nothing to lose. 'All I did was try to warn Caroline about Adrian. He is not to be trusted.'

'Enough! That is quite enough. The gentleman in question was reluctant to condemn you—'

'Condemn me, that's rich,' Beth said furiously. 'You are as blind as your daughter and I pity Caroline if she marries him.'

'Just as she said, you are eaten up with jealousy.'

'It is easier to accept than the truth, isn't it?'

'That you, of all people, should behave like this after all that has been done for you.'

'Done for me? As a child I accept that you were kind to me but then it suited you to be. In fact, Colonel Parker-Munro, you were a sort of hero until I got older and realised that your kindness was extended to me just as long as I was of use.'

She saw her outburst had surprised him.

'We took care of you after your parents died.'

'For a short time. Since it was you who persuaded my mother to let me live at Inverbrae House it was difficult to remove me. What would people say?' To her own ears she sounded breathless but she knew that she could hold her own.

'I have more than fulfilled my obligations.' He permitted himself a wintry smile.

'Let me finish, please.' Now that she had started, Beth couldn't stop herself.

'Regarding my schooldays at Rowanbank, you deliberately set out to make my life as difficult and unpleasant as possible.'

'I beg your pardon?' he said, fixing her with cold eyes.

'Miss Critchley, that odious woman, did not require to know my family history. I am not ashamed of it, nothing could be further from the truth, but you must have known that the information would not remain confidential.' She paused. 'Only a small number tried to make my life a

384

misery but I wouldn't let them succeed.' Beth smiled. 'I'm just so glad I had the guts to tell her publicly what I thought of her.'

'You made an exhibition of yourself.'

'Yes, I did and it was much appreciated by a great many.'

'The fees for that school are quite considerable and you should be grateful—'

'Grateful – grateful – always grateful, how I hate that word. Strange, I thought, that you were paying my fees when you clearly didn't want me in the school and stranger still how we come to hear things.'

'Go on,' he said sarcastically, 'this is interesting.'

'I know now that I have Mrs Cuthbert to thank for my education at Rowanbank. She persuaded you to let me go with Caroline. That is true, isn't it?'

'It is.'

For the first time Beth saw the colonel lost for words.

'You do realise that I am working my notice?'

'With no consideration for me. How am I supposed to get a replacement in seven days?'

'Mr Blair and you will just have to manage,' she said sweetly.

She saw the struggle. 'Would you consider staying another month?'

'I'm sorry, I have already accepted another position.'

'I see,' he said tersely and without looking at her went out.

Beth knew it was a victory but even so she could have wept. In spite of all the hurtful things that had been said she hated leaving this way.

There was no problem getting from Lilac Lodge to the office. She now had a bicycle. Miss Martin had told her that there was one in the shed and she was welcome to it.

On her final day but one, Beth locked up and went round to the back of the office to collect her bike. It was then that she saw him and, for a moment, the breath went from her body.

'Hello, Beth!' he smiled.

She didn't answer, just looked at him coldly and reached for her bicycle. He had put himself between it and her.

'Would you kindly get out of my way?'

'We need to talk, Beth.'

'I have nothing to say to you.'

'I've hurt you and that was the last thing I wanted to do.'

'How very touching.'

'Please don't be like that, I only want to explain.'

'I have no wish to hear.'

The patience had given way to anger. 'You might as well listen, since you can't get at your bicycle.'

'I can always get a bus.'

'You aren't going anywhere until you hear what I have to say.'

'Make it quick,' she snapped.

He spread out his hands in a gesture of despair. 'Beth, had no choice in the matter.'

'You are hoping to marry Caroline for her money?'

'Yes. Don't look like that. It happens in families like ours. And it works. Caroline wants me, her family want me.'

'She believes you love her.'

'I'll let her go on thinking it. We can all be happy, Beth. Much better, of course, if you had been the daughter but we love each other. That is what is important and, since you are no longer at Inverbrae House, it should be easier to arrange to meet.'

'Your conceit is unbelievable. It takes my breath away. If you imagine even for one moment – if you think I would dream of – of—' She found she couldn't go on and just looked at him with cold contempt.

He shrugged. 'Nothing unusual about what I am suggesting, Beth, but if it doesn't appeal to you—'

'Appeal? It sickens me. I hope and pray that Caroline comes to her senses and sees you for what you are.'

He grinned maliciously. 'Not a hope and don't try anything, my dear Beth, because Caroline wouldn't believe a word against me.' He moved away from the bicycle. 'Don't let me detain you any longer.'

He walked away with that easy grace and arrogance that she had once admired. How confident he was, so sure that she could do nothing and, of course, he was right. She had tried and failed.

Chapter Twenty-Seven

It was wonderful, this new-found freedom, and Beth was thoroughly enjoying life. At Inverbrae House she had known freedom but that had been different. No one there had cared sufficiently about her to bother where she went. By contrast, Lilac Lodge had become home, a place where she felt happy and contented. She had her own bedroom and sitting-room and could cook a meal or make a cup of tea for herself whenever she felt like it. She could also entertain friends if she so wished. When her book was going well, Anna Martin would be shut in her study for much of the day but there was always a point when they were together and theirs was an easy relationship that suited them both.

Over coffee one morning, when the writer had finished explaining changes in her manuscript, Anna Martin asked Beth if she was happy or if she felt it was too quiet for her.

'I love it here, Miss Martin. I think of it as the luckiest day of my life when I came to your door.'

'Bless you for that but you are young, my dear, and I worry that you are missing out. I was always a bit of a loner but thankfully there aren't too many like me.' She smiled and sipped at her coffee. 'You make a good cup, just the way I like it.'

'I'm learning and I'm becoming quite good at cooking.

One evening you must let me prepare you a meal.'

'Be your guest?'

'Yes.'

'I'll keep you to that.' She paused and looked apologetic. 'You must know by now that I hate stopping for meals and much prefer to work on until I finish whatever it is.'

'I do understand and I've wanted to say for some time that I don't earn my salary.'

'That you do. My manuscripts are neater than they ever were. Added to that, I like to think of someone else in the house.'

'I'm reasonably good at figures, Miss Martin, and if I can be of any assistance in that way—' she broke off and looked at her employer who was nodding and obviously pleased at the offer.

'You could, and I would be most grateful. There are financial matters that I find confusing but they probably wouldn't be to you.'

'You trust me—'

'I pride myself that I am a good judge of character and I imagine Jenny Cuthbert is too. She speaks highly of you.'

'Do you know Jenny well?'

'I got to know her well when I was ill.'

'She came to help you – that would be like Jenny.'

'Yes, as you say, that was like Jenny. Knowing that, for most of the day, I would be on my own, she called round to see how I was. I must have looked a poor soul because she had her housekeeper prepare small nourishing meals and stood over me until I ate them.'

Beth laughed, picturing the scene.

'Proper bossy boots I told her she was and she heartily agreed.'

'Jenny was so good to me when I lost my parents.'

'I did hear about your tragic loss, Beth, and the difficult life you have led since.'

'One day I'll tell you about my parents. I would like to.'

She gave a small nod of her head. 'Thank you, and now I am going to tell you something that you may think peculiar coming from me. It concerns our mutual friend, Jenny, and I tell it only because you will hear it anyway and now you will be prepared.'

Beth looked mystified. 'Jenny would never do anything wrong,' she said stoutly.

That brought a delighted laugh from Anna. 'My dear child, none of us is perfect, Jenny included, we have all sinned. It is just that some folk make a habit of it, and for others it is just an occasional slip.'

'Yes, I know,' Beth said self-consciously. 'You see, Jenny is my very best friend.'

'Such loyalty and I do like that. Jealousy, Beth, is at the root of all evil or a large part of it, and Jenny happens to be an attractive widow of independent means with a number of male admirers. In a small village like this, platonic friendship is met with scepticism. No one believes in it and, with having men friends, it is only too easy to become the victim of gossip.'

Beth could believe that.

'Should you hear gossip, don't be tempted to vent your anger. Jenny wouldn't thank you. Ignore it and treat it with the contempt it deserves.'

'Why are some people so horrid?'

'Because, my dear, their own lives are so drab that they resent others enjoying theirs.'

'I find that sad.'

'So do I. Jenny has many friends, particularly among struggling artists. More than one, on the brink of despair, has left Jenny's house with food in his stomach and words of encouragement ringing in his ears.' She smiled. 'Some have gone on to do great things.'

'Jenny's grandmother was an artist.'

'Was she? That could account for her interest.' Miss Martin got up and walked to the window where the bright sunshine was streaming in. 'Such a pity to waste the summer, Beth, and since you live on the premises the work can be done at any time. You should make use of that bike of mine and get out and enjoy the best of the day.'

Beth enjoyed cycling and the freedom it gave her. The rain had fallen overnight, leaving the countryside fresh and green. Today she would get one or two bits of shopping in the village and then take the coast road, since there was nothing to hurry her.

Cycling along, she saw the artist in the distance. There was something familiar about the figure. She propped her bicycle against a post and began walking over the stony beach. Beth stopped well short of where he was working. She had no wish to disturb but she would enjoy watching him. Eventually it was he who turned.

'Don't move, just stay exactly as you are,' he said urgently. As she obeyed, he left his easel and took up his sketching pad. Just as she was beginning to get a crick in her neck, Peter smiled. 'Relax now, Beth, and thank you very much. That was a moment I wanted to capture.' He closed his sketching pad.

'Don't I get to see it?'

'Not yet.'

'I didn't think you knew I was there.'

'I knew someone was but that someone was obeying the rules.'

'What rules?'

'Never disturb an artist when he is working. Look by all means but do not give advice. We get heartily sick of that.'

'Surely no one would?'

'You'd be surprised and they think they are doing us a good turn.'

She was about to get up and go. 'No, don't go yet. I want to know what I have done that you haven't paid a return visit to 5 Summer Street.'

'It's not an excuse, Peter, I have been very busy. A lot has happened just lately, like getting myself a new job and accommodation.'

'I know about that.' He broke off a piece of chocolate and gave it to her.

'Thanks. What do you know?'

'Some writer has given you a job.'

'Anna Martin.'

'A bit eccentric, I hear.'

'She isn't, she's lovely.'

'Could be both. I like eccentric people, usually find them a lot more interesting.'

'Who told you?'

'Jenny. Who else could it have been?' He paused. 'It was just in case I put my foot in it and said the wrong thing – but I didn't get the chance to say anything. You didn't come and I was disappointed.'

She smiled. 'Maybe I would have wept all over you.'

'He's not worth a single tear.'

'I know.'

He saw the bleak expression and knew that she wasn't over it, the hurt had gone too deep. For a while they sat in a companionable silence and gazing out to sea.

'How lucky you are, Peter.'

'Am I?'

'You can lose yourself in your work and forget disappointments.'

'That is only partly true. We all have our hopes and dreams and when they don't look much like being realised we are just as likely to be hurt and depressed as the rest.'

She looked at him in surprise. It sounded as though he had been disappointed in love.

She got up. 'I'd better get my bike and be on my way.'

Peter got up too, fished in his pocket and drew out a bundle of keys. Selecting one he took it off the ring.

'Take that.'

'Why?'

'Because I want you to have it. Take that shocked expression off your face. We are friends and friends like to help one another. Could be a change of scenery would do you good. If you want to make yourself useful, I don't eat when I am working but I do like cups of tea.' His lips curved into a cheerful smile.

She put the key in her pocket. 'Thank you,' she said. 'I make a good cup of tea.'

The newspapers made a big splash of it. Beth saw it in the local paper. It was expected but it still came as an unpleasant shock when she read the announcement of the forthcoming marriage of Caroline Parker-Munro and Adrian Scott-Hamilton.

Robert Munro returned to Inverbrae House while it buzzed with excitement over the forthcoming marriage of the daughter of the house. He was to spend ten days with his relatives before returning to Australia. Caroline pleaded with her cousin to postpone his departure until after the wedding as did the colonel and Mrs Parker-Munro. If Robert had approved of the union, he may well have done so. But he had disliked Adrian on sight and the dislike was mutual.

Robert saw behind the charm, and wouldn't have trusted Adrian an inch, but he recognised that there was nothing he could do. He hadn't expected his grandmother to be taken in but she was captivated by all that charm and his uncle appeared to be well pleased with his future son-in-law.

Adrian was glad to see the back of Robert Munro. Once he was away, he began to spend most of his time at Inverbrae House. Already he was very much one of the family but Caroline did wish that he were more ardent. Why wasn't he? she thought crossly. She could hardly throw herself at him and there were some she knew who would say that it only showed the great respect he had for her.

She wished, too, that Adrian was a bit more forthcoming. Caroline was discovering that he didn't like to be questioned but surely, as his future wife, she had a right to know what he did. And since his family was in such straightened circumstances, and he the younger son, surely he must have some occupation. It was worrying Caroline enough to mention it to her father.

The colonel looked at her fondly. 'Darling, you must have embarrassed Adrian. He wouldn't expect that kind of question from you.'

'I can't see why not. I'm not a child and, for heaven's sake, this isn't the Victorian age.'

'Most men find women more attractive when they don't try to enter a man's world. Poor boy, he feels badly enough about having so little money. I am not in the least concerned, my dear, because Adrian will be involved in the running of the estate and I'll be glad to ease off.'

'Ease off? Are you ill, daddy?' Caroline said anxiously.

'Of course not, don't be silly, I'm as fit as a fiddle but I want my future son-in-law to be able to take over when the day comes that I am not so able.'

Caroline nodded. She could forget her niggling doubts since her father had none.

'I miss Robert,' Caroline said when she and Adrian were alone in the drawing-room.

'Do you? I don't.'

'You didn't like him. Why was that?'

He shrugged. 'Fellow doesn't know how to behave.'

'Rubbish, just because he has a friendly word with the servants.'

'Didn't you find it out of place?'

'Perhaps at first I did but life in Australia is very different to what it is here.'

'Don't give me that, Caroline. There is class difference down under just as there is here. Know what I think?'

'What do you think?'

'I'd say he comes from poor stock on his mother's side.' He paused and looked at her. 'Could be that his forebears were criminals shipped out there to do their sentence and stayed on.'

Caroline was shocked and angry. 'That is a terrible thing to say. Robert's family is very nice and his mother writes such lovely letters.'

'My sweet innocent, of course she does. There is plenty of money to be made on a sheep farm and the family would have received a good education but be totally lacking in—'

She didn't let him finish. 'Since Robert's father was daddy's brother, I find your remarks insulting and to suggest he has no—'

'Breeding?' He laughed a little unpleasantly. 'Your cousin Robert is short on that.'

396

He saw by her face that he had gone too far and quickly tried to make amends. 'Darling, apart from Robert, you haven't met the family.'

'We correspond regularly.'

'Hardly the same thing.' They were sitting together and he drew her near, kissed her lightly on the mouth and sighed. 'Darling, I do love you and I can't wait to make you mine. Only I'll have to—' He gave a wry smile.

Caroline snuggled closer and her annoyance disappeared. 'I love you, Adrian,' she said pressing her lips to his.

'Steady on, darling, I am only human.'

'Sorry,' she said blushing and giggling.

'We have all our tomorrows and the years ahead, just remember that.'

'It's a lovely, lovely thought,' she said blissfully.

'Know what suddenly came into my mind?'

She shook her head.

'Wouldn't it be awful if one day Robert were to inherit Inverbrae House? Don't look like that, my love, it could happen.' He paused and looked very serious. 'We must make sure it doesn't and that means having our family right away.'

Caroline felt the cold hand of fear grip her heart. One day, but well into the future, she supposed they would have a child but a family and right away—

Adrian saw her look of alarm.

'You do want children, my children, surely you do?'

'Yes, but I don't want the responsibility of motherhood for some years. I am young.'

'Young and pretty and adorable and all the more reason to get it over in the first years of marriage.'

'This is something that should be discussed after marriage and not before,' she said frostily.

'It embarrasses you?' he said gently.

'Yes, it does.'

'Then not another word on the subject and just as well because I hear voices and your grandmother's stick.'

There was a discreet knock at the door then Nigel and his mother entered. Adrian dashed over to help the old lady into a chair.

Caroline was quieter than usual and she was shivering with a nameless fear. Only it wasn't a nameless fear, she knew of what she was afraid. Her mother had died in childbirth.

The colonel and Adrian had gone round the estate and were now back and in the drawing-room. Adrian, in country tweeds, lounged with his legs out-stretched towards the fireside. There was no fire because the day was warm. Both were smoking cigars and the nearby table held drinks.

Mrs Esslemont had arrived to whisk her niece away for the first fitting of the wedding dress. After that it would be necessary to choose lightweight costumes, gowns and dresses for all occasions. Then would come the choosing of hats that were the very latest fashion. Aunt Gwen was in her element, loving every moment, while her niece tried to hide her tiredness.

The colonel was pleased with Adrian's show of interest in the estate and the questions he put. But like his daughter, though he had hidden it from her, other areas were giving him concern. Better to have it out now.

'Adrian?'

Adrian looked across at his future father-in-law with the satisfied smile that was so often on his face these days.

'We are sorry about your mother not being well enough to come with your father and spend a few days here. But time is getting on and I think you should take Caroline to meet your family.'

'Exactly what I had in mind,' Adrian said smoothly, though it was far from the truth. Making his mother the excuse, he had hoped that their first meeting would be at the wedding. He might have known that that wouldn't have gone down well with colonel and his mother. 'Actually, sir, I was to seek your permission to take Caroline to Bankhead next weekend when my brother and his wife would be there.'

'Splendid, my boy, and I know that Caroline is looking forward to meeting your family.'

Since money was so scarce, her expectations had not been too high but would she ever forget that weekend in Adrian's home?

When they set out it was a soft summer's day with the gentlest of breezes and the countryside was at its best. Adrian drove the colonel's car, having said that it would be more comfortable for Caroline than his own. She was happy knowing that she looked fresh and pretty in a fine linen dress in a lovely shade of lime green. It had a matching jacket which was on the back seat of the car.

'Know your history, do you?' Adrian smiled as they approached Stirling.

'A little but I haven't been this way before. Oh, look! The castle,' she said pointing to it eagerly.

'Difficult to miss. That castle, my dear Caroline, has a dark history, a tumultuous past, and it was the Stewarts who built the castle as you see it now.'

She was pleased that Adrian had an interest in history. 'I believe I read somewhere that Mary Queen of Scots, married her second husband, Lord Darnley, in Stirling Castle.'

'Clever girl.'

'Have we much further to go?'

'No, not far now.'

Adrian fell silent for the last few miles then he pointed to a building. 'That, before you, is Bankhead.'

Set on a rise with the sun glinting on it, the house looked impressive and Caroline began to look about her with interest. The approach through the wrought-iron gates was pleasant since the trees lining the drive hid the untidiness behind. Only when they drew near to the house did it become apparent that Bankhead, home of the Scott-Hamiltons, was run down and in a poor state of repair. An attempt had been made to keep the garden in front of the house tidy but the rest was overgrown and had been long neglected. Broken slates lay about the ground, blown down after the recent gales and never replaced.

Caroline looked for movement from the house but there was none. Getting out of the car, she couldn't hide her dismay.

'Should have warned you, I suppose. The place is a bit of a shambles and will be for as long as money is tight.'

'Pity to let it go like this. The worse it gets, the more will need to be spent on it.'

'That is father's problem and my brother's, not mine, thank God.'

She watched him take her case from the boot and still no one appeared. 'My jacket,' she said, seeing it on the back seat. 'I had better have it with me.'

Adrian got it for her and she took it from him to carry over her arm. They walked to the heavy door which was half open. In the large, dreary hall, an elderly maid came forward and took the case from Adrian.

'Take it to the room prepared for the young lady.'

'Very good, sir.'

After the heat of the car and the few minutes in the sunshine, indoors seemed chilly. Caroline was in two minds as to whether she should put on her jacket or not. Her arm was all goose pimples but she decided to suffer the cold for the moment. No doubt it would be warmer where they were going.

Taking her arm Adrian guided her through long corridors where some of the paintwork was peeling.

'It gets better,' Adrian said with an attempt at humour.

Caroline smiled weakly. She thought it could hardly get worse.

'Only one wing of the house is used and that I can promise you is quite comfortable.'

He proved to be right. This was more like it, Caroline thought with relief. There was a brightness here denied the rest of the house, or what she had seen of it and Caroline cheered up. Adrian stopped to open a door.

'Come and meet the family.'

Caroline had heard the low murmur of voices which stopped as they entered. Adrian stood aside to let her go ahead and her immediate impression was of a comfortable but over-furnished drawing-room. Four people were there and all eyes turned to the stranger. The two women were sitting together on the sofa.

'This is Caroline,' Adrian said bringing his fiancée forward, 'and Caroline,' he smiled down to her, 'this is my mother, my father, my brother and his wife Virginia.'

Caroline smiled and, feeling her lips quivering, wondered at her nervousness. She was used to being in company, to meeting people but, of course, this was different. These people were Adrian's family and she wanted them to like her.

Both men had got to their feet, and the florid-faced man

who was Adrian's father, came forward. He was smiling hugely.

'Such a pleasure to have you here. Welcome to Bankhead, my dear.'

'Thank you.'

Roderick Scott-Hamilton was as tall as Adrian and there was a strong resemblance between father and son. Caroline thought the older man must once have been as handsome as his younger son. They had the same regular features and charm of manner but the years or perhaps the lifestyle had not been kind. The face was fleshy, the eyes slightly bloodshot, and the figure was thickening.

Caroline felt his lips on her cheek and then he was taking her arm and leading her across the room. This wasn't as it should be. Adrian should be with her and not his father but Adrian had moved away to look out of the window. For someone who complained of bad manners in others, she thought crossly, his were quite appalling at times.

Adrian's mother was not as she expected her to be and yet, if someone had asked her what she had expected, she could not rightly have said. Marjorie Scott-Hamilton was nondescript, a plain woman who made no attempt to improve herself. She wore no make-up and with her sallow skin a light foundation and powder would have made a difference. Her hair was pepper and salt and she had a slide in it to keep it off her face. She did, however, have a nice smile and an attractive husky voice.

'Caroline, I am delighted to meet you and do let me apologise for being unable to accept your father's kind invitation. You see—'

'Mother!' Adrian had turned from the window and said swiftly, 'I explained to Caroline that you have been in poor health.'

'Yes, Adrian did, Mrs Scott-Hamilton. We were disappointed you couldn't come. Are you feeling better now?'

'My wife has been in delicate health for some time but she is determined to be well enough to attend the wedding.'

Caroline was irritated that Adrian's mother wasn't allowed to speak for herself. She seemed perfectly capable.

'I'll make sure she is.'

'Yes, Virginia, you do that.'

Virginia smiled. 'You sit here beside mother-in-law,' she said, getting up from the sofa. She was of medium height and on the plump side but her soft brown eyes held a warm smile.

'Let me introduce myself. I'm Michael.' Adrian's brother came over with an outstretched hand. Caroline took to him immediately. Like his mother he was very ordinary-looking but there was a gentleness that appealed to her and a message in the eyes, a hint that he recognised this was an ordeal.

Adrian's father spoke. 'While you are on your feet, Virginia, ring that bell, if you please.' The voice was clipped and angry.

'No need, I hear someone coming,' Virginia said shortly.

It was the same elderly servant who came in with the laden tray. With her was a very young girl who had the rest of the things.

'Shall I pour, m'am?' the elderly woman asked her mistress.

'No, I'll see to it.' She smiled. 'Thank you.'

'Very good, m'am.'

Virginia touched her mother-in-law on the shoulder. 'No, you sit still and keep Caroline company. I'll pour and Michael, dear, you'll hand them round, won't you?'

'A pleasure.' He looked at Caroline. 'How was the journey?'

'Before you answer that, Caroline, tell me how you like your tea.'

'A little sugar and rather a lot of milk, please.'

'That's the way I take it too. Michael calls it baby tea.'

'I suppose it is,' Caroline laughed, 'and as to the journey, Michael, it was very pleasant. Coming into Stirling, Adrian gave me a history lesson.'

'Did you now, my boy?' His father looked pleased, then frowned. 'Virginia, what is in those sandwiches?'

'I don't know. Shall I be naughty and take a peep inside to see?'

'Safer not to. I'll let myself be surprised.'

'Roderick, that was completely unnecessary as well as being unkind,' his wife said sharply. 'With so little help in the house, I think the servants do extremely well.'

'I couldn't agree more, Mother,' Michael said.

Adrian scowled. Roderick looked daggers at his wife and Virginia's lips quirked as though she were amused.

Caroline looked from one to the other in bewilderment. She was beginning to see this as a divided house – but why? Adrian and his father appeared to be close and the mother was supported by Virginia and Michael.

Whatever was in the sandwiches was tasty and Caroline, faddy with food, enjoyed hers.

'More tea, Caroline?'

'No, thank you, Mrs Scott-Hamilton, but that was very refreshing and I enjoyed it.'

'Perhaps you would like to see your room?'

'Yes, I would, please.'

'I'll come with you, Caroline,' said Virginia, putting down her cup. They excused themselves and left the room.

'Poor you, you are wondering what to make of them, aren't you?'

'I suppose I am.'

'Families can be the limit. The maid position is pretty desperate and that upsets mother-in-law.'

The bedroom was very nice and Caroline was well satisfied.

'The flowers were mother-in-law's idea. She is rather sweet.'

'Do you always call her mother-in-law?'

'Yes, can you think of something better?'

'Tricky?'

'Exactly.'

'Do you address your father-in-law that way too?'

She grinned. 'That and a few other names.'

They emptied the case and Virginia hung up the two dresses that Caroline had brought with her. 'Very pretty,' she remarked.

'Thank you.'

'Nice to be slim and dainty. No chance for me. I am too fond of my food.'

'May I ask you something, Virginia?'

'Ask away.'

'Why won't they let Mrs Scott-Hamilton speak for herself?'

'Afraid what she'll come away with. No, no, not quite as bad as that. I don't like my father-in-law, as you may have gathered. Like Adrian he was blessed with good looks and that brand of charm which frankly makes me sick – sorry, I'm just talking of the old man. He married for money, had his fling with other women and now, I believe, he has a mistress tucked away somewhere.'

'That's awful. But surely Adrian's mother put her foot down? I mean she was bringing money into the family—'

'Until he got the money into his own hands – and women in love are fools – he would act the loving husband.'

'If he wanted he could leave her since he has all her money.'

'Which is what would have happened according to Michael if she hadn't been left money by an aunt who had the sense to leave it in such a way that Roderick couldn't get his hands on it.'

'Why doesn't she leave him?'

'She wants to keep Bankhead going until Michael takes over and that might be sooner than you think. The old boy drinks heavily and when he has the money gambles the night away. The doctor has warned him to cut down on the drink but frankly I don't think he can. Look, we'd better go down now but don't worry, there will be time for a chat later on if you want to hear more.'

'Since I am to be part of this family I had better know about them and Adrian doesn't tell me much. It won't make any difference to my feelings for Adrian,' she hastily added.

'If you are truly in love nothing else matters. Michael and I are very lucky,' she said softly.

Later on, Adrian was at his most charming and drove her into the countryside where he pointed out places of interest. Some of the amusing tales he told her had her laughing delightedly. This was the Adrian she loved and she could have forgiven him anything.

'You do love this part of the country don't you, Adrian?'

'Yes, I do,' he said quietly.

'There must be times when you wished you were the elder brother?'

'What good would that do, wishing something that can

never be? You are right though, there are times—'

'Tell me what happened to the family fortunes.' She kept her voice light.

'You are one for questions, aren't you?'

'I want to know about your family, Adrian. After all, you know about mine.'

'The sad tale of Bankhead? All right, my dearest, here it is. Once upon a time, if I may borrow the fairytale beginning, ours was one of the finest houses for miles around. But sadly my grandfather was what is now termed a compulsive gambler. We can stop here for tea if you wish,' he said, slowing down opposite a tea-room.

'No, go on, please.' Stop now and she would never hear the story of the Scott-Hamiltons. It was just an excuse to change the subject.

'Grandfather's gambling set the rot in and when he died my father inherited a load of debt and with every chance of being declared bankrupt.'

'That must have been dreadful!'

'It was and, very stupidly, my father tried his hand at gambling himself, hoping to be lucky. And he was. Luck was with him and everything would have been fine if he had had the sense to leave it at that but no, he thought his luck would hold.'

'It didn't?'

'Very nearly back to square one.'

'He doesn't gamble now?'

Adrian laughed. 'He doesn't have the money, Michael sees to that, but I am afraid it is once a gambler always a gambler.' He glanced sideways. 'Don't look so worried, Caroline. Neither Michael nor I have the least interest in gambling. We saw at first hand what it could do.'

'I'm glad you've told me, Adrian. I understand now why you didn't want to talk about your home.' She smiled and studied his profile and thought again how lucky she was to be marrying someone so handsome. Then, hoping to cheer him up, she said, 'In time Michael may bring Bankhead back to its former glory.'

'Might well have, had he married wealth instead of Virginia.'

'That wasn't a very nice thing to say and I like Virginia,' Caroline said reprovingly.

'Do you? I don't and happily our paths seldom cross. This was just a special occasion in your honour.'

Caroline was silent for a little then decided she would say it.

'Adrian, in Michael's place would you have married for money?'

'Perhaps.' Then, seeing her face, he added, 'It was a joke, Caroline.'

'I sincerely hope so.'

He took one hand off the steering wheel and squeezed hers. 'Darling, I am honest enough to admit that I am glad you are not penniless. But had you been, it would have made no difference. You are, for me, the girl of my dreams.'

She smiled tremulously. Nothing else mattered, they loved each other and once they were married and living in Inverbrae House, only an occasional visit to Bankhead would be necessary.

When they returned Caroline was flushed and happy. She would have a leisurely bath and take special care over her appearance.

In the long dress with its full skirt and sweetheart neckline, Caroline looked sweet and pretty and the gentlemen eyed her with appreciation.

Virginia gave a nod of approval and Mrs Scott-Hamilton spoke softly.

'Caroline, my dear, you look enchanting.'

'Picked a peach, my boy.'

Was it the voice or something in the older man's face that made Caroline uncomfortable? She was deciding that, like Virginia, she didn't much like her future father-in-law.

'Thank you for the flowers in my bedroom, Mrs Scott-Hamilton. They are lovely and it was a nice thought.'

She smiled. 'Flowers are my greatest joy but sadly we cannot afford the gardeners—'

'Shall we sit down?' a voice said loudly.

'Yes, Roderick, we shall all take our places.'

The dining-room was well decorated and well furnished. The silver and crystal sparkled and Caroline could not have faulted the table. She rather thought that it wouldn't be this grand most of the time but she was pleased someone, most likely Mrs Scott-Hamilton, had gone to this trouble on her behalf.

Virginia wore a long, black skirt and an emerald green blouse. She looked nice. Adrian's mother had on a cerise silk suit that when new must have cost a lot but it looked old-fashioned and where her figure had expanded it showed unbecoming bulges.

There were no awkward silences during the meal and everybody appeared to be making an effort to keep the conversation going. Dinner was as formal as at Inverbrae House, only the service was slower. Roderick Scott-Hamilton, from his place at the head of the table, had them laughing at some amusing stories and she was reminded of Adrian who had had her smiling at his. In many ways Adrian resembled his father but in what really mattered they were totally unalike. She knew quite a bit about this family but she knew there was more to learn, particularly about her future mother-in-law. She watched her when this was possible. She smiled a lot, as nervous people did, and her hands when not engaged with cutlery were never still. She said very little but when Michael spoke, the smile she bestowed on him was full of mother love. Not once did she look in her husband's direction and when he spoke she looked down at the table. How could they live like that, Caroline wondered.

After coffee Mrs Scott-Hamilton excused herself and went upstairs to her bedroom. Michael and his father disappeared to discuss some business and Adrian got up and stretched himself.

'The very last thing I want to do this evening is go out.'

'Then don't, stay in. I'm quite happy.'

'You are?' he said, looking immensely relieved. 'That makes me feel less guilty, Caroline, because I simply must get some business done while I am here and in a way you are to blame—'

'Me?'

'Haven't I been spending most of my time at Inverbrae House?'

'True,' she dimpled prettily.

'And because of it I have neglected my business here.'

Virginia shot him a look of amusement mixed with contempt but Caroline didn't notice.

'If you say so.'

It was all so easy and he wanted to hoot with laughter. His business tonight was with an actress whose voluptuous figure partly compensated for her poor acting ability. She knew to expect him and would be ready and waiting.

'May I go?'

'Of course, darling.' She held up her face for his kiss. 'Virginia and I will have lots to talk about.'

'Lots and lots,' Virginia said and saw his scowl. Caroline missed it.

★ ★ ★

They were on their own. 'Adrian did tell me about his grandfather being a compulsive gambler and his father inheriting a lot of debt and how he tried to pay it off by more gambling.'

'You know it, then.'

'Not all, and it doesn't explain Mrs Scott-Hamilton.'

'I like her but let us be brutally frank. I am no oil painting but mother-in-law is plain and she was as a young woman. No sparkling conversationalist either, so what was the attraction for the handsome Roderick?'

'Money,' said Caroline quietly.

'Exactly.'

'But you told me that before.'

'I wanted to repeat it. Her family were very wealthy and after her parents died she was brought up by her grandmother. She tried everything to stop her marrying Roderick Scott-Hamilton but she was determined and she defied her grandmother and eloped with Roderick.'

'With a happy ending, that would have been very romantic.'

'Sadly her happiness didn't last long. But she had her pride and she pretended all was well and that suited his lordship. They had two sons.'

'And Michael is her favourite?'

'No use denying what is obvious but she did try always to treat the boys alike. Their father didn't. He had no time for Michael but he adored his handsome son.'

'Adrian can't help being good looking.'

'Of course not, but I'm just trying to give you a picture of what this family was like. There comes a time in a person's life when she can take no more and mother-in-law had reached it. She did have a sort of breakdown and it resulted in depression.'

'But not mentally disturbed?' Caroline had heard her grandmother use the term for one of her friends.

'Not seriously, and she is perfectly all right now. But just to spite her husband and get her own back, and I'm sure that is what it is, she pretends not to be. Roderick is always afraid of what she will come out with.'

'Oh, dear, it is all so different from my own family.'

Virginia smiled. 'Adrian, naturally enough, wanted to keep the family difficulties from you.'

'Not much happiness in this house?'

'No, as you say, not much happiness. Michael and I have suggested that she make her home with us and she says nothing would please her more but she is determined that Michael will one day have Bankhead. For that to happen, she has to keep an eye on her husband.'

'Adrian loves this house, you know.'

'Yes, we know that.'

Chapter Twenty-Eight

The great day had arrived and, after the long dry spell, there were fears that it couldn't last. In fact, there had been short sharp showers the previous day, which had served to freshen the countryside and make this July morning quite perfect for Caroline's wedding. The sky was clear, the sun shone and there wasn't a breath of wind. Inside Inverbrae House, the servants had been up since the crack of dawn, and a great deal of the activity was coming from the kitchens.

After a lot of careful consideration, the marquee had been erected on the lawn to the side of the house. This area near to the rose gardens and flower beds was favoured because guests standing nearby would be able to smell the heady perfume drifting across. Quietly and efficiently a small band of workmen were going about the business of erecting tables and placing chairs for the less able who might require them. About nine o'clock a van drew up in front of the house and armfuls of flowers were taken indoors, while other blooms and a number of floral baskets were left beside the marquee.

Caroline had spent a restless night and woke early sick with excitement and an uneasy fear. Of what was she afraid? She kept telling herself there was nothing. After all, Adrian could hardly be held responsible for his family, indeed his reluctance to have her meet them

413

was understandable and stemmed from embarrassment.
Everything was going to be lovely and this was just silly
pre-wedding nerves. Adrian loved her, had told her so
repeatedly and he had completely bewitched her grandmother and charmed Aunt Gwen. Even daddy was won
over and he wasn't easy to hoodwink.

Why, on this morning of all mornings, did Beth have to
come into her thoughts? Was it because Beth had never
lied to her? But there was a first time for everything, and
the truth could only be that Beth was consumed with
jealousy. There could be no other explanation for her
conduct.

Had it just been Beth, she could have dismissed it. But
Caroline thought now of that other person who didn't
approve of Adrian, although he hadn't actually said so.
That, she reminded herself, had been no more than a
clash of personalities, and the dislike had been mutual.

There was a light tap at the door and a maid came in
with a breakfast tray, interrupting her thoughts and
perhaps just as well.

'Take it back,' she said sharply.

The girl looked uncertain as to what to do.

'I said take it back.'

'Yes, Miss Caroline.' She went out and returned later
with fingers of dry toast and a pot of tea.

'I may manage that. You can leave it.'

Looking relieved, the maid put the tray on a table
beside the bed and hurried out. Caroline lifted a piece of
toast and nibbled at it, then took another. She drank a cup
of tea and felt a little better.

The thought that this would be the last time she would
sleep alone and in this room gave her a peculiar lost
feeling but at least she wasn't leaving Inverbrae House.
This would continue to be her home and in many ways her

life would not change all that much. Perhaps she should start exercising her authority, insist that she was consulted on all matters that concerned herself. She had been more than annoyed, she had been extremely angry that they – her husband-to-be, her father and her grandmama – had gone over her head in a matter that concerned her personally.

Starting their married life in another wing of the house would have given them privacy and be much more romantic. She had been very much in favour of it. But, no, all that had been taken care of, and daddy and grandmama couldn't hide their delight when Adrian had expressed a wish that they live as a family and dine together. Much better, he explained and showing great concern, that Caroline should not be alone when he had to be away on business which would be necessary from time to time. What business? For all her questions, Caroline hadn't had a satisfactory answer to that one.

The ceremony was over. They were married. Handsome, darling Adrian was her husband and Caroline was blissfully happy with all the attention she was getting. She looked lovely, a radiant bride, everybody said so. Her wedding dress, with the many hours of work spent on it, was beautiful and brought gasps of delight from those gathered around the church. Eagerly they watched the arrival of guests and then the great excitement came when the bride and her father arrived. Emma Watson, no longer plump, made an attractive bridesmaid and was receiving a lot of attention from the best man, a cousin of Adrian's.

A few miles away in Lilac Lodge, Beth's thoughts were with Caroline. She hoped and prayed that this would turn out to be a happy marriage. And perhaps it had a good chance. With Adrian living in Inverbrae House and under the watchful eyes of the colonel and the old lady, he would surely have the sense to be on his best behaviour. Adrian knew on which side his bread was buttered.

Beth was at Greystanes having afternoon tea with Jenny.

'More tea, Beth?'

'No, thank you, Jenny, that was lovely and now I really must—'

'Another few minutes, do stay a little longer, dear, there is something I want to ask.' She got up and put the tray on a table ready for Miss Harris to collect, and then went back to her chair.

'Something you want to ask me?'

'Yes. Tell me, do you have any contact with Inverbrae House?'

'None at all. Have you?' she asked in surprise. She wondered if the old romance with the colonel was on again.

'Not directly, but I do hear and the news is not good. Colonel Parker-Munro has suffered a slight stroke.'

Beth looked shocked and concerned. 'That's terrible and hard to believe, I mean he always looked so – so—'

'Healthy? Yes, poor Nigel, I feel so very, very sorry about it. But thankfully it was not severe and though it is unlikely that he will ever be one hundred percent, there is no reason why he shouldn't enjoy a full and happy life. Unfortunately he is making little effort to help himself and appears to have lost interest in everything, including the estate.' She stopped to drink some tea, then put down her cup. 'Knowing Nigel as I do, Beth, I can understand it. He's never had a day's illness in his life, apart from the minor complaints we all have from time to time, and this must have been a devastating blow.'

'It's all so sad, so terribly sad.'

'You are wondering how Caroline is managing?'

'Yes.'

'Then be assured Caroline is coping extremely well. All the more credit to her since the poor girl has had such a bad time.'

'Why? What? Has she been ill?'

'Very ill, indeed for a while it was touch and go. Caroline had a miscarriage, Beth, and things went badly wrong. That could well have been what brought on Nigel's stroke.'

'That could be, Jenny. The colonel would have been nearly out of his mind with worry and Caroline would be so afraid—' Beth's voice wobbled. 'She once told me that she was afraid to have a baby—'

'Because her mother had died in childbirth? Poor little Caroline, and she would have had no one to turn to.'

'I wish, I wish, I wish I could have been there to help her.'

'It wasn't your fault that you weren't and perhaps some good has come out of it. Caroline knows now that she is perfectly able to stand on her own two feet and that will help in the years to come.'

'Is she happy with Adrian?'

'No is the short answer to that but she is pretending that all is well.' She frowned. 'In a few weeks, when I think Nigel has come to terms with his slight disability, I shall go to Inverbrae House.' She smiled across to Beth. 'The old lady, bless her, is so confused that she may even welcome me with open arms.'

Beth tried to smile but made a poor job of it.

Beth was usually the one to answer the door to callers but Anna did since she was nearest. The woman standing on the doorstep was a stranger.

'Would it be possible for me to see Miss Brown?' she asked.

'Yes, I'll get Beth for you but do come in.'

Anna Martin showed the woman into the sitting-room, got her seated then went along to where Beth was pouring over a manuscript before beginning to type.

'Don't tell me that after all this time you are finding difficulty with my writing,' Anna laughed.

'No, I can make it out but find it safer to read it over first.'

'Wise, and you, Beth, have a visitor, a woman, I've shown her into the sitting-room.'

'Who is it, do you know?' Beth asked. Aunt Anne wouldn't come here but who else could it be?

'I didn't enquire but on you go quickly and find out.'

The woman got to her feet when Beth entered.

'Mrs Murdoch!' Beth couldn't hide her surprise at seeing the housekeeper from Inverbrae House.

'Hello, Beth. I hope you don't mind me coming like this but I'm so worried.'

'Sit down, Mrs Murdoch,' Beth said gently, and when she did Beth sat down herself. 'Of course I don't mind you coming but does it mean that something is wrong?'

'Very far wrong, Beth. Inverbrae House is nothing like it used to be.'

'Is Caroline – Mrs Scott-Hamilton, ill again?'

'You heard then?'

'I heard she had lost her baby.'

'Poor lass, the doctors despaired of saving her and the master was nearly out of his mind. In a state I was myself I can tell you. But you must be wondering what I am doing here and I have to say I have no business.'

'Mrs Murdoch, if I can be of any help you have only to ask. Did Mrs Scott-Hamilton suggest you get in touch with me?'

'No, Beth, she didn't but that is just pride. Whatever the quarrel you two had was about, it is time to make it up. I'm speaking out of turn but I know the young mistress needs you. She has no one else to turn to.'

'What about her husband?'

Mrs Murdoch all but sniffed. 'That gentleman does exactly as he pleases. It's God's truth that he wasn't there when his wife was at death's door. He is away a lot and I'm glad to see the back of him.'

'Surely with Colonel Parker-Munro the way he is, Mr Scott-Hamilton should be seeing to the estate.' Beth spoke indignantly, then remembered that it was none of her business.

'That's what you would expect. There is a lass doing the job you did in that office but Mr Blair says she doesn't get through half the work you did.'

Beth smiled. 'Would you like me to come with you now?'

'Nothing I would like better.'

'I'll tell Miss Martin and get my coat.'

'Bless you, lass.'

It was as it had always been with no outward sign of the unhappiness within. Mrs Murdoch expected the old lady to be in the sitting-room and most likely dozing. She had cat-naps all day. She smiled as she said it.

They went in by the side door and Beth was left to wait in the breakfast-room. Looking around her, Beth thought of the times she had eaten in this room and then of her dismissal from the house and for some unaccountable reason began to feel nervous. She couldn't blame her sudden appearance on Mrs Murdoch since that woman had exacted a promise from Beth that her part would not be mentioned.

Beth need not have worried about her welcome. Caroline opened the door of the breakfast room and stared for a few unbelieving moments. Then, with a choking sob, she dissolved into floods of tears.

'You came! Oh, Beth, the times I've wanted you.' Caroline tried to smile through her tears as Beth's comforting arms went round her.

'If I had known you wanted me I would have come.' Now that she had her first good look at Caroline, Beth was shocked at the change. The little-girl look had gone. This was the face of a young woman who had suffered and was still suffering.

'This is my prayer answered.'

'Caroline, why didn't you get in touch?' Beth said gently.

'How could I after all the dreadful things I said? How do you like living and working with that eccentric writer, can't remember her name?'

'Anna Martin is a lovely person, Caroline, and she is both my friend and employer.'

'Come on, we can't talk here, we'll go to our own room. Would you believe, it is exactly as it was, I didn't want to change anything. When I'm feeling low,' she gave a mirthless laugh, 'which is most of the time, I go there and remember happier days.'

They were in the room they had shared as girls and Beth looked about her. 'All just as I remembered,' she said softly.

'We'll have tea brought here later but for now I just want to talk and talk and talk. You see, Beth, there hasn't been a single soul that I could confide in. Only you. Did you ever miss me?' she said wistfully.

'Often and I never stopped thinking of you as my friend.'

420

'More like sisters until things started to go wrong. Mostly my fault but there is no use crying over spilt milk, is there?'

'None at all,' Beth answered as Caroline led her to the sofa. They sat together, half-facing each other.

'So much to tell but where to begin.'

'Remember I was always a good listener.' Beth put one hand over Caroline's. Her hand was warm and Caroline's cold.

She nodded. 'Am I forgiven?'

'Forgiven and all forgotten.'

'Forgiven, I hope so, but forgetting is too much to expect.' She was very pale, her face had thinned down and her eyes were enormous in her small face. Pretty would no longer be a fitting description. Beth thought she looked delicately beautiful but as if a puff of wind would blow her away.

'All forgotten, Caroline. I have a convenient memory and I can blot out what I don't want to remember.'

'Lucky you. I have such a confusion of thoughts going through my mind that I don't know where to begin.'

'At the very beginning and take it slowly. My employer is very understanding and I can do the work at anytime.'

'The beginning,' Caroline said with a grimace. 'Had I paid attention to your warning there would be no sad tale to relate. You do know about daddy?'

'Yes, I heard and I'm very, very sorry.'

'Who told you?'

'Jenny.'

'You still keep up?'

'Yes.'

'That was all grandmama's fault. I liked Jenny and I missed her when she stopped coming. As a matter of fact, next to you, she was the only person I could have confided in. Daddy missed her too, I'm sure he did.'

'Would your father like Jenny to come and see him? She would like to, I know, but she doesn't want to upset him.'

'She wouldn't. I think he is beginning to accept the situation and the doctor has been at pains, and so has the specialist, to make him understand that this was a very slight stroke, a warning to take things easier and stop worrying.'

'Easier said than done.'

'I know. Poor daddy never expected anything like this. You tell Jenny from me that she is just the tonic daddy needs. She is both bossy and kind and he gets enough sympathy. A good talking to from Jenny will stop him feeling so sorry for himself.'

Beth was amazed. This was a new Caroline.

'I lost my baby,' Caroline said abruptly, 'and don't say you are sorry because I am not. I was glad. It was never a real baby, I mean I never held it in my arms. Beth, I love babies but I didn't want Adrian's because by the time I was pregnant I knew he was cheating on me. He had a mistress in Stirling, still has, and makes frequent visits there – it's supposed to be on business but it wasn't long before I knew exactly the kind of man I was married to.' She spoke bitterly, talking fast.

'Calm down, Caroline, take it easy. We can talk into the evening if necessary.'

'I have so much to tell you but, all right, I'll calm down.' She took a deep breath and began again but this time she spoke naturally. 'You cannot even begin to imagine what it is like for me to talk to you and know what I'm saying will never reach another soul. The baby, I was telling you about the baby—' She clutched at Beth's hand. 'Adrian nearly went mad when I lost it.'

'Then that showed—'

'That he cared about me?' Caroline's laughter was verging on the hysterical. 'Beth, Adrian cares nothing for me, even when it was touch and go as to whether or not I would live, he wasn't here. Had I died he would have wept no tears but losing the baby was different. If I can put it crudely, that was to be his meal ticket, his hold on Inverbrae House and all it stands for. With his child, the heir, his future was assured but with no child he could not be sure. He knew that I was wise to his wicked ways. Am I making sense?'

'Yes, Caroline, you are.'

'His hope was to get me pregnant again and this time produce a baby. I told him there would be no more babies. I told him I couldn't have one now but he wouldn't believe me. He told me I was a coward and called me a few choice names that he felt I deserved.'

'Caroline, I am so shocked I don't know what to say.'

'Not surprised though, are you?'

'I thought him ruthless but this is so much worse, you are painting a picture of a monster.'

'I am married to a handsome monster but one day, and very soon I hope, I'll be free of him.'

'Divorce him?'

'Yes. When I die, and since I can't have children, Robert is the next heir.'

'I begin to see now.'

'Good.'

'I don't know much about these things, Caroline, but I imagine you need proof. Are you quite sure that Adrian has a mistress?'

'His sister-in-law, who has no time for him, told me. I like her and I like my mother-in-law.' She made a face. 'Not my father-in-law though and that should have

423

warned me. Once he must have been very like Adrian, same looks, same charm, but those have gone and he just looks dissolute.'

'What about your mother-in-law?'

'She is what I could become if I don't watch myself. She has been unwell for a long time and no wonder, all her money has gone or the bulk of it. She does have some, a bequest from an aunt I think, and that is left in such a way that her husband can't get his hands on it. Michael watches that his mother doesn't weaken and let him have it.'

'Does your father know all this? He can't or surely he would act.'

'You are thinking of daddy as he was, not as he is. Honestly, Beth, there are times when I get so angry with him that I could scream.'

'When he is himself again he will come down on Adrian.'

'Better be soon then.'

'What do you mean by that?' Beth felt a cold shiver down her spine.

'Since he had the stroke daddy just signs anything Adrian puts before him.'

'You need advice, Caroline, professional advice,' Beth said urgently. 'You must not let this run on. Adrian could be ruining you.'

'Exactly. He doesn't even bother to lock up his papers because he thinks I am too stupid to understand.'

'Then he certainly under-estimates you.'

'Yes, Beth, he does.' She looked suddenly drawn and tired and put a hand to her head. 'There is so much more to tell.'

'Not until we have tea. You look as though you could do with a cup.'

'I wouldn't say no and you could do with one as well. Excuse me.' She crossed the room, opened the door and called out to someone. 'Wait! Mrs Murdoch! I'm glad I caught you. You'll never guess whom I have beside me. Beth.'

'Beth!' the housekeeper exclaimed and Beth heard the exaggerated surprise. 'Well, I never!'

'Bring tea, will you?'

'That I will, m'am, and right away.'

Caroline came back. 'Not another word about my troubles until we have had tea. Tell me about yourself. You look happy but then you are, aren't you?'

'Yes, I am very lucky. Miss Martin couldn't be nicer. I can come and go as I please but she would worry if I were very late and I like it that way. It means that she cares about me.'

The tea came and they drank it, each having a second cup and a fairy cake. Beth gathered up the dishes and carried the tray to a table near the door for the maid to collect.

'Caroline, why don't you write to Robert and get his advice?'

'I already have. That is the next bit you were to hear. Robert is married.'

'To Gemma?'

'You knew about Gemma?'

'Robert asked me to have dinner with him one evening and just in case I got any wrong ideas he told me that there was a girl back home.'

'I do love Robert, he's closer than a cousin and more like the brother I never had.' She laughed, 'This must sound so silly, cloak and dagger stuff, but I don't want Adrian to get hold of Robert's letters. He would read them you know. Imagine me asking this kind of favour of a housekeeper but Mrs Murdoch has a good idea that things are not as they should be and she has difficulty hiding her dislike of Adrian. Robert puts my letters in an envelope addressed to Mrs Murdoch and that way there is no danger of them falling into Adrian's hands. Is your head buzzing or can you take more?'

'I'll try. I want to understand as much as possible and that way I may be able to help.'

'You are, just by being here and listening.' She paused and seemed to be trying to organise her thoughts. 'Adrian's home, as you may know, is in Stirling. When he took me to meet his parents, Beth, the place was a shambles. No use going into the details but gambling debts were responsible. As I said previously, Adrian thinks he is married to a simpleton and it suits me to let him go on thinking that. It makes him careless and I have proof that he is taking money from Inverbrae and spending it on Bankhead.'

'Bankhead being the family home?'

'Yes. Gradually and at our expense, Bankhead is being restored to its former glory.'

'But that is stealing, a criminal offence!' Beth was horrified.

'He has daddy's signature and I told you daddy signs anything.'

'Then you must put a stop to it.'

'I have,' Caroline said triumphantly. 'I had a long session with our solicitor and put him fully in the picture.'

'Very sensible.'

'Nothing goes through now without my signature and a particularly big withdrawal has been cancelled.'

'How was that managed?'

'The solicitor had our doctor issue a certificate to the effect that his patient is not sufficiently recovered to be in control of his affairs.'

'I'm so glad,' Beth breathed. 'I couldn't bear to think of Adrian getting away with it though I suppose he has got away with some.'

'Not as much as he believes. I rather think the work has gone ahead on the strength of that large withdrawal and he is going to be one very worried man when he finds out.' She gripped Beth's hand with such ferocity that Beth winced. 'I sound brave and I am anything but. Beth, I'm so scared, scared of what he'll do to me if, when, he finds out.'

'There has to be a way out of this.'

'There is but it is the waiting. Robert and Gemma are due here in three weeks but that is still three weeks to get through.'

Beth gave a sigh of relief. 'Don't worry, Caroline. Your solicitor is in possession of the facts and he has the legal jargon. He is sure to come up with a plausible reason why the money must remain where it is for a further twenty-one days or whatever.'

'And by that time Robert will be here! If it works out like that, it will be wonderful.'

'It will and Robert will be well able for Adrian.'

'I've kept him informed so he's coming prepared. Beth, I'm divorcing Adrian but I'm not facing him with it until I have Robert's support.'

'How long will Robert and Gemma stay?'

Caroline stared. 'Haven't I made it clear?'

'No, not to me.'

'This is to be their home. Robert will help daddy with the estate and one day it will belong to him.'

'Caroline,' Beth said gently. 'All this has been terrible for you but soon you will be able to put it behind you and find happiness with someone else.'

'No,' she said firmly. 'I will never marry again but I

427

shall spend the rest of my life here in Inverbrae House
Gemma and I have been corresponding and I told her they
could be quite separate in a wing of the house, that we
don't have to fall over each other, and do you know what
she wrote back?'

'No.'

'She said both Robert and she are used to families and
there would be no separate wing. We would all dine
together and she would help me with grandmama since
she is used to old people.'

'She sounds lovely.'

They sat and looked at one another, the two friends
who had met as six-year-olds.

'Thank you for listening, Beth.' Her eyes were moist.

'Caroline, I am just so proud of you. Once your father is
his old self, he is going to be very proud of his daughter
and so he should.'

Caroline giggled and for a moment it was a glimpse of
the old Caroline. 'When Aunt Gwen hears about the
divorce, she is going to be reaching for the smelling salts.
In her family and ours too, divorce is a dirty word.'

'I shouldn't worry about that. Cheap at the price just to
be rid of him.' She smiled. 'Speaking of your Aunt Gwen,
how is Ruth?'

'Blooming. Happy and contented. They have two children, a girl and a boy. Ruth helps out in the practice when
she can. They live in a poor quarter of the city and do a lot
of good work. Ian is very much thought of and not only by
those he helps but others in high places. Aunt Gwen is
quite chuffed about that. I think she has hopes of some
honour for her son-in-law.'

'I'm glad Ruth is happy. She deserves to be. And now,
Caroline, I must go and get my bus.'

'You'll do no such thing. Tommy will drive you back

and promise me you'll come again and soon?'

'I promise but phone if you need me in a hurry. Remember now!'

They hugged each other and a maid was sent to find Tommy. When he came he could hardly believe his eyes.

'Quite like old times,' he said as she got in beside him. There was a baby now and most of the talk was about Tommy junior and just how bright the child was. Beth was happy to listen.

So anxious was Beth to share her worries with Jenny that, when the door to Greystanes opened, she was breathless from hurrying. As always, Jenny greeted Beth with a light kiss and a warm welcome.

The early spring day was bright and cold and Beth wore a tweed skirt in a mixture of golds and browns and over it a boxy jacket in a light shade of camel. Her dark hair was cut short and shaped to her head, and the cold wind had whipped the colour into her cheeks.

'A picture of health,' Jenny said admiringly. She gave a mock shiver and closed the door. 'You obviously don't feel the cold.'

'Only because I was hurrying. Jenny, I have so much to tell you.' She almost babbled the words.

'All in good time, my dear. Slip off your jacket and hang it up, then come along to the sitting-room. News good or bad, is better received when one is sitting comfortably. At least it is for those of us who have gone beyond the first flush of youth!' She spoke drily but with a twinkle in her eye.

'Jenny, it isn't good, in fact it is all very sad,' Beth called after her as she put her jacket on a coat hanger and hung it up on a peg.

The sitting-room was comfortably warm with the heat

of the sun playing on the window and a small fire burning
They sat in a chair at either side of the fireplace. Jenny
wore a dress in an unusual shade of mustard with long
amber beads round her neck.

'This can only concern Inverbrae House?'

'Yes, it does.' Beth leaned forward. 'Mrs Murdoch
came to see me. Anna let her in and honestly, Jenny,
nearly fainted when I saw her there, I was so surprised.'

Jenny raised her eyebrows. 'If Mrs Murdoch went the
length of calling on you then she must be very worried.
She paused. 'Unless, of course, she was just bringing a
message from Caroline?'

Beth shook her head vigorously. 'Caroline knew noth
ing of her visit and Mrs Murdoch made me promise not to
tell her.'

'And you gave that promise?'

'Yes. Jenny, I was so worried that I asked Anna if
could go back with Mrs Murdoch. When we got t
Inverbrae House I was shown into the breakfast-room an
a maid went to tell Caroline.'

'What kind of reception did you get?'

'I was nervous but I needn't have been.'

'She was delighted to see you?'

'Yes, she was. Jenny, the change in Caroline is frighten
ing.' She didn't realise what she was doing but she ha
gripped Jenny's hands.

'What do you mean?' Jenny said sharply. 'Or is it ju
that you haven't seen Caroline since she lost the baby?'

Beth shook her head slowly. 'It is more than that. Sh
told me everything, Jenny, about Adrian and the dreadf
life she has with him.'

'That shouldn't surprise you, since you had first-han
experience of the type of person he is. To your credit, yo
did your best to warn Caroline.'

'I know but I can't blame Caroline for thinking it was jealousy on my part. I may have thought the same in her place, particularly when Adrian is so well thought of by those whose opinion she values.'

They were both silent for a little while. Miss Harris came in with tea and the conversation became general.

'Let me hear the rest,' Jenny said when they were alone again. 'Then we can discuss it and see what, if anything, can be done. Help is one thing and interference quite another.'

'I know that, Jenny, but you'll want to help Caroline when you hear what I have to tell you.'

Jenny poured tea into the cups.

'This is really quite dreadful,' Jenny said looking shocked and angry. 'That odious creature must not get away with it and as to Nigel—'

'Forgot to tell you that bit. Caroline said she did wish you would come, she's missed you. Not like Caroline but she did say this, that her father gets too much sympathy and that you are the one to talk some sense into him.'

'She said that? Poor, brave little soul, I always thought there was more to Caroline than the spoilt little girl she always appeared.'

'You will go to Inverbrae House, won't you, Jenny?'

'Yes, Beth, I'll go and see Nigel. From all accounts his was a very mild stroke but it was a terrible shock to his system. Nigel was never the most patient with illness in others and he obviously hasn't faced up to his. But he will if I have anything to do with it,' she said firmly.

'You won't turn him against Adrian. He won't hear anything against him.'

'Probably no one has said anything against him and that is the trouble. An intelligent man like Nigel is bound to know that things are not as they should be. In the helpless state he considers himself to be in, though, he's just opted for the easy way out and done the unforgivable. He signed his name without knowing what he was signing away.'

The tea was cold by now but they both drank and made a face. 'Shall I get fresh, have you time?'

'No, Jenny, I haven't,' Beth said preparing to rise, 'but thank you for listening. I don't know what I would do without you.'

Jenny patted her arm. 'You would manage but, never fear, we'll get this sorted out.'

Chapter Twenty-Nine

Over in Inverbrae House, there were obvious signs of preparation for the arrival of Robert and Gemma Munro from Australia. Caroline had made no mention of it to her husband and, strangely enough, no one else had either. Had Adrian been his normal self he would have noticed and questioned what was going on but worry clouded the handsome face. The restoration of Bankhead was well advanced but accounts demanding payment were beginning to arrive. Their non-payment was causing consternation and Adrian pictured ahead the nasty scenes when no money was forthcoming.

Plausible excuses for withholding the money had been made by the smooth-tongued solicitor for Inverbrae House but Adrian was uneasy and he was no fool. Something had gone very far wrong but how? He had been so careful, and he was almost convinced that his father-in-law was not responsible. After all, wasn't he just too relieved to have his son-in-law see to everything? The old lady could be ruled out, since she hardly knew the time of day. That left his silly, bird-brained wife but had he been wrong about Caroline? Had he under-estimated her? There had been times when he had been careless about locking up documents. His face hardened. If it turned out to be the truth he would make her suffer. Already she had cheated him out of an heir and a

comfortable future and if she were to die – the doctor had
warned him about Caroline's weak heart, worsened by
that miscarriage – the thought of her death sent a shiver of
fear through him. Losing Caroline wouldn't upset him, he
had never had much time for her, but were she to die he
would have no hold on Inverbrae. That cousin Robert
would come and claim everything.

He cursed her. Caroline, and only Caroline, was
responsible for the mess in which he found himself. Had
there been a child he would not have set out on this course
of bringing Bankhead to its former glory. Now he and his
own family were to be faced with ruin and disgrace.
Declared bankrupt and when that happened, Bankhead
would fall into other hands. It didn't bear thinking about.
And it wasn't going to happen, there must be a way of
getting his hands on money. His wife had money, a
substantial amount, and that rat of a solicitor would have
to pay out if it was at Caroline's request. He smiled
cruelly. She was afraid of him, he thought contemptu
ously, and almost cringed when he was near. He drew
himself to his full height and there was a smile on his face.
He was the master and his wife would do exactly as he
ordered or else – or else what? The truth was he had no
hold over her. The love she had once had for him had
turned to hate. Now she feared him and fear of him would
be his weapon.

It was an emotional meeting. Caroline was in floods of
tears as she hugged Robert and met his wife. They were
tears of relief that she could hand over responsibility and
feel safe. So afraid was she, that she locked her bedroom
door at night and made sure that she was never alone with
her husband. This had frustrated Adrian but he could
afford to wait a little. The little money his mother had left

had bought time and her failing health was made the excuse for the length of time he spent in Stirling.

Her husband's absence had Caroline jubilant. Things couldn't have worked out better, because it gave Robert and Gemma a chance to settle in. Gemma had been utterly fascinated with the house and its history. She endeared herself to all, maids included, because she was so natural and friendly. She and her husband were very much in love. It was there in the glances they exchanged but they didn't seek to be alone, declaring themselves only too happy to be part of the family.

Robert couldn't hide his shock at the change in his cousin, and felt a murderous rage towards the man who had brought her to this. Gemma, however, thought her delicately lovely and she was. Her face, thinned by grief and illness, had achieved a mature beauty.

The decision to come and live in Scotland had not been taken lightly. It was a big step into the unknown for Gemma but she hadn't hesitated. Her place was with her husband, she said, and now that she was here her practical capabilities were being put to good use. The frail young woman needed protection from that brute of a husband and as for the old lady, there was a great deal more she could do for herself. Elderly people could rest too much, light exercise was good for them, a short walk in the grounds when the weather was good. The fresh air would help her sleep at night.

Far from rebelling, old Mrs Parker-Munro was enjoying this new experience. She was a nice girl, this Gemma. Funny way of speaking, she had, but once one got used to it, it was quite pleasant. The name, though – that was just not acceptable. Parker-Munro was the family name and Robert must take it. Gemma liked to hear about the old days, had an interest in Inverbrae's history, and she would see the importance of Robert taking the family name. One day they would have children and then it would be more important than ever. She smiled tiredly, she could die happy knowing that the family name lived on.

Jenny had made progress with the colonel and he was beginning to feel thoroughly ashamed of himself. How selfish he had been to put such a strain on Caroline and as for Adrian, he didn't know what to believe—

Adrian had been drinking. He wasn't drunk, just happy and that made a welcome change. The demands had ceased, at least for the present, and he could relax. There was time for his wife to come up with the cash or, better still, for that solicitor to release the money which had to be legal and binding since it had the colonel's signature. Time to call that solicitor's bluff.

The May sunshine was streaming through the window and, being Sunday, they had all eaten lunch in the dining-room and were now settled in the drawing-room. For the benefit of the old lady and those used to a warmer climate, a small fire had been lit and the large room was comfortably warm. Robert and Gemma had brought laughter and they were a family happy to be together.

Caroline's sharp ears had caught the sound first. Adrian must have parked the car round the back and walked round to the front door. Those were his footsteps, and as they drew nearer she caught her breath. She had promised herself to be brave but her heart had begun to hammer alarmingly. Robert heard the approach of feet and Caroline's look of alarm and whispered something to Gemma. She nodded and he got up and went to sit beside his cousin just as the door opened.

'Well! Well! Quite a party we have here.' The worry lines had smoothed out and the face was as handsome as before. He wore a well-cut suit and looked smart and relaxed. 'Caroline, my dear, you must have forgotten to tell me.'

She remained silent. Robert spoke.

'Sit down, Adrian.'

'Do I need an invitation to be seated in my own home?'

'Adrian,' the old lady said plaintively, 'close that door, if you please, you know how I dislike a draught.'

'Sorry.' He closed the door, hesitated, then sat down. He looked over at the young woman, presumably Robert's wife, and found she interested him. He liked that healthy, sporty type and she looked as though she could be fun – not like his wishy-washy wife. He would use his charm and he needed someone new in his life. His mistress was causing him some annoyance, withholding her favours and accusing him of meanness. He was tired of her anyway.

'Robert, aren't you going to introduce me to your wife?' he said. 'At least, I presume the very attractive young lady is your wife?'

'My wife, Gemma, Adrian Scott-Hamilton,' he said stiffly.

He wanted to go over and kiss her hand, the gentlemanly thing to do, but her cool nod was hardly encouraging.

Caroline had recovered. 'How is your mother, Adrian?'

'My mother,' he said blankly then remembered she was the excuse for his prolonged stay. 'There is a little improvement but she is far from well.'

'I'm sorry to hear that.'

He smiled. 'Darling, I haven't eaten. Do ring the bell and have the kitchen prepare a meal.'

'Do it yourself.'

'I beg your pardon.'

'I said do it yourself or better still wait and hear what I

have to say. It may put you off eating.'

'My poor dear, you are not yourself. Perhaps we should go elsewhere and have our talk.' He smiled. 'The others will excuse us, I'm sure.'

With Robert beside her, Caroline was gaining strength. 'I am not moving from here and now seems like a good time to tell you—'

'Tell me what?'

'I am divorcing you, Adrian. I want you out of my life.'

His face had whitened and he looked incredulous. 'What are you saying?'

'My cousin spoke clearly. It is your hearing that is at fault.'

'I'll thank you to mind your own damn business,' Adrian said furiously.

The old lady was looking outraged. 'Robert and Adrian, I'll remind you that this is the Sabbath day. You should be ashamed of yourselves, using such language. Had you been younger I would have sent you to your room.'

She got up and asked Caroline to take her to her room.

'No, grandma, I'll take you,' said Gemma.

'You'll stay for a while?'

'Of course and see more of your photographs. I would like that.'

They went out. The door closed and for a few moments no one spoke.

'On what grounds, Caroline?' Adrian said at last.

'On what grounds, you ask? Such a question only shows your arrogance. My solicitor is in possession of all that is necessary.'

'How about proof? A jealous wife would make up anything and any good solicitor would know that.'

'I have the name and address of your mistress.' Her

lips curled. 'And I am far from being a jealous wife. For a time I was taken in by your charm but I soon found out the type of man I was married to. You are a bully, a cheat, and a liar and you will not spend another night under this roof.'

This wasn't Caroline, this woman with her blazing eyes. He couldn't believe it but he had to. It was all happening.

'I would advise you to be careful what you say or you could find yourself in serious trouble.'

Robert gripped her arm to stop her answering. 'Well done, Caroline, but I'll take over now.'

'And what, pray, has the Australian to say?' Adrian said contemptuously.

'Plenty, as it happens. For what you have done you could go to prison, do you know that?'

'What am I supposed to have done?' he sneered. 'My father-in-law,' he smiled over to the colonel but he was staring into the fire, 'handed over responsibility for Inverbrae to me. Any transaction I made had his signature, nothing can alter that.'

'That is where you are wrong. Some time ago my uncle's doctor signed a certificate stating that his patient was unable to conduct his affairs at present. No document would be legal without his daughter's signature.'

Robert smiled. He was enjoying this and it gave him tremendous satisfaction to see Adrian's look of horror.

He was blustering now, desperately trying to salvage something. 'This place needs me. I have the experience to run an estate and what happens when you return to that Godforsaken land?'

'Robert isn't returning to Australia, Adrian,' Caroline said quietly. 'He and Gemma are making their home here.'

The colonel had said nothing all this time but now he sat

up straight in his chair. 'It is time I spoke up.'

Adrian gave a huge sigh of relief. 'Thank you, sir, I knew I could depend on you.'

'Depend on me to do what?'

'Speak up for me.'

'You disgust me but I have greater disgust for myself for letting things develop to this stage. I have been all kinds of a fool and I am to blame.' The speech was slightly slurred and there was a small hesitancy between some of the words but he had their attention. He shook his head. 'I prided myself on being a good judge of character, but how wrong I was to trust you. You have stolen and cheated for your own ends and believe me, Adrian, I was hard to convince. Only when I saw the evidence for myself did I believe it.' He wiped his brow and Caroline looked at him anxiously.

Robert gave a small shake of his head. His uncle was doing all right and this could be a turning point for him. From now on he would take some interest in what was going on.

'Bearing in mind your home situation, I might have been able to forgive you in time but for the unhappiness you have caused my daughter. That is something I will never forgive nor forget. Indeed, I would like to see you horse-whipped.'

Adrian got unsteadily to his feet. Ruin and possibly worse faced him but his father had come through much the same and he had survived. Come to think about it, a divorce would suit him nicely. He still had his looks and could turn on the charm when he wanted. Better to do something and quickly about finding himself a rich wife. To get his hands on money he was prepared to marry a plain woman just as his father had. Already he was beginning to feel better. Like father, like son.

Robert had the door open. 'Collect what belongs to you and get out.'

Adrian looked across to Caroline and wondered if his charm would work with her, even at this late stage. But one look at her face gave him his answer. He left without another word.

A career as a portrait artist is not easily established and is probably the most difficult to achieve. But when one does reach the heights, the rewards are great. For Peter it was a dream beginning to come true but he did not make the mistake of neglecting his other work, what had been his bread and butter. He still did small paintings of seascapes, harbour scenes and the rest which were snapped up and the monies saved.

Painfully thin though he was, Peter enjoyed good health and there were no ill effects from his early struggles. Those times spent in freezing rooms when he would have worked at his easel wearing two jumpers, a coat and gloves with the fingers cut out, would not easily be forgotten. All creative people, or the large majority, have agonising moments of self doubt and often go through deep despair. Peter had done his share but a dogged perseverance, together with a slice of luck, had put him on the path to success.

Peter knew his worth now and accepted that he was good. But these days he was achieving so much more. He felt inspired and for that he knew he had Beth to thank. Just to know she was near and he worked better. For her part, she seemed to understand his moods and never intruded other than to take in cups of coffee or tea. Food did not interest him until evening and then he would eat ravenously.

The two rooms, bathroom and tiny kitchen at Summer

Street became a second home to Beth. She spent happy, happy hours there but her work for Anna was not neglected and she continued to do the many extras she had taken on.

The house in Summer Street was showing evidence of a woman's touch as fresh curtains went up at the windows and flowering plants took up a place on the sills. At what he termed a decent hour, Peter escorted Beth to her door, kissed her lightly on the lips and left her feeling strangely dissatisfied. She wanted more, hoped that Peter did too, but could not be sure.

Peter and Anna hit it off immediately. Peter thought her delightfully eccentric, and she found him intelligent, interesting and charming. As a way of showing her approval Anna took them to the Excelsior Hotel where they dined extravagantly. It was a wonderfully enjoyable evening and the start of a long and happy friendship.

In the cool of the evening and after a long hard day, Peter needed to relax and stretch his limbs and he and Beth would take a walk along the coast road. Her eye never missed it and since she was a small child the white-painted house had fascinated Beth. From a distance and with its peculiar angle, the house looked as though it would topple into the sea. As a little girl, she had feared for the safety of those who lived in it. To reassure her and probably to stop the flow of questions, her father had taken her to the house and she had been both relieved and disappointed to find it set firmly on the ground and at a safe distance from the cliffs.

'Beth, I have to go to Edinburgh for a few days, maybe a week,' he said one day.

'To see your parents?'

'Partly. I'll be living at home – no correction, this is home – I'll be staying with my parents.' He paused and looked slightly embarrassed. 'Actually it is a small exhibition of my work.'

'But, Peter, that is marvellous,' Beth said delightedly. 'I couldn't be more pleased.' She went over to hug him. 'When is this to be?'

'In three weeks.'

'I'll be thinking of you and keeping my fingers crossed but I just know it will be a big success.'

'Hope so.' Should he ask her? No, she would just go out of politeness.

Beth was so sure he would invite her but he hadn't. Certainly it was in Edinburgh but she could have got the morning train and one back in the early evening. Why should he? Edinburgh was where he had been brought up and there would be plenty of relatives and friends to flock to see Peter's paintings. She told Anna.

'My dear child, did you show a willingness to go to Edinburgh?' her friend asked.

'Not exactly.'

'That means no and you must know that he isn't aware of our working arrangement.'

Beth looked at her enquiringly. 'That didn't apply to a whole day.'

'Of course it does. You must go, my dear, if for no other reason than to swell the numbers. I'm sure it will be well attended but he isn't to know that. One hopes but one can never be sure.'

'Anna, I'm only a friend.'

'A very special friend. Now, as you know, I am not one for interfering but this time I am going to chance it. You get yourself to Edinburgh and go and see Peter's paintings. If you don't, the day will come when you will regret it.'

'You think I should surprise him?'

'I most certainly do.'

★ ★ ★

The train thundered along the track and Beth was getting cold feet and wishing she hadn't listened to Anna. Out of good manners and kindness, Peter would make her welcome but if he had really wanted her there he would have said so.

Coming out of Waverley Station the strong breeze whipped her hair about her face. It was to be expected, it was always windy coming out of the station. Beth spent some time wandering about Princes Street admiring the fashions in the shop windows. A walk in the gardens would have been nice, but she had better get herself something to eat and a cup of tea before going out to the exhibition. Anna, it turned out, knew Edinburgh well and had drawn a remarkably clear map for which Beth was grateful. She had no difficulty finding the street and the old Victorian mansion house. Shabby but still stately, it had been divided into apartments. Outside the large ground-floor room there was a notice and Beth felt a burst of pride when she read, 'Exhibition of Paintings by Peter Nicholson'. A few people were in the spacious hallway and she saw with relief that some of the women wore tweeds. She was glad then that she had worn hers and not something more dressy. She went in.

There was low-murmured talk as people stood before the paintings and gave their opinion before moving on to the next. Beth had moved from the doorway into the room and saw him immediately. He looked very smart in a dark suit, a crisp white shirt and a blue tie and was moving about answering questions. Beth was just on the point of going over when a young blonde woman put her hand on his arm and Peter, turning round gave a delighted smile. She saw the two heads together and laughing at what could only be a private joke.

People were pushing by, she was in the way but did nothing about it. She was jealous, there was no other way to describe the feeling that gripped her. The shock of the discovery kept her standing there dumbly. She loved Peter but when had it happened? When had her feelings changed from friendship to love? She didn't know. Perhaps she had always loved him but had been blinded by her infatuation for Adrian.

He must never know. Her pain had to be private and in the next few minutes she must put on an act. Just as she was moving towards him, a set smile on her face, he saw her. She saw his start of surprise, his quick word to the blonde girl, then he was beside her.

'Beth! It really is you? I thought I must be dreaming. Why didn't you tell me you were coming?'

'Just a sudden decision. Thought I would combine it with a look round the Edinburgh shops.'

'Excuse me, I wanted to ask you—' They were all around him, all anxious to speak to the artist. A word here, a word there, he tried to get away but someone else buttonholed him and with a wry smile he caught Beth's eye and she smiled.

'You must go, Peter, I'll have a look round on my own.'

'As soon as I can I'll be with you, so don't you dare disappear.'

Beth didn't answer. She would slip away but not before she saw the paintings. Many she had seen but it was different to see them in these surroundings. People were smiling and there was a lovely atmosphere. They weren't just looking, as was shown by the large number of paintings with the small stick-on sign that said they were sold.

A small group stood before one painting that was a little apart from the others and she went over to look. The group obligingly parted to let her through and she found herself open-mouthed with astonishment. She was looking at herself, the one taken from the sketch he had made of her on the stony beach at Sandyneuk. He must have worked on it when he knew he was to be alone. There was no sold sign on this one but there was a card to the side. She read it. Not for sale.

Beth felt a lump in her throat and was about to rush away but Peter was beside her and looking at her strangely.

'And I thought it was good. One of my best. Others must have thought so too because I've had a few tempting offers. But nothing,' he said softly, 'would let me part with that one.'

'Oh, Peter,' was all she could say, her lips were trembling so much.

They were motionless, staring at one another. A smile played around Peter's mouth and Beth's eyes were shining.

'At last,' he whispered, 'at last you are putting the past behind you. I was beginning to despair that you ever would.'

'You mean – all this time—' she said wonderingly.

'All this time, from the moment I saw you as it happens. I've loved you. No, the first time you were a child but the next time, in Jenny's home.'

'You never gave a hint—'

'Of course not. I always hoped that the right moment would come and it has.'

'I've been over Adrian for a very long time.'

'There was another reason—'

'What possible reason could there be?'

'The age gap. You see, my darling, I didn't want to risk telling you of my feelings and losing your friendship. Ter years or near enough is quite a lot.'

'Ten years is nothing,' she said dismissively. Then she remembered the blonde girl. 'You were with a fair-haired girl—'

'Snakes alive, I forgot all about her,' he said dragging her along with him.

The girl was there. 'Fine one you are—'

'Sorry, Susie, I got tied up.'

'So I see,' the blonde girl said smiling to Beth.

'Susie, this is Beth from Sandyneuk and Beth, this is my cousin.'

They shook hands. 'Nice to meet you, Beth.' She looked at her cousin. 'Am I right in thinking that Beth is the reason we see so little of you?'

Peter laughed and Beth blushed.

'Not saying. All right, Peter, I'll keep your secret.' She waved her hand and left them.

'That's a joke, Susie couldn't keep a secret. I give it two hours then the entire family will know.'

'Will you mind?'

'Far from it.'

'Peter, I must go for my train.'

'Miss it and come home with me. Mother would be delighted to put you up.'

'I can't, I'm a working girl, remember. And I have Anna to thank for me being here.'

'You mean you needed to be persuaded?'

'I can't recall being invited.'

'I didn't want you searching for an excuse to spare my feelings.'

The minutes were ticking away. 'Peter, I must go.'

'I can't even see you on the train, I have to lock up here.'

'I know.' Their lips met for that first brief kiss. Then she was outside and all but running to catch her train.

Chapter Thirty

Peter was back in Sandyneuk. The exhibition had been an outstanding success and people were congratulating him. The people of Sandyneuk claimed him as their own and the small craft shop was desperate for more paintings. Everything was wonderful for Peter and Beth but their love was too new to share with others. They needed this time to themselves before shouting out their happiness to the world. As if they needed to – it was plain for all to see. Jenny and Anna had a quiet smile. They saw the way things were between the young couple and they couldn't have been more delighted.

Beth could feel Peter's excitement as they set out for a walk along the coast road. She wondered where they were going. It had nothing to do with his paintings, she knew that. What could it be? She wouldn't ask.

She had heard rumours that the white house was to go on the market but there had been rumours before and nothing had come of them. Only when they turned off the coast road to the rough path did her heart begin to flutter with excitement.

'Is it really for sale, Peter?'

'Yes, it really is for sale and we are expected.'

'You mean we—' But she didn't get to finish.

Peter knocked on the door and in a short while the bolt

was pulled back and a little old lady peered at them shortsightedly.

'Mrs Cameron?'

'Yes.'

'I'm Peter Nicholson and this is—'

'Your lady wife?'

'Not yet.'

Beth blushed becomingly and dropped her eyes to the steps.

'Come in.'

First they were in the vestibule then into the hallway. The old lady was dressed in black and looked old-fashioned and rather sweet.

'My legs are not what they used to be but then if they were I wouldn't be selling the house.'

'You must be very sad.'

'Where would be the sense in that? I am, of course I am, but relieved too. Help in the house is becoming difficult to get and expensive. I shouldn't complain, I've had a good life and if I see my home going to folk who will look after it I'll be satisfied. You look like a couple who would. Go ahead and have a good look round. Take your time.'

'Thank you,' they both said.

'May I ask what you do, young man?'

'I'm an artist.'

'An artist.' She nodded two or three times. 'You'll be the lad that has caused a wee bit of a stir? I still manage to read the papers. No artists in my family but my late husband and I had a great love of the sea. The room above this is where we sat of an evening and at the weekends. You won't find a view like it. But here I am talking and you anxious to see the house.' She smiled a little sadly. 'Comes from being so much on my own, I did have a dog and he was fine company but I had to have him put down.'

'That must have been sad and distressing for you,' Beth said sympathetically.

'Yes, but not for him. A happy release it was. He was in a lot of pain but he'll be all right wherever he is.' She turned away and they began to look around the house.

The sitting-room was large, the dining-room smaller. There was another room between them that was quite small. It had a single bed and a wardrobe and Beth thought it likely that Mrs Cameron slept there rather than climb the stairs.

Together they went up the carpeted stairs and she heard Peter gasp as he went ahead. The doors were wide open but one room drew him. It stretched the whole length of the house and could have been purposely built as a studio. Peter needed to see no more but he accompanied Beth to see the rest then they went to join the old lady.

She was smiling as she got up from the chair. 'Well?'

'It's lovely, absolutely lovely,' Beth breathed.

'Perfect, need I say more?' Peter said.

'You've fallen in love with it just as I did all those years ago. I can see by your faces that you both have.'

'Yes, we both have.'

'I'll see the solicitor and put in my offer tomorrow morning,' Peter said.

She looked pleased. 'Put in a reasonable offer, Mr Nicholson, and it will be accepted.'

'Perhaps your solicitor will want to hold out for more? It would be to his advantage.'

'That is probably true but we know each other well. We go back a long way, and he'll carry out my wishes.'

'Thank you very, very much,' Beth said as they prepared to go.

★ ★ ★

By the end of the month the house was theirs and Beth
didn't know how to contain her happiness. The two rooms
in Summer Street were given up and Peter's worldly
possessions moved to the white house, now to be known
as Cliffend Cottage. Until they were married he would
live and work there. He shut himself in the studio while
willing hands stripped the wallpaper from the rooms and
did a thousand and one jobs.

There was so much to do, so much going on, that Beth
didn't know whether she was coming or going. Peter had
taken her to Edinburgh to meet his family. His mother
had arranged it so that Alex, unmarried and three years
younger, and sister Ruby, husband Norman and their
little boy, would be there to meet Beth.

John Nicholson, Peter's father, was tall and both sons
resembled him. Mrs Nicholson was a happy-faced woman
with a weight problem which she totally ignored. Ruby
was small and slim and reminded Beth of the younger
Caroline. Husband Norman doted on his wife and son and
they could not have been more welcoming. She was
immediately drawn into the family and she loved them all.

Aunt Anne and Uncle Fred liked Peter but how could
they not, Beth thought. No one could dislike Peter.

'Fixed the big day?' Aunt Anne asked. 'Need time to
save up, you know.'

'Early September,' Beth smiled, 'and Aunt Anne,
would you and Uncle Fred take the place of my parents?'

'Oh, lass, I would and willingly but not if it is to be one
of those posh affairs, your uncle wouldn't like it either.'

'Speak for yourself, woman. With no lass of my own I'm
only too happy to give Beth away. Not to anyone mind,
but Peter, here, will look after her, I've no fears there.'

'Nothing posh about our wedding. Only close relatives

including cousins and friends. Jenny, you know who I'm talking about?'

'I should I've heard about her often enough.'

'She wants us to be married in the village church and the reception in her home.'

Aunt Anne pursed her lips and nodded. 'Since it is to be a quiet affair I'll manage to take Harriet's place.'

On her wedding day, Beth was up early to look out of the window at the lashing rain but nothing could dampen her spirits. She was too excited to eat breakfast but Anna and she had a cup of tea together.

'I was so sure it would be a lovely day,' Beth said as rivulets of rain ran down the window.

'It's early yet and it could well clear up before midday.'

'Anna, is it possible to be too happy?'

'No, my dear. You have a right to every moment of happiness. Wherever you are, we are all touched by it.'

'You have such a lovely way of putting things, such a lovely way with words.'

'Oh, I was getting quite crusty until you came into my life. I am just so glad that I am not to lose you – at least not for a while yet.'

'I want to go on working for you, Anna, and thank you a thousand times for all you have done for me. This has been home to me, you know.'

Anna patted her hand. 'Perhaps it is true to say we needed one another. But now, would you just go and take a look out of that window.'

They had been talking and she hadn't even noticed. 'It's clearing, it is going to be a good day after all,' Beth said joyfully. And it was – the clouds had dispersed, the sky was blue and the sun had appeared.

The small church was filling up and well-wishers were

gathered round the gate eager to catch a glimpse of the bride. The heat of the sun had miraculously dried up the paths and pavements and no puddles remained to wet the shoes of unsuspecting guests. Beth had decided against having a bridesmaid. She had friends, but no one she wanted in that role. Instead she would have a matron-of-honour unless Caroline refused. But she hadn't, she was touched and honoured to be asked.

Beth was radiantly beautiful, her gown simplicity itself with a froth of white net over it. Any nervousness had gone and Uncle Fred, looking proud, squeezed her arm and whispered, 'All right?'

'Just fine,' she answered as they entered the porch.

The bridegroom and best man looked smart and solemn. But Peter's face broke into a smile of pure delight as the bride, on the arm of her uncle, and followed by Caroline, came slowly down the aisle. Caroline wore a lovely gown of pale apricot. She looked frail but her eyes were clear and she looked quietly happy.

Soon they were man and wife and, leaving the confetti-strewn path, they climbed into the car that was to take them to Greystanes for the reception. Beth, with Peter by her side, had cut the cake and it was being handed round with a tray of assorted drinks following.

She looked at them, all the smiling faces and felt a lump in her throat. Once she had thought herself unloved and unwanted but all that had changed. She had a loving family and good friends, like Jenny and Anna who between them had done so much for her. Caroline had come back into her life and it was lovely to be friends or near sisters as Caroline was telling everybody.

Peter's arm drew her close. 'Darling, you are miles away.'

'Just thinking.'

'Thinking what?'

'That I am so lucky to have you beside me. I love you so very much, Peter.'

'I love you, Beth, and we will be together—'

'For always.'

'Until the end of time.'

NORA KAY

A WOMAN OF SPIRIT

Susan MacFarlane had only a few months with David Cameron, but in that time he taught her the power of passionate love – its rewards and its punishments.

Then she returned to her duty: marriage to a man who could run the family's paper mill – the mill she loved and understood but could not have for herself.

Trapped in a loveless marriage with only her children to console her, her ambition and her ability thwarted by the conventions of the time, Susan seems destined to finish her life without ever knowing again the heady excitement of her brief time of freedom.

Then David Cameron comes back to Glasgow. Rich now, ready to avenge the slights of his youth. And the implacable enemy of Susan's family . . .

HODDER AND STOUGHTON PAPERBACKS

NORA KAY

BEST FRIENDS

Fiery Agnes Boyd and quiet, motherless Rachel Donaldson have been best friends since their Dundee schooldays. Both girls are determined to escape from the poverty their families endure.

Thwarted in her ambition to become a teacher, Rachel goes to work as a maid – in the Perthshire home of her mother's estranged family. Soon she finds herself irresistibly drawn to the handsome village doctor, Peter McGregor. Who seems to be beyond her reach . . .

Agnes too becomes a housemaid, but she is determined to marry for money and status, not for love. So why can't she forget about young Tommy Kingsley?

HODDER AND STOUGHTON PAPERBACKS